MOORE
Than a Feeling

JULIE A. RICHMAN

Cover Photo: Eric McKinney/6:12 Photography
Cover Model: Will Simms
Cover Design: Jena Brignola/Bibliophile Productions
Proofreading & Formatting: Elaine York/Allusion Graphics,
www.allusiongraphics.com

MOORE
Than a Feeling

Subscribe to Julie's Newsletter

http://bit.ly/JulieARichmanNewsletter

-Dedicated to my readers-

This one is my gift to you.
Thank you for choosing to be part of my dream
and for joining me on this journey.
There will always be Moore.

xoxo,

J.A.R.

2018

CHAPTER
One

Mid-Summer

DON'T YOU DARE DIE on me, woman. Schooner Moore issued the order in his head. *Don't you dare.* He repeated his thought in case she didn't hear his cosmic command the first time. If anyone had the balls to defy him, it was her. And that was just one of the many things he adored about her. But what he adored most was the wonderful woman she raised. A woman strikingly similar to herself, who now sat in the passenger seat next to him, lost, as she braced herself, potentially for extreme pain, while trying to remain positive.

Just a glance told him she was failing at the latter.

Ocean Parkway was desolate in the hour just before midnight, its haunting and lonely beauty exposed under the unforgiving glare of a waning moon. With the beams from the Land Rover's headlights bouncing off the ground fog and obscuring visibility, Schooner Moore understood completely why this deserted stretch of beachfront highway had become a notorious locale for unsolved murders, holding tight the muted secrets of its unidentifiable victims.

Reaching across to the passenger seat, he gently pulled Mia's thumb away from her mouth, as she unconsciously chewed the skin that surrounded the edges of her fingernail. Bringing her small hand into his lap, he lovingly stroked the area at which she had been gnawing.

Mia sighed, and in the shadows cast on the car by highway-lining streetlamps that looked like seagulls perched atop weathered, wooden poles that leaned away from the ocean, Schooner could see the tension that rolled through the muscles of his wife's face. Starting at her cheekbone and moving rapidly to her jaw, a wave of worry inched toward Mia's mouth, making her lips twitch. Schooner's gut coiled watching as her tension and fear mounted with each mile they drove.

"She's going to be okay, Baby Girl," he attempted to reassure her, squeezing her hand.

"What if we don't get there in time?" There was palpable fear in Mia's voice and he ached, knowing he was never going to be able to alleviate it. At least not until they were down there.

"We're on the earliest flight out in the morning. She'll still be in surgery when we get to the hospital." He brought her hand to his mouth, gently kissing her palm. "Lois is not going anywhere, Mia. You know your mother is a force to be reckoned with." *The apple didn't fall far from that tree,* Schooner thought to himself proudly. "I'll bet you a Serendipity Frozen Hot Chocolate that she is well enough to fly up to New York for Portia's birthday in September."

Mia smiled for the first time since they'd gotten into the car at the Fire Island Ferries parking lot, hastily leaving their beach house after a call from her father, and rushing their two sleeping, young children, Nathaniel and Portia, to the nearby home of close friends, Charles and Gaby Sloan.

"Ugh. You know I hate Serendipity's Frozen Hot Chocolate. Make that some hot sex in the shower and you've got a bet." She tried to lighten her dark thoughts.

"Hmm," Schooner snickered. Giving her a side glance, "Is shower sex with me ever anything less than hot?"

"You've got a point, so to speak," Mia conceded, enjoying her own pun and giving her handsome husband's hand a squeeze as she smiled again, this time at a memory visible only in her head. "It's going to be good to be in the city, even if it's only for a night."

Mia and Schooner had been out at their beach house with their kids, working from there for over a month and only Schooner's daughter, Holly, had been in Manhattan, living in their large, sun-drenched SoHo loft.

"Yes, it will," Schooner agreed, already picturing melting into the cool, clean sheets, smooth and devoid of sand, on their king-sized bed.

He hoped they'd be able to catch a few hours' sleep before an early morning Uber ride to LaGuardia Airport. With the travel gods on their side, they'd been able to secure seats on the earliest flight down to West Palm Beach, where Mia's mom, the incomparable force known as Lois Silver, would be undergoing emergency bypass surgery first thing in the morning.

"Did you hear back from Holly?"

Picking up his phone from the car's center console and glancing at the screen, Schooner shook his head. He had left her a voice message and a text to let her know what was going on and that he and Mia were on their way back into the city and staying at the loft for the night.

"No. She must be out or have her phone turned off. Maybe she's at the movies with some friends," he conjectured.

Heartbroken, Holly had decided not to spend the summer at the beach house on Fire Island with the family, knowing that seeing her ex-boyfriend, even for one more day, in the small, beach enclave where they lived and worked, would be far too painful. Instead, she moved back into the city, where she was very fortunate, that late in spring, to be able to pick up a summer gig at NYU, teaching two classes of English as a Second Language.

Aiden McManus, the charismatic and handsome manager of Maguire's Restaurant on Fire Island had captured Holly's heart, lock, stock and barrel, several summers before. A Long Island boy from a working-class family, Aiden helped pay for his community college education in Hotel and Hospitality Management through enlisting in the New York Army National Guard.

Holly's previous love interests had all come from backgrounds similar to her own, well-educated at Ivy League schools with families of means. But Aiden was different, salt of the Earth and willing to get his hands dirty, Holly had never met anyone his age who was already a man. Aiden McManus definitely wasn't a boy, and that was the sexiest thing Holly Moore had ever encountered. There was no going back to boys after meeting Aiden McManus.

Prior to meeting, neither Aiden nor Holly would have ever seen themselves with the other, yet together they were a mutual adoration society. Holly enamored with this handsome, street-smart man's man and Aiden overwhelmed that this beautiful and brilliant California golden girl would even give him a second glance, nonetheless fall in love with him. And when she fell in love with the dark-haired, dark hazel-eyed Irishman, Holly fell hard, with her entire heart, her feelings deeper and more complex than she'd ever known.

Their break-up blindsided and devastated her. Coming just a month before Aiden's reserve deployment to Afghanistan, his harsh words tattered her heart, literally slamming her to her knees.

"Don't bother waiting for me, Holly. This is the perfect natural-ending point for us. We're just too different. So, please don't kid yourself and wait."

"You're just saying this in case something happens. You're trying to protect me, Aiden," countered Holly.

Shaking his head, his eyes never leaving hers as he delivered the killing blow, "I'm sure that makes it easier for you to handle, but the truth of the matter is, I've been wanting to end things for a while. We're really different. And I'm happier with a woman who's more like me. I've been thinking a lot about my old girlfriend, Janine, and I'd like to see if we can work things out."

Holly wasn't the only one shocked by Aiden's scathing declaration. Everyone who knew the couple couldn't believe not only that they had broken up, but how and why or that Aiden would ever treat Holly with such cruelty.

"I don't understand," she cried to her father and stepmother. "How could I be so blind to miss the signs?" She glanced from Schooner to Mia, her tear-stained eyes positively devastated. But neither had an answer for her, because they were as shocked as she was at the sudden one-hundred-eighty-degree turn in Aiden's feelings and intentions. It just didn't add up. There had been no signs.

"It hasn't been the same without her on Fire Island this summer," Schooner commented as they drove toward the city. He missed his oldest child. Holly had been the light of his life through some very dark and lonely years, supporting him, and only concerned for his happiness when he and Mia reunited after a twenty-four-year absence.

"I know," Mia agreed. Holly was such a delight to be around. She loved her relationship with her stepdaughter. They had bonded immediately over their deep love for her father. "I know Natie and Po miss her terribly, too. Maybe when the summer semester is done, she'll come back out to the beach. Aiden is already gone, so no worries about running into him."

Crossing the Williamsburg Bridge, both Schooner and Mia let out a huge sigh at exactly the same moment, turned to one another and laughed. The collective exhale had been brought on by the lights of the Manhattan skyline beckoning them home with a warm welcome. There was relief in knowing soon that they'd be in their own space to get some rest prior to leaving at daybreak for Florida, and facing the unknown of what tomorrow, and Lois' surgery, would bring.

The old freight elevator opened directly into the loft and Schooner flicked on the great room's lights.

"It's good to be home." Mia looked relieved. "I'm glad we're staying here tonight." Home was a comfort to Mia. Whether in the city or out at the beach house, being in her own space provided a level of solace well understood by Cancerians. Schooner always thought of it as her crab shell, a place she could retreat with just a moment's notice, an environment that was uniquely hers, with all the creature comforts necessary for her happiness and protection.

Coming out of the bedroom where he'd deposited their bags, Schooner picked up the remote and stood in front of the television laughing for a moment before settling onto the welcoming couch.

"Baby Girl, *Animal House* is on," he called to Mia in the open kitchen. "Come watch it with me." If anything was going to calm her down and relax her so that she could get a few hours' sleep, it was a movie that they both could recite line for line.

"Do you want a bottle of water?" she called back to him.

"Yeah, thanks. Double-secret probation," he laughed, already entranced by the show.

Sinking in beside him, Mia kicked off her espadrilles. With his arm around her shoulder, Schooner pulled Mia's head into his lap, feeling her tension immediately ease as he gently stroked her hair. Curled up with her feet on the couch, they laughed at the slapstick humor, momentarily trading in their reality for a much simpler one.

Half asleep, settled into the plush cushions, they were both roused and slightly surprised as the elevator opened to the apartment. They were more than slightly surprised when a couple kissing and laughing, wrapped in one another's arms, oblivious to the fact that they were being watched, tumbled out of the elevator and into the loft's great room.

Squinting, Mia immediately recognized Holly's long, silky blonde hair. But the man, who was he? Tall, but not as tall as Schooner, he had thick salt and pepper hair, wire-rimmed glasses and from what she could see of him, appeared quite handsome. Neither he nor Holly had yet to realize they were not alone, although the lights were on and the TV was playing.

Richard Gere. Why is Holly kissing Richard Gere? Mia wondered as she rubbed her eyes. Had she met him at some party? He was very handsome, but he was too old for her, were Mia's immediate thoughts. And what were they doing here?

Schooner cleared his throat and the surprised couple returned to reality, breaking apart to face Schooner and Mia.

The gasp that escaped from Mia's throat was involuntary and loud. It registered on the man's face as if she'd tossed him the full weight of a medicine ball, hard.

It wasn't Richard Gere that Holly had been kissing. It wasn't Richard Gere, at all.

"Mia?" There was surprise in the man's voice.

Holly looked at him, quizzically, clearly shocked that he knew her stepmother.

Mia breathed in deeply, rising to her feet and stood there for a moment, her eye contact with Holly's companion never wavering.

Finally, she acknowledged him, verbally. "Tom," she nodded, the single word, clipped. The loft took on a chill as there was not an ounce of warmth in her greeting.

Confused, Holly looked to Tom, then to Mia, and then back to Tom. "You two know each other?" She was clearly not processing how the pieces fit.

"Really, Tom?" Mia ignored her stepdaughter's question. She might not even have heard it. "You're older than her father."

"I didn't know." Tom Sheehan shook his head.

"Didn't know what? Didn't know her age? Didn't know that she was my stepdaughter? Didn't know that you were stepping too far over the line?" she screamed at the man.

"What is going on here?" Holly's face reddened, as she visibly became more upset.

"Will you tell her? Or shall I?" Mia's eyes never left his.

Tom turned to Holly, "Mia and I were involved," he stammered, "a long time ago."

"Get out of here, Tom, and stay away from my daughter." Mia took a step toward him, her small frame suddenly imposing.

Stepping forward, Holly blocked the path between Mia and Tom. "I'm not your daughter," she screamed at her stepmother. "And this is my home, you can't kick him out. My father bought this loft."

Mia felt a jagged tear in her heart as Holly drew the line. This beautiful young woman, whom she loved as a daughter, had just chosen Tom Sheehan over family, letting Mia know that they would never be blood or share those ties.

Holly looked to her father, who had been standing there watching this drama unfold as if he were observing a bad Fellini film.

"Dad?" Her tone was pleading.

Mia did not need to look at her husband to know the reaction his daughter was about to receive. She could feel his energy in every inch of her being and said a silent prayer that it didn't get physical. But one thing Schooner Moore had learned well over the years was how deadly controlled rage could be.

Not even acknowledging Holly's plea, his Caribbean blue eyes seared into Tom, a man he had forever longed to meet and one whose path he had hoped never to cross. While the loft had been filled with raised voices and emotion, Schooner Moore very quietly said two words in a tone that was both unimpeachable and deadly.

"Get out."

"You can't kick him out," Holly began to protest.

Schooner shifted his gaze from the man he perceived as his nemesis, to his beloved daughter. Locking eyes with her, he repeated what was not a request, but rather an order, one that also applied to her.

"Get out."

In the silence of the darkened cab, unspoken accusations became increasingly deafening as they hung in the humid, mid-summer night air, separating Holly and Tom on opposite ends of the back seat on what had become a painstakingly slow ride back to his Greenwich Village apartment. The relief was evident on both their faces as they shared an elevator with some of his neighbors, escaping being alone together in the confined space of the metal lift.

Not thirty seconds had passed after they entered his small flat when Holly turned to him, her face screwed up in anger.

"Did you sleep with my stepmother?" She choked out the words.

"It was a long time ago." He almost added *before you were born,* but caught the words before they escaped, and made the reality of the situation even worse.

"When was the last time you saw Mia?"

"Not in this century." That was the truth.

"Did you know? Did you know I was her stepdaughter?" With her hands clenched into fists at her side, her shoulders were bunched with tension.

With his palms upward, he shook his head, "How would I have known that? My relationship with you has nothing to do with Mia." Taking two steps toward her, "Babe, this is merely a coincidence. An odd and unfortunate coincidence."

"I can't believe my father threw me out." She began pacing the perimeter of the small living room. "I didn't give him shit when he left my mother for Mia. I just wanted him to be happy. Why doesn't he want the same for me?" She stopped and looked at Tom.

"Holly, I'm sure he wants you to be happy. Tonight was just a shock to everyone, and we all need to process this new reality and move forward." Tom sat on the well-loved leather couch and patted the cushion next to him for Holly to come and join him.

She didn't move from across the room. "What is that supposed to mean?"

"It means we all have a lot to process." Tom's tone was even, calming.

With her hands on her hips, she looked him straight in the eye. "I know what I have to process. What do you have to process?"

"That you unknowingly had ties to my past. That we are in an uncomfortable situation right now, but hopefully with time, cooler heads will prevail, and it will not be so uncomfortable for everyone. I don't want to come between you and your family, Holly."

"Is that the line you're going to use to let me down?"

Closing his eyes and shaking his head, Tom once again patted the couch next to him. "No. Not at all." Reaching out a hand to her, "Come. Come sit down next to me."

Finally, she moved across the room, lowering herself to the couch, a cushion away from her lover.

"I don't want to come between you and your family," he reiterated. "So, I am clearly going to have to walk a tightrope here. Your father is never going to like me. Being around Mia as your lover is going to be very uncomfortable, but we're going to have to figure out a way, even though it is going to be odd, but I'm sure we can make it work. If you separate from your family over this, you will resent the hell out of me. And I don't want to see that happening. We are early on in our relationship and every moment I've spent with you has been incredible. I'm not ready to give that up, Holly. You have been that breath of fresh air my life has needed for the longest time." Reaching across the empty couch cushion, Tom took her hand, threading his fingers with hers. "How did your father meet Mia?" he asked, almost as an afterthought.

"They went to college together and dated freshman year."

"In California?" Tom processed the information Holly shared.

She nodded. "When did you meet her?"

"The following year. I was her writing instructor." Tom knew it was best to get it all out now and let the chips fall where they may. "We started formally seeing one another after I was no longer her professor."

"Formally," she snickered. "I'm sorry, Tom, but I can't even think about this. I just can't think about the two of you together."

"Holly, it was a lifetime ago." He brought her hand to his lips.

"Yeah, I know, and I wasn't even born yet."

A feeling of loss spun through Holly's heart, leaving a trail of fragments at which she was not yet ready to glance. The one thing that had made her feel any happiness at all since Aiden told her it was over, was this growing relationship with Tom Sheehan. The man was smart and handsome, engaging and challenging, being with him had made her feel special. And she needed to feel special after Aiden's crushing dismissal of their relationship. And Tom accomplished that task with a finesse that fit like a custom-tailored suit.

And now she wondered if she truly was special to him or merely that summer's amusement. Had the one ray of light rescuing her from complete darkness been an illusion after all?

Hours after they had gone to sleep, Holly tried not to wake Tom with her tossing and turning, as she realized she had nowhere to go. And in his arms was the last place she wanted to be that night.

CHAPTER *Two*

Four Months Earlier

"DON'T CRY, HOLLY." Nathaniel Moore's bottom lip quivered as he tried as best he could to comfort his older sister, tenderly petting her long silky hair as he curled up into her on her bed. "Please, don't cry." Fat tears burst forth from his eyes as he failed to calm her.

"Mommy, Mommy," Portia Moore ran out onto the deck in search of her mother, who was standing at the deck's railing, looking out over the ocean and wrapping up a business call.

Mia put her finger to her lips, indicating for her young daughter to keep her voice down while she spoke to her client.

"But, Mommy," the little girl insisted.

Mia held up a finger indicating one more minute.

Standing very straight, Portia silently waited until Mia finished her call.

"What's going on, Po?" Mia was finally able to turn her full attention to her daughter.

"Mommy, something is wrong with Holly. She's in bed and she's crying, and she won't tell me and Natie why."

Looking at her watch, "It's already 2:30, why isn't she at work?" Following Portia up the stairs, Mia softly knocked on the door of her stepdaughter's bedroom before entering.

As Portia had warned her, something was very, very wrong. On her side, in a fetal position, Holly wept deeply, oblivious to her little brother's attempt at calming her.

Mia sat down on the edge of the bed near where Nathaniel and Portia were curled up behind their older sister. Gently rubbing her shoulder, Mia didn't speak, knowing Holly would share when she was able. In the meantime, there was a calming committee surrounding her with love, and Mia knew that would help.

Curled up like a little blonde angel next to her, Nathaniel surprised them all with a snore that would have made his father proud and they all laughed, including Holly. He opened his eyes long enough to give them all a smile and curled back up against his big sister for a nap.

Mia looked at her stepdaughter questioningly. "Do you want to talk?"

"Aiden dumped me," her voice cracked on the last word.

"What?" Mia's shock was apparent.

Holly nodded. "Yup. He told me I'm not the one, so for either of us to waste anymore of each other's time was not worthwhile."

"He said that?" It wasn't that Mia was questioning her, it was that she was more in disbelief than anything. Aiden appeared smitten and dedicated to Holly and their relationship and this sudden one-eighty was truly out of left field.

"I'm so sorry." Mia continued to rub her shoulder softly. "And I'm as shocked as you are."

"Mia, how could I have not seen this? How could I have misread the situation so badly? I don't understand."

"Oh Holly, I don't know what to say, except I'm so sorry. We all misread this one. My impression was that this man worshipped the ground you walked on and was never, ever going to let you go."

"Mine, too. I have never felt about a man the way I feel about him, and I think part of it is because he is a man and my other relationships have been with boys," Holly paused. "I know our backgrounds are so different. He grew up in a blue-collar neighborhood, went to school on an ROTC scholarship, served overseas. And he has worked hard and has turned the restaurant into a hot spot." She spoke of Maguire's, the restaurant where they had both worked. "And Mia, I didn't think the differences in our backgrounds were an issue for him. It wasn't for me. I just loved him for who he is." A fresh burst of tears slid down her cheeks.

Giving Holly's shoulder a squeeze, Mia stood up and left the room, returning just a few minutes later with a box of tissues and a bottle of cold water.

"This just doesn't make sense. That guy loves you like crazy. I don't think he's that good of an actor for that to have been an act. One that we all bought. Here's what I think," Mia offered as she handed Holly the tissues and water, and sat back down on the edge of the bed. "He's breaking up with you now before he gets sent up to active duty. Being called up has got to be scary with everything going on in the world. Afghanistan is still a mess. Syria is escalating. Everyone is holding their breath with North Korea. I don't know if the last time he was on active duty, he was involved with anyone as deeply as he's been with you."

"Mia," Holly began, sitting up in the bed, "that was my first gut reaction, too. And I called him out on it. He denied it and said that he didn't want me waiting for him because he knew he'd just be stringing me along and that being deployed came at the perfect time because he'd been looking for the right time to break up."

"He's full of shit." Mia shook her head. "I'm sorry but I don't believe him for a freaking second. He's older now and I think can see consequences more clearly. If something were to happen to him, either physically or emotionally, he doesn't want you tied to that. He'd feel guilty forever. I think in his head he'd rather feel guilty about breaking your heart now than the guilt he'd feel if you felt committed to stay in a less-than-perfect situation when he got home."

Inspecting a pink fingernail without looking up, Holly sniffed. "I want to believe that, but he said some pretty shitty things to me. I think he wants to get back with his old girlfriend, Janine, and that things have already started up between them again."

Mia shook her head. "Nah, I don't think so. Number one, the two of you are always together. Always. You two have been inseparable. You pointed her out when she was on the island last Labor Day. Trust me, he's not leaving you for her. She's kind of got that Nassau County skank thing going on."

With eyes widening in amusement, Holly looked at her stepmother. "I love you, Mia. I really do."

Mia laughed. "You know me, I call 'em like I see 'em. He would be around that woman for ten minutes and thinking, *Holly would have done that this way. Holly would never have said that. I wonder what Holly would think of that?* Janine could not live for one second in your shadow, sweetie."

"He wants me out of his life. He made that clear."

"When does he leave?"

"In about a month."

"Well, at least you won't have to look at him all summer and maybe Maguire's will hire a very hot new manager in Aiden's place."

"I can't stay." Holly shook her head. "Every place here will remind me of him. It will be heartbreaking. Mia, I thought I was going to marry him. I have never felt for anyone what I feel for him. He's my first thought in the morning and my last when I fall asleep. My heart wants to burst every time he smiles at me. And when he calls me Angel, which is a corny thing, but it's like there's no one in the world but me." Grabbing a tissue, she blew her nose. "Shit, Mia, I am never going to be in his arms again."

And with her stepdaughter's new round of tears, Mia opened her arms for Holly and held her tight until calm came again.

"Take a look at your cheer-up committee." Mia laughed. "Some good they are."

Nathaniel was curled up in a ball, fast asleep and Portia was stretched out on her back, snoring lightly.

Holly finally smiled and nodded her head as she looked at her young siblings. "Thank God for this family."

***

"I've thought about it and I really don't want to be here," Holly announced two days later. "I'm sure I can get a job in the city for the summer." The dark circles under Holly's eyes emphasized her lack of sleep.

"Worst case scenario, if all the college students have already gobbled up all the decent jobs, you can work at MS&A or at L9/NYC. The agency can always use a hand. It might be more on the clerical side than you'd like, but I'm sure we can use your very capable skills somewhere." Mia liked her solution, knowing that one of the family businesses in Manhattan would keep Holly occupied for the summer.

"Or I can waitress. If nothing else, I did get great experience here at Maguire's."

"How long will he be out here on Fire Island before he has to report for duty?" Mia was fearful of even asking the question, knowing bringing up Aiden brought Holly to a raw place.

"Another three-and-a-half weeks. Mia, I can't stay here for another three weeks on the island with him."

Fire Island is a sandbar. One long, glorious sandbar located off the southern coast of Long Island and acts as a barrier island, catching the brunt of the ocean storms. But what was currently playing out in the Moore house was a storm Mia hoped her stepdaughter could successfully weather. Aiden McManus was the love of Holly Moore's life. A tough, street-smart Irish kid from the south shore of Long Island and a poised, cerebral blonde beauty from a home located right on Newport Bay in Newport Beach, California. Holly and Aiden were a classic case of opposites attracting, each one entranced by the other.

Well, at least until two days before.

Three days before that, they laid entangled on the great room couch in Schooner and Mia's oceanfront beach house, binge watching *Game of Thrones*. Each one getting up hourly to get something for the other. Slices of mango, a tall, sweaty glass of iced tea, grapes. Every so often they'd get a visit from the little ones, Po and Natie, who would snuggle in for a few minutes before getting bored.

What had happened for Aiden to tell Holly he no longer wanted her in his life? Mia needed to know and slipped on some espadrilles to walk into town and give Mr. McManus a visit. And maybe a piece of her mind.

He was behind the bar, back to her, when she slipped onto her choice of empty worn, wooden barstools, their eyes meeting in the intricate antique mirror he faced.

"Mia," he said to her reflection.

"Aiden," she said to the back of his head.

"What took you so long?" he asked his ex-girlfriend's stepmother.

Watching him pour bourbon, vermouth, and bitters into an ice-filled shaker, Mia remained silent as Aiden slid the Manhattan toward her. Without batting an eye, she picked up the martini glass and sipped from it, wondering if the Manhattan was symbolic in some way of her and her family, letting her know that they were the uppity city people.

Ignoring his question, Mia put the martini glass down on the bar and looked up, locking into Aiden's dark hazel eyes. "You know I don't believe for a single second that you don't love her."

"It is what it is." He shrugged.

Taking another sip of her drink, Mia shifted on her barstool, her legs a little too short to find the right position. "I walked away from Schooner once. In my mind, I was doing the right thing. But I never got over him. He was like a ghost that followed me around and appeared in my darkest moments, making them even bleaker, because he wasn't there, and I knew nothing of his life." Sighing, she shook her head.

"Is this your way of telling me I'm going to regret this?" Aiden leaned on the bar casually.

He's certainly got game, Mia thought. "You already do."

"Mia, with all due respect, you don't know what you are talking about."

"I wish I didn't, Aiden. But unfortunately, I do. You are not going to stop loving her any more than she is going to stop loving you. And we both know that. Just don't wait too long, okay. You think you want her to move on. But you don't. You don't want to get home from whatever hellhole our government is going to send you to and come back here to see her with another man. Honestly, I can't see you standing down as you watch some guy slinging his arm over her shoulder to let everyone here know that she's now his."

A muscle right above his jawline twitched. Mia had her verification. Without another word, she slipped from the barstool and exited the restaurant wishing she could give him some of her life experience and have him learn from her mistakes.

Mistake #1 – Do not walk away from the one you love. Be honest. Communicate. And try to work it out.

But Aiden McManus was stubborn as all hell, and Mia knew the heartache for everyone would escalate before things got better.

If things ever got better.

CHAPTER *Three*

Mid-Summer thru Fall

LOIS WAS OUT OF cardiac ICU in two days and on the main floor for heart patients. It was a surprise to no one that her patience had already waned, and she was done with her hospital stay and ready to go home, whether the doctors were in agreement with her or not.

"Bridge is at our house next Saturday," she informed her husband.

Mia looked at her mother as if she were insane. Bridge, amongst their group, included a light dinner, something like bagels and lox, sandwiches, and salads or something of the like, followed later in the evening by dessert and decaf.

"Mom, you might find that you don't have your full energy back and get tired quicker than before." Turning to her father to be the voice of reason, she asked, "Dad, can you skip a month?"

"They fixed me, Mia. I'm not dead."

Leaning against a wall, half listening, half focused on scrolling through his phone, Schooner's cell rang, and he excused himself slipping out into the hallway.

"What is going on with him?" Lois asked her daughter. Even she could tell Schooner wasn't himself. "Did you two have a fight? What did you say to him?" Lois assumed her not-so-easy daughter had pissed off her wonderful son-in-law.

Mia shook her head. "This one has nothing to do with me, Mom. This falls under the category of shit you can't make up." She paused and closed her eyes for a moment. "We made quite the discovery the other night when we got back to the loft."

"What? What did you discover?"

Staring at her mother, Mia remained silent for a moment. "Okay, let me preface this by saying, brace yourself. You've just come through surgery and I'm almost afraid of what verbalizing this will do to you."

Mia's father was now at rapt attention, too.

"We were on the couch watching TV. Both of us were half asleep. Schooner had tried to get hold of Holly earlier in the evening to let her know that we were coming back to the city and would be at the loft, but he wasn't able to reach her. All of a sudden, the elevator opened and Holly and some guy tumbled out of the elevator locked in a passionate embrace, kissing. They were totally oblivious to us."

"Well, that could be embarrassing for them." Lois was checking the bruises on her arm from the multiple IV sticks they'd attempted before getting a good vein.

"At first I didn't recognize him," Mia went on.

"You knew him?

"Who was it?" Bob Silver stared at his daughter.

"It was..." she paused.

"Oh, just spit it out, Mia." Lois was losing patience with her daughter, assuming Mia was merely being dramatic.

"It was Tom Sheehan."

Lois's hand flew to her mouth and for a moment Mia thought her mother was about to be sick. Lois had never liked Tom, feeling he was inappropriate for her daughter, as he was ten years her senior.

Silently, Bob lowered himself into a chair.

The Silvers remained speechless until Mia finally broke the silence. "Yeah. I know."

"That's disgusting." The look on Bob Silver's face said it all.

Looking to her mom, who usually had a comment about everything, Mia observed the silenced Lois.

"So, that's what Schooner is understandably upset about," she explained.

"Well, I should say so," Lois finally regained her voice. "Was it the first time he's met Tom?"

"Yes." Mia nodded.

"He knew about him, though, and your involvement, correct?"

Again, Mia nodded.

"And he didn't kill him?" This time it was Bob's question.

"Surprisingly, no. He threw the two of them out of the loft and changed the elevator code, so no one can enter while we're gone. Which really isn't fair to Holly. She's got all her stuff in the loft. But I know he didn't want Tom there and he certainly didn't want the two of them there together, in our home."

"I'm shocked," Lois began. "Yet, I'm not. The man has always had a predilection for very young women." She shook her head. "At least Holly's legal." Lois gave Mia a pointed look, reminding her now forty-something daughter that she had begun her relationship with the man prior to being of a legal age.

Again, the Silvers lapsed into silence and uncharacteristically it was Bob who was the first to speak. "So, what are you going to do about this?"

"What can we do, Dad? Holly's a grown woman. We can't dictate whom she sees and doesn't see. We may not like it, but we can't do anything about it."

Bob nodded, and then surprised Mia and Lois with his next suggestion. "Get her mother into town. She'll take care of it."

"CJ?" Mia questioned, the distaste from merely verbalizing her husband's exes' name, the woman who had caused Schooner and Mia's twenty-four-year separation, made the petite brunette appear as if a fetid odor hung heavy in the air.

"Yes," Bob's response was almost a whisper. "CJ will take care of this."

Mia looked from her mother, lying in the hospital bed, back to her father, and somewhere deep in the pit of her stomach she feared the past, her past, Schooner's past, and CJ's past might end up laying their sins squarely on the feet of the next generation.

"Have you heard from Holly?"

Schooner nodded, his usual lively, oceanic-blue eyes appearing darker than usual in the restaurant's subdued light. "Yeah, she wanted the elevator code to get her stuff out of the loft."

"Oh God, I hope she doesn't move in with him."

"I hope she does." Schooner could clearly see on Mia's face her shock to his response.

"You can't be serious?" The stiffening of her spine said it all, and when she pushed away her half-eaten plate of crab cakes, that was the exclamation point.

"I'm totally serious. How old is that guy again?" *That guy.* He couldn't even say Tom's name.

Mia could see Schooner's brain churning. "Umm," she hesitated for a moment, "he's eight years older than you."

His typically vibrant smile looked more like a sneer as he let out a solemn laugh. "Yeah, well, good luck to him having a twenty-something living in his space. That novelty will wear off quickly." And then he smiled, his real smile. "I don't think we're going to be stressing out about whether or not we'll have to invite him to Thanksgiving."

"You don't think they'll make it that long?"

"Oh God, no. He's going to be gift wrapping her and returning her to us and probably paying us to take her back. There is no way having a millennial invade his apartment full-time, especially when he is not used to them, except for in the classroom," Schooner sneered again, "and in his bedroom."

Mia just shook her head looking worried. "I hope you're right."

Pointing at Mia, he smiled. "Just don't you give me any shit about having to invite him to Po's birthday party, because he is not invited. And don't tell me I'm disrespecting Holly. I don't want to see this guy again."

Holding up her hands in a sign of surrender, Mia laughed. "I can guarantee you no shit from me."

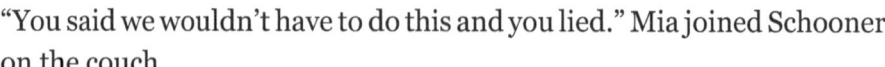

"You said we wouldn't have to do this and you lied." Mia joined Schooner on the couch.

Schooner laughed. "And you know how I hate being wrong. Especially in this case."

"So, does he get an invite or not?" Mia knew what her answer was, but this was Schooner's call.

"I don't want him here, Baby Girl. I really don't. But I don't want Holly to ever feel that she is not welcome to spend Thanksgiving with her own family."

Just looking at her husband, Mia knew the battle she was seeing rage in his eyes was probably nothing in comparison to the war being waged in his heart. Schooner Moore loved his kids and the strain between him and Holly hung over him relentlessly and had for months. Nothing would be right in his world until his relationship with his beloved first-born was repaired. This standoff had to end.

"Let me cheer you up with this thought." Mia's smile said it all. "Lois hates Tom. She has always hated Tom. Now that Lois is a senior, she says whatever the hell she wants. Not that she had a huge filter when she was younger, but she is much more brazen now. Trust me, Tom Sheehan does not want to see my mother and does not want to be in the same room with her."

Slinging his arm over her shoulder and pulling her to him, he smiled as he said, "Baby Girl, you always know how to make me feel better. God, I love Lois."

"Well, lucky for you, Pretty Boy, she has always loved you. From day one, that woman has adored you."

"I would not want to be on her bad side," he mused.

"Not possible." Laughing at the memory, she shared, "Every week when she used to call me, she'd ask, 'How's that sweet boy?'"

"And what would you tell her?"

"I'd tell her, 'How the hell should I know. I'm not friends with him. He's a jock.'"

Tucking her feet under her on the couch, Mia got comfortable against her husband. With her nose buried in his cotton shirt, she couldn't help but close her eyes and breathe in his clean scent. *Ah, my own personal aromatherapy for stress relief and relaxation,* she thought as she smiled into his shirt.

Only a moment had passed when Mia popped up in his arms, her face a portrait of astonishment. "You're going to think I'm batshit crazy, but I think we should also invite CJ to Thanksgiving."

"Have you lost your mind, woman?" Schooner couldn't believe his ears. Did Mia just actually suggest inviting CJ to Thanksgiving?

"No. Seriously, listen to me." She swatted his muscular arm.

"You have my rapt attention. Trust me."

"When we were down in Florida, right after we found out about Holly and Tom, I was telling my parents the news. Well, my Dad's response was really interesting and baffling and I don't know why I didn't question him on it, but I didn't."

"What did he say?"

"He said, 'Get her mother into town. She'll take care of it.'" Mia paused, "Do we know how much CJ knows, Schooner?"

He shook his head. "I haven't spoken to her in a while and we don't know what Holly's told her."

"Let me call her and invite her." Mia knew she was shocking her husband with every statement she made. In what universe would she ever call CJ to invite her to a family function? It had been a while since they'd seen her. But even that wasn't long enough.

Sitting very still and staring at his wife with a half-smile, Schooner wondered if he was being punked. "Why do I feel like I'm going to wake up any moment, roll over, and wake you to tell you about this weird dream I had?"

Shaking her head, Mia pulled Schooner's arm into her lap, gently rubbing his forearm where his sleeve was rolled up. "We are just going to need to keep everybody very drunk."

"Baby Girl, they are all on their own. The only person I need to keep drunk is me. Just promise to dump me in bed when I pass out." Schooner was just beginning to process what they'd discussed. "I'm going to need to go into L9 that morning and get a serious workout in just to be able to deal with this."

"Maybe you need to go do yoga that morning, so you can get all Namaste for our guests. Killing guests at Thanksgiving is not in good form. Number one no-no in the how-to-be-a-good-host manual."

"Why are we doing this? Do you hate me that much?" he kidded.

Laughing, Mia lifted his hand to her lips, softly kissing his knuckles. "This is definitely going to be a shit storm. My money is on CJ."

"You're a smart cookie. And a brave one, too." Putting his arm back around Mia's shoulders, he pulled her to him, and kissing the top of her head, he silently prayed they would come out of the holiday without family fractures that were beyond repair.

Closing the door to her office for privacy, Mia paced in front of the window, taking deep breaths as she mindlessly gazed at the Freedom Tower. There were very few people on the planet that could provoke an anxiety attack, and CJ MacAllister-Moore-Gordon was at the top of that list. Every insecurity about being a teen, and being different, surfaced with the force of a whale breaching the ocean's surface when it came to CJ. In her own mind, Mia would always be the curly-haired outcast with glasses and CJ would always be the blonde prom queen who got the guy. And in their particular version of this tale, said guy was one Schooner Moore.

Finally, she picked up her phone, put it on speaker and dialed.

"Hello."

Mia's stomach knotted just hearing her voice. *He doesn't love you. You're just a charity case to him.*

"CJ, hi, it's Mia."

"Mia?" The tone of her voice was saying *who?*

"Mia Moore." Two words that she never thought she'd be saying to CJ.

"Oh... Mia... Silver."

Don't even acknowledge that, Mia consciously told herself, as she took a breath and got to the point of the call.

"We are putting together our plans for Thanksgiving and I know Holly and Zac would love to have the opportunity to spend it with you. So, we'd like to invite you and Beau to New York to join us."

Mia did not expect total silence, and when CJ did not respond, she asked, "CJ, are you still there?"

"Yes, I'm here," and she went silent again.

Awkward.

"CJ, is everything okay?"

"Yes, everything is fine. I'm just surprised by this call, Mia. Obviously, you can understand that. And why are you the one calling me and not Schooner?"

"I told Schooner that I would like to reach out to you."

"Why?"

"Because Thanksgiving is a family holiday. My Mom had a heart attack over the summer and that was very sobering for me. People you think are just going to always be there, may not be one day. And Holly and Tom and Zac and Lily will all be here for the holiday, and Schooner and I thought it would be nice for them if you were here, too."

CJ laughed. "Schooner was not thinking that, Mia. We both know that. But I would love to spend the holiday with my children. Did you say that Holly's boyfriend is going to be there?"

"Tom. Yes, he'll be here." Mia was biting her tongue. *Bait taken.*

"I'm looking forward to meeting him. She hasn't been very forthcoming with information about him."

"No?" A war was being waged between Mia's brain and her mouth. This could all go sideways very easily and very quickly.

"No. All she's told me is that he's an English professor."

"Yes. Yes, he is." *Score one for the brain. Keep out of this, mouth.*

"You've met him?"

Mia knew right then and there that mouth didn't stand a chance. It was a losing battle.

"Yes. We've met him."

"And?"

"And what?"

"Is he a nice guy? What's he like? Does he treat Holly well?"

"So, what exactly has she told you?"

"That he teaches Screenwriting at NYU's film school."

"What else?" Mia was praying that Holly had told her something, anything.

"Nothing, she's been very close-mouthed about it. It makes coming in for Thanksgiving appealing, so I can finally meet this mystery man of my daughter's."

This time the silence was on Mia's end. She couldn't just tell her. CJ had to ask.

"Mia, are you there?"

"Yes. I'm here."

"Am I going to like this man?"

Staring out her office window, the single word was out of her mouth long before she was able to process the thought. "No."

"What do you mean, no?" ripped the edge in CJ's voice.

"Well, he's a bit older than Holly."

Staring at the Freedom Tower, Mia could not help but miss the two sentinels that had been its predecessor. She still yearned every day, each time she looked out the window, expecting them, like two arms reaching toward the sky, to embrace her, just as they had done since childhood. They had watched over her that day as she walked home to get the file inadvertently left on the dining table. The day she caught Tom and threw him out, but not until after she'd heaved his fuck partner's clothes out the window onto 14th Street, sixteen floors below.

"How much older?"

"He's older than you." Mia didn't want to tell her how much.

"What?" CJ's tone went shrill. "What else do I need to know about this man, Mia? This is my daughter."

"Well, there is something." Mia focused on a cloud floating past the tower.

"Just spit it out." She was clearly annoyed and not hiding it.

"I knew Tom years ago," Mia began.

"And?"

"And we were involved."

"Why don't you define involved?" It was obvious CJ was speaking through clenched teeth.

"It was a very long time ago." Mia forced herself to deliver the killing blow. Even though it was CJ, there was just no joy in this situation. "We lived together."

"So, you are telling me my daughter is involved with your ex-lover?"

"Yes."

"What the hell is wrong with you people? And Schooner is allowing this?"

"CJ, Schooner and I are not happy about this. But Holly is over twenty-one. What can we really do?"

"So, you just allow your ex-lover and my daughter to hang out in your home?"

"Actually, no. Tom hasn't been welcome there, but we don't want Holly to feel she doesn't have a family."

"So, she just doesn't bring him there?"

"Well, actually, she doesn't live here. Schooner threw the two of them out when we found them here."

"So, where is she living? Is she living with him?"

"Yes."

"And my ex-husband has allowed this?"

Mia could picture the disbelief on CJ's face.

"Again, Holly is an adult. And to be honest with you, Schooner thought that Tom having a twenty-something in his space would hasten the end of this relationship. Neither of us thought he'd be at our Thanksgiving dinner."

"Well, that clearly was a miscalculation."

"Yes, it was."

"How did you know him, Mia?"

There was no way to deliver this delicately and Mia wasn't sure delicate was best anyway. *Just drop the bomb. Boom. Do it.*

"He was a professor of mine in college."

"So, he has a penchant for young girls?"

"Yes."

"No wonder why she's kept him such a mystery. And I had no idea she wasn't living with you."

"So, we will see you and Beau for Thanksgiving?"

CJ waited a few beats too long before answering. "No. It will just be me. Beau and I have separated. I've filed for divorce."

Boom. The bombs were freely flying. The shit storm had already begun.

CHAPTER
Four

Thanksgiving into Winter

"YOU'RE UP BEFORE THE kids." Schooner came up behind Mia, bending to kiss her neck as she surveyed the perfectly set holiday table. "You did a really beautiful job." There was a hint of surprise in his voice as he complimented his wife. Mia excelled at many things; however, domestic goddess was not near the top of that list.

"It needs something," she insisted, not turning her sights away from the table.

"People?" Schooner ventured.

"No." She shook her head, then turned to Schooner and smiled. "We want to be without people for as long as possible."

"That's for damn sure. I'm heading over to L9 to run the SkyTrack. I'll be back in plenty of time to take the kids up to the parade. Anything you need me to pick up on the way home?" He pressed the elevator button.

"I can't think of anything. I'll text you if I do." Her back was to him as she once again stood motionless, staring at the table.

Nothing felt right about today. Nothing at all.

"Mommy."

Hearing Portia's voice, Mia turned immediately. "Hi sweetie, what are you doing up so early?"

"I heard Daddy. Is it time to go to the parade?" Only a trace of her beautiful English accent was left, matching just the mere trace of memories from her years in an orphanage in Zambia, before Mia and Schooner adopted her.

"No. We still have a few hours."

"I was excited, and I was afraid I'd miss it." Walking up to the fully set holiday table, "This looks so beautiful. Which seat is mine?" she asked.

Mia pointed to a seat at the far end of the table. "You're right over there. You're going to sit between Nana and Uncle Seth."

Portia walked over to her chair and asked, "This one?"

"That's the one." Mia smiled, thinking the kids will make the energy better today. "Daddy went running. How about you crawl back into bed with me and we'll sleep until he gets us up." As the kids were getting older, Mia missed the snuggle time that seemed to be fading away too quickly for her heart.

Portia was on her way to the master bedroom before Mia even finished the sentence. Finding her already under the covers, Mia snuggled in next to her. At least the day would have a perfect start.

"When will everyone be here?"

"After we get home from the parade," Mia explained, knowing Po wanted to know when she was going to see her older brother and sister. "You'll see Holly and Zac and Lily."

Just hearing those names, her face lit up in a beautiful smile, but her eyes were already closed, and Mia did the same.

"I can't believe you let them eat candy apples." Mia was shaking her head at Schooner as they entered the elevator. "Don't touch anything." She pointed at Nathaniel, who grinned widely, showing off his missing front teeth. "How did you eat that thing without chompers, my little toothless wonder?"

"I used my sharp ones." Pointing at his incisors, his red-stained lips stretched into a wide smile.

"You look like The Joker." Mia shook her head. "Go straight to the bathroom, wash your face and hands first, and then brush your teeth good. And don't touch anything." She screamed after him as he tore through the loft, a glucose-charged demon, capable of leaving mass destruction in his wake. Shaking her head, she just looked at her husband, "Think he's on a little bit of a sugar high?"

Shrugging his shoulders, Schooner smiled at his wife, "It's a holiday." He was a lot more relaxed with his two younger kids than he had been with raising his older two. Breathing in deeply, he commented, "It smells great in here," and headed straight for the kitchen, pulling open the oven door and momentarily closing his eyes as the fragrant aroma of fresh herbs escaped, wafting around him. "The bird looks great."

"Close the oven door," Mia ordered. "You came, you sniffed, you gawked. Now make yourself useful."

"When did you turn into such a shrew?" He smiled at his wife, enjoying this moment, before the day got out of their control.

Mia laughed and shook her head. "Hey, I think I'm holding up pretty well considering I'm making Thanksgiving for your ex and mine." Handing Schooner a bag of fresh green beans, "Cut off the ends and wash." She gave him his marching orders and a colander, then walked out of the kitchen.

"Hey, where are you going?" he shouted after her. Grumbling, "Leaving me with all the work."

"I'm just checking on the sticky bandits and want to make sure they get cleaned up and dressed. And then I'm going to get dressed, too, before our guests start walking in."

Schooner figured Mia did not want her parents to arrive and have Lois ask her, "Is that what you're wearing?" And with Tom and CJ there, he knew she was not going to be as casual as she would like to be when running around and entertaining, the way she usually was when it was just family and close friends.

The elevator door opened. "Hello. It smells divine in here." Seth called out and then stood for a moment, his eyes closed, enjoying the savory aroma. "I love Thanksgiving," he declared, stepping into the loft.

"We are definitely in the right place." Henry held up the bottle of wine in his hand, acknowledging Schooner in the open kitchen.

"Don't tease me, man. Open that thing," Schooner begged.

As Henry headed toward the kitchen, Seth went to survey the dining table.

"This looks beautiful. BBC did a great job. Schooner, you have domesticated her." Walking around the table, he noted the seating cards. "I love it, she has left nothing to chance, Tom is stuck with me and Lois. He has no idea how much he should be dreading today."

"Oh, that's right, you know him," commented Schooner. "Yeah, well, I'm dreading him being here."

"Oh yes, I was around for dark, gorgeous, brooding poet. I can't wait to see what he looks like now. And what I really can't wait for is to meet your ex." Seth leaned up against the marble kitchen counter.

"My ex, huh?" Schooner shook his head, then smiled at Henry, "I don't want to run through this one, I want to run away from it."

Henry's smile grew wide. Only he and Schooner would ever understand the comment his oldest friend just made. "I've got a ringside seat."

"Lucky man." Looking from Henry to Seth, he pointed across the kitchen to where Seth stood. "The corkscrew is in that drawer. And I think we're going to need more than wine glasses for this. Will you grab a few water glasses?"

Setting glasses on the counter for Schooner and Henry, Seth asked, "Is BBC in the bedroom?"

Schooner nodded and clinked his glass to Henry's.

"Run through it," Henry toasted.

"Mia," Seth called out, heading in the direction of the bedrooms.

"I'm in the master bathroom with Po. Come on in," she called out.

Mia stood behind her daughter, a section of Portia's thick, curly hair in her hand. "Why don't you want to let me flat iron it today?"

"Because I like it curly and fluffy."

"Last week you liked it straight."

"I did. But I don't want it that way today."

"Okay, fine. Less work for me. Go check on your brother and make sure he dresses in the clothes I put out for him."

Portia was out the door, briefly stopping to acknowledge Uncle Seth and plant a juicy kiss on his lips with a giggle.

Mia looked at Seth, "I wish they were babies again. They are growing up too fast. It's all going too fast." Mia was getting weepy.

"Stop that. You're just emotional because you're stressing out about today's guests."

"No, shit. You think?" she laughed at her best friend and business partner. "This whole thing is like a bad soap opera that needs to be cancelled."

"Well, your husband has just cracked open the bottle of wine we brought. He's clearly begun his escape route."

"That's not fair. He's not allowed to do that without me." Mia looked in the mirror. "Does my hair look okay?"

"You look good. You know I'd tell you if you didn't. What do you need me to do in the kitchen?"

"Get the sweet potatoes out of the oven and start the sweet potato soufflé. I'll be there in a few minutes." Mia stood staring at her reflection after Seth left. Having either Tom or CJ there would have been a stress-provoking situation, but having both, was pressing all her buttons, making long-extinguished, or so she thought, insecurities, float right to the surface. This was not going to be a kumbaya Thanksgiving and her stomach was already churning.

Mia arrived back in the kitchen, as the elevator opened into the great room and Zac and Lily stepped out, fresh from their ride up from Baltimore.

"Finally." Lily rolled her eyes. "The Jersey Turnpike was a hellacious parking lot. It took us over five hours to get here."

"Take off your coats and get comfortable." Mia hugged her stepson and his fiancée.

"It smells yummy in here. I love Thanksgiving." Lily smiled at her future stepmother-in-law.

"Heckle. Jeckle," Zac yelled out in the direction of the bedrooms and with screams of excitement, Nathaniel and Portia came out running to their older brother whom they hadn't seen since September. "I've missed you devils." He hugged them close.

"You didn't bring your mother?" Schooner hugged Zac and Lily.

"No, she said she'd take a cab from her hotel and would meet us here."

Schooner laughed. "Some grand entrance, I'm sure."

"C'mon, Dad. Would you expect anything less?"

"I can't wait to meet her," Seth piped in from the kitchen.

"Traitor," Mia muttered loud enough for only Seth to hear.

"Afraid I'll like her better than you?" he sneered back, as he stirred the ingredients for the soufflé's crunchy topping.

"Be nice," Henry told his partner.

"I'm always nice. I'm just so excited to meet this person I've heard about for years." He spread the topping over the soufflé. "Will she out-bitch me?"

"It'll be close. You might have met your match," kidded Henry. "I'm sure she's as anxious about today as you are, Mia. At least you have the home-turf advantage."

"It's going to be a shit storm," Mia muttered, getting Seth the lid to the casserole dish. "Please control my mother, Seth. You know how she's always felt about Tom."

With a snicker, he looked at her like she was crazy and put the sweet potato soufflé in the oven. "As if anyone could control what comes out of Lois Silver's mouth."

"That's my fear." She looked through a cabinet, not finding what she needed. "Hey, Hon," she yelled out, "please bring me a bottle of cognac."

Schooner appeared with a bottle of Hennessy. "Starting the hard stuff a little early, Baby Girl?"

"I wish. Still too much to do." Holding up a measuring cup, she poured in a small amount of the amber liquid before putting the open bottle under her nose and smiling as she breathed in deeply. "I'll meet you for one of these tonight, before we go to bed." Smiling at Schooner, she put the stopper back in and handed him the bottle.

"You've got a date." He bent down as Mia got on her toes for a quick kiss, then turned around with a smile as he left to return the bottle to his office.

"I'm excited for today and a little afraid. Does Tom know I'll be here?" Seth asked.

"I don't know. I don't think so." Mia and Seth stood there very still, smiling at one another. "Do you believe this shit is happening?"

"You couldn't make this up. And what's it been? Like twenty years?"

"Something like that," Mia confirmed, as she slid the tray of stuffing into the oven.

"How do I look? Do I look okay?" Seth squared his shoulders.

"Princess, do not tell me you want to look good for Tom?" Mia was amazed.

"No, I don't want to look good for him. I want him to see how good I look." Seth wiggled his shoulders.

"You are such a tart."

"Bitch." His smile began to curl into a snarl, but was cut short by the unpleasant buzzing of the intercom.

The guests were arriving. Mia pressed the button, activating the video.

CJ.

In what alternate universe would CJ MacAllister be coming to her home in New York for Thanksgiving. CJ. Her nemesis. The woman who had cost her and Schooner twenty-four years of their lives with her lies. Her stinking lies.

Mia pressed the button to open the elevator and bring CJ to their loft.

"Zac, your Mom's on her way up," Mia called out to him.

Rising from the couch, he walked across the room to the elevator, just as the doors parted. Emerging with the elegance of a pageant girl, she cut a striking figure, head-to-toe in winter white, in what appeared to be vintage Chanel. Class, elegance and beauty, CJ MacAllister-Moore-Gordon certainly lived up to her reputation for knowing how to make an entrance.

Giving her son her cheek and a brief side hug, CJ surveyed the room. She crossed toward the open kitchen to Mia, awkwardly holding out an arrangement of fall flowers in front of her, like a shield, saving her from any real contact with the woman who had been her archenemy since they were teens.

"Thank you for inviting me." She handed Mia the flowers.

"These are beautiful. Thank you. You really didn't have to."

"Is Holly here yet?" she asked her hostess, without even acknowledging Mia's comments.

Mia shook her head.

"Hello, I'm Seth," he introduced himself, as Mia forgot he was standing next to her.

"Seth." She nodded, extending her hand with a close-mouthed smile.

"I see you've met my better half." Henry came up behind her.

Turning at the familiar voice, CJ broke into her first real smile. "Look at you, how handsome you're looking." She gave Henry a hug, whispering in his ear, "At least I have one friend here."

He gave her a squeeze to let her know that she did. He had never liked CJ and knew in his gut that she was behind Schooner losing Mia in college. And he'd been right. CJ was manipulative, self-serving, and self-absorbed. But that's not all she was. She was the woman who made him organic pureed food when his psychotic lover broke half the bones in his face. And on the darkest day of his life, the day he buried his beloved partner, Quinn, CJ took over, hiring and directing a catering staff to ensure that neither he nor Quinn's mother had to lift a finger or worry about anything but making it through that brutally heartbreaking day. So, for all the wrong she had done, Henry knew that when the chips were down, CJ could be counted on to come through, without ever having to be asked.

"What can I get you to drink?" Seth asked.

"White wine."

Even her drink matched her suit. Sitting down next to Zac on the couch, CJ took notice of Portia and Nathaniel for the first time.

"You look just like my son did," she said to Nathaniel, who appeared confused. "I'm Zac's mommy," she explained.

Natie looked from CJ to Zac and then turned around to look at Mia.

"You're Zac's mommy. That's my mommy." Portia pointed to Mia.

"Yes, dear, I could tell. You have the same hair. And you wear it just like she wore it in college."

Not understanding CJ's true intent, Portia took the words as complimentary, smiling broadly at the woman. Entering the room just in time to hear the exchange between his young daughter and his ex-wife, Schooner shook his head.

Leaning down from behind the couch, it looked as if he were going to kiss the cool blonde's cheek, but instead he whispered in her ear, "You are a guest in our home. I expect you to be civil."

Craning her alabaster neck, she smiled, a close-mouthed smile, at her ex-husband. "Always a pleasure to see you, too, Schooner."

Standing, she smoothed down her pencil skirt, and walked toward the kitchen, without a second glance at her ex.

"Mia, may I have a moment with you?"

"Sure, give me one sec." She put down the slotted spoon and washed her hands. "Let's go talk in Schooner's office." Mia led the way, closing the door behind them, not really knowing what to expect.

Being in a room alone with CJ had only happened once before in her life and the results had been disastrous for her as CJ convinced her that Schooner never loved her and only saw her as an obligation and charity case, causing Mia to flee before ever confronting Schooner. That conversation was the life-altering genesis of a twenty-four-year separation from the man she loved.

"I wanted to talk to you before Holly gets here," CJ began.

"Her well-being is something you and I share."

"Good, then will you please fill me in on the details. I need to know what I'm dealing with here."

"We had no idea that she had met Tom. I had not seen the man in like twenty years, so we were really shocked."

"What's he like?"

"Intelligent, charming, talented, handsome. Female students love him. Male students want to be like him. He's not very good at monogamy." Mia strained to find the right words, not really knowing what they were.

"Is that why you broke up with him?"

"Yes. I caught him in our bed with one of his students. Keeping his dick in his pants was not his strong suit." There. It was out.

"Once a cheater, always a cheater." CJ nodded, as she stared at a spot on Schooner's desk. Inhaling deeply, she looked back at Mia, pointing a finger at her. "I'm going to take one for the team. So, don't you forget it."

"What are you going to do, CJ?" Mia, of all people, knew the lengths this woman would go to in order to get her way.

"It's best you're not complicit."

"Well, thanks for that." Not knowing what she would pull, it was a relief to know that.

"Thank me later." CJ brushed past Mia, exiting the office.

Mia stood there for a moment, not moving. *This certainly is going to be a shit storm,* she thought. Taking a deep breath, she forced herself to leave the quiet office, knowing that this moment alone would be her one and only peaceful stretch of the day.

As Mia walked out, the elevator call buzzed. Seth was closest to the intercom.

"It's Holly and," he paused, "Tom," and proceeded to push the button. "And Lois and Bob." His eyes were wide as he turned to Mia.

"What?" Mia raced over to the intercom screen for a visual. "I almost feel sorry for him." She watched the four enter the lift. Laughing, she turned to Seth, "Now that's poetic justice. Too bad we don't have a 'Get Stuck Between Floors' button."

"Just pray she doesn't come out of the elevator with his balls. We don't have room in the oven for another course."

There was a collective holding of breath as the door to the elevator opened. Holly and Lois emerged first, and shrieks of "Nana" and "Holly" drew all attention away from the men entering the apartment, except for CJ. As she slowly stood, waiting for the melee to subside before approaching her daughter, her eyes were locked on Holly's lover. He was a *fine-wine man*, one of the few, like her ex-husband, who aged well, and just becomes sexier to women of all ages, with every year that passes. *But what was Holly doing with him?*

Watching as Holly started to make her way around the room to greet each person, CJ, and everyone else in the room, could not help but notice the uncharacteristic reception she received from her father. Their usual, warm hug and camaraderie was merely a wisp of a memory on this day.

"Mom, what did you bring?" Mia nodded toward the box in Lois's hands.

"I stopped off at Macaron Parlor Patisserie. You can't expect the children to eat pumpkin pie."

"Or me," muttered Schooner under his breath.

"That's right, or you." She handed him a small brown bag.

Peering inside, Schooner smiled, his nose to the bag in a nanosecond. "I love you, Lois. These are my guilty pleasure." He looked in the bag again.

"I know and I love you, too. You know I'd never walk out of that shop without kitchen sink cookies for you." She kissed his cheek.

Tom looked on at the evident lovefest between Schooner and Mia's mother, mentally noting that Lois had never brought him anything all the years he and Mia were together.

"Hand over the bag." Mia crooked her finger at him.

Reluctantly, Schooner parted with his future dessert. "Who needs drinks?" he asked his tense guests and was met by a unanimous chorus.

With a newly refilled glass of wine, CJ sat down on the far end of the couch with Holly and Tom. "You look good," she told her daughter.

"That's because I'm happy." Reaching over, Holly slipped her hand into Tom's, twining their fingers.

"Mm-hmm. And what are you doing to make my little girl happy?" CJ directed the question to her daughter's lover.

Tom choked on his red wine.

"Mom!" The color rose in Holly's cheeks, her wide eyes silently pleading with her mother not to embarrass her.

"Oh, stop it, Holly," CJ promptly shut down her daughter. "What do you expect me to do? Dance around the elephant in the room?" Focusing her sights on Tom, "What is going on here?"

"CJ," Tom began, "when we met, neither Holly nor I realized there was a single degree of separation between us. Considering there are eight-and-a-half million people in New York City, the odds of being struck by lightning are probably better than this situation happening."

"Maybe it was fate, Mom." Holly's taunt caught her mother off guard.

"Or a stroke of bad luck," Lois muttered from a few feet away, loud enough for Holly, Tom, and CJ to hear.

Directing his comment in Lois' direction, "Mia and Schooner were very gracious in extending a holiday invitation that included me, and I'd like to thank them by being a gracious guest." Shifting on the couch, he focused his attention back on CJ. "I know that this is a bit unconventional, and Lord knows it was not planned. You have raised an exceptional woman who is bright, eloquent, fiercely independent, and yet has maintained a sensitivity and an amazing amount of empathy. She is truly remarkable." His last statement punctuated with a squeeze of his young girlfriend's hand.

"You don't have to tell me about my daughter. I know her quite well. And you have to know that I'm obviously concerned about this." She waved her hand in front of them.

"What can I do to ease your concern, CJ?" Tom was smooth.

Again, Lois muttered under her breath, "Try finding someone your own age."

Out of nowhere, Schooner appeared, handing CJ a scotch on the rocks, disappearing as quickly as he had arrived.

Henry, Schooner, Mia, and Mia's mother. CJ mentally tallied up her very surprising list of allies in the room, realizing if you are the hated enemy entering an adversary's territory, always make sure there's someone else there with a bigger target on their back than yours. *Love and war make strange bedfellows,* she mused.

Seth placed two trays of assorted hors d'oeuvres on the coffee table.

Mia popped her head out of the kitchen. "Use toothpicks and napkins, you two. No fingers," she directed the two little ones.

"We've got it," Lily called back, as Zac handed Natie and Po each a green, pastry-looking triangle and a napkin.

"What is that?" CJ asked.

"It's got Brussels sprouts." Natie held out his half-eaten appetizer. "You could have a bite."

"Thank you, but you finish that one. Zac, would you please hand me an hors d'oeuvre?" CJ took a bite of the green triangle.

"Do you like it?" Nathaniel asked, standing right next to her leg, waiting for a verdict.

"It's quite good."

"I knew you would like it." With a smile that would someday stop women dead in their tracks, he turned from her and went back to the tray. Picking up a toothpick and napkin, he carefully speared another green triangle and brought it to her. Through long lashes, reserved just for little boys, he looked up and smiled, shyly. "In case you get hungry."

Everyone laughed, including Nathaniel, who had no idea that his flirtation had eased a tense moment.

"He reminds me so much of you at that age," CJ reminisced.

Grabbing an appetizer, Henry laughed. "I don't think so. I remember this guy," he looked at Zac, "hauling off and punching Quinn when he was a little younger than Natie."

Zac laughed. "I did that?"

"You did, but then Quinn charmed you and you became best buddies." Henry smiled at the memory. Quinn had been gone so long now, he could barely remember the sound of his voice, but knew, if he were ever to hear it again, he'd recognize it immediately. *Someday. Somewhere. Somehow.*

"Excuse me." Tom got up from the couch, heading toward the kitchen where Mia and Seth had just pulled the turkey out of the oven to cool.

"Well, this is a familiar scene. The three of us in the kitchen. Can I help you two with anything?" Tom appeared to be relieved to have escaped.

"CJ giving you a rough time?" Mia smiled, standing next to the oven.

"Your mother's right up there." Tom smiled back at his former girlfriend.

"You didn't expect her to mellow with age, did you?" She turned to Seth. "Can you get me one of the Brussels-ricotta things?"

Knowing Mia as well as he did, he picked up on the clue to give her and Tom some privacy. Or as much seclusion as you can get in an open kitchen.

"Thank you for including me."

"Schooner never wants Holly to feel as if she is an orphan, especially on the holidays." She pulled the green bean casserole out of the oven and placed it on the stovetop, added the crunchy French's crispy fried onions to the top and put the casserole dish back in to cook.

"He's a big man."

"That he is." Mia smiled at Tom. There wasn't hatred in her heart. They'd shared some wonderful memories and he was just what she had needed at that time in her life. Tom Sheehan, and her friend, Rob Ryan, were lifeboats for a very adrift young woman who was barely treading water as she pretended to the world that she was an Olympic swimmer. But she had learned how to swim and that was a choice she had made, even though the work was hard. It was slow at first, as she barely stepped into the shallow end. But then she met Michael, and he coaxed her into deeper waters, although she remained fearful of being over her head, and remained merely neck deep no matter how much she wanted to totally submerge. In that moment, she felt bad for Tom. Unlike her, he'd never put in the work to fix what was broken, the thing that held intimacy at only the physical level for him. He was still wading at the water's edge trying to catch guppies with his hands. Who was going to be there for him? Certainly not any of his young students.

"I've seen that storm in your eyes before, Mia." It may have been years since they'd seen one another, but one doesn't forget the nuances of a love affair. Or of a lover.

"I'm just thinking, who is going to be there for you in ten years, twenty years. Not a twenty-something millennial. Tom, what are you doing? Find some great forty-something, she'll still be ten years younger than you and will wear you out in bed. It can be lasting. You'll have someone…"

"To grow old with?" he finished her thought.

"Yes. Or you are going to find yourself a lonely old man." Mia's eyes never left his. "This really can't still make you feel good."

"She's an exceptional young woman." he began.

"Don't you think I know that? So, I'll answer the question I asked before. You're doing what you've always done. And it's selfish. And self-serving. I don't want you hurting her. And you will." Picking up a wooden spoon, she stirred the gravy, scraping down the sides of the saucepan. "But I'm also thinking about you. I don't hate you and I'd like to see you happy. But you have no clue how to find it. I can guarantee you, it's not with someone who is young enough to be your daughter."

Holding her eye contact, it appeared he was going to answer her several times, but chose to internally censor his responses.

"Just say it," Mia urged, one hip leaning against the counter, arms folded defensively over her chest, wooden spoon still in hand.

"I'm in your home. I'm not going to insult you."

"Say it."

"You're not always right, Mia." He waited, knowing she might show him the door, or in this case, the elevator door.

"I know that, Tom. But, this time, I am," and in a low voice, hissed, "so, fix it." Handing him a bowl of homemade cranberry sauce, she added, "Please bring this to the table."

As he placed the bowl, she could see he took note of the place cards at each of the table settings.

"You really do hate me," he returned to the kitchen grumbling, commenting on sitting at the end of the table near her parents and Seth.

She laughed. "Not at all. Our ending wasn't good. But endings generally aren't. And we definitely made a lot of good memories along the way, too." Mia couldn't help but smile at the recollection of her young, handsome professor who pushed her to explore her talent, while pulling her out of a dark void.

"Yes, we did."

"I have something for you."

"For me?" He was surprised.

"Be right back." She held up a finger indicating one minute, but returned even sooner, with a small, clear plastic bag.

The moment he saw the silky brown strands in the bag, he knew what it was. Deftly, Mia slipped it into one of his front pockets.

"This is yours. You should have it."

"Thank you and thank you for hanging onto it and not getting rid of it. I really appreciate that." Sticking his hand in his pocket, he could feel the long strands of the tassel within the plastic bag.

"Well, it was important. An MFA from Cornell is an impressive thing in the writing world. I'm glad it's back with its rightful owner." Surprisingly, Mia felt herself getting emotional.

"I entrusted its well-being to a very special woman." He smiled at her, warmly.

Holding out his phone toward Mia, Schooner entered the kitchen. "My mom wants to say hi."

Wiping her hands, she reached for the phone, "Tom, can you bring those bottles of wine to the table," she pointed to the counter, then turned back to Schooner, handing him the wooden spoon, "Keep stirring so the gravy doesn't clump."

"Dee, Happy Thanksgiving," she walked out of the kitchen, slipping into Schooner's office, to wish her in-laws a happy holiday.

"Hey, thanks for including me." Tom walked back into the kitchen, facing Schooner alone for the first time.

Picking up his glass of scotch, Schooner took a sip, regarding Tom over the rim. "You disrespected Mia when you cheated on her. But I wasn't here, and she wasn't my wife. And we were all a lot younger and stupider then. This... this is my daughter, man. I witnessed her get her heart ripped out last spring, and when it's your kid, it is a brutal thing to watch. There are just some things that Dad can't fix. She has gone out on a limb with her entire family for you. Do not disrespect her or I will take that personally." Schooner trained his sights back on stirring, and then as an afterthought, "Even if this thing with Holly wasn't happening, you can't expect me to like you after what you did to Mia."

"I was with Mia during that first year after California, Schooner. And if she wasn't writing, she would be dead. I made sure she didn't do anything destructive with that pain, but instead channeled that talent to help her heal."

Schooner nodded. He had never given Tom credit for being there for Mia or for being a positive influence in Mia's life. Just knowing how crushed he was when she didn't return to school, it hurt to even think about what Mia had been going through back then, thinking he never loved her, and that what they had shared had been a lie. He knew that Tom was telling the truth. The man had met a broken Mia and helped her move on, and not only survive, but thrive.

"Thank you for that," Schooner acquiesced, and looking Tom straight in the eye, "I can only imagine her pain that first year."

Mia returned, handing Schooner his phone. "Okay, that looks done." She turned off the gas on the stove. Handing Schooner a large chef's knife, "Carving time."

Tom's eyes widened, he wanted out of the kitchen. "Can I take anything else to the table?"

"I think we're good. Can you grab Seth for me?"

"Sure thing." Tom was all too happy to get as far away from the imposingly large figure of Schooner Moore, and what he was sure was a recently sharpened for the occasion, eight-inch chef's knife. He left the kitchen on what he knew would probably be the most civil moment that would ever pass between the two men.

"There's something so hot about you butchering that bird." Seth entered the kitchen and stood there staring at Schooner. "But you're not doing it right."

"All yours," he gladly surrendered the knife to Seth. "Mia, should I bring the sweet potato soufflé and stuffing to the table?"

She turned her head and nodded, and he grabbed the two dishes.

Looking out from the open kitchen, Seth watched Henry laughing at something CJ said. It was hard for him to imagine that they had a history he wasn't a part of, that she had known Henry and Quinn as a couple. "She is very beautiful. There's no denying that. And you were such a mess when I met you. I shudder to think of what you looked like in college."

"Et tu, Princess?" Mia shook her head.

"I think Henry is protecting her," he observed.

"That woman does not need protecting. Does she look like she needs protecting?" Mia was losing her cool. Ms. Namaste was gone.

"Chill, BBC. The evening is still young."

Picking up the scotch glass Schooner had left on the kitchen counter, Mia took a healthy swig, the glass still resting on her lips when he walked back in, surprised to see his wife belting down a single malt.

"C'mere, Baby Girl." He opened his arms to her, pulling her in for a tight hug. "I'm right there with you." He kissed the top of her head.

"Why did I think this would be a good idea?" She looked up questioningly into eyes that were an exact match to the mid-morning sky out at the beach house after the sun burned off the early fog from the horizon.

Smiling down at her, "Just sit back," he said in a soft voice, "and keep drinking. The only thing we'll have to do is clean up the mess," he laughed, "oh, and the dishes." He genuinely seemed amused anticipating what might transpire at the dinner table. Looking at Mia with a conspiratorial smile, he shared their pre-entrance trademark, "Showtime."

"Let the shit storm begin," Mia couldn't help but share the smile with her husband as they exited the kitchen area and made their way to the dining table.

"Oh, place cards, Mia. How fancy," Lois noted, as she walked around the festively decorated table.

"Nana, I get to sit with you and Uncle Seth." Portia ran to her chair, standing behind it as she waited for the other guests to take their places at the table before sitting down.

With Schooner and Mia's arrival, everyone took their seats, Schooner at the head of the table, the end closer to the kitchen and Bob, Mia's father, heading up the far end of the table.

"Are we going to get one of your famous speeches tonight, Schooner?" his mother-in-law asked from her seat next to her husband.

"I wasn't planning on it." He laughed.

"Oh c'mon," Seth urged, "we haven't had one of your speeches in a long time."

"I don't think he'll ever top the one from right after Nathaniel was born," Bob sounded skeptical.

Mia shook her head laughing. "Oh God, now we're never going to get to eat. What is wrong with you people?"

"Be quiet, BBC, and let our host speak," Seth admonished his business partner.

"Okay, okay." A smile slowly overtook his handsome face, "I wasn't planning on doing one of these today." Looking reflective, he took a deep breath. "With the exception of my parents, who we'll see in a few weeks, and Yoli and Debbie, and Charles and Gaby."

"And Paola," Portia added, reminding her father.

Acknowledging his little girl's contribution with a smile, "And Paola. Everyone I love is sitting around this table, which makes me a very fortunate and thankful man." Shifting to his right to address Lily and Zac, he paused for a moment. "Lily, having you become a member of our family is truly an honor and something we are all looking forward to. We are so proud of you as we watch as you fulfill your dream at Johns Hopkins. Our families are so intertwined. Your father's work led us to Po." Looking down the table, Schooner smiled at his adopted daughter. "When you're ready to start the wedding plans, the two best wedding planners in the world are sitting down at the end of the table." He smiled at Seth and Lois and laid his hand on top of his future daughter-in-law's, giving it a squeeze. Looking Zac in the eye, "You know how proud of you I am, right? I will be the first to admit, getting kicked out of Bryson was the best thing that could have happened to you, allowing you to experience things that were more aligned with your passions and you took those opportunities to make your own dream a reality. I know you will never cease to amaze me. I am thankful that you two have found one another and embarked on this wonderful path together and I'm so proud of the man you have become." He looked from Zac to CJ who was sitting on the other side, "Well, we obviously did something right." He smiled at her. "I'll bet you never thought we'd be sitting at the same Thanksgiving table again so soon. Holidays are for families and loved ones and this is where you should be, surrounded by your children." He gestured to Zac and Holly flanking their mother. "Please don't ever think you can't spend the holiday with the kids because they are here. I am thankful for the two wonderful children you gave me."

"Are you actually going to pick up the phone and invite me?" CJ stared into her ex-husband's eyes.

"Probably not. But Mia's a lot nicer than I am."

Schooner shifted his gaze from CJ to Holly. The table fell silent as father and daughter locked eyes. Finally, Schooner spoke, his voice gruff. "I miss you. I miss you so damn much it physically hurts."

Mia looked down at her plate so no one would see her eyes well up. She had felt Schooner's pain, day in and day out, for the past few months, a hole in his world that sucked out oxygen and sunshine. He had been emotionally gasping in the dark as he tried to sort out how to come to terms with his beloved daughter's choices.

"I hate that there is distance between us," he went on. "My world and my heart have had a gaping hole in them for months now. I want that to end. Now. I *need* that to end now. Can we do that?"

With tears streaming down her cheeks, Holly nodded and was out of her chair the moment her father rose. Wrapped in his arms, she cried into his shirt.

Dipping his head, Schooner whispered in her ear, "This has to be behind us, okay."

Looking up, Holly nodded, fighting to hold back the next torrent of tears.

"I miss you, too, Holly." Natie surprised everyone with his declaration as he watched his father hug his older sister. While Nathaniel could not grasp the circumstances of Holly's absence, he only knew that he missed having her as a constant in his world.

"Me, too," Portia chimed in.

Sitting down again, Schooner continued, "Holly, I am thankful we are all together as a family." His gaze moved down the table. "Tom. What can I say? This is as awkward for me as it is for you. I don't think there are any circumstances we could have met under that wouldn't have been strained, but we've managed to take it to the next level. Despite that, I hope you enjoy your Thanksgiving meal."

"You're too kind," Lois muttered.

Schooner smiled at his in-laws. "Lois, I'm glad you love me," he laughed, thinking Mia did something really mean putting Tom down at the end of the table with her mother and Seth. Everyone thought she was so sweet to invite him, but a single holiday was about to turn into a season from hell for that man. *Mia knew just what she was doing*, he mused. "And I love the both of you. Lois, you gave us quite the scare earlier this year." A very serious look overtook Schooner's face. "Don't do that again." Pausing, he played to his audience before his trademark smile overtook his handsome face. "I am so thankful you both are healthy and felt well enough to come up for the holiday." Moving his attention to Portia, "Well, young lady, you and your little rascal brother," he looked at Natie, "are absolutely the Fountain of Youth. And I know you're thinking, 'Daddy, what are you talking about'?"

Portia nodded, and everyone laughed.

"Yeah, I know. You two make me feel younger and more connected to the world than I ever imagined possible and I'm thankful that you both make me laugh every single day." Setting his sights on Seth, "I am thankful that you are Mia's wingman in every part of her world. But more than anything, I'm thankful you keep her in line."

Mia swatted him in the arm as everyone chuckled.

Directing his attention to Henry, he continued, "I don't think anybody but the two of us can understand what we have weathered together. I'm thankful that through business and through Seth you have become part of my everyday world again. It's comforting to know there is someone out there who will always have my back and lend a hand when the surf gets rough. You've always been that for me for almost my entire life. Yeah, I am definitely fortunate and incredibly thankful."

Finally, he had made his way around the entire table to Mia. The long way. But he had made it. Reaching out, he took her hand.

"Everything I want, I have, whenever you are in my arms. Everything. Thankful doesn't even begin to describe my level of gratitude. You make me whole, happy and content. And for that I am thankful." Leaning toward one another, he placed a soft kiss on her lips.

Mia looked around the table at her guests, "He really doesn't need much egging on. Next year you'll keep your mouths shut, and the food will still be hot when you eat it."

Looking at Schooner, she shook her head in mock disdain, but the smile on her face told the real story. She had hung on his every word and would forever be thankful, for second chances, and for Schooner Moore finding his way back into her life.

Turning back to her guests, Mia smiled. "Please help yourselves and dig in, everybody."

With everyone focused on the food, the tension eased.

"The turkey is delicious. It is so juicy. Did you brine this, Mia?" Henry asked.

Before Mia could speak, Seth answered for her. "BBC has the best brine recipe and she actually created it herself, without my help."

"The white meat is delicious," Lois commented. "I can taste the citrus and herbs. It's so juicy it doesn't even need gravy."

"Nobody likes a dry turkey." The words were out of Mia's mouth, and although meaningless to everyone else at the table, flooded Mia with a Thanksgiving Day memory that made the back of her throat burn as she held back tears.

"Excuse me." Forcing a smile, Mia stood and left the table.

Escaping to the master bedroom, she sat on the edge of the bed hoping for a moment where she could sit in silence, take a deep breath, and gather the strength to keep smiling. The past, which usually just danced around the corners of her mind, had ventured out of the shadows into full light, promenading underneath the chandelier illuminating her Thanksgiving table. Either Tom or CJ would be enough to conjure up old memories of pain and rejection long ago dismissed, but having them here together was rousing emotions best left buried. As positive as she tried to be, Mia could feel her edges fraying.

Nobody likes a dry turkey. She shivered as those words poked into her mind again. Hugging her arms tightly to her chest she told herself, *pull it together.* He was the only one from her past whom Mia would have loved to have sitting at her Thanksgiving table. And he was the only one who wasn't there.

"Someday in Heaven, Michael, I'll tell you all about this crazy Thanksgiving." She sighed, "I wish you were here and not them. My past may be in that room today, but you're here with me, in my heart."

As she walked out of the bedroom, Schooner approached. "I was just coming to look for you. Are you okay?"

Nodding, she smiled up at him.

"C'mere, Baby Girl." Schooner opened his arms for his wife, pulling her to him, his lips in her hair.

"I needed this hug," she said into his cotton shirt, breathing in deeply, and letting his clean scent activate whatever it was in her brain that told her she was safe.

"You know what?" he smiled. "Me, too."

As Mia took her seat, Nathaniel turned to her. "Mommy, can I have more?"

"You ate everything on that plate?" She was surprised to see his entire plate cleaned off, vegetables and all.

"If we had a dog, I would think the dog licked your plate clean. But we don't have a dog, so it must be you," Mia kidded her son. "What would you like more of?"

"Everything," he exclaimed dramatically. "It's so delicious."

"We're going to have to have an eating contest, because I think you can eat more than me, Natie," challenged Zac.

"I can." Nathaniel started on his second plate of the heavy Thanksgiving food.

"Natie, you're a pig," Portia called from down the table.

"I'm not a pig. You're a pig." He didn't skip a beat eating to answer his sister, who responded by snorting.

"Mia."

Mia could hear the tone in her mother's voice saying *discipline your children.* With Mia being an only child, Lois hadn't had the experience of raising multiple children, with one being all boy.

"Oh Mom, this is mild, we haven't gotten to the burping and farting portion of the show yet."

An appalled CJ just stared at Mia and the younger generation of Moore children, as if she'd never seen small children find bodily functions hysterical. Certainly not from her well-bred children.

And then her son chimed in, egging on his younger brother. "It's probably best you don't burp the alphabet, Natie."

Not needing any further encouragement, he burped the letter A.

Stifling a laugh, Schooner quickly morphed into his serious dad face. "Enough of that, Nathaniel. That is not appropriate at the dinner table."

"You got me in trouble," Nathaniel called out Zac.

"Yeah and you fell for it," the older brother shot back, regressing fifteen years in a mere matter of minutes.

Lily regarded her fiancé with a disturbed look on her face, "I feel like I'm in the movie *Big* and you're twelve years old. Are you the same guy with the Masters in Engineering from Berkeley?"

Mia laughed, "Get used to it, Lily. Men can morph into teenage boys in a nanosecond."

Lois couldn't pass up the opportunity to piggyback an insult on the last comment, "Is that why they remain attracted to teenage girls?" Her eyes were trained on Tom.

Tom appeared to be poised for a comeback and then thought better of it.

And Lois went on. This man had hurt her daughter deeply and a mother never forgets that. "You've grown old, Tom. Why don't you grow up?"

There was silence at the table, everyone waiting for the person next to them to grab the conversation and expertly steer it to a neutral subject. A moment of silence passed, only to be punctuated by the unmistakable growl of vomiting as Nathaniel heaved his dinner, all cast in a red glow onto his plate and down the front of his shirt.

"Ugh, that candy apple. Too much sugar." Mia grabbed her son leading him from the table quickly.

Schooner jumped up and grabbed the offending plate off the table.

"Well, that concludes the dinner portion of tonight's show," Seth announced. "Please make yourselves comfortable in the great room and we'll have coffee and dessert in a little while." He grabbed some plates and headed toward the kitchen to help Schooner.

"That child has impeccable timing." Seth began to place bowls on the counter.

"I know, doesn't he?" Schooner looked up from the sink with a smile. "So, how much has my mother-in-law had to drink tonight?"

"I don't think much at all." Seth shook his head.

"Seriously? She's been even more outspoken than usual."

Giving Schooner a conspiratorial grin, he confided in a low voice, "She may have given you your favorite cookies as a gift today, but you gave her an even better present," he paused. "You handed her on a silver, no-pun-intended, platter, a guest she could make an appetizer out of. She has been chomping at the bit to chew him up and spit him out for nearly two decades." As Schooner listened, Seth went on. "He was actually around before me, but even when I came along, I remember Lois never liking him at all. And then with cheating on Mia, that woman has had a lot of years of pent-up, I-told-you-so anger going on. Add on top how upset you've been about Holly, and how much she loves you. So, when you think about it, she's actually been kind of restrained tonight. But the evening's still young." He laughed.

Henry entered with an armful of dirty dishes, "Well, that all went better than expected." He looked at Seth and Schooner and the three men laughed. "Are you serving popcorn for dessert?" he kidded his old buddy.

Laughing, "That would have been a good thought, so everyone could sit back and enjoy this warped psychodrama unfold. You just can't make this shit up."

"Exactly," Henry nodded at his old friend. "I'll help Seth with the clean-up so that you can go see how Mia and Natie are doing."

As Schooner exited the kitchen area, he noticed Tom looking around.

"Bathroom?" Tom asked.

"Follow me." Schooner led the way through the vast loft space. "The first door on the left," he pointed out and continued to the master bedroom suite.

Locking the door to the guest bathroom, Tom drew in a deep breath. He knew today was going to be rough, but he'd just been thinking about his interactions with Mia and Holly's father and mother and had not even factored Lois Silver or Seth Shapiro into the equation. Seth had been pretty controlled, and he assumed that he was maintaining a low profile in front of his significant other. But Lois, well, that woman was relentless. And something was way off with Holly's mother. The woman was seriously beautiful, but he couldn't get the vision of a coiled-up snake out of his head, and he was on edge, waiting for her to spring. Or maybe it was just his imagination. Maybe she'd already said her peace before dinner and now was just going to enjoy some rare time with her children. He smiled thinking about little Nathaniel flirting with CJ earlier in the evening. She looked like his Holly, so he was drawn to her, not even noticing that the woman possessed none of the warmth of her daughter.

Locking the door behind him, Tom took refuge in the small space. *Anything just to get away from these people,* he thought. Absentmindedly gazing into the mirror over the streamlined pedestal sink, he pumped soap from the dispenser onto his hands and was hauled from his thoughts as the wafting fragrance filled his senses. The scent was unmistakable.

Picking up the bottle of *Bath & Bodyworks' Summer Sail,* he eyed the label for a moment. *Shit, I smell like Holly's father now. Great, that should make the rest of the evening even more pleasant. I have the scent of him on me.*

And shaking his head, he realized it was just a doomed day. And frankly, that came as no surprise. Unlocking the door, he grasped the knob, poised to turn it as he felt the smooth metal handle move within his grasp although he hadn't turned his hand. Still holding on, he took a step backward as the door jerked open and she slipped in, closing it behind her with a mere flick of her wrist. Her back was against the door before his mind could even process what was happening. His initial reaction was, *Oh, thank God, Holly.*

But it wasn't Holly. Not even close.

"CJ." He was surprised. "I was just leaving."

"Not so fast, Professor."

As he moved forward, she stopped him with a hand to his groin. Bullseye. She had him cupped in her hand and he immediately began to twitch. CJ had plucked a classic out of her bag of tricks, recycling a variation of what she had once pulled on their host.

"You want to know what I think?" her voice was breathy, her eyes trained on his, as her hand began to apply slight pressure and her thumb started a steady up and down motion, resulting in his hardening in her hand.

"I think you're going to tell me." His voice was calm and even, holding her stare, it appeared as if he were oblivious to what was going on between his legs. But they both knew that was impossible.

"I think you are afraid you won't cut it when a real woman drags you to the edge. Afraid you won't be able to play there." Loosening her grip on his pants, his body immediately reacted to the void left by the lack of contact and he pressed forward into her touch.

"Why are you doing this?" his voice was little more than a whisper.

As her hand slid up the front of his pants, she smiled, answering, "Because I can." Working her way up to his zipper, she stopped to squeeze, pleased with herself that the man was rock hard in his pants. It only took a moment to unzip his fly and have her hand wrapped around his flesh. Holly's boyfriend, Mia's ex, was now exactly where she wanted him. It was time she made her mark and left him with very few good options.

"Have you ever been with someone who doesn't look up to you as a god, someone you have to work hard," she squeezed him for emphasis, "to impress. Someone who challenges you and stimulates you," she stroked him while maintaining eye contact, "on every level."

"And what makes you think I don't have that with your daughter?"

CJ ran a well-manicured finger over the top of his crown, applying slight pressure and pausing as she reached the slit, then slowly removed her hand from his pants and gazed down. Tom's eyes followed hers down to her glistening forefinger. Looking back up at him, she smiled, a smile almost identical to her daughter's, but not quite.

As if in slow motion, she raised her finger to her lips and grazed her lower lip as if she were applying lip gloss with his semen. Her tongue flicked out the corner of her mouth, tasting with just the tip as the rest remained slick on her full bottom lip.

"Oh, come on, Tom. My daughter is in her twenties and we both know how," she paused, looking for the right word, "*unformed* we were at that age. Hell, you were sleeping with Mia when you were that age." Her nose wrinkled in disdain at the mere thought. "And tonight, when you're fucking my daughter, you'll be fighting yourself just trying to stay present, because we both know what you'll be thinking about." She licked the rest of her bottom lip. "I've tasted you."

"Maybe it will get me off even more to know both mother and daughter have tasted me." He was fighting fire with fire.

"Really?" CJ called him out on what she knew was a lie. "Well, I can guarantee you my daughter won't think it's so hot. She is her father's daughter and has a very different sense of right and wrong than you and I do."

"I'm not like you." He shook his head.

CJ looked down at what was now a semi poking out of his fly and reaching out, she grazed it with the tips of her nails, smiling as he responded with a visible throb.

"Actually Tom, you're just like me. It's really all about us and having what we want, when we want it." Again, she swiped her finger across his slit, and brought it to her lips, but this time, she sucked it into her mouth fully tasting him.

CJ turned to the door and with her hand on the knob, looked back at her daughter's lover. Pointing to his open pants, she wagged the finger that had just been in her mouth and reminded him, "Don't forget to zip up before you come out." And with the sweetest smile she could muster, CJ left the guest bathroom feeling she'd accomplished her mission.

She gave Tom and Holly a week – tops. Finding another hot twenty-something would take him no time and there was not a shot in hell he was going to subject himself to Holly's family again. Not her father. Not his ex. Definitely not his exes' mother. But more than anyone else, if he didn't know it before, he knew it now, being around Holly's mother was going to cause him more problems than he'd signed up for and CJ was convinced he'd never be at another family gathering. If he had any conscience at all, which she suspected beyond his narcissism he did, there was no way, after today, things would ever be normal between him and Holly.

Passing Mia, as she walked through the kitchen toward the great room, CJ paused, and whispered in her ear, "You owe me one."

Looking up from slicing a pecan pie, Mia was caught by surprise at her nemesis' smile and wink. *Lord knows what she did.* Mia wasn't sure if she should feel happy or disturbed or some combination of both. Peering out into the great room, she looked for Tom, who appeared to be deep in conversation with Seth and Henry. *He probably sought out Seth as an ally,* she thought. *His only ally. Besides Holly.*

As if sensing her stare, Tom turned, his eyes connecting with Mia's. With almost an imperceptible nod of her head and flash of her eyes, she clearly transmitted her message to a man who had learned to read her signals long ago. Excusing himself from the conversation, Tom strolled into the kitchen.

"Are you holding up okay?" Mia felt bad for him.

"It's been a long afternoon." Tom smiled at Mia. He was exhausted. "How's Natie feeling?"

"Much better, thank you. He had way too much sugar earlier today."

"Your children are beautiful, Mia. I'm glad you're happy." Reaching out he gave Mia's shoulder a squeeze.

"I am happy, Tom. I'm sorry if this has been an awful day for you."

"It hasn't been pleasant, but on the other hand, Holly's reconciliation with her dad was well worth it." He looked out into the great room where Holly sat with her brother and parents, "They really are beautiful, aren't they?" he commented, his eyes trained on Holly, who was engaged in a conversation with her family.

Mia followed his gaze and nodded. She had to agree, they looked perfect together, the four of them, in a way that her diverse family unit with Schooner never would. And then Tom verbalized her next thought.

"But all that glitters is not gold." Tom shook his head. Turning back to Mia, he smiled. "You are married to a really good man and that makes me happy, Jailbait." There was warmth in his tone as he vocalized a nickname he hadn't uttered in nearly a lifetime. "I know that he's a good man because he raised an exceptional daughter. And it doesn't take a rocket scientist to know it was his influence on Holly, because it definitely wasn't hers." He gestured his head toward CJ.

"Do I even want to ask?" Mia was afraid to know.

"No. You don't. Let's just put it this way, this may be my personal enactment of *No Exit*."

Mia burst into laughter. "Oh no, Sartre's *No Exit*. My Thanksgiving is like being trapped in Hell, huh?"

Laughing with her, he added, "This is one for the books."

Schooner turned at the sound of his wife's laughter, surprised to find that the person she was laughing with was her ex. Making his way to the kitchen, he came up behind Mia, putting both hands on her shoulders. "Anything I can help you with?" he asked, his eyes trained on Tom.

"Yeah, let's start moving the desserts onto the table. We'll do it buffet-style." Mia grabbed two pies off the white marble counter and handed them to Schooner. "Tom, can you grab that bread pudding and the box of macarons."

"Don't forget my cookies," Schooner called into the kitchen.

"Seth ate them," Mia yelled back.

"BBC, you lie," Seth chimed in. "Schooner, would you let me eat your cookies?"

Shaking his head as he took the bag Mia held out. "Not even a taste, buddy."

"You are such an only child," Seth rolled his eyes at Schooner.

"Say it, Seth," CJ joined in. "He's selfish."

"There's a reason I divorced you." Pulling a kitchen sink cookie from the bag, Schooner took a bite out of it, without breaking eye contact with his ex.

"Do I need to go hide the knives?" Mia asked, looking from CJ to Schooner, who continued their staring showdown.

"It might be best," he nodded.

"My money's on CJ," Seth continued to fan the fire.

"I'm going with Schooner," Henry added. "He's still the one signing my paychecks." He laughed.

Finally turning his gaze from his ex, Schooner looked at Henry and laughed. "I sign your paychecks? So much for loyalty, man."

"Gotta be pragmatic. This one's got expensive tastes." He gestured toward Seth.

"Yeah, I know. He trained Mia well," Schooner kidded, savoring another bite of his cookie.

"Well someone had to train her. She had this big bridge and tunnel hair when I met her."

"Sounds like someone I knew in college," CJ added her two cents.

"Do you even know what bridge and tunnel hair is?" Mia tried to soften her tone, but her New York attitude could not be smoothed away as she addressed CJ, a rush of all the horrible feelings still haunting her from freshman year bubbling to the surface.

They were all skating on very thin ice, and as the tempers heated in the room, the fissures were expanding.

"Remember that day I took you shopping for the first time?" Seth reminisced as he scooped up his first bite of pecan pie, his eyes closing with delight as the flavors filled his mouth.

"Like it was yesterday." Mia caught Tom's eye.

Catching the look, Seth commented, "Oh, that's right, Tom, that's the night I met you."

Nodding, he smiled at the memory. "You did a good job. Mia looked very beautiful that night."

"Yeah, well..." Mia's voice trailed off as she plucked a pistachio macaron from the box and took a bite. That night. That night held memories, very hot, raw, carnal memories. Memories she didn't want to think about at the Thanksgiving table with her husband sitting next to her. And her stepdaughter across the table.

Holly looked from Tom to Mia to Seth. She didn't say a word, but the crevasse that formed between her eyes spoke volumes. It was apparent that these people held memories that she would never be part of. They had a past and although that wasn't news to her, witnessing the tightrope they were walking made it real. Uncomfortably real.

Sensing the ice cracking, CJ turned up the heat. "So, how long were the two of you together, Mia?"

"A few years." Mia left it vague.

"And you were how old when you two met?" she pressed.

"Seventeen."

"Isn't that statutory rape?" Her eyes were wide with delight.

Giving CJ a hard look, Mia shifted her eyes to the small children at the table, indicating the inappropriateness of her question.

Tom stepped in, "Mia was of legal age before we became a couple."

Holly and Schooner became mirror images, their tense jaws twitching.

"You know what I loved about those days," Seth broke in. "We were just starting the company, and anything seemed possible as we brought on new accounts and worked crazy hours."

"Kami was a selling machine, delivering new clients at warp speed," Mia smiled at the memory and Seth's ability to steer the conversation back to the shores of the pond.

"How is she?" inquired Tom.

"She's doing great. She's spending the holiday with her family in Birmingham."

"Imagine that. She gave up this shindig to be with her family." Schooner put the last bite of kitchen sink cookie in his mouth.

"We may want to start limiting your sugar intake, too." Smiling at her husband, Mia's eyes were shouting at him, *Behave!* They already had enough craziness at the table, she didn't need Schooner, typically Mr. Controlled-Deadly-Calm, to lose the controlled-calm part of that equation. She was beginning to fear that being at a table with both CJ and the man who had slept with both his wife and his daughter might, at any moment, turn lethal.

Standing abruptly, Mia picked up her dessert plate and grabbed Schooner's, too, then snatched Lily's as soon as she lifted the fork off the plate with the last bite of pie.

Following his wife into the kitchen, Schooner put a hand on Mia's shoulder, "You okay?" He was trying to read her eyes.

"I think it's time for Thanksgiving to end. If I take away their dessert plates, they can't eat anymore. I need today to be over, Schooner. We need today to be over."

"We certainly do, Baby Girl. Let me go gather the rest of the plates and set our guests free."

The clearing of desserts was like the school bell ringing at the end of class on the last day before summer break. Zac and Lily were the first to say their goodbyes.

"We're driving up to Darien, Connecticut to spend the day tomorrow with Liz and Hayley at Liz's parents' house," Zac explained. "Kylie and her friend, Dev, will be there, too."

"How is Kylie doing?" Schooner asked. "I miss seeing her."

"I'm sure she has bad times. How could she not? But Liz told me, for the most part, she really seems at peace."

"Please give her my love." Schooner hugged Zac.

Mia's parents and Henry and Seth left right behind Zac and Lily, leaving Holly, Tom and CJ.

The wrong people left. Mia couldn't help but be amused at the three who were still remaining in the loft.

"Why don't the two of you come up to my hotel and have a nightcap with me in the bar. I'm staying at the Four Seasons." CJ suggested to Holly and Tom as she shrugged into her coat and pulled on a pair of smooth leather gloves the color and feel of butter.

"It's been a long day, I think we'll pass." With a piercing look at his girlfriend's mother, Tom answered for both of them, before Holly had a chance to respond. The edge in his voice was unmistakable.

Cocking her head to the side, CJ smiled at him. "Oh, what a shame. I was hoping we'd be able to continue our conversation from earlier. It was positively *stimulating*." Her emphasis lay solidly on the last word as she let her gaze drop for a moment, scanning his fit frame top to bottom and back up again, terminating at his eyes.

Tom turned to Mia, regarding her for a moment before breaking into a smile most pronounced at the crinkled corners of his eyes. "I am so happy to see you so happy."

Mia nodded, unable to speak. Even after all these years, she knew from his expression exactly what he was thinking. And then he confirmed it with a fleeting narrowing of his eyes. With a barely perceptible nod, Mia let him know that she understood and stepped toward him with her arms open as they met and fell into an easy embrace, punctuated by silent gasps. Holding one another a second longer than what they both knew they should have, Mia's heart felt surprisingly heavy. She knew.

Releasing Holly from a hug, Schooner took her face in both his hands. "I will talk to you tomorrow," his tone was absolute.

Holly nodded, smiling and threw her arms around her father again.

"I love you, sweetheart," Schooner's voice was thick with emotion.

"Love you, Dad." Holly stepped back.

Turning to Tom, Schooner extended his hand. Without a word exchanged, the two men shook before Tom turned to Holly and ushered her into the waiting elevator.

"Hold the door for a moment," CJ ordered. Glancing from Mia to Schooner, the look on her face was disturbingly similar to the cat who ate the canary. "Remind me to go to Cabo next year," she directed the barb to her ex.

"With pleasure," Schooner answered to CJ's back.

She had already turned away from them, heading to the elevator, and without turning back around, threw her hand in the air in a backwards wave, wiggling her fingers. Her back was still to them as the elevator doors closed.

"We're going away next year, too, and trust me, it will be as far away from Cabo as we can get." Schooner shook his head. "What was that weird look about before she left. Did you see that? You saw that, didn't you?"

Mia nodded. "Earlier she told me we owe her one. So, she did something. What she did, I'm not quite sure."

"Trust me, you don't want to even think about it, Baby Girl."

"You're right, I don't. The only thing I want to do is get on the couch with those two." She gestured to Natie and Po, who were snuggled under fleece throws, laughing hysterically at a Thanksgiving episode of *Rugrats*.

"Hey, shove over, you two, there's no room for us." Schooner smiled down at the kids, who immediately split apart making room for their parents between them.

"Mommy, Daddy, the turkey is in love with Spike," Nathaniel explained, as he burrowed into Mia's lap.

Kicking off his shoes, Schooner raised his long legs onto the coffee table. Looking over at Mia, "Well, we survived."

Smiling at him, she commented, "Yes, we did. I just don't know if everyone else was so lucky."

"Baby, that's your phone." Mia poked Schooner. She had heard it ringing in her dream. But it wasn't a dream. The phone was actually ringing.

Looking at the phone screen, "It's Holly." He tapped answer. "Hi sweetie, is everything okay?... You're downstairs?... Yeah the code is 1-3-6-2. Of course, you can come home. Come on up." Hanging up, he turned to a now fully awake Mia. "It's Holly. She's here."

"What time is it?"

"A little after 3 a.m." Jumping out of bed, he pulled on sweatpants and went out to meet the elevator.

Mia followed Schooner, entering the great room just as the doors opened. Dragging two large duffel bags, Holly's tear-stained face answered the unasked question as she fell, sobbing, into her father's arms.

"Daddy," she choked out against his chest, her back heaving from the torrent of sobs.

"Shhh, sweetheart. It's going to be okay," he whispered, tightening muscular arms around her and letting her cry it out.

Retreating to the kitchen to give them a moment, Mia filled a glass of water for Holly. The look Tom had given her when they were saying goodbye flashed before her eyes. She knew. That moment would be their final goodbye. She knew that even before he, Holly, and CJ stepped into the elevator. She knew. What had CJ done to move Tom from agreeing to put himself in the crosshairs so that Holly could spend the holiday with her family, to telling her it was over? That was a big leap to go from one to the other — in the same day. *What had CJ done?* Mia wasn't sure.

Reentering the great room, a glass of water in one hand, a box of tissues in the other, Mia handed Holly the water, and placed the tissues on the coffee table.

"Thank you." Holly tried to smile at Mia.

"I'll let you two talk." Mia wanted to give them space, and given the circumstances, she didn't want her presence to make it even more awkward.

"No, Mia, please stay." Holly's eyes were pleading. "First, I want to apologize for being so nasty to you. You've been nothing but wonderful to me from the moment we first met, and I said some really horrible things."

"No need for an apology." Mia sat down next to Schooner. "I think we all found ourselves in uncharted waters. Very emotional uncharted waters."

Holly nodded, wiping a fresh stream of tears with the back of her hand.

Handing his daughter a tissue, Schooner asked, "So, what happened? Can you tell us?"

Focused on a spot on Schooner's L9 tee-shirt, Holly shook her head. "I'm not really sure what happened. I knew from the time we left that things weren't right, but I just thought it had been a trying day. He took a lot of heat." Turning to Mia, "Your mother really hates him."

Mia nodded. "And my mother, who never had much of a filter to begin with, has had even less of one since her heart attack."

"Damn, I'm glad that woman loves me." Schooner smiled at Mia.

"You can do no wrong." Mia rolled her eyes at Holly. "So, was it my mother getting in his face?" Mia knew Tom may have been annoyed by Lois's hostile behavior, but that wouldn't have been enough for him to end his relationship with Holly.

"No. It was *my* mother." Holly reached for another tissue as the room became dead silent.

"Oh God, what did she do?" Schooner finally asked.

Shaking her head, Holly's voice cracked, "I'm really not sure. He wasn't specific. He said something happened with Mom and that it was best if we went our separate ways."

Something happened with CJ. The hairs on the back of Schooner's neck stood on end as the floodgate of his memory burst open. *Something happened with CJ. Is this déjà vu,* he wondered? He had been too ashamed to tell Mia. Oh God, what had she done this time? And although the result was something he was not unhappy with, Schooner actually felt for the guy. When CJ MacAllister-Moore-Gordon wanted to accomplish something, she justified her actions, no matter how morally askew they were, or how much carnage was left in her wake. He knew that firsthand. And so did Mia.

"He didn't say anything else?" Mia's voice was tight.

"I asked if she'd threatened him and he said no, it was nothing like that."

"No elaboration? He didn't give you any explanation?" Schooner's voice was as tight as Mia's.

"He wasn't very forthcoming with information. I asked if she didn't say anything, did she do something? And he turned away from me and wouldn't answer. So, I knew she did something and then I said don't you think I deserve an explanation?" Holly's voice became wrought with emotion. "And he said, 'Yes, you do, and I'm ashamed that I don't have the guts or the heart to give you one, but we need to say goodbye and go our separate ways. Let's just leave it at that.' That's what he said to me. Can you believe that's what he said to me?" She paused to dab her eyes and then looked at her father and Mia, her voice a near shriek, "What did she do to him?"

"Entrapment." Schooner shook his head. "You probably really don't want to know and I'm glad he spared you the details." A look of disgust marred his handsome face.

Without knowing the specifics of the act that took place, Schooner Moore knew in his gut the tactic CJ used, as it was one she had successfully performed on him shortly before his nineteenth birthday. How could Tom touch Holly after that? He couldn't. And CJ was banking on that. Yeah, the guy liked women who were too young for him and liked having his ego stroked, but the position CJ put him in was morally untenable, even to him. Saying goodbye to Holly was the only play CJ left him with.

"Why would Mom do that to me?" Holly searched her father's eyes.

"Because she loves you," muttered Mia.

Stunned by the comment, Holly turned to Mia. "She loves me so she betrayed me this way?"

"Your mother and I don't see eye to eye on very much, and I would not have chosen her tactics, but her heart was absolutely in the right place." Mia shocked herself at her defense of CJ.

"Her heart? Mia, clearly you are giving my mother too much credit. You, of all people, know that the woman doesn't have a heart." As Holly's volume rose, her face flushed.

"She loves you, Holly," Mia repeated, heart sick for everyone involved and hoping the family fissures didn't create irreparable cracks.

Turning to her father, "And I'm the only one who has never been to Africa," she spat out angrily, on the verge of hysterics as more tears began to flow.

Caught off guard by both the non sequitur and Holly's feeling of being left out, Schooner assured his daughter, "If you want to go to Africa, I will put you on a plane tomorrow. I'm sure Sonkwe and Bupe would be thrilled to have an extra pair of hands. If you want to get away from him..."

"Get away from him? I don't have to worry about getting away from him. He no longer wants me in his life. Which is becoming a major freaking theme for me. Why do they no longer want me in their lives?" she cried. Looking from Mia to her father, her breath rapid, "Do you think he wants Mom? Do you think he went to the Four Seasons after I left?"

Clasping his daughter's hand, Schooner shook his head. "No, Holly, I don't. I think he said goodbye to you to ensure he would never have to see your mother again in this lifetime."

"What's going on?"

They all jumped hearing Portia's voice. So involved had they been in tonight's psychodrama that not one of them saw or heard her enter the room.

"Did we wake you, sweetie?" Mia reached out a hand for Po to come sit between her and Schooner.

Rubbing the sleep from her eyes, she smiled, "Holly, you're home."

"I am, Po."

"For real?" the little girl asked.

"For real."

Stretching out his arms along the back of the couch, Schooner pulled them all into his sides for a hug. "I've got all my girls here." He smiled.

They knew he was happiest when he felt he could keep them all safe.

And for that, they were thankful.

"Were you serious about Africa?" Mia asked Holly several weeks later, as she set a fragrant cup of oolong tea on the table in front of her.

"Honestly, I don't know where that came from," she admitted. "I would like to go someday. But I would really love to do it with Portia."

"Now that would be pretty amazing." Mia loved the idea of the two sisters visiting Po's birth land. "Are you coming out to Newport Beach with us for Christmas?"

Shaking her head, "No. I'm going to stay here in the city. A lot of my friends from Brown will be home and in town." Holly grimaced, "And I don't want to be within striking distance of that woman."

"I understand, but I do hope you two don't go for too long without talking. That's not good either. Has she reached out to you?"

"She texted. But I didn't answer." Holly shrugged.

"We both have mothers who did not want us with Tom Sheehan." Mia laughed.

"We do have a lot in common," Holly agreed

"Here's another thing you and I have in common. Tom came into our lives when we really needed someone, because our hearts were decimated. And he's handsome, brilliant, amusing and, yes, hot. I know that is weird hearing me say that, but he is, and he was a great person to take us over the hump, so to speak." Mia laughed. "And that was his reason in our lives. And he did a good job with that."

Holly smiled. "You're right. Now I feel like we should thank him. Were you over my father when you and Tom split up."

Mia shook her head, sighing as she sorted through words and feelings before speaking. "In my heart, no, that never happened. In my head, mostly. I couldn't allow myself to think about him because he was years in my past, and probably married with kids, which it turns out, he actually was. But the ghost of him would show up out of the blue and I'd try to shoo him away, always knowing that when I least expected it, he would be invading my thoughts again. I remember the day I graduated from college," Mia stopped to swallow the lump in her throat. Decades later and just the memory could evoke the sadness, making her eyes sting as they misted. "All I could think was he was in a cap and gown three-thousand miles away and how handsome he must look, and that I wasn't there with him. It wasn't us celebrating that moment together and my heart hurt just thinking that. I wanted to see him in his cap and gown that day." Mia brushed aside a tear and smiled. The emotions were running high tonight. After a moment, she spoke again, "Tom absolutely kept me afloat in those days. And that was exactly what you needed after Aiden."

Holly let out a sob. "Why did he leave me, Mia?"

"Aiden?"

She clarified by nodding.

"Holly, I think your initial gut reaction was right on target with him. I think he is afraid he will come back a changed man, and that man won't be one whom he feels is deserving of you, and he loves you too much to burden you with that."

"So, you really think he dumped me because he loves me?"

"Yeah. I think he did." Plucking a tissue from the box, Mia handed it to Holly. "I believe he did this in a chivalrous, albeit misguided, way. My gut feeling is that he was fearful that the man who returned would be damaged, and I think being emotionally damaged scared him even more than being physically injured or incapacitated. He didn't want that for you because he loves you. Personally, I don't believe any of that crap he said to you."

"I don't think I'm going to get over him. And you are right. As I'm sitting here thinking about what you said before, obviously Tom was a rebound, but he was really interesting and challenging and a lot of fun to be around. He definitely helped me get past hurting so badly. It still hurts, but not like it did at the beginning."

It was now a few weeks past that tumultuous Thanksgiving, and Mia was glad to see Holly not obsessing over her break-up with Tom, but seeing the relationship for what it was, her segue to healing her heart and trying to move past Aiden.

If that was even possible.

CHAPTER
Five

Spring thru Memorial Day Weekend

LOADING THE LAST DUFFEL and beach bag into the back of the Land Rover, Schooner turned to Mia and Seth. "Are you two going to be able to handle getting all of this onto the ferry?"

"We'll be all right. We've got the easy end of things for the next few days." With her devilish grin, she informed him, "You've got all the tough stuff, Pretty Boy. Don't forget Natie has the dentist tomorrow afternoon." She reminded him for the fifth time.

"Got it, and Portia has dance on Thursday." And with a devilish grin of his own, "I'm going to make Yoli take her."

"You might want to rethink that." Seth laughed. "Payback is going to be hell." Putting out his hand, Mia handed him the car keys, and he got in and started the engine, leaving Schooner and Mia to say goodbye.

"I'm going to miss you." She took his face in her hands as he bent down to kiss her.

"It's smoochal, Baby Girl. Call me when you get out to the house. I love you."

Heading out of Manhattan, Mia played with the radio. "No kids. I get to listen to Bruce." She quickly switched the dial to E Street Radio.

"We should be listening to beach music," Seth complained, as they drove an uncharacteristically freely moving, half-empty Long Island Expressway.

"Beach music it is, as we're setting up the house," Mia conceded.

"A rare BBC compromise, hmm. What am I in store for over the next few days?"

"An empty beach house with just the two of us." Mia smiled, enjoying seeing trees that were finally green. It had been a long, gray, and emotional winter.

"Is that supposed to make me feel good?" he snarked. "If it were an empty beach house with just me and Henry, that would make me happy."

"So, buy a beach house of your own, freeloader." She gave it right back to him.

"Now why would I do that when my BFF already owns one of the best houses on the entire island?"

"You've got a point." She smiled. "And we'll have more room than ever with Zac and Lily down in Baltimore and Holly coming out just for weekends. She's doing a full load of summer classes up at Columbia."

"She certainly is getting as far away from the NYU campus as she can this summer without leaving Manhattan island," observed Seth, as he exited the Long Island Expressway, heading south on the Sagtikos Parkway.

"I think her goal this summer is to not get her heart broken again and to avoid her East Coast exes."

As Seth exited on Merrick Road, Mia cracked the window, letting in the cool, spring air. "I cannot wait to see the ocean and wake up to the sound of the waves crashing on the shore."

"You and me both, sista."

"Thank you for helping me do this, Princess. Seriously. I really appreciate it." They were unpacking the kids' summer clothes and putting them away.

"Are you up to tackling the kitchen next?"

"No. I think we should go drink." Mia smiled at him. "I am never without kids. This may be my only adult vacation all year."

"Should we uncork a bottle? I saw some Silver Oak in the wine rack."

Mia shook her head. "Maybe later when we're hanging out on the deck. Let's go into town. Why don't we go to Castaway. I am dying for baked clams and a grilled romaine salad."

"And a Rocket Fuel?" Seth taunted Mia with the Fire Island specialty drink.

"Oh God, I'm going to be shitfaced. I haven't had anything with that much alcohol in it for a very long time."

"I'm buying."

"In that case, let me go grab a sweatshirt and my wallet."

As they walked into town, Mia took deep breaths. "That air. There's nothing like it."

"Yeah, well that air hates your hair. You already look like a Chia pet and we're not even there yet."

"Ah, who gives a shit. I'm going to be drunk in a few minutes."

"This really is your happy place," Seth conceded. "You don't even care how frizzed out your hair is."

"Not like I'm trying to find a man."

Opening the door to the restaurant for Mia, "You're already with the best man this side of Cherry Grove."

"Schooner really is, isn't he?" Mia pretended not to understand Seth.

"No, BBC. Not Pretty Boy. Moi. I'm the best man this side of Cherry Grove."

"If you say so." She smiled sweetly at him.

"Bitch. Buy your own drink." He laughed as they entered the rustic restaurant.

"Hey, you two. Welcome back!" Maddie yelled from behind the bar. "Are you back for the season."

"Not yet. We just came out ahead of everyone to get the house ready," Mia explained.

"Grab a seat anywhere," she motioned toward several empty tables. Coming out from behind the bar, she dried her hands on the towel hanging off her apron. "How's that handsome husband of yours? And the little ones?"

"Everyone's great."

"Don't take this the wrong way, but he is just so much fun to look at," she admitted, blushing slightly.

"Please don't tell him that," Mia begged.

"Deal." Maddie winked. "How's Holly doing? Is she okay?"

"Yeah, just buried in school work."

"I'm sure she took the news real hard. Even though they're not together anymore. It's still gotta be rough."

With a glance across the booth at Seth, the look in his eyes telegraphed the same fright Mia could feel deep in the pit of her stomach. As her abdominal muscles started to knot, she braced herself for news she didn't want to hear. *Please God, please let him be alive.*

Maddie's dark eyes misted. "You haven't heard, have you?"

Mia felt the searing pain stab at her chest as her heart skipped a beat. Shaking her head, the lump lodged at the base of her throat began to block her airway.

"Aiden was wounded overseas."

"Is he alive?" The air rushed out of Mia.

"Yeah, he was in the hospital overseas and then in and out of VA hospitals, including the one up in Northport a couple of times. But he's out now." Maddie nodded reassuringly.

"What happened?"

"Not sure of the details, but I know he's had some surgeries to remove a lot of shrapnel, and," she lowered her voice to a whisper, "I understand he's lost an eye or his eyesight or something."

"Have you seen him?" Seth asked, looking from Maddie to Mia, his mouth hanging open.

"No, but I know he was out like two weeks ago. Billy saw him." She turned to the bar to catch Billy's attention. "Billy, come over here a sec," she yelled across the room.

"Hey, Billy, make us two Rocket Fuels first," Seth called out to him.

"Good idea, I think we're going to need them," Mia said to her friend. Looking back at Maddie, "I'm just glad he is alive. Holly is going to be devastated."

"Hey, guys, good to see you." Billy arrived with two tall glasses, filled with frozen white *help me cope with this news* Rocket Fuels.

"I was just telling them about Aiden."

"Yeah, poor guy," Billy commiserated.

"What happened? Is he okay?"

"Yeah, I mean he's been through some bad shit. One side of his face is pretty messed up. They've been doing reconstructive surgery on him so that they could fit him with a fake eye. I think his arm on that side was pretty scarred up, too, but he was wearing long sleeves, so I don't know for sure. But that's what I heard."

Mia tried to process what Billy was telling her. The memory of Johann Baer making prosthetic eyes at the clinic in Zambia flooded her thoughts. "How was he? Did he seem okay?" Mia patted her hand over her heart.

"Yeah, he was just kinda like himself, you know. A little on the quiet side for Aiden. He still had the patch on his eye, so he kinda looked badass. And he's bulked up, I think they had him working out a lot in the hospital. You know, doing therapy on his body and stuff. Considering everything, he did seem okay, Mia. He was a little distant, but I know I'd be fuckin' bitter if it were me."

Seth pushed Mia's drink toward her. Pulling out the straw, she picked up the glass and took a healthy swig.

"Holly didn't know?" Billy asked. "I know they broke up and all, but I figured she mighta heard, you know."

"She has no clue. She is going to be devastated for him. Do you know if he's coming back? Is he going to be out here this summer?"

"I dunno, he didn't say." Billy shook his head. "We talked about my new boat. I got a racing boat and I showed it to him and that was about it. Excuse me. Customers." He gestured to the couple walking in and left to greet them.

"What can I get you to eat?" Maddie asked.

"I don't think I can eat after that news. But you might want to go ahead and get us another round of these."

"I'll give you a few minutes to finish those and then I'll bring you round two."

"Thanks, Maddie," Seth called after her as she headed back to the bar.

"Oh my God, Seth." She just stared at him for a moment. "Poor Aiden. My heart is just breaking for him." Squeezing her eyes shut, she shook her head. "Imagine the scars we can't see."

"I was just thinking that. He didn't want Holly to have to go through this with him if it happened."

"Yeah, I know that is what he was fearing. How are we going to tell her, Seth?" Mia put her head in her hands

"I don't know." He shook his head.

"I just feel like I keep slamming into brick walls no matter which direction I turn." Holly's bottom lip quivered. It had been two weeks since Mia had shared with her the news on Aiden. "His old cell number isn't his anymore and his parents haven't returned any of my messages."

Schooner winced hearing that neither Aiden nor his parents had acknowledged Holly's attempts to find out how he was doing, and just to let him know that she was thinking about him. "C'mere." He motioned for Holly to join him on the couch. Pulling her to him, she put her head on his shoulder.

"Oh, Dad, I just want to know he's okay."

"Next weekend is Memorial Day. Maybe he'll come out to Fire Island for the weekend. He has a lot of friends out there, I'm sure he'll be invited to several barbeques. And maybe the folks over at Maguire's know something or have a newer phone number for him."

Recognizing the pain in his daughter's eyes, he hurt for her, knowing firsthand the heartache of losing the one who is the star of all your hopes and dreams. This guy wasn't just a break-up. This was the soul crusher, where you don't know your heart is walking a tightrope, until you are careening to the cement fifty feet below and shatter. Wishing he could somehow make this better for her, and knowing there wasn't anything he could do, frustrated him.

"I know this is rough, sweetie. But with all the acquaintances we have in common, we'll know something pretty soon. I'm sure of that. Are you coming out for Memorial Day weekend?"

The disappointment was evident on Schooner's face as soon as Holly shook her head. He wanted his whole family together. Nothing made the man happier. The beach house, the ocean, Po and Natie keeping them all amused, and even Zac and Lily were going to be there. He had told Zac, "You'll have to leave three days in advance or you'll spend the weekend sitting in Jersey shore traffic trying to get here."

But no Holly.

"Everybody will be there." Dad-speak for we're all there to support you if you are having a rough time.

"I know, but I told my lab partner, Jenna, that I would go to her barbeque on Sunday." Holly nervously played with her hair.

Reaching out, Schooner took his daughter's hand and held it in both of his. "You're afraid he'll be there this weekend." It wasn't a question. "Do you want us to text you if we see him?"

Nodding, "Yeah. Will you let me know how he's doing?"

"We haven't seen him yet, so he may not be there." They'd been out every weekend since Mia and Seth had set-up for the season.

"But this weekend is it. It's the official start of summer and everybody's out there."

"We'll miss you, kiddo." Schooner wished he could do something, anything to help her heal from this heartbreak. It didn't escape him that she hadn't stressed over her break-up with Tom, but it was Aiden who was absorbing her every thought since Mia and Seth had delivered the news of his return and the few details they knew of his ordeal.

"Busted," he whispered in her ear, coming up from behind, just as Holly sent a text to Mia saying, **Anything?**

Sticking her phone into the back pocket of her worn jeans shorts, Holly smiled at Jenna's very handsome older brother, Pierce. Man buns were not usually her thing, and pulling one off was reserved for seriously hot men, but this guy totally rocked it. With a casual, laid-back vibe, a few days' scruff, a very colorful full-sleeve of ink on his left arm, and hazel eyes that leaned more toward green than brown, rimmed in enviably long, dark lashes, this man was hard not to notice.

Holly immediately felt eyes on them — from everywhere. The glare of all the other single women at the party felt like an undertow of bitchy female energy, making Holly feel more alone than she already did. Alone in a crowd was not an alien feeling to her, though it would probably surprise most people. It generally took Holly a long time to find her crowd, and it typically wasn't what people might expect her to gravitate toward.

"It's a party. You gotta mingle." His accent was thick New York. He took a swig of his beer. "Or I could just keep you to myself," he flirted.

Feeling self-conscious, she changed the subject to neutral ground. "This is my first time in Carroll Gardens. I've been in Brooklyn a bunch of times, mostly in the Heights. We have a close family friend there, but I've never walked this far down. I love all these brownstones, and the outdoor space your sister has is amazing. Do you live nearby?" She was rambling, and she wasn't sure if it was because she was so uncomfortable or because he was so good-looking.

Jenna's ground-level-floor-thru apartment had exclusive use of the small rectangular yard, which held enough space for a grill and fifteen guests. At the very back of the yard she had a plastic blow-up kiddie pool filled with water. Holly wondered if, as the afternoon heat and humidity climbed, the party-goers would be stepping in to cool themselves off.

Taking a swig from his beer bottle, Pierce shared, "Not too far. I'm in the Slope. No private backyard, but I'm not too far from Prospect Park."

"That must be nice." Trying hard to stay in the moment, Holly searched her brain for something to say to this handsome, seemingly nice guy, and her mind just blanked out.

"So, let me ask you a question," he began, filling in the silence. "My sister tells me you're not involved with anyone. How is that possible?"

Holly smiled, Pierce had obviously been inquiring about her. New Yorkers were so direct. That had initially taken some getting used to, but it was actually refreshing, and moved things from superficial to real at warp speed, and that was something she liked. "Bad break-up. Still recuperating."

"Is he fucking nuts?" Pierce took another swig.

Watching his throat muscles and Adam's apple in motion was oddly erotic. *Maybe it's the sheen of sweat covering them*, Holly thought, followed immediately by the memory of Aiden's salty skin waking the taste buds on her tongue.

"I'll volunteer to be your transition guy," offered Pierce with a smile.

"Thanks. Appreciate the offer, but you're a little late to the party." Holly laughed.

"Well, he's not here, what happened to that guy?" Pierce was persistent.

Reaching out and taking the beer from his hands, Holly took a swig. "I think we're going to need some Jack for that story."

"You, I like." He laughed. "I don't think my sister's got any, but there's a liquor store up on Court Street, we can take a walk up there and get a bottle."

"Let's do it." Holly wanted to get away from the stare of female eyes that were taking on an increasingly hostile glare, especially those of a brunette who was going to regret her dark microbladed eyebrows when, in a few years, she looked back at pictures of herself.

As they walked down Second Place, Holly asked, "So, what's with you and the lady in the revealing pink halter."

Pierce started to laugh and began to cough. "Holly, that ain't no lady."

"No? Now I'm intrigued. I'll bet you have a lot better stories than I have."

"I don't know how she got an invite today. She's my version of a stalker."

"Did you deserve it?"

He thought for a moment. "Yeah, probably."

"Drive-by?"

"Yeah, I couldn't pull out fast enough."

Holly's eyes widened, as she looked at him, the front of her sandal catching on the uneven sidewalk. Reaching out and catching her shoulder, Pierce steadied her.

"Oh shit, that didn't come out the way I wanted it to."

"So I gathered." She laughed.

"Woman, I am tongue-tied around you. I was trying to sound really smart and hit you with a driving metaphor, but I fucked that all up." He gestured to a store, and grabbed the door, holding it open for Holly. "Whiskey aisle all the way to the right. Not that I would know that."

Holly turned around and smiled. "I like a man who knows his way around."

Grabbing a bottle of Jack from the shelf, he turned to Holly who was checking out the single malt scotches. "Anything else?"

"No, I think Jack is enough." She ran her fingers slowly down the side of a sleek scotch bottle. "Single malts just remind me of my dad."

"Have you not seen him in a while?"

"No, I see him all the time. He's just out on Fire Island this weekend."

"Your parents are on Fire Island?"

Holly nodded. "Yes, we have a house in Ocean Beach."

"And you are not there because?" He paused. "You like humid, sweltering days in the city where the heat rises off the sidewalk and bitch slaps you in the face?"

"It's complicated."

"Family complicated?"

"Oh no, family is great. Ex-boyfriend is not so great."

"So, the heartbreak guy is out on Fire Island?"

Pulling the phone from the back pocket of her shorts, she checked Mia's message. **No sign of him at all.**

"No, doesn't look like he's there."

"Someone is sending you messages about it?" He was surprised.

"Yes." Holly laughed. "My stepmother."

Opening the low wrought-iron gate leading to Jenna's brownstone, Pierce headed up the stone stairs and sat down on a step instead of heading back through his sister's apartment to the yard. Joining him, Holly watched as he opened the Jack, still in its paper bag. With the black cap now off, he handed Holly the bag for the first swig and she didn't disappoint, downing a hearty swallow and handing it back to him.

"Woman, you just keep impressing me more and more." And he followed suit putting down a healthy swallow before handing the bag back to Holly. "So, do you know what we're doing here?"

"Getting shitfaced?" Holly ventured.

"Yes, that, too. But what we're doing right now is stooping. Have you ever stooped before?"

Wide-eyed, Holly shook her head. "No. I think I'm a stoop virgin."

Mid-swig, Pierce started to choke at Holly's comment. "Thank God, I'm not too late to that party. In case you are wondering, what you are sitting on is called a stoop. And we are stooping." Elbowing

Holly playfully, he reminded her, "So, wait. You were supposed to tell me about transition guy. The guy who stole my spot. What happened to him?"

"My mother happened to him."

"Give me that bottle back. Your mother? What did she do to him?"

"You might want to take another slug of that first."

Smiling, he brought the bag to his lips. "This better be a good one."

"Trust me, you can't make up this crap." Holly reached out for the bag, taking a courage swig before continuing and spilling family dirty laundry to a virtual stranger. "My mother has no moral compass. I will start off by telling you that. It's like not even shattered, she just straight up doesn't have one. Whatever means necessary to get the results she wants, is fair game to her. She didn't want me seeing this guy."

"Why?" he interrupted.

With her already inebriated courage propped up, and doing just a slight lean, she smiled at her friend's too-damn-handsome brother. "True confession time. She didn't want me seeing him because he was, well, he was a lot older than me." And then in a rush, "He was also my stepmother's ex-boyfriend."

Spitting out the Jack in his mouth, they both laughed at his reaction. "No freaking way did I expect you to say that. You are full of surprises. I had you pegged for wholesome, a little aloof, maybe snotty. Totally wrong on all counts. Your stepmother's ex? Really?"

"In my defense, I didn't know that at the time. And we were all surprised. It was just kind of this random thing."

"Okay." He drew out the two syllables. "So, what did your mother do to him?"

"Ah, that is the big mystery. Only the two of them know that for sure. He wouldn't tell me. But I know it was bad."

"Like threatened him?"

"Probably more along the lines of blackmail. And I wouldn't doubt that there is a sexual element to it. One that she initiated, and he might not have been a totally willing participant."

"I'm really confused." His brows knit together as he tried to follow the story. "Do you think she slept with him?"

"No, but something happened. Like I said, my mother gets what she wants by whatever means she needs to employ." Pulling out her cell, she scrolled through pictures and handed the phone to Pierce.

"That's your mom? Wow. She's beautiful. You look like her." He continued to stare at the picture.

Reaching for the phone, she scrolled and handed it back to him. "And that's my dad."

"Man, he's in good shape."

"He owns health clubs."

"Health clubs plural."

Holly nodded.

"Like franchises?"

"No. No. He would never franchise out the business. Each facility is his concept. He's very protective of the brand. He's meticulously built it over like twenty years."

"What's the name of it."

"Level 9."

"Your father owns L9?"

Holly nodded again.

"Beautiful, smart, nice, and rich as shit. This guy who broke your heart is one dumbass."

"Thanks." She took another swig.

"Okay, so now that you confessed to dating your stepmother's ex who was then, we think, sexually molested by your MILF mama, I have a confession to make. But I'm warning you, it's not nearly as good as yours. You definitely win confession of the day."

"'Fess up, dude." Holly elbowed her new buddy.

"I've never been to Fire Island."

"What? No way! And you grew up here, right?"

"Born and raised."

"And you've never been to Fire Island?"

"No, I usually go out to the beaches on the east end. My band has played semi-regularly at EBI."

"What's EBI?" Holly asked.

"Ahh, you are clearly not a native of the area. EBI is a place you totally need to go. EBI stands for Echo Beach Inn. It's a club/bar out on Echo Beach. Big summer hangout."

"So, you're in a band. I should have guessed. You look like a musician." Holly waved at a young couple walking with a baby jogger who waved back at her and Pierce, wishing them a happy Memorial Day. Drunk stooping was fun.

"Thanks. I think."

"Why aren't you playing out there this weekend? This is a big weekend. Shouldn't you be out on the beach?"

"Because two of my bandmates have mono."

"Remind me not to kiss you." Holly looked at the bottle of Jack, pondering if she should be sharing it with this stranger, but decided, in her already drunken state, that the 80-proof alcohol would be the victor, obliterating any mono germs.

"I'm too drunk to remember to remind you." He hit her with a slightly crooked smile.

"Do you have a day job?" she wondered aloud.

"Now I do, since I'm not making money off my music this summer." The look on his face clearly said he was not thrilled about it.

"What do you do during the day?"

"I'm a programmer." Then he added, "But I'd rather be sleeping after a late-night gig."

"You've really never been to Fire Island?" Holly's mind had circled back to their earlier conversation.

"Never." He shook his head.

"Let's go." The spontaneous thought made her smile, and in the moment seemed like the most brilliant idea she'd had in forever.

With a look that said, *Are you serious?* He asked, "Like now?"

"Yeah. Like right now. We could take the train out and then a cab to the ferry."

"I have to go home and get stuff." It was difficult to get his brain clear enough to work through the details.

"Go do it," she urged, nodding him on.

"Bossy," he smiled. "Are you sure? Your family won't mind?"

Waving a hand at him, "My family totally embodies the more the merrier philosophy."

"And what if we run into the heartbreaker?"

"Mia said he's not there."

"And Mia is who?"

"My stepmom."

Pulling out his phone, "Okay, I'll get an Uber back home. What do I need?"

"Shorts. Tee-shirt. Bathing suit. Toothbrush. Flip flops." It was taxing Holly's brain to try to come up with a list.

"Can I buy the stuff there? Then I don't have to go home."

"Yeah, there's shops right when we get off the ferry."

"So, an Uber to Penn Station?" he suggested

"Totally, I'm too trashed to get on the subway."

"Let's go tell my sister we're leaving." Pierce suggested.

"Is that girl in the pink halter going to scratch my eyes out?" Holly was envisioning the stalker chick chasing them out onto the street.

Thinking for a moment and realizing Holly had a point, "Maybe we should just leave. We'll text Jenna once we've made our getaway." He ordered the Uber. "There's a car three blocks away."

Unsteady on their feet, they stood. As a small white car pulled up outside the gate, they made their way down the steps.

Laughing, "I can't believe we're doing this." Pierce smiled at Holly.

Pointing to the bag sitting on the stoop, "Don't forget Jack."

"My faux pas." He laughed, running back up the steps to retrieve the catalyst to their journey.

"Wake up." Holly shook Pierce. "This is our stop."

"Wow, that went fast." Rubbing his eyes, he looked out the train's window as they pulled into Bay Shore station. They had talked most of the trip, Holly sharing the Aiden/Fire Island saga before they both dozed off somewhere around Bellmore. "Holy crap, I'm still drunk. Are you still drunk?"

Picking up the bag between them on the seat, Holly uncapped the Jack and took a gulp before handing it to Pierce.

Following suit, he took a swig and then laughed. Looking at Holly, "Your parents are going to wish transition man was back in the picture when they get a whiff of me. I smell like a human distillery."

Looking at her watch, "Most likely they'll be out on the beach for a bit, so we'll have time to clean up our acts and maybe sober up a little, too."

Exiting the train, they could already smell the salt on the breeze. "Okay, so we can take a cab, or walk it. It's about a mile. And we'll have enough time before the next ferry, even if we walk."

Pointing to a concession stand, Pierce suggested, "Why don't we grab a couple of water bottles and hoof it."

"I like the way you think."

"I like everything about you." He gave her a side-eye. "Too bad you're still in love with someone else."

Looking at him sad-eyed, she sighed. "Maybe I just need closure. I just want to see him and talk to him."

"He could show up this weekend."

"Not likely. He would've been there already."

"Well, we're just getting there," he remarked.

"You have a point." Taking a sip of her water, "I am really dehydrated from drinking." Leading them out to Fourth Avenue through a semi-industrial area, "It gets prettier and a lot shadier once we cross over West Main Street," Holly promised.

"This is fine, I'm sweating out some of the alcohol," he commented, taking in his surroundings.

"The breeze on the top deck of the boat should wake us up."

"Are you sure it's okay for me to stay. I can always take the ferry home tonight."

"If you want to leave, I'm not going to make you stay. But seriously, Pierce, trust me, you will be totally welcome. My family will be thrilled that you got me out here. The only thing to worry about is that you might never want to leave."

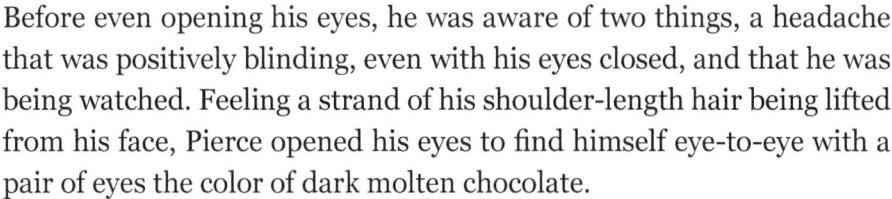

Before even opening his eyes, he was aware of two things, a headache that was positively blinding, even with his eyes closed, and that he was being watched. Feeling a strand of his shoulder-length hair being lifted from his face, Pierce opened his eyes to find himself eye-to-eye with a pair of eyes the color of dark molten chocolate.

"You must be Po," his voice was hoarse.

She nodded and silently held out a bottle of spring water in her left hand and a bottle of aspirin in her right. Sitting up, he took them from her, shaking three pills from the bottle and downing them with the water. Closing his eyes, he took a deep breath, the journey to his current location slowly coming back to him. When he opened his eyes, he heard a rustle from the foot of the bed, and discovered a second set of eyes that had been watching him. In contrast to his sister, his were a clear blue, almost white surrounding the pupil.

"And you must be Natie."

Giggling, the little boy jumped on the bed, a motion Pierce felt excruciatingly in each and every dehydrated brain cell trapped inside his exploding skull.

"Holly said you probably had a headache."

Pierce smiled, hearing the remnants of a British accent in the little girl's voice. Holly had told him about Po's adoption from a Zambian orphanage.

"I'll bet she's got one, too," he commented.

Portia's eyes opened wide as she nodded her head. Reaching out, she stroked his hair, "You've got really pretty hair."

"Wanna see what I do with it?" Pierce grabbed his hair tie from the nightstand and quickly twisted it into a man bun.

"I wish my hair was long enough to do that." Natie looked on enviously.

"Don't let your mom cut your hair all summer and it might be close to long enough."

"Do not corrupt my brother and sister." Holly was at the door looking in, holding towels.

Pierce laughed. "I'll leave the corruption to you. Jack was your idea after all."

Sitting next to Pierce on the bed, Natie ran his fingers through his own loose blond curls trying to figure out how to twist them into a bun.

"Okay, you two, let's give Pierce some space." She ushered them out and handed her new friend the towels. "There's a great private outdoor shower on the deck right outside those French doors." She pointed across the room.

"I should probably look at the ferry schedule back."

"Tonight? You just got here. And then we passed out. There's still so much to show you."

"I don't want to crash your family's weekend."

"My family would be pissed if you left. Like I said, this beach house is about the more the merrier and good times. They love having people."

"Are you sure?"

"I'm positive. My brother and his fiancée are here. Family friends Seth and Henry and Yoli and Debbie are here, too."

"I don't want to put anyone out."

Rolling her eyes and shaking her head, "I won't make you stay if you really want to go, but this house has seven bedrooms, so you are not putting anyone out."

"Seven bedrooms? Wow. It felt like we were walking into the Kennedy Compound when we got here earlier, but I thought that was just because I was so drunk."

"Don't say that in front of Seth. He's done most of the decorating and would consider being compared to the Kennedy Compound an insult. But anything Jackie, he'd be more than thrilled with. So, you'll stay?" With a smile, she left the room before he could answer.

A beautiful beachfront house on Fire Island with a menagerie of people I don't know, *this is either going to be epic or the scariest fucking weekend of my life,* thought Pierce, as he headed out the French doors to the shower.

Streams of warm water cascading down the back of his head alleviated the muscle tension in his neck and shoulders, easing what was left of his dehydration headache. Straightening up, the droplets before his eyes prismed in the sunlight, their sparkle so brilliant he decided that it was an omen that the weekend would end up being epic.

"Two more for dinner," Holly announced, walking into the living room with Pierce following a step behind.

"So, what are we now? Fifteen instead of thirteen?" Schooner Moore looked around the room for confirmation as he approached his daughter and wrapped her in a bear hug. "I'm so glad you're here, sweetheart." Reaching out his hand, he shook hands with his daughter's new friend, "Schooner Moore."

Just introducing himself, he commands the room, thought Pierce. "Pierce Cooper." Taking Schooner's hand, it was impossible not to feel his energy. He oozed power, but in a very understated, yet charismatic way.

"So, we're fifteen now?" Schooner pulled out his cell. "I should just buy that damn place," he muttered, stepping out of the room as he called the restaurant.

As Holly introduced Pierce to their sizeable crowd, she couldn't help but notice the consistency of the questioning looks, the unasked question crowding the forefront of everyone's mind. *New boyfriend?*

"Pierce is Jenna's brother, you know, my lab partner, and he was telling me earlier today that he's never been to Fire Island."

"So, you just decided to hop a train?" Mia looked amused.

"Well, after half a fifth of Jack Daniel's, it seemed like a good idea." Holly leaned against the island of the open kitchen.

The room erupted in laughter and disbelief.

"Wait a minute. A fifth of Jack and I'm the one everyone considers the problem child," Zac piped in. Looking at Pierce, "Don't let her fool you with that brainy, Ivy League stuff. She's the troublemaker, I'm just the one who got blamed. The truth finally comes out," he kidded, ribbing his sister.

"Jack Daniel's?" Schooner's upper lip curled with disgust. "Didn't I teach you better?"

"We were sitting on a stoop and it was in a paper bag," Holly explained.

"You were stooping?" Mia was amused.

"Yes, I stooped today." Holly bragged to Mia as if she'd just been invited to sit at the cool kids' lunch table. Pointing to Pierce, "He stole my stoop virginity."

"Jack and a bag are definitely appropriate for stooping," Mia gave her approval. "Ah, memories," she smiled wistfully. "And you did it in Brooklyn. I'm proud."

"You are such a derelict, BBC." Seth was looking at Mia the same way Schooner was looking at his daughter and her new tatted-up friend.

"What is stooping?" Yoli asked. "I am totally lost."

"I live on arguably the street with the best stoops in all the five boroughs and you'd never catch anyone stooping on my block." Seth was mortified.

"Is anybody going to tell us what stooping is?" Henry looked as confused as Yoli.

Laughing, Mia looked at Pierce. "They are all Californians. Not a game of stoopball between 'em."

Pierce smiled at Mia. He knew by her accent and her attitude that he liked her. "Now, that's a shame. Imagine not having stooping memories?" he asked Mia.

She shook her head. "No, I can't. Hot summer nights stooping. I can't even imagine not having those memories."

"Right," he acknowledged.

"Okay, you two, enough of the *I Love New York* moment, tell us about stooping." Schooner had opened one of the distressed, white clapboard kitchen cabinets and pulled a bottle of Johnnie Walker Blue from the top shelf.

"Stooping," began newly minted stooping expert, Holly Moore, "is the art of successfully hanging out on the staircase, or as it is known, a stoop, in front of a building. Seth's brownstone has a stoop. Gaby and Charles's brownstone has a stoop. And today Pierce and I stooped in Carroll Gardens."

"And got shitfaced," Zac added, more than slightly surprised by his generally good girl sister's escapade.

"Yes, and got very shitfaced," Pierce confirmed.

"As witnessed by the fact that you guys got on a train." Mia was very amused and thrilled to see Holly letting loose and having some fun for a change.

"And then walked from the train to the ferry." Holly filled in that detail.

"No way," Zac was laughing at his sister. "You must've still been shitfaced."

"We were," Holly and Pierce announced in stereo.

Shaking his head, but wearing an entertained smile, Schooner rejoined them, handing Holly and Pierce each a glass with two fingers of Johnnie. "Hair of the dog. This will actually make you feel better."

Taking sips, Holly and Pierce looked at one another, smiling.

"Man, that's good. Thank you, Mr. Moore."

"Schooner," he corrected.

"Schooner." Pierce nodded. "That is so smooth."

Mia looked at her watch, "I think we need to get ready to move on out and head to the restaurant. Charles, Gaby, and Paola are meeting us there."

As they walked toward town, Pierce took in the houses set behind the scrubby beach pines. "This is really not like anyplace I have ever been." He was mesmerized by the beach community with no cars that had been a stone's throw from him his entire life. Assuming it was just another Hamptons, he was pleasantly surprised by this laid-back community. While obviously affluent, it didn't rely on glitz for its charm, but rather embraced a more down-to-Earth ethos than the East End beach towns.

"It's great, isn't it? I remember the first time I came out a few years ago, I didn't want to leave," Yoli confessed.

"Are you hanging in there?" Mia asked Holly.

"I'm a little freaked out. But that shot of Johnnie Walker that Dad gave me helped not only with the after-effects of Jack, but also my confidence." Turning to Pierce, she explained, "The place we're going for dinner, Aiden managed it for years. And I worked there during the summers."

"So, everyone there knows you as a couple."

She nodded.

"You'll be fine. You've got quite a posse."

The staff reception was warm and loving as soon as Holly entered the establishment, her former colleagues showering her with love and concern.

"Hey, Holly, we need extra help tonight. I understand there's a party of fifteen," kidded Sheila, a waitress with twenty years under her belt at this beach establishment. "Oh, wait, it's you." She gave Schooner a flirtatious sneer.

"How's my girl?" He embraced her in a side hug.

Sticking her nose into his fresh cotton shirt, she breathed in deeply. "Better now that I've gotten a whiff of you, handsome." Breathing in loudly a second time, "I missed this." And then she turned to the group. "Let me show you to your table."

They were seated for no more than two minutes when Sheila reappeared with a glass of scotch for Schooner that he had yet to order.

"You take such good care of me." He hit her with his heart-melting smile.

"If you ever want to kick him out, I'm just saying," she said to Mia.

"Watch what you wish for," quipped Mia, causing everyone to laugh, including Schooner.

"You're new and very handsome." Sheila took notice of Pierce.

"And a younger model," Seth was quick to point out without looking up from his menu.

"Damn millennials are replacing us everywhere," Schooner muttered with a smile as he picked up his menu.

After ordering, Holly quickly excused herself and headed toward the bar where Sheila welcomed her with a smile as she loaded drinks onto her tray.

"Is that your new boyfriend?" Sheila was curious.

"No. No. He's a friend's brother. He's never been to Fire Island, so I invited him out to see it." Pausing, Holly took a deep breath before spitting out the question haunting her. "Have you seen him?"

Him. There was only one him that Holly would be referring to, and sadly, Sheila shook her head. "The one time he was out here, he didn't step foot in this place to say hello to any of us, that stinker. We were like his family for years. No. Let me correct that. We were closer than his family. And he doesn't even come in to let us know he's back."

"I know the feeling. I've been trying to reach him since I heard he had been out here. And nothing. Even his parents won't respond." Holly's eyes filled with tears.

"Hey, gorgeous." Tommy worked his way over from the far end of the bar where he finished serving two women.

Leaning across the teak and brass bar, Holly gave her former co-worker a big kiss. "How are you, handsome?" She continued their repartee.

"Much better now that I'm looking at you." His eyes crinkled with his smile.

"We were just talking about our former boss," Sheila filled him in.

"Have you heard from him?" he asked Holly.

"Not a word. You didn't see him when he was out here?" Holly was dying for information. Any tidbit, just something.

The older bartender shook his head. "No. He avoided this place. He clearly didn't want to see us." Tommy wasn't hiding his hurt. "He was like a son to me."

"I know." Holly reached across the bar, taking his hand.

"And what he did to you. That's just crappy," he added.

"Was she with him? Do you know?" Holly referred to Aiden's ex, the woman he dumped her for. *Please say no,* she silently begged.

"I don't think so. I didn't hear anything about her being out here with him." Leaning across the bar, Tommy whispered to Holly, "You're still hung up on him, aren't you, doll?"

Nodding, "I know it's probably stupid."

"Not stupid. You loved the guy. That was very evident."

"Was I a fool, Tommy, to think he loved me, too?" Holly searched his eyes.

"Ya know, Sheila and I were just talking about that the other day. The guy worshipped the ground you walked on. He acted like he was the most fortunate son of a bitch on Earth because he had you."

"Maybe that's it. Maybe he was just acting."

"Nah, he loved you, Holly. Maybe too much," he added.

"Do you think that scared him?"

"I dunno. All I know is the guy was crazy in love with you. And then he wasn't. Just like that. Doesn't make sense. And like Judge Judy says, 'If it don't make sense, it ain't the truth.'"

"If he shows up this summer, can you tell him I really need talk to him, I just want to know he's okay." It was painful even talking about Aiden.

"Sure thing, doll," Tommy promised.

"You're the best," she flashed him a smile before leaving to go back to the table.

Sitting down next to Pierce, Holly was glad to see he was involved in a conversation with Zac and had blended in well with the Moore party. From down the table, their family friend Gaby mouthed, "He's hot," to which Holly mouthed back, "Just a friend." Caught mid-mouthing, Holly turned to Pierce and confessed. "Everyone wants to know if we're a thing."

Looking down the table to Gaby, "I wish. But she's hung up on another guy and I've already missed the transition guy spot."

"And that's a damn shame," muttered Schooner.

Mia gave him a pointed look.

"Well, it's true. Think of how much better Thanksgiving would've been if Pierce had been there."

"Do you mean I wouldn't have thrown up?" Natie chimed in.

"No, sweetie. That was some strategically timed vomiting, and we all were thankful for that," Mia explained.

"I was thankful we weren't there," laughed Charles. "Although you do realize I'm the only one who's never met him." He referred to Tom.

"That's right. I met you the night I threw him out." Mia smiled at the memory. "What a great night that turned out to be. We ate tuna at Kiev."

"They are talking about transition guy," Holly explained to Pierce in a whisper.

"Next subject," Schooner declared, just as pots of steamers were delivered to the table.

"Clammies," squealed buddies Portia and Paola from the far end of the table, reaching into the heavy aluminum pot closest to them.

"So, Pierce, we know you're a stooper, and that you and my daughter both arrived in a stupor today. What else should we know about you?" Schooner looked directly at the younger man.

Meeting his gaze, "I'm a struggling musician who pays my bills programming for a small, tech start-up."

"What does the company do?" Schooner cleaned a clam, swirling it in a bowl of broth, the sand vortex settling to the bottom.

"We provide automation synchronization with cloud-based solutions," he explained.

"Interesting. And the music?"

"I've got a three-piece band. Guitar, keyboards, and drums. And unfortunately, we've got no gigs lined up because both my keyboard player and drummer have mono." He dipped his clam in a bowl of drawn butter.

Schooner slowly chewed the steamer in his mouth, staring at Pierce. Finally, he spoke, "Don't kiss my daughter."

"Dad!" Holly stretched the plea into three syllables.

Holding onto his serious expression, it was a moment before Schooner broke into a smile. "Eh, even with mono, he's a drastic improvement."

"Let's get rid of some of these empty pots and bowls." Sheila arrived a few minutes later. "I've got your dinners coming out of the kitchen now." Turning to Schooner, "Chef says you need a smaller family."

Laughing, "You tell Chef my big-assed family just helped pay for his daughter's first semester at Swarthmore."

"I think that might be true." She turned to the server arriving with the first tray. "Those go to the far end of the table." A second tray arrived, and she placed the dishes. "Natie, I will pay you five dollars if you eat something other than chicken nuggets."

"Okay, I'll have ice cream." He smiled at his favorite waitress.

"Oh, you are too smart for me, young man."

"We're going to go out and see if anyone good is playing in one of the bars after this, you guys want to join?" Zac asked Holly and Pierce.

"Definitely. I'd love to see who's playing out here."

"Anyone want to come?" Holly asked.

Mia shook her head, "I need to get these two into a bath and to bed."

Yoli laughed. "We're all thinking about shoes off and hanging out back at the house."

"I'm thinking about bra off." Debbie laughed.

"Oh, yeah. Can we leave now?" Mia replied to Debbie. Looking at Pierce, "Feel free to say anything around this crew. We're clearly dysfunctional."

"You guys are really funny," was his observation.

Bidding their parents and family friends goodbye after dinner, Zac, Lily, Holly, and Pierce headed out in search of a bar band. As they walked, Holly's eyes scanned the throngs of holiday weekend partiers. *He's about Aiden's height. That haircut. Who is that smoking a cigarette in the doorway of Ocean Beach Hardware?* She could barely breathe, choked by illusions existing solely for her. *Where are you, Aiden? I need to see you.*

"Where are we going?" Pierce asked.

"Want to try the Schooner Inn first?" Zac suggested, looking at his sister.

"Your dad owns a place?" Pierce asked.

"No. Purely coincidence," Holly explained. "Ocean Bay Park actually has a bar/restaurant named The Schooner Inn and here in Ocean Beach is another named CJ's."

When his sister's new friend didn't get the reference, Zac chimed in. "Our mom's name is CJ."

"Seriously. Wow, that's quite a coincidence."

"You want to walk all the way over to Ocean Bay Park?" Lily asked.

"Babe, it's a mile and after all we ate tonight. Plus, Pierce will get to see more of the island."

"Okay," she acquiesced, happy to get the fresh air after long days in class and clinicals in med school, and less and less exercise as she studied more.

"I'll tell you what, we'll take a water taxi back to Ocean Beach, so you only have to walk one mile. One measly mile. We'll be there in eight minutes. Actually, seven now, since we're already walking."

"We used to walk miles and miles every day," she reminisced, thinking of their time together in Africa, walking trails on the savannah to their work sites.

"We need to start walking more," he threw his arm over her shoulder. "I miss our long walks."

"Hey, you guys! Good to see you. Been way too long," the ginger-haired bartender greeted Zac, Lily, and Holly, spotting them as they found space along the bar.

"Hey, Mikey, this is our friend, Pierce."

Mikey extended a hand, "Nice to meet you, man."

"Four Rocket Fuels," Zac called over the din, pulling Lily closer to him at the bar.

Looking around at the wood-planked walls, Pierce leaned over and shouted into Holly's ear, "I love places like this."

"Me, too." She smiled, taking a drink from Mikey and handing it to Pierce.

Leaning over the bar, Mikey whispered in Holly's ear, "New boyfriend?"

"No. No. Nothing like that. Just a friend." Sucking down a swig of her Rocket Fuel.

Mikey's breath was hot on her ear when she heard him say, "I saw Aiden."

Grabbing onto the bar to keep her knees from buckling, Holly didn't say anything, but her eyes told Mikey every single question she had.

"Tonight?" The word was choked as it came out of her mouth.

"No. About a month ago. I was over in Ocean Beach, grabbing some stuff at the hardware store. It was great seeing him, but Holly, he got pretty fucked up over there. Have you seen him?"

Holly shook her head.

Mikey went on, "The right side of his face got chewed up pretty bad. He seemed okay and all, but he was really tense and kinda jumpy."

Holly's eyes widened, tense and jumpy was not Aiden McManus. He could be intense, because he was driven, but jumpy was the antithesis of Aiden, who handled life's issues, big and small, with a laid-back confidence and swagger.

"I'm worried," she finally spoke, her eyes misting over as she looked up at the ceiling in an attempt to curb her tears. From Mikey's description, it sounded like Aiden's internal scars rivaled, and probably eclipsed, any external disfigurement.

"Yeah. Me too," Mikey confided.

"Did he say if he'd be back out?" Holly tried to slow her heartbeat as she was flooded with a myriad of emotions. Deep, deep sadness was the one that bubbled to the top, pushing anger way down the stack.

The bartender shook his head, his concern mirroring Holly's. Mikey and Aiden had been buds, tight for years, having worked together at many an island bar before Aiden became General Manager at Maguire's. It now appeared Holly was not the only one Aiden had locked out of the fortress. Which made her worry even more.

"Hey, who's playing tonight?" Zac called over to Mikey.

"No one. The douchebag I had booked cancelled a couple of hours ago with a totally bogus reason."

"We've got a musician right here." Holly touched Pierce's arm.

"You wanna step in?" Mikey asked. He was totally serious. "Can you play covers?"

"With the best of 'em, but I don't have my guitar and you don't even know if I can sing." Pierce laughed.

"I've got an acoustic back in my office. You just need to tune it," he offered, wiping his hands.

"Are you serious?" *This weekend just keeps getting more and more, or should I say Moore and Moore, unexpected,* thought Pierce. The fact that he was even here, having drinks with people who were basically strangers, staying in their beach house, dining with their family, and now an impromptu gig at a packed, bayfront bar. He had started the day dreading going to his sister's party, fearing Stalker Nicole might be there waiting for him. And she was. Then Jenna introduced him to her lab partner, a girl way too beautiful to be hiding away in a microbiology lab, and way too heartbroken to be anything more than a new friend.

"Totally. I'll pay you $250 cash if you play now and a set later."

Pierce looked at his hosts, *was this for real?*

"Do it," Holly urged. "I've always wanted to say, *I'm with the band.*" She flicked her hair over her shoulder with attitude and smiled.

Back in Mikey's office, Pierce fiddled with the tuning on the guitar, getting the pitch perfect.

Taking hold of Holly's shoulder, "Are you okay?" Mikey asked.

"No. Not at all," shaking her head. "My heart hurts. He's never even tried to get in touch with me. Not once. And all I want to do is talk to him. See him."

"Not for nothing, Holly, but I think he's afraid to see you."

"I should be with him through this, Mikey. I should be there for him."

"You know what I think? I think he's afraid he's going to ruin your life. And he doesn't want to saddle you with his shit."

"Or he loves that other girl." The sadness in Holly's expressive blue eyes said she believed Aiden loved someone else.

"Impossible." Looking up from the guitar, Pierce added his two cents. "Holly, I've known you twelve hours, and I'm telling you this guy doesn't love another girl. Trust me." *And if he does, he's a putz.*

"Okay, let's get you set up out on the deck." Mikey led the way. "If we've got a full band, I put them by the dance floor. But since you're solo, I think out here will be better." Setting up a stool, microphone, and small amp, Mikey looked at him. "I'll introduce you."

"Pierce Cooper," he supplied the name knowing Mikey probably didn't remember his first name, and never knew his last.

"And where are you from?"

"Park Slope."

"In Brooklyn?" Mikey looked pleased with himself that he knew that.

"Yeah."

Mikey turned on the microphone, immediately met by a momentary screech of feedback until Pierce turned down the amp. The noise got everyone on deck to look in their direction, a perfect way to get everyone's attention.

"Are you guys having a good time tonight?" Mikey's amplified voice boomed. "Yeah? You're all enjoying your Memorial Day weekend?" He was met with enthusiastic shouts. "Well it's about to get better. Joining us on guitar tonight is Park Slope's own, Pierce Cooper." Along with cheers, there were shouts of Brooklyn and The Slope, by fellow residents.

"Hey, everybody," Pierce called out to the crowd as he took a seat on the stool and adjusted the mic down to his height. "So, this is really beautiful getting to play and look over the Great South Bay. I have a confession to make," he paused, pulling the tie from his hair, and shaking loose his thick waves, sending the estrogen in the crowd sky high. "I've never been to Fire Island before today."

"And now you're never leaving," someone yelled from the crowd.

"It could happen." He laughed and started strumming. "Have we got any Soundgarden fans here?" From the screams he knew this would be a good opener. By the time he hit the first chorus of "*Black Hole Sun,*" the crowd was singing with him.

"He's got a really good voice," Lily said to Zac and Holly. "And the women are totally digging the hair. He's pretty hot, Hol."

"He's the guy they want to be sleeping with and not their wimpy boyfriends," was Zac's observation, as he scanned the crowd watching the new singer.

"I wouldn't call you a wimp, babe," Lily kidded her fiancé.

"Check out the audience," Zac continued. "He's a total chick magnet."

"Threatened?" Holly chided her brother, slurping the last of the Rocket Fuel through a straw.

Zac laughed. Nobody could bust you like your own sister. "A few years ago, I definitely would have been competing with this guy or wanted him as a wingman. But now, I don't care if he nails half the island, just as long as he steers clear of what is mine."

"I'm now a what?" Lily protested.

"Baby, baby, baby, you're *my* what." Zac pulled her close, tipping her face up for a kiss.

"Ugh, I can't watch this." Holly turned, heading toward the bar to get another Rocket Fuel. As she approached the bar, the thought struck her that she'd drank more today than she had in four years of college.

"Your friend is really good." Mikey wouldn't let Holly pay for her drink. "I wonder if he can play the next two weekends. I had the guy who stood me up tonight lined up. He's history in my book. You fuck me over on a holiday weekend, you don't get another chance."

Finishing his first set, Pierce made his way to the bar where Holly was standing.

"You were great." She touched his upper arm.

"That was so much fun. I don't think I've ever done a solo gig before. I hadn't even thought about going it alone with the guys down."

"What are you drinking?" Mikey called to him from behind the bar.

"How about a couple of cold bottles of water."

"Coming up, my friend." Placing two large bottles of Evian on the bar in front of Pierce, Mikey asked, "So, what are you doing the next two weekends? Would you want to do Friday and Saturday nights here?"

"Thanks for asking me, but I'm just out here for the day. I don't have a place out here or anything."

"Stay at our house." The solution seemed simple to Holly.

"Will you be here?"

"Probably not." She shook her head thinking how hard it was for her to be here, waiting for a moment that might never come.

"I can't stay at your house without you there." He hardly knew her, to stay with her family without her, would be an imposition. The Moores had already been so nice to him, her father refusing to let him pay for dinner. "You offered. That's a good thing and he'll remember that. But don't push it," Holly had advised him.

"My dad and Mia would be totally cool about it. They'd probably get a sitter for the kids and come watch you play."

"No, Holly, I can't," he protested.

"Yeah, you can," she countered.

"Only if you're out here both weekends."

"I can't do that. I thought I was ready for his ghost. But I'm not. It's everywhere. We're everywhere, he and I. Everywhere I turn, I'm choked by a memory. Everywhere. And it hurts. It physically hurts. It feels like he just broke up with me all over again. And I keep looking, Pierce. Everywhere. Like he's going to come around a corner or out from an alleyway between the shops and just be there. Just walking over here from the restaurant tonight, it felt like I was on high alert, scanning the doorways of every shop, bar, and restaurant. And I could see him standing there. But it was just a mirage. And if I keep coming out here, it will drive me crazy."

It wasn't until the last words were out that Holly let go, tears brimming over her lashes. He could feel her pain and it was overwhelming. This girl he had just met, and he hurt at her heartbreak, feeling how painful this was for her. *What a jerk*, he thought. Imagine having a girl like this, love you that much.

"Holly," he pulled her into his arms. "I am so sorry you are having such a rough time and it's because of me. I'm so sorry."

"Because of you?"

"Yeah. You didn't want to be out here, and you came so that I could experience it, and it was too soon for you."

"Don't be sorry, Pierce. This is not your fault. This hurt and pain, this is between me and Aiden. I will talk to my dad and Mia when we get home. If they have the slightest hesitation about you staying there without me, I promise to let you know. But I really think they are going to be fine with it."

"Holly, they don't know me. Heck, you don't know me."

"I know enough to know that I just watched you doing what you love. And you should be here doing it. And we can help."

"You may be the single most beautiful person I have ever met."

"Thank you." She smiled at her new friend, knowing full well he was not referring to her looks.

"And I'm going to repay you right now." His look said he had something up his sleeve. Quickly scanning the crowded bar area, he turned his attention back to Holly. "Would you say there are a lot of people in here who know Aiden?"

She thought his question to be odd, but looked around before answering, "Quite a few, I guess."

"Good," he smiled at her, taking her face in his hands. "Then we can assume this will somehow get back to him." And with that, he brought his lips to hers for a kiss, taking a shot that while it may not be heard around the world, it certainly would be resounding throughout Fire Island.

CHAPTER
Six

July 4th Weekend

"IT'S A HOLIDAY. You should be spending it with us and not worrying about running into him. Besides, he hasn't been out all summer, so I doubt he'll start on the most crowded, touristy weekend of the season. Natie and Po miss you, sweetheart. And so do I." Schooner was becoming concerned by Holly's obsessive fear of running into her ex-boyfriend. "You should not be changing or altering your life because of him."

"I know. I know." Her dad was right, and she knew that, but mourning the loss of her relationship with Aiden had become an addictive and pervasive thought pattern in her mind. She was able to push him away for short bursts of time when she was studying, but this overwhelming sadness continued to creep in, cradling and lulling her, yet robbing all her joy at the same time, as she waited for something she knew would happen, eventually. But until then, she was stuck, in a place she'd never been before in her life.

"Well, if you know, then get your tush on a train and come spend the holiday with your family. I know you don't have classes this week."

"Tush?" She laughed. "We really have become New Yorkers. You said it and I understood it."

Holly needed some tough love. Schooner knew that. And he was going to give it to her. As empathetic as he was to losing the one you love and not having closure, their family was going to be summering on

Fire Island for a very long time — this was their second home, so she needed to move past the fear that was strapping her down and holding her back. It was that reticence that concerned him, because one of Holly's attributes, one he was extremely proud of, was her fearlessness. But this breakup with Aiden had broken her. And standing by, watching her not heal and making stupid mistakes like Tom to avoid the pain, made him want to fix things. That was something he was exceptionally good at, and yet understood it was not a good thing to do for your adult children. But to know Schooner Moore was to know that backing off, especially when it came to his family, was not an easy thing for him to do.

"Okay, I'll come out," she finally acquiesced. "Is your third son going to be out there?"

"My third son?" *What was she talking about?* "Should I be paying child support to someone?" he joked.

Holly laughed. "Pierce."

"We haven't heard from him since he thanked us for those two weekends. He's your friend, why don't you ask him? You know he's always welcome here."

Any chance this is another long holiday weekend where you don't have plans? Holly texted Pierce later that night.

Hey there. I was just asking my sis about you yesterday. Doing ok?

Hanging in there. Want to come out to the beach this weekend?

Serious?

I'm as serious as a bottle of Jack.

Hahaha. I think your dad had a better idea with the stuff he was drinking. But yeah, I'd love to. I can come out over the weekend, but I can't actually stay for the 4th. I'm working.

A gig??? ☺

Ha ha. I wish. Client is doing a system upgrade and they chose the 4th because staff wouldn't need access to work files. So I get to babysit the process. Big fun.

Well come before that.

I can come out on the 1st, leave on the 3rd.

Awesome. I'll already be out there. Let me know what ferry you're on and I'll meet you when you get in.

You just made my day. And my weekend.

"I need to go shower and meet Pierce's ferry. He gets in at 3:10," Holly announced, sticking her Kindle in her beach bag, and getting up from her turquoise-and-white-striped beach chair. Lost in afternoon naps and books, headphones on, no one actually acknowledged what she had said.

Seeing movement out of the corner of his eye, Schooner pulled out a wireless earbud and turned to Holly. "You off to meet Pierce?"

She laughed. "Yes. We'll be back in a little bit."

Nodding, he put his earphone back in, his attention immediately refocused back on his book. Standing there for a moment before walking back to the house, Holly took in the afternoon haze on the horizon, lazily lounging on the water, the way the Moores did on the sand. Smiling to herself, she thought her family was in their afternoon haze, everyone so relaxed from the sun and salt air, a sandcastle her dad had built with Natie and Po in ruins, a victim of the relentless surf.

He was right, she thought, walking to the house. Her dad was usually right, though. Being out here and not letting the fear of seeing Aiden dictate her plans made her feel stronger, as if she were propelling herself out of limbo, where she'd been held hostage for over a year now.

Over a year. That was a sobering thought. A year of her life. First hiding all grieving and feelings by burying them in a relationship with Tom. Looking back, that even seemed crazy to *her* now. And then finally nursing a broken heart, that she hadn't given the intensive care it desperately needed after their breakup. But these last few days out at the beach had been healing, surrounded by those who loved her and made her laugh, she felt like herself for the first time in way too long.

The crowd thickened as she approached town, slow-walking groups of friends and families, meandering along the narrow pavement. It was amazing to watch the population swell from just a normal summer weekend out here, which was filled with weekend warriors, to the holiday weekend crowd, where half of Manhattan seemed to descend on the tiny sandbar island. Laughing to herself as she walked, leave it to Seth to make sure, way back in early May, that they'd had restaurant reservations through Labor Day weekend. That man could organize anyone's life. And right now, she was glad as she thought how long all these people were going to have to wait to eat dinner tonight, if they could actually get in at any of the handful of restaurants in town.

Glancing at her watch as she approached Bayview Walk, she had twenty minutes to kill until Pierce's ferry arrived. The shops were all packed, overflowing onto the streets. Who were these people? *Go to the beach,* she wanted to scream at them all. *It's a perfect day, great breeze, awesome waves. What are you people doing shopping? If you're going to do that, you all need to go back to Manhattan.*

Ah, a friendly face, *finally.* Holly could see Billy on the far side of Bayview Walk, just past Ocean Beach Trading and headed toward him. As she moved past a slow-moving group of tourists, she felt the stab in her chest, and simultaneously, an invisible plastic bag descended quickly, shrouding her head as it was tightly bound around her neck, cutting off all air. Stopping in her tracks, she bent forward, grabbing her thighs just above the knees and reminded herself to breathe until the panic subsided. Straightening up, she saw Billy was still there. *Thank God.*

And this time, it wasn't a mirage.

Stunned, even though she'd played out this scene in her head a million times, over what seemed like a thousand lonely nights where she saw him standing in almost the exact same spot. This time it was no illusion, though, as she stood motionless, initially unable to move from her spot, and shivered, the chills embarking on a trail through the hair on her arms, rustling them from their usually prone position.

Taking a deep breath, Holly slammed all the insecurities of the past months to the pavement under her feet, stomping on them as she cut a determined path to the center of the thoroughfare, stepping in front of Billy, where she now stood toe to toe with the over-a-year-long, sole obsession of her thoughts, fantasies, and dreams. Engrossed in conversation, he never saw her approaching.

In all her reveries, never did she react the way she did now, surprising herself, and him, as she wrapped her arms around the man she loved, the man she lost, and held onto him as tightly as she could, burying her face into his shirt, and hugging him, whether he wanted to be hugged or not.

Breathing in deeply, the first thing to hit her limbic system, unleashing flashes of memory, was the slightly musky scent of his skin. *My Aiden* was the accompanying thought entering her brain, as she tightened her hug even more. *New detergent,* was the second thought, followed by *new detergent equals new girlfriend.*

"Holly, what are you doing?" his voice was gruff, clearly caught off guard.

"I'm hugging you, Aiden." Her face was still pressed to his chest. "Whether you want me to or not. I'm hugging you."

"Holly…" his tone was pleading, as he stood there, arms hanging at his sides.

"What?" She held on tightly, not ready to look up and lose the familiar feeling of him in her arms.

"Holly…" he repeated.

Finally loosening her hold, she leaned back to look up at him, her body still pressed against his. She noticed he made no move to sever their body contact as she took in the new landscape of his face. Reaching up, he stopped her hand before it made it to his cheek and held it mid-air.

"I don't want you feeling sorry for me."

"Feel sorry for you?" She looked at him as if he'd uttered gibberish. "Screw that — I feel sorry for me, you dumped me, and you broke my heart. No way do I feel sorry for you."

He opened his mouth to speak, but then processed what she had said, realizing it wasn't the reaction he thought she would have.

And Holly didn't wait for him to utter a sound before continuing. "There's never been a day, since the day you said goodbye, that I haven't thought of you, wondered where you are, if you're okay, what you are thinking, or if anything reminds you of me. Of us. Ever." Her voice, just more than a whisper, tensed. "Does it, Aiden? Do you ever think of me? Of us?" It was time to say her peace. The obsessive, pent-up thoughts tumbled off her tongue.

His hand tightened around hers, still suspended mid-air, their eyes remaining locked. Riveted, he found himself staring into a kaleidoscope that rapidly swept through every emotion he had felt since he had told her goodbye, except they weren't his emotions, they were hers. The prevalent one being pain, her pain, deepening his own.

"Why do you care whether or not I think about us, you've got a boyfriend."

Shocked. *What?* And then it dawned on her. Pierce. He knew the word would get around.

But even more shocking was that this was the first thing Aiden said to her. *Umm, jealous much? Perfect. You're only jealous if it's someone you want.* Holly's heart exploded with joy. *This can definitely be fixed,* she thought. *He feels it, too.*

"I don't have a boyfriend."

"Bun Man." He didn't hide his animosity.

Bun Man.

She could feel the corners of her mouth twitching as she fought back a smile. "This is Fire Island, Aiden. Don't believe everything you hear."

"Okay, Malibu Barbie, get your nasty claws off my man."

Both Holly and Aiden jumped as the woman yanked Holly's arm, tearing her hand out of Aiden's. Neither had seen her approach.

Face to face. *And this is why I was dumped? Could she be any more different than me?* were Holly's initial thoughts, followed by, *That's a lot of eye make-up for the beach.* Holly looked down at her arm where the woman had grabbed her and then up at the woman, dismissing her the next second as she turned back to Aiden.

"Janine, it's okay." Aiden held up a hand, indicating she should stand down.

"No. It is not okay. Back the fuck off, bitch."

Continuing to ignore her, Holly reached up to Aiden's cheek again, this time his hand was too late, covering hers after she had already begun to softly run her thumb over the scars and dimpled flesh of what appeared to be skin grafts.

Her voice hitched as she muffled down a sob, a single tear breaching her lashes. "You should have called."

Taking her hand from his face, he moved them both to her cheek, gently using his thumb to wipe away her lone tear. Closing her eyes, Holly leaned into his touch. In that moment, there was nothing but that small point of connection, no Fire Island, no tourists, no girlfriend, no scars, and for one brief second, it all faded into a blurred, impressionistic background.

With arms crossed over her chest, Janine drummed her impossibly long, curved fingernails against her own upper arms. Watching Aiden wipe Holly's tear, Janine reached her tipping point. Her right hand lashed out in a claw-like manner, yet again pulling Holly's hand from Aiden's.

Shaking her off, Holly glared at the woman, but didn't utter a word, then momentarily turned her attention back to Aiden, before looking back to the woman again for a long, hard second. Finally, turning back to Aiden, she held his gaze for a brief second.

She didn't speak to him either. She didn't need to. The silence clearly enunciated her point.

As Holly turned and walked away, Aiden could hear her voice in his head saying, "You've got to be kidding."

She didn't look back.

"Are you okay?" were Pierce's first words when he debarked the ferry.

"Yes. No." Without another word, she steered him by the arm, negotiating them away from the tourists crowding Bay View Walk, and veered down a side alley.

"What's going on?"

"I just saw Aiden. And met my replacement."

"And?" Pierce was dying for more details.

"And he knows about you. He brought you up."

"Awesome. I knew that would somehow make its way back to him." Pierce looked pleased with himself. "You do realize that is a good thing. If he's hitting you with that, he is not emotionally detached from you."

"I thought the same thing, but it's good to hear it from you. To get a guy's perspective. Plus, I'm a little too close to it to see things clearly."

"When you don't care, you're not jealous. Honestly, you wanna know what we think?"

Holly nodded.

"We think, 'Great, she's got a new dude, now I know she won't be bothering me. Thanks, Bro.' That's what we're thinking. But if another guy coming into the picture bothers you, you'd better figure out how to get her back. Trust me, no guy wants another guy nailing his woman. We get really territorial that way."

"You sound just like my brother. He's always saying almost the exact same thing."

Walking into the beach house, Pierce was greeted like a long-lost son. *How did this happen?* Holly wondered. *He gets treated like family already.*

Stepping into the kitchen area to see Mia, Holly shared her news. "I saw Aiden."

"Oh my God, he's here this weekend?"

Hearing Mia's voice, Schooner looked at them from across the room, and seeing Holly's face, made his way over to the two women.

"Aiden's out here?" Schooner's voice was calm, the muscles in his face told a different story.

"Remind me not to piss off your father," Pierce whispered to Zac.

"He tends to be a tad overprotective."

"Yes, Aiden is out here," Holly addressed the whole room so that she would only have to repeat it once. "And so is his girlfriend."

"How is he? Is he okay?" Mia asked.

"He's obviously been through an ordeal." Her eyes filled just verbalizing what she'd witnessed.

"Not to slight Aiden and all he's done for this country, but let's get to *the* thing everyone in this room wants to know." Pausing, Seth dipped his head, giving Holly a look, punctuating the moment. "The girlfriend. What's she like?"

"Umm," Holly struggled, appearing to start a sentence several times, only to change her mind.

"Come on, you're more dramatic than us old queens," referring to himself and Henry.

Finally, Holly smiled. "Okay, Seth, I really don't want to be ugly…"

"Do you have a choice?"

"No," she shook her head. "That witch called me Malibu Barbie."

"And what did you call her back?" Seth was now an incensed queen.

"I don't think I called her anything. I did not say a single word to her. What do you say to someone with, as you would call it, 90's bridge and tunnel hair, purple eye shadow, and claw nails. I just looked at her and then turned back to Aiden."

"I'd call that unfuckable." Zac smiled at his sister.

"Umm, we have little ones here," Mia reminded him.

Zac laughed, "Sorry, but I was overcome by that description."

"Malibu Barbie, my ass. You're like Grace Kelly." Seth was still stewing over the insult.

"Are they out here for the weekend?" Mia asked.

"I don't know. We really didn't talk. Well, I talked and did a mini-unload on him. And then his girlfriend showed up and yanked my hand out of his."

"What did he do when she did that?" Schooner wasn't pleased Aiden would let anyone treat Holly poorly.

"She told me to get my hands off him and he told her it was okay. It all happened really fast."

"And he even brought me up," Pierce chimed in from the couch. "Thought I was Holly's new boyfriend."

Mia smiled, "Ooo, I love a jealous guy."

"Lennon or Ferry?" Schooner asked his wife.

Smiling, "You know we are the only two people in the room who get that, don't you?" she answered her husband.

"Umm, musician in the house." Pierce chimed in again. "And I'm a purist. So, I say Lennon. And, Holly, you have the coolest parents who make the best musical references. I want to be adopted by them."

"Stay a few more weekends and they'll have the papers drawn up." She laughed.

"Maybe they were just day-tripping," surmised Pierce as Holly walked with him to the ferry two days later.

He, Holly, Zac, and Lily had been out partying all weekend and there had been no sightings of Aiden and Janine, not in the restaurants or the clubs and not down at the beach. He was curious to check out the guy who held Holly's heart captive, but they never crossed paths with him.

"You know you've friend-zoned me. And I'm really not used to women doing that." He shoulder-butted Holly as they walked. "But you know what?"

"What?"

"It's really nice to have a lady friend where we actually are friends and there's no overtones lurking around that make you wonder. It really takes a lot of pressure off. Know what I mean?"

"I do. And I think that is why I feel so comfortable with you. You know how much I love getting your perspective on things." They continued to walk, a smile breaking out on Holly's face, exposing her amusement at the thought running through her head.

"What? What are you thinking? 'Fess up, woman."

"I'm thinking about what a chick magnet you are and how many women you must have slept with in your life." They had been over at the Schooner Inn the night before and the minute they walked through the door of the crowded bar, Pierce was surrounded both by women who had seen him play there, and others who were setting their eyes on him for the first time.

Nodding, Pierce tried to suppress a smile, "Well, friend, if I'm being truthful, a ridiculous amount. I've heard the word manwhore bandied about on more than one occasion."

"That's hysterical." They turned onto Bay View Walk.

"Not to the women I've been involved with," he admitted.

"Like the one who was at Jenna's party?"

"*That* was the universe telling me to keep my dick in my pants."

"Well, have you listened to the universe."

"Like most men, I'm a terrible listener." He laughed, thinking about the phone numbers he'd gathered the night before.

"So, am I cramping your style here?"

"Bun Man says no." He smiled, shaking his head. "You and your family have provided some much-needed balance in my life. I really appreciate being asked out here."

Arriving at the packed ferry terminal, Holly looked around at the crowd, scanning quickly for Aiden. "I wish you could stay for the 4th. My father is really spectacular with a grill. One of his many talents."

"Hey, if I could've snuck one of those tomahawk ribeyes and a lobster into my bag..." he kidded. "He was so serious making his secret marinade."

Holly laughed. "He is a bit intense," she said lovingly.

Looking at the line moving onto the ferry, "Okay, looks like we're boarding." Pulling Holly in for a hug, he whispered, "There's a lot of people here today and we've got rumors to spread. This should throw him over the edge." Taking her chin in his hand, he brought his lips to hers, "Get ready for a kiss, friend." Brushing her lips softly, he lingered a few seconds longer than he should have. "Now I'm off to go find a woman to keep me company tonight. Something tells me she's on this boat."

"Manwhore," Holly kidded as he stepped away.

Stopping, he turned around, pointing at her, "It's Bun Manwhore to you." And with a smile and a wave, he boarded the ferry.

"Mommy, how many more hours until the fireworks start?" Natie asked again, for the fourth time since lunch.

"Not until dark." Mia looked from her Kindle to her watch. "So, about six more hours."

"That's a long time away." He looked crestfallen.

"C'mere." Reaching out her arm, she plucked a piece of seaweed from his loose curls. "You're wearing the ocean."

"I wish it was night time already." The frustration in his voice was clear. Today was the day he had been looking forward to all week. Starting in the morning with the parade through Ocean Beach's small downtown, they stayed in town to enjoy hot dogs and cotton candy served by the town's volunteer fire department, before coming back for an afternoon on the beach.

Looking up from his Kindle, Schooner asked, "You up for building a sand fort, buddy?"

"Yeah." Nathaniel ran over to his father, his smile appearing as easily as if someone had flipped a switch.

"C'mon, let's go do it." He ruffled his young son's hair as they walked toward the wetter sand closer to the shoreline.

"He really is the best dad ever. We are all so lucky." Holly raised her sunglasses as she watched Schooner and Nathaniel find the right spot for their fort.

Mia smiled as she looked on from her beach chair. His focus and patience with both Nathaniel and Portia was something she truly admired, whether it was helping them with math homework, teaching them tennis, or helping them spend an afternoon engaged in designing and building incredible sand structures, Schooner was right there. When she looked around, she saw too many fathers more interested in what they were reading on their phones than in paying attention to their children. Those fathers may have been physically there, but that was the extent of it. And then there was Schooner Moore, who possessed the uncanny ability to shut out the world and not let it interfere with his family time. The way he engaged his children, and the lessons they learned through his interaction were peerless.

Nodding, Mia looked at Holly. "We are more than lucky. He is one very special man. And this is perfect, because they won't be done until it's time to head into the house to shower before getting the barbeque started."

"They will be there for hours." Smiling at her dad with her little brother, Holly recalled a memory and began to laugh. "I remember this one time when I was little, still in elementary school, and was upset about something. Some friends had been mean, and I was the only one in the group not invited to a birthday party, and I was so hurt by it. He took me down to the beach and we sat there for hours building a Rapunzel castle and talking. It's one of my favorite childhood memories."

Slipping her Kindle into her beach bag, Mia grabbed her sunglasses and stretched in her chair. Portia was with Gaby, Charles, and Paola, Schooner was keeping Nathaniel engaged. "I think it's time for a beach nap."

"Grab it while you can." Holly laughed and glanced back down at her own eReader.

"We couldn't have asked for better weather this weekend." Billy walked over to them a few minutes later.

"I know, this is so perfect," Holly agreed. "You're not working?" she asked the Castaway bartender.

"I'm on all night, so I've got a few hours off this afternoon and the surf was calling my name." He looked out at the ocean, smiling, before looking back down at Holly. "That was quite a little meeting you had with Aiden and Janine the other day."

Holly just shook her head.

"You handled it really well. I don't know many women who wouldn't have gotten into it with her right there in the street."

"Definitely not my style," Holly confessed.

"Yeah, and that is what was so evident. You two are like night and day. She was looking for a fight and you weren't going to give her the satisfaction." Billy appeared to be proud of Holly.

"Damn right, I wasn't. Do you know if they are still here?" Holly had been wondering if they had been on the island only for the day or if they were here for the entire holiday.

"I saw them a couple of hours ago, they were going into Castaway for lunch," he confirmed. "Holly, I know he's with her now. But I just don't see it. I was standing right there during the whole thing the other day and when he reached over to wipe your tears, that look on his face, man, that was the first time I saw the old Aiden. He was back, just for that second, and he wasn't looking at you like he was over you. You know what I mean?"

"He's here with her." Holly sounded resigned to the fact that the man she loved had moved on.

"I don't see it. I just don't see him with her, you know. And I think now that he's seen you, he knows it, too. I think he's known it all along on some level, but seeing you, Holly, that look on his face." Billy was getting emotional. "I could see he was in there, and I want my friend back."

Holly nodded, her face solemn. "Unfortunately, it doesn't matter what I want, Billy. If Aiden and I don't want the same things, there's not a damn thing I can do about it, except live with it."

"The fat lady hasn't sung on this one. I know it in my gut."

As she watched her friend wade into the ocean, all she could think was that Aiden was still here. She knew if he was on the beach, he would avoid the stretch right outside her family's home, knowing she and the rest of the Moore crew would be there. He wouldn't do that to her and he wouldn't do that to himself.

Besides not wanting to see her, Schooner and Mia were probably the last two people he wanted to run into. Her dad could be quite intimidating, and Mia was not someone whose wrong side you ever wanted to be on.

I love my family. Holly smiled to herself, and with a last glance toward her dad and Nathaniel's latest masterpiece, she went back to the juicy tale on her Kindle.

"Nathaniel, come here right now." Mia meant business.

"I don't need it," he whined.

"Natie, listen to your mother," Schooner wasn't kidding, and his young son knew not to defy him.

Begrudgingly, shuffling over to Mia, Nathaniel stood still for a moment while Mia sprayed him with bug spray.

"Portia, Paola, you two are next," she called out to the girls.

It was twilight and they had finished their barbeque, now it was time for the mosquitoes to begin their feast. Her children already looked like they had the chicken pox from all the mosquito and sand fly bites covering their little arms and legs.

"Mommy, are the fireworks going to start soon?" Nathaniel's body was high-wired with excitement.

"Just a few more minutes," Mia assured him, noticing how crowded the beach in front of their house had become. With the fireworks being shot from barges out on the water, their deck overlooking the ocean was prime viewing space.

Billy's bombshell that Aiden was still there had haunted Holly from the moment the words were out of her friend's mouth. *Why was he still here?* she had asked herself. But even she knew the answer to that. He'd been a Fire Island regular long before the Moores bought their beachfront retreat. Initially working summers while in school, and then moving to the island full time, managing restaurants and bars in town, this was his home, much more than it ever was hers.

As dusk turned into darkness, singles and families packed the beach, some set up on their blankets and towels, others in beach chairs, and toward the back of the sand, farthest away from the ocean, it was five or so deep, people standing shoulder to shoulder.

Scanning the crowd, Holly didn't see Aiden or Janine. In past summers, when they could get off from work, they would watch the July 4th display with her family from the Moore's deck. She couldn't help but wonder how far away from them he had situated himself tonight.

"I'm going to go take a walk. Check out the crowd," she told Mia.

"Are you sure you want to do that?" She knew exactly what Holly was doing.

Nodding. "I just can't stand here. I'm jumping out of my skin." She felt like Nathaniel had acted all day, energy bursting in anticipation of the fireworks. The waiting...

Rubbing her stepdaughter's arm, "Be careful." Mia knew Holly had to go look. If it had been her during the years when she and Schooner were apart, and she'd known he was nearby, she would have done the exact same thing.

"I will," Holly promised, knowing it was her heart that was causing Mia concern and not her physical safety walking alone on the island.

As the first fireworks went up, the static crackles and little light bursts overhead filled the sky, followed by a deafening boom and silver, red, and blue cascades raining down into the ocean. A series of collective ooo's and ahh's filled the night at the appearance of each colorful blast.

Walking quickly, she searched the crowd, weaving her way through the bodies, and trying not to get in anyone's way or block their view, as she passed.

"Hi, Holly," a friend from Maguire's yelled, waving at her.

"Hi, Drea," she called back waving and kept on her way, wondering if she should have stopped and asked her if she had seen Aiden, then decided that probably was not the best idea.

It only took a few minutes to get to the far edge of town, where the size of the crowd watching the fireworks was only a fraction of what it had been several blocks back. Looking out over the last groups of people and not seeing a single familiar face, Holly realized she was looking for a needle in a haystack and the question occurred to her, *what was she going to do if she saw him?* Really. Suddenly she felt like a dog chasing a car. What does the dog do if it ever catches up to the vehicle? And in that moment, there was nothing else to do but turn around, and go enjoy what was left of July 4th with her family.

She hadn't noticed most of the fireworks on her outbound walk, as she had been focusing on the crowd lining the beach. But now, as she leisurely strolled back toward the house, the sparkling lights in the sky brought back childhood memories of sitting on her father's shoulders, high above the crowd, watching the display over Newport Beach. *I should be watching Natie and Po enjoy this,* she thought, hastening her speed.

It was during the next sonic-like boom that something at the back of the crowd caught her eye and she stopped. Standing very still, she waited for the next blast, again seeing what caught her eye the first time, and realizing her own body had jumped and stiffened. She wasn't sure if her reaction was from the sound or from what she was witnessing. Assuming the latter, her suspicions were confirmed with the next explosion.

Watching him was painful, even though all she could see was his back, jolting with every blast. It looked like his hands were clenched in fists at his sides, tightening with each shoulder rise, right before the spasm hit. This was killing him.

Not being able to help him was killing her.

She could see Janine standing slightly in front of him and she appeared to be oblivious to his reaction. *How could she not know what this would do to him and why isn't she paying attention to what is going on with him?* Each firework that went up made Holly cringe, followed by another jagged tear in her heart, every time he jumped.

Should I go up to him? Or will I cause him more problems? Her anxiety was reaching a fevered pitch as she internalized his fear. *I need to do something.*

But the something she needed to do quickly vanished the moment his girlfriend flung her arm around his waist.

Don't stand here and watch this. Don't do that to yourself.

Janine's arm dropped a moment later when she pointed to the sparkling gold waterfall gently floating down from the sky. *Don't you see what's going on?* Holly silently screamed in her head at the oblivious woman.

Leave, Holly, she then ordered herself and turned on Ocean Breeze Walk heading away from beach. The pain she felt watching his anxiety had been overwhelming. It was something she hadn't been prepared to see and never could have anticipated how deeply she would feel his pain. Leaning against a large driftwood sculpture, she hung her head for a moment, allowing the sadness and the gravity of the situation to roll over her. Aiden was in trouble, deep trouble, and all she could do was hope that Janine was aware enough, and supportive enough, to make sure he got the help he needed to cope and adjust, or he was going to go under. Of that, Holly was sure. Just the thought tore another shred in what she already knew was a badly frayed heart.

Pushing her hair from her face, she watched Aiden's back move away from her rapidly down Ocean Breeze Walk. Realizing he must have passed her when she had her head down, she watched him recede into the night, surprised that he was leaving the beach alone. Half running, she followed him north of Midway Walk, where it looked like he turned into an alley. The fireworks display was still in full gear, and she assumed he had hit the threshold where he couldn't keep it together anymore and needed to get away from the crowd.

Reaching the alleyway, she peered down the narrow passage. His back was to her, his right shoulder leaning up against the weathered cedar-shingle of the building. As she watched the heaving of his hunched shoulders, it looked as if he was imploding with each firework that exploded.

Slowly walking down the alley toward him, she spoke when she was still a few arm's lengths away, so as not to spook him. "I'm here now. I'm here with you." Seeing him react to the sound of her voice with what appeared to be sobs, she approached, sliding her arms around him and lying her head against his back, tightening her grasp with each blast. It only took a moment for Aiden to surrender, his weight fully leaning into Holly for comfort and protection.

They both knew what was coming, and as the grand finale began, Holly tightened her hold even more and whispered in his ear, "I'm hugging you whether you want me to or not."

He didn't answer and when he began shaking in her arms at the torrent of noise, she knew that he couldn't respond.

"It's okay, Aiden. I'm with you. I've got you. I'm not letting go. This will be over soon. I've got you. I've got you."

But the blasts continued, his body nearly convulsing in her arms. "It's okay," she repeated over and over again.

When it was finally silent, they heard the cheers from the beach and Holly could feel him go lax in her arms. "You're okay, Aiden. It's okay now. It's over."

"No, it's not." He finally spoke. "I don't want you to see me this way."

"Yeah, well, that ferry has sailed, my friend," she smiled into his back. Loosening her hold, "Aiden, look at me."

Turning around he faced her, his eyes cast to the ground in a look she could only describe as embarrassment.

"Please look at me."

"I can't."

Reaching out, she placed a hand on each cheek, taking his face in her hands and lifting it until his eyes met hers. Brushing her thumbs softly over his cheeks, she was too overcome to speak and hoped her touch told him she had never stopped loving him.

And he read her, like a beloved book with favorite passages memorized.

"Holly, can't you see, I'm no good to you or for you."

Shaking her head, she corrected him, "No Aiden, you are no good without me. That's all I see." He didn't answer, and she went on. "So, what is it? You think you're broken now and I can't handle it?"

"No. I know you could probably handle just about anything." His face crumbled, "I don't want you to have to handle it."

Finally, after over a year, the truth.

"So, what are you saying? It's better that I remain broken, too? You think this is some gallant form of protecting me? Because you are sadly mistaken if that is what you think."

The anger that spiked in her voice was impossible for him to ignore, and this time it was Aiden reaching out to touch her cheek. "You need to forget me, Angel."

Angel. A shiver ran up her arms, as her eyes filled. How long had it been since he had called her that? Angel. *I love watching you sleep with your hair fanned out on the pillow. It's like watching an angel. My own special angel.*

"You want me to forget you? Just like you've been able forget me?" she called his bluff.

"Holly, I'm..."

"You're a mess. A fucking mess," she cut him off. "I get that. You've been through Hell and now it's going to take a boatload of work to get back to you. And you're worried that you'll never get back to you. Well, here's a newsflash, you will never, ever get back to you. Not the same person you were before this tour. He's gone. We both know that and need to accept it. And yes, I can accept it. You know why?" she didn't wait for him to answer. "I can accept it because the Aiden McManus who owns my heart would do the work to come out the other end of this a stronger, wiser, more badass guy than he already was. The Aiden McManus I know is one tough, resilient, stubborn-as-hell Irishman who can slay demons, even his own. And *you* need to find him, because he is in there." She punctuated her words by poking him hard in the chest with her index finger, "And that's the Aiden McManus I want back. Do you hear me?" she was practically yelling. "I want him back."

"It's not that easy."

Calming herself down, "I know. I suspect it's impossibly hard. But you need to fight, Aiden. You need to fight for yourself and don't back down. Not now. Not ever."

Looking at his feet, he shook his head.

"Now I know the real reason you don't want me in your life. It's not because you don't want me to have to go through this, is it? You don't want me around because I would push you too hard. I wouldn't allow you to drown. So instead, you chose someone you know will let you wallow and not even see that you've slipped under the surface."

"No, that's not..."

Again, she cut him off. Like her father, it was best not to get Holly Moore mad. "Oh, yes, it is. If that woman was even thinking about you and your needs, you never would have been on that beach tonight, and the minute you reacted to that first blast, she would've had you out of there so fast that your head would have been spinning. But she didn't even notice, Aiden. How could she not notice that you were freaking out? I'll tell you why, because she's too absorbed in herself to notice or care about what you need."

"Oh, so is that your diagnosis, Dr. Malibu Barbie?" Like nails on a chalkboard, Janine's voice got louder with each step she took down the alley.

As with their previous altercation, Holly ignored her, staying focused on Aiden. "If you can't do it for me or for us, please love yourself enough to do it for you. You are more than worth it. Promise me you'll never, ever forget that." Reaching for his hand, she gave it a squeeze knowing this moment was their goodbye.

Loosening her grip, she turned to leave, but Aiden did not release her hand. Surprised, she looked back over her shoulder at him, knowing with her anger now dissipated, the only emotion left for him to see was the pain she could no longer hide. Their eyes met, each mirroring profound sadness, Holly realizing he would probably never find his way back to her, and Aiden acknowledging how truly lost he was. With a final squeeze of her hand, Aiden's hold lessened and Holly's hand slowly slipped from his until only their fingertips touched. Curling the last knuckle of her fingers in his, he squeezed again, not releasing her. Not ready to. Just one more second. And then it was just one finger left connecting them.

Please let me go, Holly silently begged.

And he did.

Still a few feet away, Janine stepped to the left, placing herself directly in Holly's path. With her arms crossed over her chest, there wasn't enough room on either side to pass without banging into her and she was daring Holly to walk past her.

With the practiced finesse only a true California girl could master, Holly tossed her head, initiating a perfect hair flip, as her sheath of long hair slapped Janine across the face like a flogger. It was a skill developed to torture Zac when they were little, and was coming into very good use now.

"Bitch." Janine grabbed Holly's arm as she attempted to pass.

Jerking her arm to disengage from the other woman's claw-like grasp, Holly opened her mouth to tell Janine not to touch her, but the words never got out.

From behind her, Holly heard Aiden's voice loud, clear, and very angry. "Janine, take your hands off her now." The emphasis was on now and his girlfriend was shocked. Following his orders, she dropped Holly's arm, allowing her to pass.

The forty feet to the end of the alley was a never-ending walk. Holly straightened her spine and walked slow and deliberately like the pageant girl her mother had always wished she'd become. As soon as she reached Ocean Breeze Walk and was clear of the alleyway's view, she picked up her pace, heading back toward the house.

Hoping the family was all still outside on the deck enjoying the holiday evening, Holly decided she would pack her bag and leave a note on the kitchen island, telling everyone she had left. Special holiday schedule ferries and trains would be running late to shuttle the July 4th crowd, and even though she'd get back to Manhattan in the wee hours of the morning, she'd at least be far away from Aiden and his girlfriend, and wouldn't have to worry about running into them and having yet another altercation with the unpleasant Janine.

Playing over in her head what had just happened in the alleyway, Holly felt confused by the mixed signals. Not letting her hand go when Janine was already there. The way he spoke to Janine telling her to leave Holly alone. And calling her Angel. *Why would he do that?* Angel was his term of affection for her. Yet he was very clear about not wanting her in his life.

As she approached the house, she prayed that they would all be outside, that she wouldn't have to talk to anyone and recount the details of her encounter with Aiden and Janine. She'd just grab her backpack and a few items and be gone before anyone was the wiser.

Opening the front door, she stepped from the darkness of night into the bright lights of the people-filled great room.

"Holly, you're just in time for dessert," Henry called out from the kitchen island where he was helping Mia scoop ice cream.

Standing in the threshold, Holly didn't move as she glanced around the noisy room while her eyes adjusted to the light.

On his feet the moment he saw his daughter's face, Schooner took three, long-legged strides toward her, and opened his arms.

"Daddy." She rushed to him.

Holding her tight, he assured her, "It's okay, sweetheart. I've got you now."

CHAPTER
Seven

Late July thru Labor Day Weekend

HOW DID YOUR exam go?

Holly had just walked out of her last final of the summer semester when the text arrived from her dad.

Waiting in the hall for Jenna to finish, she texted back, **Done. I think I did well.**

No surprise there. When are you coming out?

Not sure. Holly could feel the pressure. Just the thought of being out at the beach sent her angst through the roof.

Kids miss you and so do I. You have over 5 weeks off.

Yeah, but... Her shoulders tensed just thinking about the scene in the alleyway.

They haven't been here since July 4th. And that's no reason for you not to spend time with your family.

You're right. He was generally right. She knew that.

So when will you be out? The man was relentless.

Tomorrow afternoon.

Why not tonight?

Because tonight I am drinking margaritas!

Totally valid reason. Let us know what ferry you'll be on.

Will do. Love you.

Love you Moore. ☺

Dad I'm rolling my eyes at you. Holly smiled as she typed.

"Who's making you smile like that?"

She hadn't seen Jenna approach. Holly laughed. "My dad. He is such a goofball."

"My brother totally has a guy crush on your dad."

Holly laughed. "That's because my dad makes Pierce drink single malt scotch with him."

"Yeah, that would absolutely constitute love for my brother. No wonder why he wants to be adopted by your family."

Strolling down Broadway, with the heat from the pavement rising up to greet them with every step, the subject remained on Pierce.

"So, he texted me that his bandmates are better and they've got weekend gigs out in the Hamptons," mentioned Holly.

"Yeah, they've got a few bookings between now and Labor Day weekend at the Echo Beach Inn. They've played there in the past and something happened with the house band, and the owner called and asked if they could fill in. He's even letting them stay at one of his properties."

"My parents are going to miss him. Not sure how I'm going to break this to my dad," she kidded.

Finding two open barstools at the Taqueria, the lab partners ordered their end-of-semester celebratory drinks.

"Here's to acing the semester," Jenna toasted, clinking glasses with Holly and taking her first icy sip. "When you and my brother left my party, I really thought something was going to happen with the two of you."

Holly could feel the rush from the tequila coursing through her veins. "Your brother is really cute, but I wasn't over my ex, and honestly, I can't imagine Pierce even wanting to be in a committed relationship."

"Is that what you want? A committed relationship?"

Taking a moment to answer and another sip of her drink, Holly licked the salt from her lips. "Maybe your brother has it right. Maybe I should be looking for something casual."

"Would that make you happy?"

Holly loved that her friend was such a straight shooter. Shaking her head, "No. Not at all. I'm definitely the monogamous type."

"And the ex?"

Holly sighed. "He's moved on." Taking a healthy gulp of her drink, her face screwed up, appearing at first to be from the icy cold liquid, but when she spoke, it was evident that the grimace was actually caused by her thoughts as she added the detail, "With his ex." Taking another sip, this time Holly smiled. "And she hates me."

"I'd hate you, too, if you were my boyfriend's ex. I mean, look at you." Jenna took a sip of her drink and then laughed. "I can tell you this, all the women at my barbeque hated you when you left with my brother."

"That's so funny, especially because we are just friends."

"Yeah, well you were the new girl who stole him."

"He's not stealable. Is that a real word, stealable? Or did I just make that up?" Holly laughed, feeling the effects of drinking on an empty stomach.

"I'm a microbiology major, I have no clue. I dreaded undergrad English courses."

"Anyway, your brother is not stealable. But I do think he's probably a thief of hearts."

"I'd love to see him with someone he's crazy about. Maybe he'll meet someone out in the Hamptons."

Mia waved to get Holly's attention as she got off the ferry. It had been several weeks since Holly had been out to the island and Mia was anxious to tell her news that she had just learned on her walk into town.

"It's so good to see you." She hugged her stepdaughter, before helping her hoist her oversized duffel bag into the family's little red wagon.

Taking a deep breath of sea air, Holly closed her eyes for just a moment. "I didn't realize how much I missed it here. And coming off finals, I already feel more relaxed."

"Well, don't relax too much yet," Mia lowered her voice so people surrounding them wouldn't hear. This was a small community and news traveled fast.

"What?" Holly asked, halting.

"I just saw Billy on the way here. Aiden's back. And he's alone."

Holly let out an involuntary gasp, "Mia, what do you mean back and alone?"

"From what I understand, he's going to be splitting his time bartending at Maguire's and Matthew's. He's rented a studio apartment at one of Andy Metzger's rental houses, and, last but not least, the piece of information you've been waiting for..."

"Mia, I'm going to kill you. Spit it out!"

Mia laughed. "No Janine. Janine is history. He told Billy he ended it several weeks ago, so that's got to be shortly after July 4th." Mia smiled brightly at Holly. "Welcome back, baby."

"Oh my God." Holly's eyes were wide. "Do you know when he got back?"

"Sometime earlier in the week, I'm guessing." Mia shrugged. "Not sure. We definitely didn't see him last weekend."

"Oh my God. Wow. Living and working here. He's really back." Holly repeated. "Mia, what should I do?"

"Well, let's get you home and unpacked." They had only taken two steps when Mia turned to Holly with her signature devilish grin, "Oh, and I just happened to mention to Billy that you'd just finished finals and were on your way out and that I was meeting you at the ferry. I'd give it another hour, tops, before that news makes its way to a certain someone. So, I don't think you have to do anything except sit back and let it play out. If he didn't want to see you, he wouldn't be out here, Holly. He'd be making himself scarce like he did for months when no one even knew he was back. You want to know my guess?"

Holly nodded.

"He couldn't stay away. As much as he may have wanted to, he couldn't."

"From the island or from me?"

"I don't know that you can separate the two of you. Fire Island is where his heart is, this is home for him. And you are the one who holds his heart."

"I don't know about that. He was quite the player before we were together. There were always girls hanging around until closing, waiting for him to lock up. And it was always a different girl. The man could flirt."

"Yeah, but that stopped the minute you told him you were interested in him. He was totally monogamous."

"He was a good boyfriend. Until he wasn't."

"Well, he's back, so we're going to be running into him. This is a small island and even a smaller town."

They turned up the path to the house.

"Oh God, I bet he's dreading running into Dad."

Mia nodded. "And with good reason."

Aiden had always looked up to Schooner, admiring that he was a self-made man who focused on making his dreams come true and taking care of his family, while Schooner appreciated Aiden's strong work ethic and convictions. The two men enjoyed an easy camaraderie and shared a love for Holly. But decimating his daughter's heart was not something Schooner took lightly, and both Holly and Mia worried his reaction to seeing his daughter's ex-boyfriend might be less than cordial.

He was pacing the great room with his characteristic, long-legged strides as he talked to a business colleague when Mia and Holly entered. Looking up, he flashed a breathtaking smile and mouthed the words, "Welcome home" to his daughter before returning his focus to the call.

The house was quiet, with Natie and Po in summer camp, as Holly made her way upstairs to her bedroom.

Standing before the window, watching the ocean's foam form lacy patterns on the shoreline, she tried to think through what Mia had told her just minutes before. He was here. Right here. On this tiny little sandbar of an island with her, and it was inevitable that they would be running into one another. A lot.

Do I wait for him to contact me? Approach me? Or should I just go for it, balls to the wall, and go find him and make him talk to me?

Janine was history. Holly couldn't help but smile. The woman was a piece of work. But it wasn't just that or the fact that she was sleeping with the man Holly loved. It was her lack of sensitivity to his needs, to what clearly was PTSD. She had not made Aiden's needs a priority and that is what angered Holly more than anything.

As she watched the water intricately weave its way onto the beach, Holly wondered, will Aiden let me in like the water rushing over the sand? And it was in that moment she realized that although she wanted to flood his world like a tidal wave, take over and fix everything, which she acknowledged was a very Moore trait, she knew there was a fragility to this situation that was going to require restraint and patience, and with only a little over five weeks before she had to leave again, this was going to be a balancing act.

Sitting on the edge of her bed, she continued to stare at the sea, silently hoping that riding in on the crest of a wave would be the answers to questions that her experience and knowledge were ill-equipped to handle. PTSD was very serious and very real, and she knew that she needed to be sensitive to that above all else. Her emotions needed to take a backseat here, and she was fearful that her love might also demand to be shelved, too, although she was sure, with every fiber in her being, that it was her love that had the best chance of saving him.

Let me in, Aiden. Please let me in.

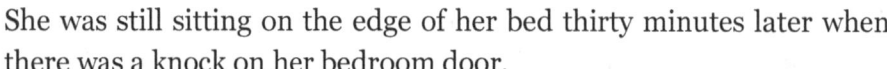

She was still sitting on the edge of her bed thirty minutes later when there was a knock on her bedroom door.

"Come in," she called. Looking over her shoulder, she smiled as her father entered. "Hi, Dad."

"Hey, sweetheart. I thought you'd be down on the beach already trying to get rid of that bio-lab pallor." He sat down next to her and slung an arm across her shoulders.

Holly looked at her forearms, "I really am pale, aren't I?"

"Mia told me Aiden's back." He cut to the chase.

"Yup."

"How do you feel about that?" He, too, stared out the window at the mesmerizing ocean view.

"Well, I've been sitting here thinking about it."

"I thought that might be the case."

"And although I want to go all bull in a china shop all over him, like I did the first time I saw him, I realize I have to tread very lightly. The man I saw on July 4th is clearly suffering from PTSD, and I need to pull myself out of the equation because there will be no chance for a me and Aiden if Aiden doesn't get healthy again." Sighing, Holly leaned into her father.

"You are so smart and so sensitive." Schooner smiled at his oldest, his pride worn on his sleeve.

"I also have to face the possibility that he meant what he said when he broke up with me." Holly's cornflower blue eyes widened, the sadness evident.

"Do you think that's the case?"

She shook her head. "Not after what happened in the alley. That didn't feel over." She thought for a moment. "At least, not to me."

"PTSD is a really serious thing."

Holly recognized the tone in her father's voice. It was the preparing tone.

"I realize that, Dad. And I really think that is why Aiden pushed me away. He never wanted to talk much about his previous tours. But if he'll let me in, you know I'm going to be all in."

Schooner nodded, his brows furrowed with worry.

"Mia's been really open about what she went through in her twenties with PTSD from sexual assault. If Zac and I hadn't been in the picture, and you reconnected with Mia at that time, would you have left because she was going through a really rough time?"

"Not a chance. I would have stayed by her side trying to help her through it."

His daughter was more like him than anyone in the world, and he ached watching her in pain, frustrated by the fact that he needed to stay out of it. This was something only she and Aiden could fix.

"I hope he lets me."

"Let me know if I can do anything to help." He kissed the top of Holly's head and stood to leave.

As he reached the door, Holly smiled at him. "Just promise me you won't kill him."

"That's an easy promise. I'll just torture him a little, instead. It's much more fun anyway. Maybe I'll tell him I bought Maguire's." Schooner laughed, and before closing the door, "By the way, we have reservations there tonight at seven. We made them yesterday, before we knew he was back."

Holly bit her lip anxiously. "Maybe he's working at Matthew's tonight."

"Maybe, but if he's at Maguire's, you can bet he's seen tonight's reservations list." Schooner smiled and closed the door.

His back was to them when they passed the bar on the way to their table. Holly stopped short, unable to take another step, her eyes riveted to his broad shoulders narrowing down into his black work pants that hugged his muscular butt. The memory of what it felt like in her hands when she was holding him, doused her with a wave of sadness. His hair was much shorter this summer than she'd ever seen it, but it only served to make him look more manly, as did the scars on the right side of his face.

Holly's eyes immediately shifted as she was watching her father's back as he approached the bar. Hearing footsteps, Aiden turned.

With an extended hand, Schooner greeted the younger man. "Welcome back, Aiden. It's good to see you."

"Schooner," Aiden extended his hand. "Good to see you."

"Thank you for your service and I'm sorry you've been through such a tough time."

Aiden nodded. "I appreciate that."

"Good to have you back."

With a wave, Schooner turned to leave. As Aiden's gaze followed him, there was Holly standing outside the bar area. He smiled at the sight of her, an involuntary, visceral reaction as their eyes met. Raising a hand to give him a small wave, she followed her father as they went in search of their table where Mia and the kids were already seated.

"What happened to you two?" Mia gazed up from the menu.

"I welcomed Aiden back." Schooner reached for a menu.

"And you?" Mia turned to Holly.

"I waved."

"Very good," she approved. "Are you two starting with clam chowder?" Mia asked Natie and Po.

Nathaniel nodded, without looking up from coloring.

"I would really prefer lobster bisque." Portia informed her mother.

"Would you now?" Schooner looked up from his menu with a smirk. "You've got some champagne taste there, young lady."

Looking up through her lashes, adoringly, "Come on, Daddy. You know you're raising a foodie."

They all laughed at the precocious little girl.

"Lobster bisque, it is." He could not help but smile at his sweet, smart little girl. Alone with her in Zambia in the weeks leading up to her adoption, the two had formed a special bond. Although her initial attachment had been to Mia, by the time Schooner and Portia arrived in the states, she was Daddy's girl and that had not changed.

"A little something special for my boyfriend." Sheila placed a glass of scotch in front of Schooner.

"How's my girl?" he greeted his favorite waitress.

"Better now that you are here. So good to see you back, Holly. Have you seen our friend?" Her eyes shifted toward the bar.

"Just in passing as we walked in."

Sheila smiled at her, "Are you ready to give me drink and appetizer orders?"

"A lobster bisque for the young lady over here. And I'll do the same. Clam chowder for these two. Holly?"

"Nothing for me."

"Wine?" her father asked.

"No. I'll just do an iced tea and the crispy skin salmon as my entrée." A few minutes later, she excused herself from the table.

Wandering into the bar, his back was to her again and she couldn't help but admire his broad shoulders and the way his light blue cotton shirt stretched over them. She felt an overwhelming desire to lay her cheek against his back. Sliding onto a barstool at the far end of the bar, she watched him until he caught her reflection in the bar's ornate mirrored back.

Turning to her, their eyes met, and he didn't miss a beat. "What can I get you?"

"Surprise me."

"Okay." He accepted the challenge with a smile and started pulling bottles and measuring shots into an aluminum shaker, before giving the tumbler a vigorous workout. Reaching above, he slid a martini glass from the rack and set it on the bar, filling it with the icy, pale lavender cocktail, and finishing it with a piece of lemon peel, before sliding it across the bar to Holly.

Picking up the glass, she motioned, as if toasting him and took a sip. "Mmm, this is good. What is it?"

"I dunno." He smirked. "Maybe I'll call it a Malibu Barbie."

"You're an asshole." She laughed.

"It's not the first time you've told me that."

I hope it's not the last. "I don't taste rum in this."

"That's because there isn't any."

"Then you can't call it a Malibu Barbie because that implies Malibu rum, of which there is none."

The look he was giving her was one she recognized. *Get your ass over here, Angel. I need to fuck your brains out.* It was also overwhelming.

"So, I will call it the Violette Elderberry Sapphire Barbie."

"Barbie." She shook her head, not even attempting to hide her disgust.

He leaned on the bar, halfway breaching the space between them. Holly remained sitting straight-backed on the barstool, maintaining her distance.

"I'm really sorry about the way Janine attacked you."

Holly still didn't move. "Aiden what are you doing with her?"

"I'm not with her anymore." The words tumbled out rapidly.

"Why were you with her in the first place?" She didn't wait for a response. "Do you love her?"

The moment he hesitated, Holly began to move off her barstool. Reaching out, he grabbed her hand, pulling her toward him on the bar, their faces inches apart, her hand still captive in his.

"Do you love her?" Her voice was barely more than a whisper.

"No. No, I don't."

They looked at one another for a long moment before Holly broke the silence. "Do you have any vision in that eye?"

Shaking his head, he was surprised by the non sequitur. "It's prosthetic."

"Really? It looks really good." Holly picked up her drink. "If I were just meeting you, I'd never know. It has such great movement."

He smiled and gave a little laugh.

"What?" she asked. "What's so funny?"

"You. You're just never afraid to go there with me. People dance around everything these days, nobody wants to ask me anything. But not you."

"Is that a good thing?"

"Yeah."

"Hey, flirty bartender, you're needed down here," called one of the new, young waitresses.

He gave Holly's hand a squeeze. "Excuse me."

The girl handed him the order and leaning against the polished wood bar, openly checked out Holly head to toe before training her sights back on Aiden as he mixed drinks.

"You're still coming out with us after closing tonight, right." It wasn't a question. "I'll wait for you to finish and go with you," she offered, her head dipped flirtatiously as she leaned her store-bought rack on the bar.

Shaking her head, Holly pushed her half-finished drink away and began to dig in her pocket. Placing a ten-dollar bill on the bar, she stood and walked out.

She was already out into the dining room when she heard him call her name. She didn't stop.

Sheila was just delivering dinner when she got to the table. "Great timing," Holly said brightly, trying to hide her wildly churning emotions and desire to flee the restaurant.

"You okay?" Mia asked.

Holly nodded, but it was clear she wasn't. Picking up her fork, she started decimating her fish.

Reaching out, Schooner put a hand on her arm. "Rome wasn't built in a day. Try to have patience."

Shaking her head, "It's not that, Dad. It's..." She never finished her sentence.

Delivering her half-finished drink, he set the martini glass in front of Holly, "I'd hate to see you waste your money."

The furrow between his brows told her he was angry. That was his tell. Though, in all their time together, he had rarely been angry at her.

Turning from Holly, he walked around the table to Mia. Taking his hand in both of hers, she greeted him, "It's good to see you, Aiden. Welcome home."

"Thanks, Mia. It's good to be back."

Portia couldn't contain herself, popping up from her chair and running to him with a smile. Her crush on her older sister's boyfriend was well-known.

"Aiden," she hugged his waist, "I've missed you."

"I've missed you, too, Po."

Stepping away she looked up at him, "What happened to your face?"

Mia, Holly, and Schooner exchanged mortified glances.

Aiden laughed. "It's pretty messed up, isn't it?"

"Yeah." She nodded, as she visually inspected the multiple scars on his cheek and around his right eye.

"Do you still think I'm cute?" He openly flirted with the little girl.

Portia's smile grew wide, and she looked down, embarrassed. "Yes." Everyone at the table laughed.

"Enjoy your dinner, everyone." And with a wave he was off.

"What was that about?" Schooner asked Holly as he stabbed a piece of Ahi.

"He's mad at me."

"Why?"

"Because I walked out." Holly put down her fork. She couldn't even look at her food.

"What happened?" Mia asked.

"Some girl, a waitress, was making plans with him for later tonight and I just didn't want to hear it."

"I don't blame you," Mia commiserated. "That's not cool."

"I don't know what to do here. I'm really lost. Should I give him time and stay away or should I just dive in and tell him what I want? Which he may not care about considering he dumped me." She pushed her plate of uneaten food away.

"What exactly is it you want?" Mia wanted her to verbalize it.

"I want us to be together and I want to help him get through this and help him heal emotionally." As the words came out of her mouth, the realization became clear that not only did shrapnel cut and scar Aiden in ways that might never fully heal, but like secondhand smoke, she was no longer immune to the ravaging effects that were preventing her own recovery.

"There's no shame in telling him that," Schooner weighed in.

"You can't lose, Holly. There's only an upside. If he tells you that is not what he wants, you haven't lost anything from where you are now. You can only gain in this situation."

"I just don't want to get my heart stomped on again. At some point I'm going to have to start believing him when he says, 'Go away.'"

"Can I clear away some of these plates?" Sheila approached the table. "Something wrong with the salmon?" She regarded Holly with concern.

"No. It was fine. I just lost my appetite."

"Do you want me to box it?"

Holly just shook her head.

"Would anyone like dessert?" Sheila addressed the table.

"Mom, can we go to Scoops for ice cream?" Natie asked.

"What? You don't like my ice cream?" Sheila teased him.

He shook his head. "You only have two flavors. Scoops has like a trillion." He was very serious.

"Well. I certainly can't compete with a trillion." She laughed. "Check?" She looked at Schooner.

"Trying to get rid of me already?" He hit her with a real smile.

"Not on your life, mister. Stay all night." She paused, "I might charge you rent. Let me go grab your check."

Seeing the kids were getting restless, Mia stood, "We're going to head over to Scoops while you pay the bill."

"I'll join you." Holly pushed her chair back from the table.

Portia immediately skipped ahead, while Mia ushered out Nathaniel. Glancing into the bar as she passed, Holly's initial thought was that it was good to see Aiden smiling, until she saw the reason for his smile. He was leaning across the bar and she was leaning against it, the same waitress from earlier.

Without skipping a step, Holly exited the restaurant never stopping to say goodbye.

It was nice to see Aiden smile again, but those smiles were not being given to her. They seemed to be reserved for the new waitress.

He was inventorying a wine shipment, several days later, when Mia entered the empty bar and made herself comfortable on a stool. With his head still down in a box, he called out, "I'll be with you in one sec."

"Take your time."

The moment the words were out of her mouth, his head popped up, as he had recognized the voice. "Mia?"

She smiled at him and raised her brows.

"Afternoon drinking?" He had never known Mia to drink in the afternoon. Ever. She was either always working or with the kids, and usually doing a fine job of juggling both.

"I think I will. Will you join me?"

Her smile was infectious, and she made Aiden feel like he was in tenth grade, and she was trying to get him to cut school with her. That was part of Mia's charm.

"I have a long night in front of me, but yeah, I'll join you for one." Fear was the first emotion to crowd the corners of his mind, knowing he was going to be no match for Mia, and worrying that he would spill more than he had yet shared with anyone.

Pointing to the far corner on the top shelf of the bar, Mia gave Aiden a conspiratorial grin. "Didn't my husband buy that bottle?"

Aiden nodded, "Yes, I think he did."

"Well good, let's drink his booze."

"If you insist." Aiden pulled down the bell-shaped Hennessy bottle and slid out the cognac snifters with fluid ease, setting them on the bar and pouring reservedly, until Mia motioned to make the pours heftier.

Picking up her glass and holding it up between her and Aiden, she toasted, "To having you home."

He nodded to that as they clinked glasses and both took sips.

"That is nice." Aiden looked at the glass in his hand.

"Thanks, Schooner." Mia laughed.

Aiden regarded Mia for a moment before speaking. "I'm not sure if I'm hoping for a crowd to walk into this bar any second or for no one to walk in for the next hour. A crowd could save me…"

"…And if it's only me and you, you might just save yourself." Mia cut him off.

"Highly doubtful, Mia. That's not even a remote possibility." He twirled the stem of the glass between his thumb and forefinger watching the viscous amber liquid slowly recede down the curved sides of the glass, forming legs in its wake.

"That dark?"

"You can't even imagine." He looked her dead in the eye.

Mia waited a beat and picked up the bottle of Hennessy, refilling their only half-emptied glasses.

"Unfortunately, I can. No, I'll never know what *your* personal dark space looks like, but I know what dark space looks like and I know what a solitary prison PTSD is. Obviously, our sources are vastly different, yours from a battle situation and mine from sexual assault."

"Oh, Mia, I'm sorry. I didn't know."

"I didn't even know what PTSD was and I certainly didn't know I was suffering from it. But I was. And I have to tell you, that if it wasn't for Seth, Kami, and my friend, Rob, I would be dead. No doubt in my mind, I would have been long gone by now. I was lost, speeding recklessly down a very dark road."

"Well, you are lucky you had good friends."

"You have good friends, too, Aiden, if you'll just let them in. Everyone in this town loves you. We love you." She paused, regarding him seriously. "Let us help."

Taking a sip of the smooth cognac, Aiden remained silent and she continued.

"And while we're sharing truths, let's just get this out in the open. You leaving Holly because you didn't love her is a crock of shit. You know that, and I know that. Your gallant heart was absolutely in the right place for not wanting Holly to have to suffer the second-hand effects of battle, but the reality is, Aiden, she already is, and that's not going to change. So, either the two of you suffer alone, or you work together to try and navigate your way out of the darkness."

"That's a big assumption, Mia."

Bringing her glass to her lips, she asked, "What is?" before taking a sip.

"Assuming that I didn't break up with Holly because I don't love her."

Mia shook her head, giving Aiden a look that said *seriously, dude?* And then she remained silent, waiting for him to speak, knowing silence would surface the truth.

"What am I supposed to do? Drag her into this for the ride? I'm not the guy I was when we met. He's gone and he's not coming back, and that's the guy Holly loved. Not me. She doesn't even know who I am now. She may think she's still in love with me, but she doesn't know me."

"Maybe you don't know you."

"You're right. Maybe I don't." He paused, closing his eyes for a moment. "This was my first tour where I had to leave behind someone I loved, besides family. My two other deployments, there was no one special in my life, no one I loved. I wanted her to move on. And if I got back and was okay, and she wasn't married or anything, I would have gone after her. Relentlessly. That was my plan. But I didn't come back okay. I don't think that I will ever be okay, and you want me to drag her into that, and ruin her life. I'm not going to do it, Mia."

"You know what I loved about Aiden McManus. Aiden was a scrappy kid from the wrong side of the tracks who was smart, and a risk-taker, and way mature beyond his years. He had guts and balls and was protective of those he loved. You reminded me of Schooner in so many ways, and I think that Holly probably saw a lot of the attributes in you that she admires in her father."

"I don't think Schooner was from the wrong side of the tracks." Aiden smiled.

Laughing, Mia nodded in agreement. "Very true. In Schooner's case, he was from the right side of the harbor. And I think for him, that provided the impetus to try even harder, to prove that he was a self-made man, and not a spoiled rich kid who was handed everything." Mia picked up the bottle of Schooner's booze and refreshed their glasses. "Aiden, I'm not going to bullshit you. If you want your life back badly enough, you're going to have to work your ass off. And my point before about the Aiden I knew, was that Aiden was so driven, nothing could stop him when he set his mind to something. And I know you have to be ready, you have to want this more than anything else. And I hope you get to that place. Because when you do, you won't have to go it alone. We'll be there for you. But you have to be the one who is ready to fight."

"How long did it take you to get to that place?" his voice was soft.

"I got there after I hit rock bottom. I was a fucking mess." This time when she picked up her glass, she took a hefty swig. "And that was when I decided that the two pieces of shit who raped me had controlled my life for long enough and I was done handing it over to them."

Aiden was clearly floored by Mia's candor. "And what did you do? How did you take the control back?"

"The first piece of it was making the conscious decision that they didn't deserve the power. I did. The second piece was finding a therapist who specialized in treating PTSD in victims of sexual assault, and the third, and by far the hardest piece of it, really working my ass off in therapy, being honest with both myself and my therapist, digging deep and facing truths about myself, and then living what I learned, and employing the strategies my therapist and I had discussed."

"You know I've always liked you and respected you, but now, even more so. You are truly a badass."

"Are you talking to anyone? A professional?"

"I am, but the VA doctors are so backed up and overloaded. And the last thing I want to do is start taking drugs on a regular basis."

"What about groups? There have got to be vets' groups on Long Island with guys, and women, who have been through similar things. I would think those would be tremendously helpful."

"There are. I just haven't really looked into them."

"Aiden, you don't have to do this alone. And it's not a sign of weakness to ask for help. As a matter of fact, it's a sign of strength. It shows you're ready to fight for what's important and that is you."

"If you say so."

"Are you telling me you don't think you're important?"

He shrugged.

"People don't walk away or stop loving you just because you've been through a shitty situation. And if they do, well, those are the people you don't want in your life anyway. Do you really think Holly's going to stop loving you because you are in a dark place or have some scars and a prosthetic eye?"

Aiden's head snapped back at the mention of his prosthesis. And then he smiled. "You know, Mia, I think the thing I love most about you is that you don't shy away or pussyfoot around things. You just put it right out there and I really appreciate that. People are just so afraid to address what happened to me, that they pretend nothing has changed. I don't have conversations with people about it because it makes them uncomfortable. But something has changed and I'm so tired of everyone pretending it hasn't."

"Well, your eye looks great. Let me just start by saying that."

"Thanks."

"When I was over in Zambia for the groundbreaking of the physical therapy rehab center, Lily and I met an ocularist named Johan Baer, and we spent some time with him that trip and got an education on prosthetic eyes." Mia picked up the bottle again. Feeling the effects of the cognac, she looked at Aiden and smiled. "Wow. We've really made a dent in this." Digging in her wallet, she pulled out a credit card. "Can you order another one to set aside for him? He won't even know we've been having a good time with his booze." She laughed. "Maybe this falls under community property-law booze."

Aiden swiped the credit card and handed it back to Mia. "You do understand why I can't drag Holly back into my life right now?"

Mia shook her head. "I think, you think, you're doing the right thing. But neither of you are going to truly heal staying apart from one another. Trust me on that one, too." Mia referred to the twenty-plus-year gap that she and Schooner had spent apart. "Aiden, it breaks my heart to know you are emotionally struggling." Mia's eyes quickly filled.

"I'm not struggling, Mia. I'm drowning."

Mia nodded. His candor was painful to hear, and yet, his last statement sparked hope. He had finally slid open the bolt securing his door. Now if she could get him to just crack the door open.

"And I can't let her follow me down this rabbit hole. I can't."

"Well, you can't stay in the rabbit hole either, Aiden. You either crawl out or you die. Those are the only two options. And the second one is not an option. So, you need to fucking claw your way out."

Picking up his glass, he regarded her for a second before taking a sip. "I don't know how to start." Feeling the muscles in his face begin to twitch with emotion, he turned away, embarrassed to let Mia see him crumble, even a little bit.

"Aiden," she whispered. Reaching across the bar, she slipped her hand into one of his, squeezing it. "You just did."

"I don't know what to do, Mia."

"I want you to listen to me. Really listen." She paused to make sure she had his attention. "You are not alone. I hope you know that you are family to us and we're not going to let you drown. We are not. We are just not. And we're not going to let you drown in self-pity, either, okay. So, will you let us help you? Will you let *me* help you?"

"I don't know how you can."

Mia released his hand and picked up her drink. "Well, the only way I can is if you're willing to help yourself. If you are, then I can help you. But I'm not going to lie to you, it's a shitload of work and hard as hell. But it works, Aiden, it really does. Just the fact that I'm sitting in front of you proves it works. It just depends on how badly you want it."

"I wasn't having a whole lot of luck with the doctors I was seeing."

"Well, then, let's find you someone who can help."

"I've got to go through…"

"No, you don't." She cut him off.

"Yeah, I do. I can't afford…"

Waving dismissively, she cut him off again. "Let's make that the least of your worries."

Squinting at her, he wondered if he was too drunk to follow the conversation. "What are you saying?"

"I'm saying let's find you a great doctor who specializes in cases like yours, someone you feel comfortable talking to, and I don't want you to worry about the money."

"Are you saying..."

"Yes." She cut him off again.

"I can't."

She knew he was too proud. He'd been supporting himself from the time he was a teenager. "Yeah. You can, and you will. If you want this just to remain between us, I'm fine with that."

"How am I going to..."

"Repay me?" Mia asked, as she watched him breathe in deeply through flaring nostrils. "You're going to repay me by working your ass off to get better. That's what I want back from this. I want you. You in?" Mia picked up the bottle again, refilling their glasses and then smirking as she observed how much of the bottle was gone. "I'm glad he loves me." She giggled.

"You are a force to be reckoned with. You really are."

"That's what my husband tells me."

"Can this just be between us?" He needed confirmation.

"Of course."

"I should be able to handle this on my own. I'm a man. I'm a soldier."

"And you're human, and there is no shame in asking for help when you need it. Are you afraid of what Schooner and Holly might think?"

He nodded.

"They'll think you're really brave. Trust me, they will not think less of you. Quite the opposite. They'll be really proud that you took the hard road. Believe me, I'm right about this. But if you'd like this to remain between us. I'm fine with that. Give me a couple of days to do some research. I'll see if my therapist can give me some recommendations, if that's okay with you?"

"Yeah. I'd appreciate that."

"It's going to be okay, Aiden. We're not going to let you drown. And you are one of the best swimmers I've ever met. You've got this." As Mia went to get down from the barstool, she grabbed onto the bar, realizing just how drunk she was.

"One sec." Aiden pointed a finger at her, opened a cooler, and pulled out an ice-cold bottle of Evian for Mia. "Drink this on your way home. I wouldn't want you dehydrating in that heat."

"Thanks. Someone is going to need to feed those kids dinner, I'm too wasted to do anything but crawl into bed."

Aiden laughed. "I'm on until eleven. I need to make a pot of coffee."

"And get some food into your stomach," she called over her shoulder, staggering out of the bar.

Standing behind the hostess stand, Sheila looked at Mia questioningly.

Nodding, Mia smiled her devilish grin. "Okay, you can start letting people back in the bar now," she told the older woman. "But I think you might need to get another bartender for the night and send this one home to sleep it off."

"I've already called Tommy." Sheila winked at Mia.

"Thanks," Mia whispered.

"Well done."

The two women exchanged a hopeful look.

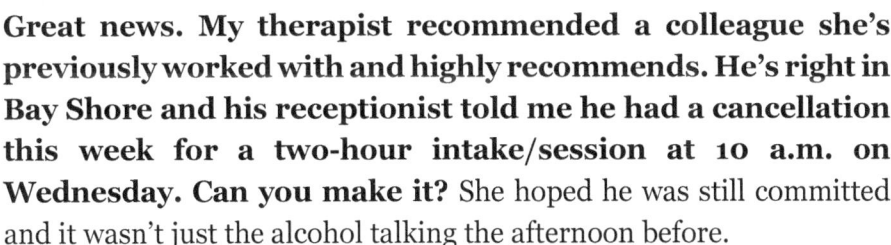

Great news. My therapist recommended a colleague she's previously worked with and highly recommends. He's right in Bay Shore and his receptionist told me he had a cancellation this week for a two-hour intake/session at 10 a.m. on Wednesday. Can you make it? She hoped he was still committed and it wasn't just the alcohol talking the afternoon before.

Wow. This week. Yes. I'll take it. What do I need to do? Who do I need to call?

Mia texted him the information. **Aiden, I'm really proud of you.**

I haven't done anything yet.

Oh, but you have. And what you've done may be one of the hardest parts. She pointed out.

Something you said to me the other day keeps playing over and over again in my head. Kind of like a mantra.

What is that? They had talked about so much and were quite drunk. She wasn't sure how much or what was actually going to resonate with him. Or that he would actually remember.

You said, it depends how much you want it.

Keep asking yourself that question.

I will.

☺ **I hope things go well on Wednesday and you like this guy.**

I'll let you know, okay.

She was glad he was willing to keep her in the loop. That was certainly his choice and she would have respected it either way.

I look forward to it. She waited a moment and then sent a final text. **I know I said it earlier, Aiden, but I am really, really proud of you.**

An appointment this week. Not bad for a morning's work, Mia thought to herself, before diving into a string of emails from Seth and Kami.

With the kids in summer camp and Schooner back in the city until the weekend, Mia spent the remainder of the morning taking advantage of the rare calm and quiet to focus on a client proposal that was due at the end of the week.

Three hours had passed when Holly knocked on the door.

"I just made a huge salad. Do you want me to bring you up a bowl?"

Mia stretched in her chair. "Oh, excellent. Thank you. I need to get away from this PC for a bit, so I'll come down and join you."

As Holly grabbed the salad from the counter, Mia took two bowls to the long, rough-hewn driftwood table. Placing a bowl next to her stepdaughter's laptop, she noticed a piece of paper with a list of PTSD symptoms.

"Are you researching PTSD?" Mia asked, sitting down.

"I was just looking at the different symptoms to see how many I'd observed in Aiden."

"And?" Mia immediately felt guilty that she couldn't share with Holly the conversation she had with Aiden. It had to come from Aiden, but she was torn in protecting one person's trust, she was potentially jeopardizing another's.

"Well, I haven't been around him enough, but I think there's quite a few that would substantiate it." She pressed a key on her keyboard, waking her screen. "Okay, so here's what it says. The first area they talk about is reliving the event. I don't know if he does that. I'm assuming he probably does, but also in that category it talks about having intense and discomforting reactions to objects or situations that remind you of the event. Well, we know he has that. The fireworks on July 4th practically did him under."

"Wow. What else does it say? By the way, this dressing is delicious."

"Thanks. I used the Meyer's lemons, garlic, and that champagne mustard Henry and Seth brought us." She scrolled down the page on her screen. "Okay, so the next section is about people and places and feeling emotional detachment. I'd say yes to this one since we know he avoided the Maguire's gang for months and months. He even came out here and didn't stop in to see anyone."

"Yeah, I would check that box, too," agreed Mia.

"Loss of interest in everyday activities. I don't really know. Feelings of hopelessness. Not sure about that one either." Holly continued to scroll.

"If he truly has PTSD, which I suspect he might just based on what we know he's been through, I wouldn't be surprised if he has feelings of hopelessness." Mia focused on her salad, pretending she was digging for certain things mingled in with the bibb lettuce and finally settling on a large chunk of gorgonzola cheese.

Shaking her head, Holly grimaced, as if a physical blow had been landed. "That makes me so sad to think that."

"Hopefully he's getting the help he needs and will come out the other end of this okay. Aiden is a strong man."

"I hope so." Her eyes didn't leave the computer screen as she ate. "Hyperarousal." Holly smiled for the first time and looked at Mia. "And they don't mean that in the good way."

"What a shame." Mia looked amused.

"I know. Right?" She kept reading. "Well, this fits, too. It talks about being easily startled. And I've seen that firsthand."

"Although we are not mental health professionals, I'd say based on a combination of several factors, it's safe for us to assume Aiden is suffering from some degree of PTSD. And he, for sure, does not have an easy road in front of him."

"I don't even know how to deal with this, Mia. On one hand, I want to go to him and convince him to let me in to help him. And then I think how many times do I need for him to tell me that he doesn't want me before I start believing him?"

"You know I have felt from the start that Aiden did this as some grand gallant gesture and was actually doing it, breaking up with you, etcetera, out of love. I have always thought that." She wasn't telling Holly anything they hadn't discussed before her recent conversation with Aiden. "And I think what happened to him overseas just solidified that for him, really making him believe that he's doing the right thing in distancing himself from you and not burdening you with what is a really heavy load for him."

"Mia, I wouldn't have walked away."

"I know, sweetie. And that was his big fear. He didn't want you to stay out of obligation."

"But I wouldn't be. I'd be staying out of love."

"I know you would. But in his mind, he feels unlovable and can't even fathom that you would be by his side by choice."

"How could he not know how much I love him?"

"Somewhere in there he does, Holly. And that's why he wants you to walk away and find happiness with someone who doesn't carry the baggage that he does."

They ate in silence for a few moments, Holly continuing to scroll through PTSD info on her laptop.

"Speaking of Aiden," Mia began, "The kids wanted to go to Maguire's for steamers tonight."

"Would you mind if I didn't join you? I'm just too emotional right now to see that waitress flirting with him."

"We could go someplace else," Mia offered.

"No. Take them there. Natie and Po love their steamers. And there's plenty of food in the house for me to eat."

"Are you sure?"

Holly sighed. "Yes. No. Maybe. As much as I want to see him and talk to him, I think it's best I don't go."

"I understand." Mia wanted to tell her, *just wait for him, he wants this badly enough, he wants you badly enough,* but she couldn't betray Aiden's confidence.

***

"Mom, I'm old enough to go pee by myself."

Mia's head snapped to attention at her daughter's eye roll. The future was coming too fast, way too fast, as actions like this reminded her that her two little ones were not so little any longer and a teenage daughter was going to be in her future sooner than she'd ever be ready for it.

"Go to the bathroom and come straight back," she instructed Portia and remained at the table to watch Nathaniel.

As she skipped past the bar, Aiden looked up and waved at her. Smiling, she waved back and headed toward the restroom. After her dad, Aiden was the most handsome man she'd ever seen, but now he was no longer at their house all the time, and she missed him swinging her around, playing airplane with her.

Passing by the bar on her way back to the table, Aiden smiled at her again and waved for her to come in.

"I thought you and Natie might like these." He slid two Shirley Temples across the bar to her.

"Is the one with two cherries mine?" Portia was all smiles and giggles around her crush.

"Do you even need to ask?"

"No." She laughed.

"Can you carry those both or do you need a hand. I might have filled them too much."

"I'm okay." She took a sip from hers and then a sip from her brother's to ensure she wouldn't spill them.

"If you had a third hand, I'd send something for your dad. But you don't have a third hand."

Portia giggled again. "I don't need one. I only need two. My dad's not here."

"No?"

"No, he's back in the city until this weekend. And Holly stayed home tonight. So, it's just me, Mom, and Natie."

"Holly didn't come?"

Portia shook her head, but didn't say anything.

"Is she feeling okay?" he asked.

"Yeah."

He could tell the little girl was feeling uncomfortable talking about her sister's absence from the family dinner, so he let it go. "You'd better get those back to the table before all the bubbles fizz out and Natie has a flat drink."

"Okay." She nodded. "See you later," and walked carefully from the bar, trying her hardest not to spill the drinks.

What the heck? Holly rolled over and reached for the phone. *Who is texting me in the middle of the night?* The noir ringtone let her know it was a text.

Hey Holly, it's Billy. Did Aiden come to your house?

I don't think so. But I've been sleeping. She looked at the clock on her phone. It was only 12:45 a.m., but she'd gone to bed early, around 11:00, and had been in a deep sleep. **What's going on?**

He was in here and left about 30 minutes ago. He was really drunk and a mess. He kept talking about ruining your life. He was saying he needed to apologize to you, then started talking about the world being a better place without him. And that freaks me out. I'm working 'til 2:00 and there's no one here tonight to cover for me, then I have to clean and lock up. Can you check on him?

I don't even know where he lives? You want me to just knock on his door???

Do you remember the Andy Metzger house my ex lived in on Denhoff Walk two summers ago?

LOL the ugly green one?

That's the one.

Aiden's living there???

Yes. If you go around the stone walkway on the side of the house, there's a door there for a studio apartment and they keep a key behind the big terracotta planter.

Holly was sitting up in bed now with the light on, talking into her phone doing voice to text as she pulled on cut-offs and a tank top.

Billy, you seriously want me to just let myself into Aiden's apartment in the middle of the night.

Well, I'd knock first. Maybe he'll answer. I'd use the key if he doesn't. Just to make sure he's ok.

Crap Billy you're scaring me. I'm leaving now.

Text me if you need my help with anything.

k.

Heading downstairs quietly, so as not to wake anyone, she grabbed her keys off the kitchen counter and slipped out the front door. Walking toward Midway, Holly felt more secure walking alone at this hour as she began to pass people who'd been out at the bars, making the streets feel less deserted as she headed toward Aiden's. At the corner of Denhoff and Midway, she stopped, standing in the glow of a streetlamp, taking a moment to think, and formulate a strategy. *I'll knock first and call his name. Hopefully he'll answer, even if he tells me to go away. If he doesn't answer, then I'll find the key.*

Please God, please let me find him safe. With each step the dread built, fear cramping her stomach as she silently prayed he hadn't done anything drastic.

The winds were beginning to kick up as she walked down the street toward his house, heat lightning flashing in the distance. Crossing her arms over her chest, she wished she'd grabbed a jacket before leaving. It had been awhile since she'd been on this end of Denhoff Walk, but she recognized the house immediately and located the path that curved around into the side yard. With the scrub pines growing up against the house, she couldn't get close enough to peer into the windows, but it didn't look like there were any lights on. *Maybe he's not even home. He could have gone to that waitress's place.*

When the path ended at the door, she just stood there for a moment, taking a deep breath before knocking.

"Aiden. Aiden, are you home?" Waiting a moment, she put her ear to the door, but heard nothing and banged again. "Aiden, open up." She banged harder and continued to be met by silence.

"Shit," she muttered and reached behind the planter, searching with her fingertips for a key in the night.

"Aiden." She banged again before inserting the key into the lock.

Opening the door, she stood very still waiting for her eyes to adjust to the pitch-black studio. In the quiet, Holly could hear Aiden's deep breathing, his fast-asleep breathing, a comforting sound she knew so very well, one that had lulled her to sleep on many a night. She stood in the doorway, relieved, as she listened to the familiar sound. Billy had said he was drunk, and now he was passed out, but at least safe and sound in his own bed.

Closing the door gently, so as not to make a sound, Holly pulled out her phone and swiped the flashlight function, illuminating a conical path. Across the room was a queen-sized bed and Aiden was on the left side, his side of the bed, sleeping on his left side, the way he always slept. Slowly, she walked over to the bed, approaching on the right side, and looked down at him, thankful to see him sleeping peacefully, and sleeping off whatever caused the alarmedly drunken state that had concerned Billy enough to text her at 12:45 a.m.

Her heart began to swell with emotion just seeing the peace on his handsome face, an inner tranquility that defied his external scarring. Even in the darkened room, she could see the purplish-pink scars that told the story of the hell he was trying to hide. Continuing to gaze at him, she silently hoped he was someplace pleasant in his dreams, somewhere far from the reality that had altered his life so drastically.

Slowly, she sat down on the right side of the mattress, careful not to disturb him. How many nights had she watched him sleep, just like this? *Too many to count,* she smiled. With her eyes now acclimated to the dark, she could see his eyes darting back and forth behind his lids, indicating he was dreaming. Not ten seconds had passed when his lips began to move, and unintelligible words emerged, the tone indicating strife, and she immediately felt like a guilty intruder.

He's safe in bed. I need to leave.

As she planted both feet back on the floor, the room illuminated simultaneously with a crackling sound from a startlingly close bolt of lightning, followed immediately by a sharp clap of thunder.

"No! No! Get out now!" Thrashing, Aiden shouted the words clearly, internalizing the summer storm, immediately transforming what had been a dream that had turned stressful into a full-blown nightmare.

His scream was piercing as a second nearby clap of thunder rattled the windows of the small house.

Her reaction was instinctual. "Aiden, you're okay." She leaned into him, her hand gently grasping his shoulder to shake him awake and pull him from whatever was closing in on him.

His reaction was instinctual, too, and with a guttural scream he shot up, his hands wrapping around her neck, his fingers digging in, as his chokehold on Holly tightened.

"Aiden," she wanted to scream, but his grasp snuffed out the air needed for the words to make it up from her vocal cords.

Flailing, she punched at his shoulder, trying desperately to make him stop, but she could see from his face, which was screwed up in anger, that his eyes were still closed. That is when she realized this was all happening in a dream for him. But it was no dream for her. This nightmare was very real, as real as his, and as his face started to swim before her eyes, the thought racing across Holly's consciousness was, *I can't die this way. Please God, don't let me die this way.* Knowing it was her last-ditch effort before she blacked out, she thrust her left knee forward praying she still had the strength for it to hurt him and jolt him into an awakened state.

Please God, she silently begged.

"Ahhh," he screamed, as her knee made a hard-enough contact with his genitals and he fell backward off her, his hands immediately releasing her neck, and rushing to his groin.

A sickening gasp arose from Holly's throat, followed by a series of heaving sounds as her lungs strove desperately to replace the air that had been robbed from them.

"What the hell is going on?" A now awake Aiden dove for the interloper in his apartment.

As he went to jump her again in the dark, she was able to croak out, "Aiden. No," making him stop before he was on her again.

"What the..." He appeared disoriented.

"It's me," her bruised vocal cords produced a harsh whisper.

Backing off, he sat back on his haunches, his sight finally focusing. "Holly?"

Her answer was a strangled sob as Aiden flicked on the lamp, his eyes wide with confusion.

"Holly? Holly, what are you doing here?"

Her eyes searched his face in disbelief as her hands went to her bruised neck.

"Oh my God, did I do that? I just did that to you, didn't I? Oh my God." Her bruises were turning purple before his eyes, the bile rising in his throat as he oriented himself to the situation. "What have I done? What did I do to you?" As he moved toward her, he could see the substantiated fear in her eyes. "I am so sorry."

Her lips moved, as if she were going to respond, but the only response from her body, were pronounced twitches from her tensed muscles as she put her hands out in front of her to stop him from getting any closer.

"Holly, I am so sorry," he repeated, looking at her in disbelief, wanting more than anything to hold her as he apologized, but he could see the fear still in her eyes. Fear of him and the monster that he had become. "Let me get you ice."

Springing up from the bed, he crossed the studio to the refrigerator, and pulled a tray of ice out of the freezer at the top. Quickly opening a series of drawers, he found a large plastic bag and dumped a whole tray of cubes into it.

As he went to put the ice pack against her throat, she again put her arm out to stop him, and took the bag, placing it against her own throat, and wincing at the initial pain before the cold began to numb her burning skin.

Sitting down on the bed next to her, he shook his head, closing his eyes as he said, "I am so sorry. You cannot even imagine how sorry I am. Can you tell me what happened? How did this happen? Oh God, Angel." He shook his head. "How did I do this to you?"

They both jumped at the next clap of thunder. But this time Holly made no move to comfort him. Instead, they both sat silently, seemingly listening to the rain relentlessly pounding the windows, while all the while, each listened to relentless screaming in their own heads.

"Please, look at me. I need you to look at me. I need to know you don't hate me for what I just did to you."

"Aiden, if I harbor any negative feelings toward you, it's not because of anything that happened here tonight." The ice was cooling down the burning of her skin, but the bruising inside her throat and the pain in her heart, far eclipsed the stinging of the bruises. "Do you have any anti-inflammatories and some water."

"Yeah, yeah, sure. Oh, sorry, I didn't even think about that." He brought her back three Tylenol and a bottle of water. "So, what are you doing here?" Again, he sat down next to her and twisted the cap of the bottle before handing it to her.

"Billy texted me. He was worried about you tonight. Afraid you might do something to hurt yourself and he couldn't get out of work, so he texted me, and asked if I'd come and check on you. So, I did. When you didn't answer the door, I used the key behind the planter to let myself in."

Aiden looked away, his face filled with emotion. "So, you came to make sure I was okay, and I practically killed you for caring about me. Please tell me you know I would never hurt you."

"Never hurt me? Are you serious?" The anger quickly swept across her face.

"I mean physically hurt you. I would never lay a hand on you. Please tell me you know that, Angel."

Holly just stared at him, then nodded. "I know that, Aiden. I know you would never intentionally hurt me physically." No matter what had gone down between them, Holly knew, one-hundred percent, that Aiden would never be physically abusive. That wasn't in his make-up. But if anyone saw the bruises on her neck, they would never believe that. Flashing across her mind was the thought that she'd better find somewhere to go this weekend before her father got back to Fire Island. She knew all he'd see were the purple fingerprints on her neck and the circumstances behind it wouldn't matter to him at all.

"But, unintentionally, I did. And I am so sorry. I'm a mess, Holly." He raked his fingers through his thick, dark hair in an exasperated gesture. "And I know I keep saying this, but it's really best for you to stay away from me. I hope you can see that now."

"Do you also not want me near you because you don't love me? Tell me the truth, Aiden. Now is the moment for the truth."

Remaining silent, he met her angry glare.

"For God's sake, you almost killed me. Just tell me the truth." Her already hoarse voice was tightening with emotion.

"You can't be near me. Emotionally, I'm a timebomb. Never in a million years did I think I had the capacity to hurt you physically. That's never what this was about. But I did. Tonight, I did."

"Aiden, you weren't even conscious when it happened. And it was just crazy circumstances. Even I know that. But you still haven't answered my question." She stood her ground.

"Because I need you to stay away from me."

"And I need you to answer my question."

Raking his hand again through his hair, he just shook his head. "I don't want to ruin your life," his cadence was slow, emphatic. "Don't you see that. I'd rather hurt myself than hurt you, Angel."

"Well, you're not succeeding."

"I know. And I hate myself for that. And I hate that I ever met you."

"You hate that you ever met me? Nice, Aiden. Really nice." Holly had enough. Taking the ice off her neck, she placed it on the nightstand, and swung her long legs over the edge of the bed, ready to head out the door into the raging storm, anything to distance herself from the torrent that was raging in her heart.

Reaching out, Aiden grabbed her arm, pulling her to him.

"What are you doing?" She tried to wrench away, but he used the motion to tug her to his chest.

"I'm hugging you. Whether you want me to or not," he whispered softly, mirroring the words she had used on him twice.

"I need to go," she insisted.

"No."

As he shook his head, she felt his chin moving through her hair in a massaging motion.

"No," he repeated. "I can't let you go." And he tightened his embrace.

"If only you meant that," she said against his bare chest.

"Look at me, Angel."

She shook her head, still smarting from the comment that he wished he'd never met her. Tonight had been painful enough already, both physically and emotionally, she didn't need any more.

She just needed to leave.

"Angel, look at me." His hands slid to her shoulders. "I need you to look at me." His third plea was a whisper. When her eyes met his, he continued. "I think you misunderstood my intent when I said I wished I'd never met you."

Her only response was the slight tremble of her bottom lip.

"I wish I'd never met you because then I never would have caused you pain. And I know I have and I'm sorry," he paused, "and the answer to your question is no."

"No?"

"No, I don't want you to stay away from me because I don't love you."

"So, what does that mean?"

"It means I want you to stay away from me because I'm not in a good place. And it's probably going to take me a while to get to a good place."

"If you really think pushing me away is going to pull me out of Hell, think again, Aiden."

"I just don't want to take you to Hell with me."

"Where do you think I've been since the day you told me you didn't love me anymore?"

Leaning his forehead against hers, he just sighed. "I've really made a terrible mess of all this, haven't I?"

Holly nodded, her forehead still against his.

"I'm sorry, Angel. For everything. Well, everything except loving you. I'm not sorry for that."

"Then let me help," she pleaded.

"Please listen to me." Gently, he stroked her hair. "I have so much shit to go through before I can open that door."

"That door?" she questioned. "The one that lets me in?" *But you let Janine in,* she wanted to say. Instead, "I need to go."

"Holly, I'm not letting you walk home in a storm in the middle of the night. Just stay here. I'll sleep on the couch."

Sleep on the couch? She knew he was just trying to be a gentleman, but after all the other comments of the evening, it carried the sting of rejection.

"I really want to go," she insisted.

He just shook his head. "Not happening. Let me get you a tee-shirt." He rummaged through a drawer before pulling out a faded gray tee that said, "ARMY Est. 1775" in navy blue lettering. Walking back over to her, he placed it in her hands. "Bathroom is over there."

He was covering the couch with a flat sheet when she came out of the bathroom, his shirt fitting more like a short dress. Looking up, he smiled at her in his shirt.

"That doesn't look very comfortable. I feel bad making you sleep on the couch. Why don't you just sleep in the bed with me." Pulling the covers back, she sat down on her side of the bed.

Straightening up from where he'd been tucking in a corner of the sheet, Army-style, he raised his brows, looking at her questioningly. "Are you sure? I mean, the couch is just fine."

"Whatever you want." Worn out from what she perceived as continued rejection, Holly settled in under the covers, and turned off the light on the nightstand, plunging the room back into the darkness she had entered less than an hour before. Only this time it doubled as the perfect cloak to hide the pain that had been steadily mounting. *How overwhelmingly sad,* she thought, *we're finally in the same room, and yet, separated by terrain that neither of us know how to successfully traverse.* Quietly wiping tears she didn't want him to know she was shedding, she strove to make her tone sound normal. "Goodnight."

"'Night."

It was maybe five minutes later when she heard the rustling of his sheets, followed by footsteps and the motion of his side of the bed yielding under his weight. She rolled over to face him.

"It's just crazy. For four-hundred-and-ninety-three nights, all I thought about was falling asleep with you in my arms. That dream got me through more dark nights than I care to admit. And here you are, in my bed, and I'm sleeping across the room. That's just insane." Reaching out, he pulled her close to him. As he went to push the hair from her face, his hand brushed the wetness of her cheeks. "Please don't cry." He wiped her cheek with his fingers.

"That ferry's sailed."

"You feel so good, you know that. I've missed you. I know you don't think I have. But I have. It's been four-hundred-and-ninety-three nights." His voice was thick with emotion.

She was shocked that he knew how many days it had been, that he'd been counting their time apart. He was the one who left her. *Why would he count days?*

He continued, "I am stuck in a rabbit hole right now and I don't want to drag you down there with me. What you saw July 4th, which, by the way, I hate that you saw, is just the tip of the iceberg."

"Why do you hate that?"

"Oh, Angel, do you think I want you to see me that way?"

"I'm sure you don't, but do you really think that would make me love you any less? You saw what my reaction was. I couldn't stay away."

"And I loved you for that. But trust me, when it's not an isolated incident, it gets old."

In that moment, Holly realized that for Aiden, the darkness was not a cloak, but rather his safe space to lay bare his demons without the light of judgment shining upon them.

"What can I do to help?" *Please let me in. Please.* She silently begged.

"Stay away from me, Angel."

The irony of his words with their bodies pressed together didn't elude either one of them.

"I don't think that I can do that, Aiden. You're like a drug for me, and it's an addiction I haven't had much success kicking."

Even in the darkness, she could see his smile before his head dipped to her neck. "I am so sorry I did this to you." His words were muffled as he slowly worked his way around her neck placing a chain of kisses over the line of bruises left by his fingers.

With every kiss, Holly's breath hitched. Four-hundred-and-ninety-three nights, longing, dreaming, needing his touch. "Aiden," she whispered. "Aiden." Burrowing her fingers in his hair, she lifted his face from her neck until his lips were right above hers, and then on hers with a forcefulness, and an urgency that matched her own.

Breaking the kiss, he pushed up on his forearms. "I can't be this close to you, Angel, and not be inside you."

That was her Aiden talking. She saw him. He was there.

Rolling onto her back, Holly pulled him on top of her.

"Ditch the shirt." His voice was gruff.

Raising her arms, she looked at him, indicating she was going to need a little help since he was on top of her.

Rolling over and pulling her on top of him, he smiled up at her. "Next position, please." It was an inside joke, from a long day they'd spent together at the Motor Vehicle Office, where the lady behind the counter would move people through the line saying, "Next position, please."

Lifting his shoulders off the bed, he reached for the hem of his Army shirt and pulled it over Holly's head, eliciting an involuntary moan at the sight of the tan lines on her gorgeous breasts.

"I'm still not inside you," he reminded her.

"That's not my fault." She got off him and sat on the bed, then reached over and snapped the elastic waistband of his boxer-briefs. She marveled at how easy it was to slide back into *Holly & Aiden*. How easy it was to be *them*.

Reaching down, he pulled his underwear off in one fluid motion, and was back on top of Holly in the next. *Please forgive me, Lord. I'm dragging her into the rabbit hole with me, leading her by the hand, and I just can't stop myself.* "You really should have stayed away from me."

There was no foreplay. There was none needed.

"That ferry's sailed." Her words were mixed by a gasp as she felt him fill her.

With his eyes closed, he drove into her fast and hard, his need to unleash fueling the relentless pace. The thought of asking her if he should pull out fleeted across his mind, and he batted it away ferociously, needing to fill her, to reclaim a life that was once his.

"You feel so freaking good," he growled. "I have missed fucking you."

"You're not deep enough," she told the man who was always pushing her away. "I want you deeper."

"Like this?" He rammed her hard.

"Just like that," she gulped.

Leaning back on his haunches, he pulled her down onto him and with his hands at her waist driving her up and down, he buried himself deep inside.

"Is that deep enough?"

She shook her head, her long silky hair whipping his face, eliciting a primal groan that emanated from deep in his chest. There was no one who made him feel the way she did, and he knew there never would be anyone else who could.

"No? You need it deeper, Angel?" He rammed her down hard, filling her completely.

"Damn, I've missed your cock," she said into his neck as she hung on for the rough, insane ride.

"Yeah, and I've missed ramming it into your tight, little hole."

Pulling her face from his neck and looking at him, she sneered, "Good."

"I love when you get bitchy."

Without saying a word, her mouth went to his neck, her teeth scraping his skin hard, and then biting down, claiming and marking. *Let that new little waitress ask who gave you that.*

"You nasty little bitch." He rammed her down hard...

...and she bit harder, only letting go when he began to lie her on her back. This was them, and for right now, she had him back, the comfort, the rapport, the passion. There was no other world. This was their world as it was before. Holly and Aiden. Aiden and Holly. Air. Water. Each other. That had been all they ever needed.

Taking his face in her hands, she looked at him, sorting out the light and the shadows playing upon his face and trying desperately to etch a visual memory that would always bring her back to the overwhelming pitch of this moment. This very second needed to be committed to memory.

Burying his face in her neck, he groaned, "Come with me, Angel."

And like a thousand nights before, hearing those words, words she didn't know if she'd ever hear again, she let go and let him take her over the edge.

Staying inside her, he laid his head on her chest, and her arms immediately wrapped around him.

"You hugging me?" he asked with a smile she couldn't see.

She laughed. "Yeah, but I think this time you might want me to." And she kissed the top of his head.

"I think you might be right." He remained in her arms and inside her, silent, for what felt like a while before getting up to head to the bathroom.

Feeling an immediate sadness, she knew this wasn't basking in a post-coital glow, because there had been so much pain in their joy tonight.

Returning with a warm, wet towel, Aiden sat down next to her. "Spread 'em, Angel." His touch was soft as he ran the cloth between her legs, causing her to jump a little. "I was kinda rough tonight." Lying back down, he pulled her to him, spooning her and whispered, "I've got an appointment in Bay Shore in the morning. It's with a shrink. I'm hoping he can help."

Holly smiled in the dark. "My money's on you, McManus."

"You always were the optimistic one." There was a tone of resignation in his voice and a heaviness indicating he was already falling asleep.

Lying awake for a long time, she listened to his breathing, not wanting to miss a single note from his symphony of sounds. Her nights had been silent for too long. But as the night moved toward dawn, the sinking feeling in Holly's gut told her that the telling glare of daylight was going to be harsh.

She ached everywhere. Her neck, her insides from the roughness of his thrusts, her heart. His ability to open up in the darkness had dissipated in daylight, just as she had feared, replaced by a detached aloofness.

Inspecting her bruises, they looked even worse than they had the night before and she hoped the truly garish color was just a result of the bathroom's fluorescent lighting. She had to get home and into her room before the kids got up for breakfast and camp so that they wouldn't be alarmed at the sight of her neck. And more than anything, she was well aware that she needed to be gone before her father got out to Fire Island, or all hell was going to break loose the minute he saw Aiden's fingerprints all over her throat.

"Do you have a hoodie I can borrow?" she asked, stepping out of the bathroom, devising how she could pull her hair forward with the hood up and hide some of the bruising.

"Yeah, sure." He tossed a sweatshirt to her. This too was gray and emblazoned with the Army logo.

Pulling it over her head, she immediately put the hood up and pulled her hair out the front.

"I'm sorry about last night."

"I know you didn't know it was me."

"Yeah. That, too. But, I mean, I'm sorry about everything."

"Are you talking about us being together last night?" She could feel her anger rising.

"Yeah. It shouldn't have happened. I should have had more self-control."

"So, let me ask you something. What was that last night?"

"What was that?" He thought for a moment. "What happened between us was really hot sex. We fuck great together. We always have."

"We fuck great together," she repeated his words in disbelief, shaking her head. "Nice, Aiden. Real nice."

Shrugging his shoulders, he didn't even attempt contrition. "Hey, I've warned you to stay away from me."

"Keep pushing me away. And I *will* go." Walking to the door, she did not look back, afraid the hurt would show in her eyes, and not wanting to give him that power.

As she walked home, she tried to let go of the hurt and anger as she played the night over and over in her mind, and became more convinced than ever that she could help him. He'd shown her glimpses that he was still there, and fighting to escape what she could only think of as a POW camp in his mind.

If only he would let her in.

But she feared that ferry might have already sailed, too.

It was late morning when there was a knock on her bedroom door.

"Come in," she yelled from the bathroom, where she'd spent the past half hour semi-successfully applying make-up to her bruises. "I'm in here."

"Hey, just checking on you, it's not like you to sleep late. You're usually finishing your run when we're first getting up." Stepping through the bathroom door, Mia saw Holly in the mirror dabbing her neck with a cosmetic sponge. "What the..."

"I know this looks bad."

"Oh my God. Are you okay? How did this happen? Did someone attack you when you were running this morning?"

Holly shook her head, followed by a short bitter chuckle. "No. This was no stranger." She paused. "Or maybe it was."

"I'm sorry. I'm not following you."

Blending in the last few dabs of make-up, she put the sponge down and turned to Mia. "Let's go sit."

Holly sat down in the middle of her bed, with Mia across the room in a chair, and recounted the night's events starting with Billy's text, through Aiden waking in shock, and finally his disgust and remorse when he was conscious of what had happened. She intentionally left out the rest of the night and the morning's conversation.

"I just didn't think he'd be violent," Mia stammered, shocked by what Holly had recounted.

"I don't think he is. I think this was just a bizarre circumstance. He was not awake when this occurred. He was still in a dream state."

"Sounds more like a nightmare. Holly, I'm concerned this could happen again."

"I'm really not, Mia. Obviously, I don't know that for sure. But I just think this was one of those perfect, or imperfect, in our case, storms. I don't think he's violent, and believe me, if I had any doubt about that, I'd be scared, and I'm not."

Cocking her head, Mia gave her an *are you serious* look.

"Really." Holly nodded. "I'm more scared of him when he's awake."

"Why?"

"Well, just what he can do to me emotionally. But I do know he's trying to get help. He told me he's meeting with a psychiatrist this morning and I think that's a great step. I don't think he wants to let himself get too optimistic in case he doesn't make progress."

Mia nodded. It appeared that although Aiden had confided getting into therapy, he hadn't mentioned her involvement.

Getting up from the bed, Holly went to the closet and pulled out her duffel bag.

"Where are you going?"

Holly sighed. "I called Jenna and she's going out to the Hamptons. Pierce is out there, playing a place called the Echo Beach Inn and is staying in a big house with plenty of room, so I'm going to meet her on the 2:33 train out of Bay Shore. I can't be home when Dad gets here. He will go apeshit if he sees me and I don't even want to think about him getting into it with Aiden." She sighed again. "Nothing good can come from that."

Holly moved around the room quickly, grabbing clothes for the weekend. "Is Dad still getting in at his usual time tomorrow?" The weeks Schooner was in the city, he'd always be on the 3 p.m. ferry on Thursday afternoons.

Mia nodded, but remained silent for another minute. "Holly, how am I not going to tell him this?" Mia's gut was churning. Not only was she keeping her involvement in Aiden's therapy from Holly and Schooner, now she was asked to keep Aiden practically choking Holly from her husband, too. It was too much of a burden knowing everyone's secrets.

"If you tell him, I'd really appreciate it if you could just play it down."

"I wish I could unsee your neck without make-up. I really do."

"Mia, he felt terrible. He really did. If he didn't have remorse, I'd worry. But he was devastated by what happened." And now she was devastated by the aftermath and being relegated to a great fuck. "I've just got to get away."

"I understand. And you'll have fun in the Hamptons. I have some very good, albeit hazy," she smiled, "memories of hanging out at the EBI."

"EBI?"

"Echo Beach Inn. It's a Long Island landmark for fun. Pretty infamous and very cool that Pierce is playing there."

"It's my first time in the Hamptons. Do you think I'll like it?" Holly zipped up her duffel after throwing in her makeup case and blow dryer.

"The Hamptons are beautiful, and actually you are a descendant of one of the founding families. Your branch of the Moores settled in Southampton in the 1640s."

Holly stopped moving. "I didn't know that. So, this is where we started in this country?"

"Your dad and I did a bunch of research way back, and if I remember correctly, John Moore was born in England and then was in the Massachusetts Bay Colony before settling on Long Island. I think there was also a Southold branch of the family, too. That's on the north fork of the island. And I think that branch of the Moores had been in Salem. But to answer your question, the Hamptons are beautiful and historic, just a really different vibe than here. This is infinitely more laid-back, the Hamptons are more see and be seen. You'll need clothes and makeup for the Hamptons."

"Good to know." Looking sad, she slung the bag over her shoulder, and confessed. "I am worried about Aiden, Mia. Not because of this." She pointed to her neck. "I'm worried about what's going through his head when he's awake."

"Hopefully he'll be able to do good work with this therapist."

"I hope so. He's really such a good person."

"I know he is," Mia agreed, saying a silent prayer that his session this morning steered him to the right track.

"I really miss the guy who could make me laugh and had so much charisma he could charm an eighty-five-year-old nun. I see glimpses and I want to unlock the cage. Is that crazy?"

"No. It's not crazy at all. This is going to take more patience than, I think, any of us can imagine. One day at a time is going to be tough, but then at some point you'll realize that the glimpses are longer and more often. But, for now, get off this island, have some fun with Pierce and Jenna, try to stay in the moment with the Hamptons. Fire Island and all the drama will still be here when you get back. Now, go have fun. And I'm going to try and forget that I ever saw your neck."

Mia was on a conference call when Schooner walked through the front door. Looking up, she gave him a small wave and felt her heart bloom with *that feeling* that she still got every time the man walked in a room. It had been an emotional week. First her talk with Aiden, then the situation with Holly. She was glad he was back, knowing his calm, centering presence was the energy she needed surrounding her. That and his arms.

Tipping her head back for a kiss, she mouthed the words, "I missed you."

"It's smoochal," he whispered, smiling, his real smile. "I'm going up to shower and change."

"Don't use all the mango butter lotion," she whispered after him.

Stopping on the third step, he looked back over his shoulder, his smile wide. "Never without you," he promised, before continuing to climb the stairs.

Smiling, she turned her focus back to what her client was saying.

Seated at the table talking to her client when the doorbell rang, Mia looked toward the stairs to see if Schooner was possibly out of the shower to answer it. When he didn't appear at the top of the steps, she took her cell to the door. Opening it, she was surprised to see Aiden standing there. Motioning for him to come in, she held up two fingers indicating she'd be off the phone shortly.

Standing with his hands in the pockets of his cargo shorts, Aiden stared out at the ocean crashing against the shore, waiting for Mia to finish up. This was the first time he'd been in the Moore's house in well over a year. It had been his second home for a long time, a place of comfort and laughter, and now he felt agitated and apprehensive standing in the great room.

Hanging up the phone, Mia headed to the refrigerator. "Water?" she asked.

"Yes, please. I'm not drinking the hard stuff with you anymore." He took the bottle from her. "Oh, by the way, the new bottle of Hennessy arrived this morning."

"Oh, good. I've already got too many secrets from people. That doesn't need to be another one. Come sit."

He followed, sitting on a chair across from her. "Did Schooner come in on the three o'clock?" Even Aiden knew his schedule after all these years.

"Yeah, he's just upstairs showering."

"Okay, good, I wanted to talk to the two of you."

"I'm sure you do." Mia gave him a pointed look.

"Is Holly out on the beach?" After he spoke to Schooner and Mia, he wanted to make sure she was okay.

"No." Mia shook her head. "Holly's out in the Hamptons."

"The Hamptons?"

"A friend of hers is playing this weekend at the EBI, so she went out."

"Bun Man?" There was more than a note of derision in Aiden's voice.

"Yes, Bun Man."

"She went to be with Bun Man." He was now visibly upset.

"C'mon Aiden. You know she couldn't be here. She was petrified of her father seeing her."

"Why would Holly be petrified for me to see her?" Schooner was at the top of the stairs, his voice filled with alarm.

Aiden stood. "That's why I'm here. I wanted you to hear about it from me."

"Hear about what from you?" Schooner's fuse was fraying quickly.

Meeting his glare, Aiden didn't sugarcoat his response. "I hurt Holly this week, Schooner."

"You've been hurting Holly for well over a year now, so why should this week be any different." It wasn't a question.

"This week was different. This week, I hurt her physically."

"What?" Schooner's tone was sharp and loud as he quickly traversed the space between him and Aiden. Springing up from the couch, Mia interjected herself between the two men.

Holding out a hand that landed mid-chest on her husband. "Sit down," she ordered, her voice as authoritative as his. "Holly is okay. Let's hear what Aiden has to say."

"You hit my daughter?" Schooner hissed through clenched teeth.

"Actually, I choked her." Aiden looked resigned, ready to receive Schooner's wrath as if it were some form of penance.

"You choked her?" His body pressed hard against Mia's hand and outstretched arm. Schooner was quickly losing control.

"Hey, hey, hey." Mia held him back. "Sit down," she ordered her husband. "Let him talk."

Schooner remained standing, looming a couple of inches over the younger man, adrenaline and testosterone stoked to a fevered pitch.

"Sit." Mia was not kidding, and at a foot shorter than her husband, was cutting an imposing figure.

Muttering under his breath, he sat on the couch, leaned back, and crossed both his legs and arms. Looking at Aiden, he spoke one word before entering his dead-calm mode. "Speak."

"I figured you might be on the three o'clock ferry, so I wanted to get over here immediately to talk to all of you. I knew you'd be upset."

Mia was waiting for a sarcastic "You think?" out of her husband. But Schooner remained silent and motionless, the only visible muscle movement in his entire body resided in his left cheek, where it was thumping like a cinematic drumbeat.

"Tuesday night I was having a rough time and went over to Castaway to drink. I drank way too much, and I was really down, and said some stupid things. Things that led Billy to think I might hurt myself. I'd also mentioned wanting to talk to Holly. He texted Holly at some point to ask if she'd seen me and when she said no, he asked her if she would check on me because he was the only one working and couldn't leave the bar. I had gone back to my place and passed out. I never heard Holly at my door and she used an extra key. Billy had told her where it was, and she let herself in. I guess I was having a bad dream, I have them a lot, and a thunderstorm kicked up and it was close, and well, I have a really rough time with loud noises these days, and I guess it affects me even when I'm sleeping. Which I didn't know until the other night. Holly saw me having a rough time and tried to wake me to tell me it was okay. And when she touched me, I grabbed her, and it just integrated into my nightmare. And I almost killed her." He looked down for the first time and shook his head. "I almost killed her."

They all sat in silence for a few minutes processing what had occurred.

Looking at Schooner, Aiden added, "You'll be happy to know your daughter kneed me in the balls and the surprise and pain woke me. And I was shocked to find her there and even more horrified by what I had done."

Schooner remained silent, stood, and walked to the open kitchen. From the top cabinet, he pulled out a cobalt blue bottle with a gold cap and liberally poured himself a Johnnie Walker Blue Ghost and Rare. He didn't offer a glass to anyone else. Sitting back down on the couch, he still remained silent as he took a sip of his scotch.

"Schooner, I don't even know how to express how sorry I am. I would never intentionally harm Holly." Schooner just looked at him and Aiden went on, "I saw a new psychiatrist this week. Mia, thank you for helping me get that set up." He looked toward Mia.

Slowly turning his head, Schooner glared at his wife.

"Oh, stop that." She gave him a disgusted look, then turned back to Aiden. "How did it go?"

"Really good. He's very easy to talk to and it was just hours after this had happened, so I just spilled it all."

"What did he say? If you don't mind my asking," Mia inquired.

"He said it falls under what they call Disorders of Arousal."

"Sorry to hear that," Mia snickered.

Schooner just looked at her and took a sip of his scotch.

"C'mon, lighten up. You know I have the sense of humor of a teenage boy. The term Disorders of Arousal is funny." She looked at Aiden. "I guess unless it is happening to you."

"Yeah, it definitely wasn't so funny the other night. I told him I was concerned about hurting someone and he felt that the circumstances of what happened just all converged at the right time, and that more likely than not, it would be an isolated incident."

"And how do we know that?" Schooner finally spoke.

"We don't. Not for sure, anyway. He did say that it is a very rare occurrence and he put me on some meds to help with the sleep terrors."

"Rare doesn't make me feel better."

"I know. Believe me, it scares the hell out of me. I've wanted Holly to stay away from me because I'm no good to anyone at this point. Just dealing with everyday stuff is a real challenge. This is a lot to take on. And I don't want her doing that."

"What if she wants to do that?" This time it was Mia who spoke.

"Well, I don't want it for her. At least, not now. I need to be significantly better before I can even consider being back in her life."

"That's an understatement." Schooner was not cutting him any slack.

"I know," Aiden agreed.

"Excuse me." Schooner stood and walked out of the room.

When he was clearly out of earshot, Mia said, "He wants to pull you apart, but he also sees how standup it is for you to be here. It took a lot for you to come today to talk to us face to face. Trust me, he appreciates that. Right now, he's just concerned for Holly, emotionally and now physically."

"I know, and I don't want this for her. She shouldn't have this stuff in her life."

"Maybe she should. We really don't know what someone's life path should be."

As Schooner reentered the room, he heard Mia's last comment and shook his head. "What are you reading these days?" he asked her. "Her life path?" he scoffed and picked up his drink.

Ignoring him, she asked Aiden, "So, you liked this guy?"

"Very much. He had some sound strategies for me that I've just started trying to use to make it through the days and nights. And he thought it would be beneficial to see him twice a week and I committed to that."

"That's great. It sounds like you're on the right path." She turned to Schooner, giving him her devil smile. "Oops, I said the 'p' word again."

"You're obnoxious." He finally smiled at his wife.

"Well, that's what I came to say. Schooner, Mia, all I can say is that I'm sorry. I really think it was just a freak thing. I would never hurt Holly. But it was bad, and I realize that, and I'm really sorry I hurt her."

"So, what do you want, Aiden?" He needed to know.

"I wanted everything out in the open. I wanted you guys to know."

"And what do you want from Holly?" Schooner leaned forward.

"I want her to stay away so that I'm not her problem."

"You know that's not true, Aiden. What do you really want?" Mia cut to the chase.

"What I really want is for Holly to wait for me, but I can't ask her to do that. Because realistically, I may never be whole enough again, and she doesn't deserve that. And I don't deserve to waste her time. What I really want is to be happy again. And to make her happy."

"That may be the most honest thing you've said to me yet," Mia acknowledged.

Aiden shrugged, palms up. "I'm trying. I really am."

"Good. Stay focused on that."

Mia rose when Aiden did, but Schooner remained seated, clearly not getting up to give him a proper goodbye.

Seeing him to the door, "Nice hickey," she commented quietly, so that her husband wouldn't hear.

Aiden leaned down and whispered, "Don't let that sweet face fool you. She bites."

And with a smile that gave Mia a glimpse of the young man they were all so fond of, he was off.

Closing the door behind him, she turned to Schooner. "Well, you were pretty tough on him."

Schooner shook his head. "Nah. Not really. It's just man-code stuff. If he needs to work for it, he'll work harder. That's the way he's wired."

"Work for your approval and acceptance?" Mia needed clarification.

"Yes, exactly that. He'll work even harder to get our relationship back on even keel and to get himself back, too." He smiled at Mia. "Trust me, I know what I'm doing. And by the way, it was very nice of you to help him find a therapist." He wasn't being sarcastic.

Standing, he pulled his phone from his pocket and opened the french doors to the deck. "Now, if you'll excuse me, I need to FaceTime with my daughter, see her bruised neck, and have a little chat with her."

Hey, I think you should come here and hang out. It was a text from Billy.

Special reason? Or you just miss me?

Both

Billy, you are such a match maker. She knew this was his way of telling her that Aiden was there.

I like seeing my friends happy

Well, I'll be bringing a friend. My friend Jenna is out. Maybe that will make you happy, friend.

Is she cute? ;-)

Very

Then get your asses here now. I'll keep our friend occupied.

"Want to meet Aiden?" Holly asked Jenna.

"Was that him?"

"No. That was our friend Billy. He bartends at Castaway and he was letting me know a certain someone is there. And I told Billy you were here and you're cute and he said we should get our asses there now." Holly laughed.

"Do I need to change my clothes?" Jenna was in a gauzy white peasant blouse, cut-offs, and flip-flops.

Holly laughed again. "No. You're probably overdressed."

"This is so the antithesis of the Hamptons. I could seriously get used to this."

"Anytime you want," Holly offered. "I'm just going to let Mia know we're heading out." Holly had successfully missed seeing her father, who was already back in Manhattan by the time she and Jenna arrived on Fire Island after their long weekend in the Hamptons. Her dad had called her every day since Aiden had told him of their incident.

As they were walking into town, Jenna asked, "How will I know which one is Aiden?"

"He's tall, with dark hair. Really handsome. And he's got some pretty nasty scars by his right eye and on his right cheek."

"You know your voice changes when you talk about him." Jenna smiled at her friend.

"Really?" Holly was surprised to learn that. No one had ever mentioned that before.

"I can tell you really love him," Jenna observed.

She just rolled her eyes to indicate *understatement*. "This is the place." Holly took a deep breath as they entered, bracing herself for their first encounter since the choking incident.

The bar had a decent crowd and was well on its way to being packed later in the evening. Billy was down at the far end and a female bartender, whom Holly didn't know, was covering the section closer to the entrance.

"We're going to head down there toward where Billy is."

"Billy's kinda cute," Jenna screamed into Holly's ear.

Making their way through the crowd, Holly and Jenna were stopped several times by guys asking if they could buy them drinks. Politely they declined and kept moving. They were almost down to where Billy was when they were stopped again by two guys who also offered to buy them drinks.

"We're good. But thanks," Holly told one of the guys.

"I'm sure you're very good." He eyed her up and down. "But you'd be even better with a drink in your hand."

"Thanks, but we're meeting some friends."

"Have a drink with us first." He turned to Billy. "Can I get two Rocket Fuels for these lovely ladies."

Making eye contact with Billy, Holly shook her head slightly.

"I think the ladies have already been taken care of."

"I don't think so. I don't see drinks in their hands." The guy slapped a twenty on the bar.

"He said the ladies have been taken care of." Aiden tossed a twenty of his own on the bar, which Billy scooped up.

Holly tried to move past the guy, but he closed his hand around her upper arm, which Holly unsuccessfully tried to yank from his grasp.

"What? You're too good for me, blondie?" His tone was belligerent.

"Get your hands off me." Holly snarled at him, finally freeing her arm from his grasp.

"Lay a hand on her again and I will beat your brainless pinhead into the bar. You got that?" Holly felt hands cupping her shoulders and Aiden's unmistakable voice as he moved into position behind her.

"Shut up, Scarface." The guy was a bulked-up gym rat ready to do battle.

But he picked the wrong soldier to go to war with.

In one swift move, Aiden was out from behind Holly and removed the guy's beer from his hand and slammed the bottle down onto the bar. "I think you're done. Time to go."

"You can't tell me to leave." The guy countered.

"Yeah, I can. And you're leaving. Now." Aiden looked at the guy's friend who had remained silent. "You need to get your buddy out of here before we have a real problem."

"Dude, you can't kick me out." The guy reached for his beer on the bar.

"Yeah, he can." Danny, a long-time Ocean Beach regular was right there, and behind him was his buddy, Carter, and half a dozen more guys who had known Aiden and Holly for a long time.

"Problem over here?" Carter asked.

"No problem," the guy's friend finally spoke.

"You were just leaving, weren't you?" Aiden asked him.

"Yeah, we don't want any problems. C'mon, Anthony, let's get out of here."

Aiden stood guard, arms crossed over his chest, watching until the guys were out the door before turning back to Holly, "You okay, Angel? Did he hurt you?"

"I'm okay. I just seem to be getting manhandled a lot lately." She tried to smile, but was unnerved at how quickly things escalated. She wondered if she was the only one who heard the timebomb ticking. This was so different than it had been in the past. Managing restaurants and bars, Aiden had always been the epitome of cool and calm, but tonight it felt as if he were hypervigilant.

"I've got a couple of Rocket Fuels here for you two ladies, compliments of the house," Billy called from behind the bar. "Take your money back," he said to Aiden, handing him back his twenty. "And I'll take his," Billy laughed, throwing the guy's twenty into the till.

"Thanks, Billy." Holly handed Jenna one of the plastic cups. "Welcome to Castaway. It's usually a pretty chill place. Billy, *this* is my friend Jenna."

"Well, it's about time you introduced us." Wiping his hands on a towel hanging from his waist, he extended a hand to Jenna.

"And Jenna, this is Aiden." She turned to her ex.

They acknowledged each other with shakes of their heads, but neither one said a word.

"So, Jenna, tell me, is this your first time in Ocean Beach?" Billy was very interested in Holly's new, cute friend.

"Actually, it's my first time on Fire Island."

"I didn't realize you hadn't been out here before, either," remarked Holly, as she took a sip of her Rocket Fuel. She could feel Aiden's body right behind hers, drawing her like a magnet.

"Either?" Billy asked.

"Yeah, my brother had never been here until he and Holly got drunk and decided to play escape from New York in the middle of my Memorial Day barbeque. And now he loves it here and can't wait to come back."

"I think my father wants to adopt him." Holly immediately felt Aiden tense behind her the minute the statement was out of her mouth, and instantly regretted verbalizing it. Mia had shared with her that her dad had been pretty rough on Aiden, and when he called her that night after Aiden left, he didn't tell her to walk away from him, but he did urge her to be cautious and careful.

"Your brother's the guy with the bun?" Aiden asked, inching his body even closer to Holly's.

"Yeah. That's my brother." Jenna looked directly at Aiden who didn't acknowledge her answer.

"Hey, Billy, can I get some water? I'm feeling a little dehydrated from being on the beach all day." Holly fanned herself.

"Sure." He reached under the bar and grabbed a bottle, loosening the cap before handing it to her.

"Want this?" She held up her Rocket Fuel for Aiden.

"You don't want it? You feeling okay?"

"Yeah, we were just on the beach all day and I can tell that I'm a little dehydrated." She handed him the drink. "Excuse me, I need to go to the ladies' room."

With Billy serving customers, Aiden and Jenna were left alone, their silence uncomfortable in the noisy bar. He scanned the crowd, checking out all the patrons, as if he were on some kind of watch, looking out for the next potential troublemaker, before returning his attention to the woman standing in front of him.

"So, Holly was with you over the weekend?" he finally asked.

"Yes. We went out to the Hamptons to see my brother play, and we stayed with him and his band."

Aiden just looked at her in steely silence. He knew she was fucking with him, throwing in the detail that they had stayed with Bun Man *and* his band.

"I don't like you," she finally said. With her first Rocket Fuel under her belt, Jenna's already questionable filter had all but disappeared.

"Well, that's your problem." His tone made it clear the feeling was mutual. Another moment of silence passed before Aiden asked what was really on his mind. "So, what's your brother's story? Does he like Holly or what?"

Jenna took a sip of her Rocket Fuel. "Of course, he likes Holly. She's beautiful, smart, and fun, and they totally get along." Smiling, she added, "And they look great together, too."

Aiden silently regarded her, and Jenna went on, "My brother is very protective of Holly and he was not happy to see what she looked like last weekend. What you did to her. If he could have canceled his gig for this weekend, he would have, just to be here with her." She didn't mention how Holly's emotional state had been, because it was none of his business.

"She doesn't need his protection." Aiden was liking this woman less and less. He knew she just wanted to protect her friend. But she didn't know him. And she had no clue how he felt about Holly.

"Well, that's not our opinion. I'm here this weekend. He'll be here next."

"Whatever." Aiden turned and walked away from her.

Heading toward the back of the bar, he turned down the hallway toward the restrooms.

Holly was emerging from the bathroom just as he got there.

"Are you okay?" He thought she looked tired.

"Yeah, I'm fine. Like I said, I think just a little dehydrated."

"Come with me." He put his hand on her shoulder and led her through the doorway toward Castaway's private offices and storage area. As a longtime employee of all the establishments in town and a friend of the owners, he knew nobody would have any issues with him slipping back there.

Stopping outside of one of the office doors, he turned to Holly, and she leaned up against the wall.

"I just wanted to talk to you alone for a second. You don't need to be afraid of me and you don't need to bring friends out here to protect you from me." His tone revealed he was upset that Holly felt she needed bodyguards when around him. And he was even more upset at who she had chosen to help keep her safe.

"What?" Holly cocked her head to the side, her long hair cascading down her arm.

"Your friend and her bother coming out to guard you."

"That's not why I invited them out, Aiden."

"Well, that's their plan."

Holly shook her head and sighed. "That was not my intention."

Running a hand down her arm, he asked, "Are you okay? Really? I've been thinking about you all week and what happened."

Looking into his eyes, she admitted, "Yeah, I've been thinking about you, too."

"I'm really sorry."

"I know. I know you didn't mean to hurt me."

"Yeah, well, I'm sorry about that, too."

Holly looked at him questioningly, waiting for him to continue.

"But what I'm most sorry about is what I said to you in the morning. I don't know if I said that stuff to protect you or to protect myself. It doesn't really matter, either way, it's not true."

Feeling her heart starting to race as he leaned over her with an arm on the wall, she looked down and nodded.

"Angel, it never has, and it never will be just a fuck with you. And no matter what moronic stuff comes out of my mouth, I hope you know that." Leaning down, he whispered in her ear, "I'm sorry. I'm sorry about so many things."

"Including meeting me?"

His hand immediately went to her chin, tipping her head up so he could see her eyes. "That just might be the stupidest thing that has ever come out of my mouth. And we both know I've said some stupid shit in my time." As his eyes flashed regret, his hand swept slowly from her chin to her jaw, and then down the curve of her neck. Sliding his thumb softly back and forth across the front of her throat. "Are they healing?"

She nodded. He didn't move, and she was vaguely conscious that his hand on her throat was pleasurable, not scary.

"I'm glad." His voice was soft.

"Oh, hey, I'm sorry. I didn't mean to barge in on you." The busboy looked as surprised to see them there as they were to see him.

Clearing his throat, Aiden straightened up and stepped away from Holly, dropping his arm from the wall. It felt to him like someone had flipped on the lights and it was way too bright, making it hard for his vision to adjust.

"I should get back to Jenna," Holly mumbled, immediately saddened that their moment had evaporated with the intrusion.

He just nodded, and held open the door for her, scanning the area as they walked through the door.

"Sorry I was gone so long," Holly apologized to her friend.

"No worries. Billy's kept me company. I figured you got detained by a certain someone."

Looking over Jenna's shoulder toward the front door, Holly rolled her eyes.

"What?" Jenna asked with a laugh.

"A couple of the new waitresses from Maguire's just walked in, and one of them is always hanging all over Aiden. Ugh. If you don't mind, I don't want to stick around to watch."

Jenna nodded. "I think we've had enough excitement in this place for one night."

"Flipping understatement," Holly agreed. "Do you want to check out one of the other bars? There's a bunch of places we can go."

"Don't think I'm weird, but you know what I really want to do? I want to go to that ice cream place we passed, get a giant waffle cone, with sprinkles," she added. "And then the part you're going to think is really, really crazy, I'd rather go back to your house and hang out with Mia. She is hysterical."

Holly laughed. "She is very amusing. Especially when she's with her best friend, Seth. This weekend you'll meet him and his partner, who is my Uncle Henry."

"Let's go get ice cream," Jenna urged. As they were about to work their way through the crowd, she asked, "Who's the one who hangs all over Aiden?"

Holly motioned her head to the right. "The short one with the purple and blonde hair."

As they passed by, Jenna handed her empty plastic cup to the purple-haired girl, who took it from her, and was left with a perplexed look on her face, as if she were asking, *Why did this chick just give me her cup? And why did I take it?*

"You look like you need something to hang onto," Jenna told her over the noise, and kept walking.

As they stood in line waiting for ice cream, Holly felt her phone vibrate in her back pocket.

He left as soon as he realized you were gone. I think crowds really put him on edge. Once he knew you were gone, he bailed

Is that purple-haired girl still there?

Yeah, I think she's looking around for Aiden

Ugh!

A wave of nausea hit Holly as she silently hoped the girl didn't follow him home — and that she didn't know where the extra key was hidden.

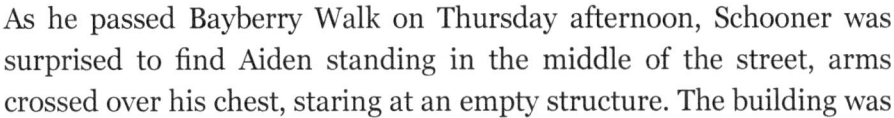

As he passed Bayberry Walk on Thursday afternoon, Schooner was surprised to find Aiden standing in the middle of the street, arms crossed over his chest, staring at an empty structure. The building was like many others on Fire Island, at nearly a century old, the cedar shake shingles had taken on a rustic appearance, having been weathered by the harsh winter elements, sun, and salt. What differentiated this place from the other buildings on the street, was a porch running its entire length, and the fact that it was vacant.

Approaching slowly and stopping a few feet away, so as not to catch him off guard, Schooner too stood in the middle of the road, crossed his arms, and regarded the building.

"What do you see?" he eventually asked Aiden.

"Tapas."

"Yeah." Schooner nodded. "That would absolutely work. Nothing else like it around. Perfect for a beach community. I like it."

Smiling, Aiden nodded.

"Mia would love a tapas place. You just need to feed her olives and she's happy." Schooner laughed at the thought.

"And a nice Albarino to go with them. Spain's always had such great wines."

Could work, thought Schooner. Aiden's knowledge of wines and his palate had been well developed over years in the restaurant industry, and he certainly had the purchasing expertise and contacts.

"I'll let you get back to your envisioning." Schooner walked away. His weekend duffel slung over his shoulder. He'd been in the city for three days and was anxious to get home and see Mia and the kids, including his oldest daughter, whose neck he was very interested in seeing up close and in person versus on his phone screen.

No one was inside the house when he arrived. Looking out onto the deck, Mia, Holly, Seth, Henry, and Holly's friend, Jenna, whom he hadn't met yet, were all stretched out on lounge chairs soaking up the sun. Nathaniel and Portia were still in day camp.

"Looks like I'm a little overdressed for this party," he said, stepping out onto the deck in a pair of well-worn cargo shorts and a pink, cotton button-down Ralph Lauren rolled at the sleeves, exposing tan, muscular arms.

"I vote you get naked," Seth commented, looking up from his Kindle.

Schooner laughed and bent down to kiss Mia. "Missed you, Baby Girl."

"It's smoochal, Pretty Boy."

"Hello, sweetheart." He walked over to Holly's chair and tipped her head back to inspect her neck. A look passed between the two, but he made no comment, and kissed her forehead. He would talk to his daughter alone later.

"You must be Jenna." Schooner extended a hand to Holly's friend.

"So nice to meet you. My brother has told me so much about you." She couldn't take her eyes off Holly's handsome father.

"It's been fun having him here." He smiled at her.

Still in work mode, he looked across the deck at Henry. "You wanted to talk about Carlsbad?" The facility was in the middle of a remodel and as most construction projects go, they'd hit more than a few unexpected glitches.

"Yeah, let me just run upstairs and grab my laptop."

As soon as they were both inside, Seth looked over at Jenna. "It's okay, you can say it."

Jenna shook her head. "I can't. That's Holly's dad and Mia's husband."

Without looking up from her Kindle, Mia gave her permission. "It's okay, you can say it."

"No wonder why you're so beautiful, Holly."

"Actually, I look like my mom. My brother looks more like my dad."

"Is he married?" Jenna perked up.

"He's engaged. And I would not mess with his fiancée," Holly warned with a smile.

"Understatement," Seth chimed in. "She'll cut you."

"Oh my God, Princess, I can't believe you just said that," Mia admonished her BFF.

"Oh, get over it, BBC. Lily could kick all our asses. That girl is more than a little scary." Seth removed his sunglasses with the sole purpose of rolling his eyes at Mia.

Jenna looked on, amused. "You're right, they are funny together."

The french doors opened, and Henry came back out, "Holly, your dad would like to see you."

"I was afraid of that." She got up from her chair.

"What is he, like The Godfather, where everyone goes in one by one?" Jenna asked, amused.

"I know what ring I'd like to kiss." Seth smiled at Mia.

"Don't hold your breath," she shot back.

"Years of practice, I've learned to breathe through my nose."

Mia picked up a tube of La Mer suntan lotion and threw it at his head. Hitting him smack on the ear.

"Ow, that hurt, you bitch." He looked at the tube. "Ooo, La Mer, the good stuff. Thank you." He slipped it into his beach bag and went back to reading.

"Jenna, please accept my apology on behalf of these two morons." Henry sat back down and picked up a bottle of water.

"Is it always like this?" she asked, totally amused by the rapport and camaraderie.

"Believe it or not, they're actually on their best behavior right now." He shook his head.

"You rang?" Holly asked her father as she entered the house, referencing Lurch from the old *Addams Family* reruns her dad used to watch with her and Zac when they were kids.

Schooner smiled at the reference and at the memory of his two older children laughing like crazy, throwing themselves against the back pillows of the couch, whenever Cousin Itt or Uncle Fester came on.

"You look good. I don't know what you looked like a week ago, but I feel better now that I've seen you and I can see that you're alright."

"I am okay, Dad. It was just one of those perfect storm situations and I really don't think Aiden is violent. I just know he would never physically abuse me. The only one I worry about him hurting is himself."

"Do you think that's a possibility?" Schooner's brow furrowed. That was an alarming thought.

"Honestly, I don't know. He really hasn't let me close enough to find out." Pulling a peach out of a glass bowl on the table, she watched it as she rolled it back and forth between her hands. "All I know is that twenty veterans commit suicide every single day and Aiden is definitely suffering from PTSD."

"Hopefully therapy will give him strategies to help manage things."

"I hope so, Dad. We saw him last night at Castaway and some guy grabbed me and I thought Aiden was going to smash his head into the bar. There's an anger in him now that there wasn't before. Aiden was the diffuser, the roll-with-the-punches guy, the one who could calmly handle any situation, even with the biggest jerk. I've seen him do that a million times. Now you can see the fuse is just poised for him to blow. I'm not going to lie, it's more than a little scary. He's much more aggressive. Zero to sixty immediately. Things escalate fast, and that's not Aiden."

"Are you seeing anger management issues?" Schooner probed.

"I don't really know. Like I said, he won't let me close enough."

"Well, I think that's pretty typical with PTSD. Pulling away emotionally from people, that is."

"I feel like a puppet on a string. One minute he's being sweet and protective and the next he's pushing me away. My head is spinning, and I just don't really know how to act or what to do."

Schooner just listened and nodded. They sat silently for a moment and he finally asked, "What do you want?"

"I want to be part of his healing."

Schooner's heart ached for his daughter, but he understood it would be impossible to let someone she loved so deeply flounder and not try and help. "Here's what I think."

Holly listened attentively, her father's advice was usually very sound.

"I think you need to heal, too." His statement was very matter-of-fact and he continued, "What has happened to Aiden is beyond comprehensible. Without knowing specific details, I think we can safely assume he has been to Hell and is probably to some degree still trapped there. But what has happened to Aiden has had a profound effect on you, too, sweetheart. Whether he wants you to be part of it or not, you already are, and I think he might know that, at least on some level, but admitting it adds another level of guilt for him."

Holly stopped rolling the peach and looked up at Schooner. "Yes. You are right. It has. It has had a huge effect on me. I feel like I'm feeling his pain, Dad. And it hurts so deeply I can't even describe it." It was clearly an epiphany for Holly as she took a deep breath, pondering her father's words.

"How do you feel about you finding someone to talk to, to help give you strategies to cope with some of this? These are some big issues, one's you've never dealt with before, and having someone trained to talk with might give you some clarity and grounding, so that you don't feel like you're blowing in the wind with all this, which is what I'm hearing from you. I think there are some emotional boundaries you might need to establish as you work through this with Aiden."

"That might be a good idea. I'll definitely think about it," she promised.

"And speaking of Aiden. I ran into Mr. McManus on my way home tonight."

"Oh, you did, did you?" Holly sat up straight, alert, eager to hear about her father's encounter with him. "And what did he have to say for himself?"

"Tapas." Schooner smiled.

"Tapas?" Holly was lost, she tossed the peach back into the bowl and looked at her father questioningly.

He nodded. "Tapas. You know the place with the really nice porch on Bayberry Walk?"

"Yeah."

"He was standing in the street, looking at the place and I asked him what he was thinking. And he's thinking he'd like to turn it into a tapas place."

"Tapas would be good. There's nothing like it out here. But wouldn't it be expensive to buy or rent the building and renovate it into a restaurant?" She knew her father would know about this, considering how many Level 9 facilities he had built.

Schooner nodded. "I would think it would take a significant amount of capital."

"Well, I hope it happens. I think it would be good for him to throw himself into a project like that. I bet that would help him feel more connected. I don't think he feels very connected right now."

"I think you're right, sweetheart."

Schooner hoped the seed he had planted in Holly's mind about getting into therapy was something she would start to consider seriously. He was worried about her and knew he didn't have all the right answers. But he did know one thing, he knew his daughter, and could see she was suffering deeply, and if there was such a thing as PTSD by proxy, she had it.

Over a week had passed, and after the moment they had shared in the hall by the offices at Castaway, Holly thought for sure she'd hear from Aiden, and that they'd have the opportunity to talk. But there had been radio silence. Compulsively, she checked her phone for texts and emails that never came. Midweek, she and Mia took the kids to Maguire's for steamers, but it turned out to be Aiden's night off. The purple-haired waitress wasn't working that night, either.

And now it was the start of another weekend, and as she waited for Pierce's ferry to arrive, her mind and stomach both churned from conflicting emotions gnawing at her heart.

Should she have uninvited Pierce? No! He had proven to be a good friend and uninviting him because her ex had a baseless dislike for him would just be wrong.

Should she be more empathetic to Aiden's feelings about this? Aiden had left her for another woman. He had been sleeping with that other woman. Pierce was just a friend. A friend whom Aiden was unfoundedly jealous.

Should she have texted him during the week to initiate a conversation. She didn't even have his new cell phone number.

Should she just have stopped by his place? Did he need his space? Or was space the worst thing in the world for him? If she stopped by, she was again the one making the overture to connect. If he really wanted to connect, he'd seek her out. *He* actually had her cell number and could contact her, if he wanted.

But obviously he hadn't wanted to.

If he wanted to see me or talk to me, I'm easy to find.

"Whatcha thinkin'?" Pierce whispered in her ear.

Holly jumped. She hadn't even seen him approach and there he was, standing toe to toe with her.

"Hi." She smiled at her friend.

As Pierce pulled her in for a big hug, all Holly could think was he's hugging me whether I want him to or not. And she wondered, is there anything that happens that *doesn't* remind me of Aiden?

"Oh, man, I missed this place. I've always loved playing the Hamptons in summer, but this has really spoiled me."

"Well, it's good to have you back." She patted him on the shoulder as they started toward the house. "Good trip out? Even though you had to do it sober."

"Yeah, just put on my headphones and chilled."

Crossing Bayberry Walk, Holly couldn't help but look down the street at the building with the porch, hoping that Aiden was moving forward with his dream, and feeling tremendous guilt that Pierce was with her, and that Aiden might find that upsetting. She was already wondering if the weekend family dinner at Maguire's was something she and Pierce should miss. He'd already had a few dinners there with the family on weekends before Aiden came back, so he would know something was off. *He's just a friend. Get out of your head with this stuff,* she silently screamed at herself.

"I thought maybe we'd take a walk over to Ocean Bay Park tonight to The Schooner Inn and see Mikey."

"I like that idea. I had so much fun playing there. That is such a great crowd."

"I think we're grilling lobsters tonight."

"I definitely showed up on the right night." He looked around, breathing the sea air in deeply. "It is so good to be back. Jenna loved it out here."

"Jenna loved my dad." Holly laughed.

"I love your dad. We're having a total bromance."

"You really are." She looked at him. "It's sick."

"She told me she wants in on the adoption."

"Hey, I just need to stop here at the bakery. I promised Heckle and Jeckle I'd bring them back cookies."

"Who?"

Holly laughed. "Family joke. Zac always calls Natie and Po Heckle and Jeckle."

"Yeah, I can see it. Totally fits them." Looking at the pastry cases and menu, Pierce pointed to a tray of bars with roasted marshmallows on top. "What are those?"

"Those are a mouth orgasm. They're s'more brownies."

"Hey, let me buy the stuff for the kids and dessert for everyone tonight. It's the least I can do for freeloading half the summer."

"I'm sure that will be much appreciated and devoured. If you get the crumb cake, Mia might expedite the adoption papers, and she'll definitely be your best friend for life."

"And what about you? What does it take to make you my best friend?"

"Well, that's pretty obvious." Looking at him, she laughed. "A bottle of Jack."

As they walked out with a filled bakery box, Pierce commented, "So, I hear my sister met Aiden."

"And you're about to right now," she muttered only loud enough for Pierce to hear.

Just several yards away, turning off Denhoff Walk on his way to Maguire's, was Aiden, dressed for work in black pants and a light blue shirt.

"Hi." Holly's smile came naturally. It was impossible not to smile. Just like it was impossible for her to slow down the racing beat of her heart.

Aiden's face lit up for a second, until he processed what was going on and the light immediately extinguished. He acknowledged Holly with a nod of his head and silence, walking past them, and not looking back.

"I just ruined his day," Pierce commented.

Holly couldn't help but hurt for him.

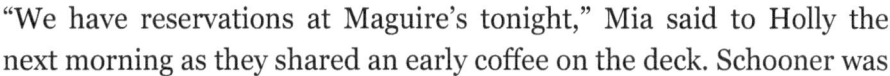

"We have reservations at Maguire's tonight," Mia said to Holly the next morning as they shared an early coffee on the deck. Schooner was already on the tennis courts for a match, Henry had gone to a sunrise yoga class, and everyone else was still sleeping.

"I know. I don't know what I should do. Even though Aiden knows Pierce is out here, I don't want to rub it in his face."

"I know. And if you don't want to go tonight, I totally get it."

"But there's another part of me, Mia, that says, why should I miss a family dinner because Aiden doesn't like one of my friends?" She stared out at the ocean, hoping she'd have some clarity.

"Holly, whatever you decide. There's no right or wrong here. If Aiden sees you with Pierce, he's not going to be happy. But if you and Pierce skip dinner, and we're all there, that might make his imagination run even wilder and cause him even more anxiety."

Pulling her hair up into a messy bun, she shook her head. "I hadn't even thought about that," she paused. "But that is under the assumption that he cares."

"I think we're past assumption on that. I wonder how his therapy is going." Mia raised the steaming mug to her lips.

"No clue. He lets me in for really brief snippets, where I have this beautiful glimmer of hope, and then boom, the door slams in my face again. I know I said this before, but I feel like a puppet on a string." Holly took her hair down, twisted it again, and put it back up into another messy bun.

"And in this case, the puppet master is the one hanging on by a string. So, you do know what that means, don't you?"

"That I need to take back control?" It was a question and not a statement.

Mia nodded.

"Okay, so there's my answer. Pierce and I will be joining the family for dinner tonight." Picking up her mug, Holly took a sip, crinkling her nose. "Does this taste off to you? Is the milk bad?"

"No. Tastes fine to me." Mia took another sip. "I need to get Natie and Po up." Mia stood and stretched. "Looks like we've got another perfect beach day on our hands." Smiling at Holly, she laughed, "Paradise does not suck," and she turned and went into the house.

It sucks if you're inside my head. It sucks if you're on an island that is nothing more than a large sandbar and the man you love spends day after day ignoring your existence. It sucks if you know he's emotionally drowning and you can't get close enough to save him. Maybe paradise is not all it's cracked up to be.

Walking past the bar area with her heart squarely lodged in her throat, Holly caught Aiden's eye, giving him a smile and a small wave, which he returned with an acknowledging nod. She noted his look harden the moment he saw Pierce with her family.

Sheila greeted them to take a drink order. "Hello, handsome," she greeted Schooner, "and handsome's family. Oh, and version 2.0. Welcome back."

They all laughed at the greeting and Holly relaxed a little.

"Are you okay here," she asked Pierce, not having considered that dinner in the same place where her ex worked might be uncomfortable for him.

"Yeah, I'm fine. No worries."

Sheila returned with their tray of drinks, when she came to Holly, she placed before her the iced tea she'd ordered and a tall, frozen drink the color of sunshine.

"What's this?" Holly asked.

"That is from the bartender. He said to tell you it's called a Malibu Barbie and that it's made with Malibu rum."

"A Malibu Barbie." She laughed, shaking her head. "Tell the bartender he's an ass..."

"Hole." Aiden finished her sentence, surprising her when he walked up. "Not the first time you've called me that." He smiled.

"Something new for you to try." He handed Schooner a glass of scotch.

Lifting the glass, Schooner studied the color and clarity, before placing the glass under his nose, his eyes serious as he tried to identify the whisky's notes.

Looking up at Aiden, he said, "Oak and smoke are the first things I'm picking up, but there's something else. What is that?" He placed the glass under his nose again and took another whiff. "Coastal?"

"Very good." Aiden was impressed. "Coastal peat."

Taking a sip of the scotch, Schooner let the initial sweet tone wash over his tongue, savoring it as it turned peppery, and enjoying the single malt's lingering, smooth finish.

"That is nice," he concluded. "What is it?"

"It's a Talisker thirty-year-old, matured in both American and European refill casks."

Schooner took another sip, appreciating the subtleties of the scotch. "That is really special. Thank you."

"I thought you might appreciate it." He looked at everyone sitting around the table with his gaze finally settling on Holly. "Enjoy your dinner, everyone."

As he went to leave, Portia called to him, waving him over and motioning for him to bend down where she whispered something in his ear that made him smile and give her shoulders a little squeeze before leaving.

Watching the entire encounter, from the moment Sheila had delivered the drinks to Aiden's departure, all Pierce could think was that Holly's ex had just pissed all over the table, from one end clear to the other, marking his territory, and making it abundantly clear that this was *his* family. Everything that had just occurred had been for Pierce's benefit.

Territorial motherfucker, mused Pierce.

"Excuse me," Pierce got up from the table after they'd placed their order, heading toward the men's room, before diverting to his actual destination.

Taking a seat on a bar stool, he watched as Aiden greeted customers, mixed drinks and traversed the entire length of the bar, several times, without acknowledging his presence.

"What does it take for a Bun Man to get a drink?" he asked as Aiden was passing him for the third time.

"A different bar."

"You're a funny guy."

Aiden finally stopped and crossed his arms over his chest. "What do you want?"

"Besides Holly?" Pierce baited. Craning his neck to look past Aiden at the line-up of local craft beers lining the bar, he said, "I'll take an Illegally Blonde."

"Why am I not surprised." Grabbing a cold bottle from the cooler, Aiden flipped off the cap, and set the dark Belgian blonde in front of Pierce. He didn't offer the man a glass. "Should I put this on Schooner's bill?"

Smirking at the barb from Holly's ex, he picked up the bottle and took a healthy swig as he slid off the bar stool. Reaching into the pocket of his shorts, he threw a ten on the bar. "You might want to remember what I drink." Inferring Aiden would be seeing more of him. "Oh, and keep the change."

Game on, thought Pierce. *Fight for her, man.*

Do you know where Aiden is?

Holly pulled her buzzing phone out of her beach bag and read Billy's text.

No. The last time I saw him was over the weekend at Maguire's. I haven't seen him since.

Did he mention anything to you about going away?

No, but I didn't really talk to him. With Pierce out here over the weekend, I only saw him the night we were at Maguire's. *And that was damn uncomfortable,* she thought.

We were both off today and were supposed to go golf at Bergen Point in West Babylon. We had plans to take the 10:10 ferry and he totally no-showed.

Oh wow. That doesn't sound like Aiden. Officially worried.

And I just ran into Sheila and she told me that before he left work on Saturday night, he pulled himself off the schedule for the rest of the week and he's not working this weekend either. I can't imagine he'd give up his weekend shifts.

Red flag. Holly knew from her years at Maguire's that weekend tips were more than most people made a week in full-time jobs. People fought for those primo shifts.

What about at Matthew's? Maybe he picked up extra shifts there??? She was hoping there was some simple explanation. But blowing off a scheduled trek to the mainland for a round of golf was sticking in her craw as something was wrong.

I checked over at Matthew's, same thing there. Just pulled himself off the schedule with no explanation and didn't even try to grab slots for Labor Day weekend. That's weird shit.

Over holiday weekends they would make a ridiculous amount of money and everyone fought for those shifts.

That is weird. Did you call him?

Yeah. No answer.

Did he say anything about going away? Maybe he went to see his family??? She ventured another guess.

He didn't mention anything at all about going away. Can you give him a call or text him? He might answer a message from you.

I don't have his number. She confessed.

631-485-3699

**Do you want me to try his parents too? (Not that they
return my calls either)**

**Yeah. I'll go bang on his door. See if he's around
and I'll let you know. Maybe I can see in through the
window. I'll let myself in if I have to.**

Between last time and the fear of finding something devastating,
she was glad that Billy was going to be the one to check. *Don't even
think that.* She banished the thought from her mind.

**Ok. Let me know. And I'll let you know if I get in touch
with him,** she promised.

Laying her phone in her lap, Holly stared out at the ocean, trying to
quell the fear that was beginning to choke her. *Be okay, Aiden. Please
be okay.* She knew this was exactly what he didn't want for her, the
worry that layered on top of everything else. And this was a piece she
hadn't factored into the equation. *I feel sick,* she thought as she finally
dialed his number. It rang a few times and went to voicemail.

*Leave a message or hang up? He'll know it's me anyway by my
phone number.*

"Hey, Aiden, it's me. Billy gave me your number. I hope you don't
mind. He's a little worried about you. He thought you were meeting
for golf and you didn't show up and you're not on the work schedule
anywhere. So, umm, just let me or Billy know you're okay. Okay? Umm,
well, that's it. I hope everything is alright."

She then texted the same number. **Is everything okay? You
were supposed to meet Billy for golf. We're a little worried.
Get in touch with one of us.**

Fifteen minutes later, her phone buzzed with a text. Taking a deep
breath, she looked at her phone. It was from Billy.

Looked in the windows. Didn't go in. He's not in there.

Could you see into the bathroom or closet? She couldn't believe she was typing such a thing.

Oh, shit, Holly. I didn't. Should I go back? I think the bathroom door was open so I would have seen something.

Breathing a sigh, but nowhere near totally relieved, she responded, **Yeah, you're probably right. I left him a voicemail and a text. I'll try his parents now.**

As with their son, she hit another voicemail. "Hi, Mr. and Mrs. McManus, this is Holly Moore. It's Wednesday morning and I'm looking for Aiden. Can you please have him get in touch with me. Thanks. I hope you are both well."

And now the waiting game begins.

She knew she'd be checking her phone incessantly 'til either she or Billy heard from him.

Sitting on a barstool in Castaway, Holly confessed to Billy and Maddie, "I am so worried about him. I can't eat. I can't sleep. I've left him so many messages that I feel like a stalker. Do you think we've made a huge mistake not reporting him missing to the police? I feel like we're missing something."

"Maybe he just needed a vacation and went someplace without cell service." Maddie conjectured trying to put a positive spin on the situation and allay Holly's fear.

"I feel so guilty. I had Pierce out here last weekend. I'm just so afraid that it really upset Aiden. I know when we were having dinner with my family at Maguire's that Pierce went into the bar to get a beer, and now I'm wondering if something went down between the two of them that made Aiden leave." Holly was wracked with guilt, her emotions slaughtering any positive thought in her overtired brain.

Maddie put a steaming mug on the bar in front of Holly. "Drink," she ordered, in a motherly tone.

"What's this?"

"Chamomile tea. It will help you feel a little calmer. Your nerves are frayed, Holly."

When Billy walked away to serve a customer, Holly confided, "Maddie, I haven't slept in three days. I am so worried that he drove off someplace remote and did something to himself and I know I should be doing more to find him. I just don't know where to look or what to do. And on top of that, I have the worst PMS ever. I want to bite everyone's heads off. I yelled at Natie this morning over nothing. He was doing this stupid grabbing boobies thing that the kids were doing in camp, and I just went crazy on him. And now I feel like crap about that, too. I shouldn't have yelled at him."

Maddie just shook her head. She had never seen dark circles under Holly's eyes before. "There was nothing in his apartment that indicated where he might have gone?"

"I didn't go in. Billy looked through some of the windows and said everything looked okay and that Aiden wasn't in there."

"But neither of you have been inside to see if there is any clue as to his whereabouts? Something he might have left."

Holly shook her head.

"Before you call the police, you should go over there and look around. Maybe there's something. A brochure for someplace or some directions he wrote down or a phone number. Maybe he's having a tough time and checked himself in someplace. You really need to go over there." When she saw Holly tense up, she added. "Take Billy with you. I'll cover for him. If there's anything that feels wrong to either of you, call the police immediately."

"We have to stop for a second," Holly told Billy on the walk over to Aiden's place. "I can't breathe." Putting her hands on her knees, Holly took deep breaths to calm herself.

Rubbing her back, Billy tried to talk her down. "Just breathe, Holly. It's going to be okay. For all we know, maybe he's back and will answer the door and then we'll give him hell. I really don't think we're going to find anything devastating."

Nodding, Holly straightened up and slowly blew air out through her lips. As she looked at the surrounding houses, she realized they were already close to Aiden's place and that she had no recollection of anything they had passed on their walk over there.

"Are you okay to go on?"

Again, Holly nodded.

"Maybe he was just afraid I was going to pummel his ass on the golf course and couldn't take defeat. You know how competitive he can be. He hates losing. He's an asshole to play poker with." Billy tried to lighten the mood as they reached the house and followed the path around the side to Aiden's entrance.

"Aiden, are you in there?" Billy knocked on the door hard. "Aiden, open up."

When they were met by silence, he reached behind the terracotta planter and found the key. Trying one more time, he banged on the door, the sound reverberating. "Aiden, open the door." When there was no response, he inserted the key in the lock. Pushing the door open, he once again called out Aiden's name, before flicking on a light switch on the wall, as he stepped inside. "Hey Aiden," he called out again.

Stepping in behind him, Holly scanned the studio. Nothing appeared to be out of place. His bed was made, there were no dishes in the sink, no clothes hanging on the backs of chairs, the place was spotless, which was typical of Aiden.

Holly pointed toward the bathroom, the door was ajar with a partial view, and Billy made his way over. "Aiden," he said again as he inched the door fully open and flicked on the light. Stepping in, he took a deep breath, and said a silent prayer, before pulling open the shower curtain. The tub was empty. Aiden's hair and bathing products neatly lining the tub's edge.

Both Billy and Holly audibly sighed, the first wave of relief washing over them.

"The closet." Holly said, pointing to a door along the wall. She turned away as Billy yanked open the door to the last place they hadn't looked.

"That motherfucker," Billy declared.

And Holly felt her heart sink. *Oh God, no!*

"Who the hell color coordinates their shit in their closet? That's just plain weird. All his blues are together, all his whites. What a fucking girly-man. I'm gonna rip his ass over this one." He laughed. "Who even fucking hangs up their clothes?"

Holly began to laugh, as tears streamed down her face and a second wave of relief washed over her. The worst of her fears had just been allayed. "He's very organized. Between the Army and running restaurants, everything has its place."

"Yeah, well, there's a difference between organized and anal. When I see him, the dude's gonna take some shit from me on this." Billy closed the closet door.

"The dude's going to take some shit from me, too." Holly shook her head. *Where the hell are you, Aiden?*

"Holy shit, Holly, look over there." Pointing across the room was the first of their answers.

They both walked over to a small, worn, wood corner table. Sitting on top of several magazines was a cell phone, plugged into a wall outlet next to the table.

"Is that his phone? Did he leave it here charging?"

Pulling out his own cell, Billy called Aiden's number. They both jumped when the phone rang, its screen lighting up, even though that is what they were anticipating.

"So, maybe it's just as simple as he left his cell phone on the charger and forgot it when he left for wherever he was going," Holly surmised.

"Yeah. That definitely could be it." Billy looked relieved. "And now it makes total sense why he wasn't returning messages."

They had both been so geared up to discover the absolute worst, that the possibility of their friend just forgetting his phone while it was charging, was something that hadn't presented itself into the realm of thoughts that had been haunting them for several days.

"I wonder where he is."

Holly just shrugged and shook her head. Looking over at the bed, she couldn't help but think about the last time she was here — the storm inside the room had left more debris in its wake than the violent thunderstorm that swept across the island that night.

He loves me. He loves me not. He loves me. He loves me not. The childhood flower petal game played in her head.

Aiden, where are you?

Staring at the perfectly made bed, a large, spiral-bound notepad caught her eye. It felt out of place to Holly, laying on the nightstand, askew, as if it had been haphazardly tossed there, defying the straight lines and right angles of everything else on the bed and nightstand. As she approached, Holly was surprised to see the manufacturer's label *Sketch*.

Grabbing the sketchbook off the nightstand, she sat down on the edge of the bed. His side of the bed. As she ran her right hand over the cover, she felt as if opening it might be an intrusion Aiden wouldn't want. *But if he's in trouble and this contains an answer to helping him, I'll be mad at myself for leaving a stone unturned.*

Gently, she opened the pad. The first page was blank, and she guessed that was so the drawings would not smear against the cover. The paper was thick and textured, a warm white in color versus the stark white of computer paper. Flipping the page, she gasped at what was before her eyes.

"What is it?" Billy asked.

"It's a drawing. A rendering of a restaurant."

Billy sat down next to Holly. "Wow. That's really beautiful." He studied the intricate pencil drawing. "I didn't know Aiden could draw."

"Neither did I." She was shocked. How could she have been with the man for so long and not know he possessed such a fine talent.

Billy pointed to the corner. "He's initialed it."

There in broad, confident pencil strokes were the initials *ASM*. Aiden Shaun McManus.

"And these notes are definitely his handwriting," Holly pointed out. Looking at the notes in Aiden's distinctive hybrid of print and cursive.

The drawing clearly laid out his vision for his tapas restaurant. The entire length of one wall was a bar lined with barstools and set up for dining, the back of the bar ran to the ceiling with patches of exposed brick and a large window at the center giving patrons a view of the kitchen. The opposite wall of the restaurant appeared to house a glass wine cellar. The detail in the drawing was exquisite, down to potted palms placed throughout the main dining room. Hints of color were added sparingly, bringing the drawing to life.

Slowly she flipped the page and the next one was blank. Turning that, they came to the second drawing. The weathered cedar shingle outside of the building with the porch running the entire length.

"That's the place on Bayberry," Billy commented.

"Yes, the space where he wants to open his tapas bar." He had added ceiling fans and palm trees to the porch. All the tables had little kerosene lamps. Again, this rendering was signed *ASM*.

The next drawing laid out the kitchen from prep area to the pass and included the deep freeze. Aiden had made notes about the foot traffic flow of staff in the kitchen.

"Are you thinking what I'm thinking?" Holly asked Billy.

He smiled. "I don't know. What are you thinking?"

"I'm thinking a man who has obviously invested a lot of time and thought in putting this together is someone who is hopeful. Someone with a plan. A guy who is looking toward the future."

Billy nodded. "You're absolutely right." He stared at the picture for a moment and then asked, "Are there anymore?"

"I don't know. Let's see." The next page was blank and so she turned it over.

The next drawing was the simplest of the renderings. Facing the entrance, it appeared the wood-paned double doors presently on the building had been replaced by what looked to be flat, distressed wood doors with small rectangular windows set high. The windows themselves were covered with ornate bars and Aiden had noted they were black wrought iron.

Above the entrance was a rectangular sign, the restaurant name appearing in thick, bold calligraphic-like letters. **Acebo**

Trying to control the corners of her lips from being drawn down by the quivering muscles of her chin, Holly was beyond holding it together.

"Is that a made-up word?"

Holly shook her head. "It's Spanish."

"What does it mean?" He looked up at her, but her eyes remained focused on the drawing.

"Holly. It means Holly."

They both jumped at the sound of one of Holly's tears going kamikaze and splatting on the paper in her lap.

"Holy shit." Billy instinctually grabbed the pad, causing the tear to roll a little farther than its original landing spot, already blurring the restaurant name.

"Put it down and don't touch it. We need to let it dry by itself," she instructed.

"Damage is done. That was one big-assed tear."

"Shit." She looked at it. "Maybe after it dries, I can try to fix it with a pencil and eraser, but if we try and touch it now, it will smudge more."

Billy looked at his watch. "I've gotta get back to Castaway."

"I'm going to wait for this to dry. I'll lock up and put the key back when I leave."

"So, what should we do? Do you want to call the police, or should we wait out the weekend and if he's not back on Monday, we'll regroup?"

Holly nodded. "I think that's a good idea. I mean, I could be wrong, but after being here and knowing he was probably charging his phone and forgot to grab it, and then seeing the drawings, I feel like he's okay. AWOL, but okay."

"I'll text if I hear anything," Billy promised, as he opened the door.

"Same here." Holly got off the bed and locked the door after him and then went back to look at the **Acebo** drawing.

She felt herself get choked up again and stepped away, afraid another tear would go splat and do even more damage.

"*Acebo*? And you don't love me? You are so full of, as you would say, malarkey, McManus. Who names their first restaurant after their ex? Umm, I'll tell you. No one. No one names their business after their ex." Stepping back to look at the rendering again, she shook her head and smiled. "Let me do this with you, Aiden. We should be building this dream together."

Sitting back down on his side of the bed, she opened the nightstand drawer and immediately saw the tin of artist's pencils and a green rectangular eraser. Pulling them out, she placed them on the table.

Grabbing her phone, she dialed his number and watched the phone across the room light up and ring, then waited for it to go to voicemail. "Message 973," she began. "Well, maybe not quite that many, but it feels like it. I'm sitting on your bed right now. Yes, I'm on your bed. Again. I know, I know, you're thinking *I need to change the locks*. Billy and I came over, because we were worried. And you weren't returning calls. And I just wish I knew where you were and that you were okay." She hung up and listened to his phone beep, alerting that there was a new voicemail.

Putting her phone down on the nightstand next to his pencils, the exhaustion following the adrenaline burst she'd had earlier was starting to settle in. As she leaned back against the pillows, the pervasive scent of Aiden comforted and calmed her in a way she hadn't felt in days. Grabbing the top pillow and pulling it to her, she rolled onto her side, hugging the pillow as if her head was on his chest. *I'll just close my eyes for a second while the drawing dries.*

She was disoriented when she heard her phone ringing and it took more than a moment to figure out where she was and where she had put her phone. It was Mia, but by the time she swiped the screen, she'd missed the call. It was 3:30 a.m.

Calling her right back, "Hey."

"Are you okay? Where are you? I woke up and you weren't here."

"Yeah. Sorry. Billy and I came over to Aiden's earlier to see if everything was okay. He's not here. And I guess I fell asleep."

"Any clue as to where he is?"

"No. But it looks like he was charging his phone and forgot it and that's why he hasn't been returning messages."

"I'm glad you are okay. I had a panic moment when I realized you hadn't come home."

"I'm sorry. I just crashed out here. I didn't mean to, I guess I'm just so emotionally fried, that I just passed out."

"I'm glad you're okay."

"Thank you. Sorry I worried you. I guess I'll just go back to sleep here and come home once it gets light out."

"Okay. I'll see you later."

Crawling back into Aiden's side of the bed, Holly turned off the lights before snuggling into his pillow and falling into a deeper, more restful sleep than she'd had in days.

Stepping into his apartment, Aiden put down his leather duffel bag on the chair just inside the door and flipped on the light.

Immediately he tensed at the shock of finding someone in his space, in his bed. It took only a moment to realize that the someone was Holly, and she was fast asleep on his side of the bed, with his pillow hugged to her. Taking a moment to process what he was seeing, he consciously told himself to count to five.

One...this is a situation you were not expecting.

Two...not all unexpected situations are bad or hostile.

Three...this is not a situation that requires you to be on guard.

Four...correct response to this situation does not include anger or fear.

Five...dude, there's a beautiful woman in your bed.

"Someone's been sleeping in my bed." He said aloud, with an amused look on his face. "Goldilocks." He had always loved the way her hair fanned out when she slept. *There's an angel in my bed.*

Closing the blinds to keep out the morning light, the room immediately darkened. Quietly, so as not to disturb his guest, he crossed the main room to the bathroom, splashed water on his face and brushed his teeth. He had dozed a little bit on the redeye, but not enough to feel rested.

He wondered what Holly was doing in his apartment and had she been there the whole time he was gone. Stripping down to his boxers, he lifted the covers, slipping onto the edge of his side of the bed, and moving her body with his toward the center. He carefully reached over her and grabbed a pillow from the other side of the bed.

Turning her head back to look at him, her eyes fluttered, "Aiden. You're back. Are you okay?"

"Yeah, I'm fine. What are you doing here?"

"We were worried about you. Billy and I came over to check on you and I guess I fell asleep."

"You're wearing all your clothes," he whispered, pulling her to him. "I think you're overdressed." Reaching around her, he undid the button and zipper on her jeans shorts and started inching them down her hips.

"I guess I just kinda passed out in them."

"Drinking tonight?"

"No. Coming down off an adrenaline rush. I was scared to come in here. I was afraid maybe you'd hurt yourself."

Those were thoughts he hadn't had in a while, and even though he was at the beginning of his journey with therapy and medication, he wasn't going to that dark a place any longer. But that was not something either Holly or Billy would know. He pulled her closer, burying his face in her hair. "I'm sorry I worried you, Angel."

Rolling over, she looked at him, his face in the shadows. "Where were you?"

"I was out in Los Angeles. I took the redeye home and then got the first ferry back this morning."

"What were you doing out in LA?"

"One of my wine distributors had mentioned me wanting to open a tapas bar here to some restauranteurs in LA who have had a lot of experience with the concept, and when they heard it was on Fire Island, they immediately wanted to meet. It was kind of an impromptu thing."

"How'd it go?"

"Really good." His face couldn't conceal his excitement.

It was a smile she hadn't seen in a long, long time. A smile she used to see all the time, every single day. Reaching up, she gently ran her hand down the side of his face and he leaned into her touch. "I'm so glad you're okay."

"You were really worried?"

"That's an understatement. When you blew off Billy for golf and then didn't answer any messages from anyone, we got really concerned. I even called your parents and left a message for them. We've been going crazy for days, Aiden."

"Crap. I totally spaced out on the golf thing. This trip happened so fast. I literally packed and left for Kennedy Airport in a blur. I was standing in this long-assed security line when I realized I didn't have my phone with me and had left it sitting on the charger. There was no way I could come back out here to get it without it taking three hours, and missing my flight. And honestly, after the initial freak-out of not having it, it was kinda nice to not be tied to it for a few days. It's really kinda freeing from reality." He stopped for a moment to stroke her hair. "My folks are up in Vermont until the end of September, and I doubt they're checking the messages on their home phone. Not that they had any clue I was on the West Coast." Taking her hand from his cheek, he brought it to his lips, kissing her palm. "I had no idea anyone would be worrying about me."

"Aiden, I haven't slept in days. Well, until I got into your bed."

"I'm sorry." Pulling her to him, he held her tight. "I'm really sorry I worried you."

"I don't think you have any idea how many people were worried about you, how many people love you."

"I think you're right. I forget that too often."

She nodded. "Yeah, you do." Snuggling her head into his chest, she added, "Oh, and Aiden, I promise not to enter your apartment again by myself, unless you've given me a key."

"Are you sure that is what you want?"

"I want you to open the door and leave it open long enough for me to walk through." It was clear she wasn't talking about the door to his apartment.

"Holly, you have to understand, I'm not back to me yet. And it's probably going to be a long time before I'm there. If I'm ever fully there. And that frustrates me, so I can only assume it is going to frustrate the heck out of you," he paused, kissing the top of her head. "Is that what you want?"

"It is exactly what I want," she spoke without hesitation.

He shook his head. "I want more for you. And as much as I hate the thought of it, you should go to him. He can give you what I can't."

She knew he was referring to Pierce and wondered what was said in the conversation they'd had in the bar the weekend before. "But I can't give him something you already have. He can't have my heart. Sorry, dude, it's non-transferrable."

His laugh was so hearty, her head jostled on his chest.

The Aiden laugh. She couldn't help but smile. Hearing it felt like a gift. The return of a long-lost friend. *He's coming back. I know it. It may be little by little. But I know I will hear that laugh every day again. I know he can get there. I know we can get there.*

"You know, you're not the only one who got hurt in battle, Aiden. It changed your life and it changed mine. I know you keep saying you don't want this for me, but that ferry's sailed, my friend. It's happened to me, too, and while I've only been focused on how to help you, I haven't even started to acknowledge that I, too, need strategies on how to move forward in a way that is productive." Burrowing her head a little deeper into his chest, she added, "But I do know one thing, I'm in this, Aiden. And it's not just your problem. It's our problem, whether you want to admit it or not, and that is something that needs to be acknowledged in the same way, just like you acknowledged having PTSD."

Lightening the moment, he ran his hand up and down her arm. "Wow. And I thought we were just going to have wild sex." But what she had said was reverberating in his soul. *I have been such a narcissist.*

She swatted his chest and he grabbed her hand, bringing it to his lips.

"You're relentless, you know that." He ran his lips from her forearm to her wrist, then grazed the inside of her wrist with his teeth.

"I do. It's a Moore trait. I'm going to wear you down, so you might as well give in now."

And again, there was that laugh.

"Like I ever stood a chance against you."

"Why would you want to?"

"Good question," he agreed, his lips now on her palm again.

"Aiden, you're used to putting together missions. Well, the new mission is us."

Pulling her hand away from his mouth, he was stunned by her words. So simple, yet something he could easily wrap his head around. *The new mission is us.*

"Mr. McManus, if you choose to accept this mission," he began in a deep, announcer-like voice. Tightening his arms around her, he whispered. "Mission accepted."

Waking up with Holly Moore sprawled across your bed, snuggled onto your stomach like a pillow, doesn't suck, was Aiden's first thought when he woke. Sliding his fingers down a lock of her hair, he stopped, weaving his fingers between the silky strands until his fingertips reached her scalp. Gently he rubbed in a soft, circular motion.

Why would you ever not want this woman in your life, putz?

She stirred, and he stopped massaging her scalp, afraid he'd wake her. She'd told him she hadn't slept in days. He had no idea his trip, and then forgetting his phone, would cause such a chain reaction here in Ocean Beach.

"Don't stop. That felt good."

"I woke you. Sorry about that." But they both knew he wasn't.

Moving her head from his stomach, she crept up onto the pillow next to him. Reaching out, he brushed the hair from her face.

"What's that look you're giving me?" she asked.

"It's not too late to bail." He searched her eyes.

"You accepted the mission." A deep furrow appeared between her brows.

"Yes, I did. But I couldn't live with myself if there wasn't full disclosure."

"Okay, so disclose."

"Angel, most days I don't know whether I'm coming or going. Shit freaks me out that shouldn't freak me out. I'm a lot more paranoid than I ever was and you've seen first-hand how loud noises can totally incapacitate me, even though I know it's damn fireworks or thunder. I'm moody, volatile, and when I retreat into my head, it is dark. Really freaking dark in there. I'm still having night terrors." Taking her chin in his hand, "This is no picnic, Holly. I want you to know what you're signing up for. And I want you to know, you can bail at any time, and I will understand."

"Are you done?"

"Yeah, I mean, that's the gist of it."

"Okay, good. You've warned me. Done. Here's the thing, Aiden. It's no picnic without you. I thank you for the warning, but I think I have a pretty good idea of the situation. Is it going to be tough? Yeah. But it's tough without you. So, I have two words for you."

"What, fuck off?" He smiled.

"No, you asshole." She smiled back. "The two words are mission accepted."

"C'mere you." Pulling her to him for their first kiss since he'd arrived home and crawled into bed with her, there was a tenderness to his touch, so different than the raw angst of the last time they came together. "I'm going to say this, because after the last year and a half it might not be evident. But it's the truth. I love you, Angel. And no, I have never stopped loving you. Lord knows, I tried."

"Promise me you won't do that again. Because seriously, Aiden, I can't go through losing you another time. The pain was everywhere. It was in me. It was surrounding me. It was pressing me down and in, with so much force, from every single angle. I can't live through that again. I can't lose you again. I just can't."

"You know, I'd honestly convinced myself that I've been protecting you. Doing the right thing for you. The day before I left for California, I was telling that to my therapist and he made me dig, and in there was a truth I'd never admitted to myself. I was also protecting me. And I don't really think it was my ego. It was my heart that I knew wouldn't be able to handle losing you. So, look what I did to you. I'm not proud of that, Holly. Honestly, I don't know how you could still love me."

"Well, I do. Still. And I'm not going to lie to you, I'm very scared about getting back together. And it's not the PTSD stuff, Aiden, that scares me, because I know we can work through that and there are resources to help us. What I'm really afraid of is that you'll tell me you don't love me again."

Taking both her hands in his, he brought them up to his lips. "I don't know what the future holds, but I will commit to you right now, that I will never again tell you that I don't love you, because I will never stop loving you. Not ever. And that may be the only thing of which I am absolutely certain. I will love you every day for the rest of my life. I promise. Please believe me." He moved her hands, still within his, to his chest and covered his heart with them. "I know I have to prove it to you and I will."

She was silent. The moment she'd dreamed of for so long was in reality, scary, raw, and painful — three emotions that had never surfaced in her dreams. "I'm so afraid."

Nodding, Aiden gave her a sad smile. "Me, too."

Pulling her hands from his, she held out her right pinky, pointing it at him. Smiling, he locked her pinky in his for a pinky swear.

"Leap of faith?" She was asking him to join her.

"Leap of faith," he committed. Smiling, he brushed the hair from her face. "Now there's only one thing I need to prove."

"What is that?"

"How hard I can make you come."

"Mission accepted." She wound her arms around his neck.

Aiden lifted his arm, looked at his watch and nodded.

"You're looking at your watch? Seriously?" *What the heck is that about?*

"Mmm-hmm. This is going to be so torturously slow, you're not going to remember you missed me," he said with a wolfish grin.

"Yeah, well, then you'd better get started, we've got a lot to make up for." She took his hand and moved it between her legs.

"Feels like you started without me." He smirked.

"For someone who once told me he can't be this close to me without being inside me, you're very late to this party."

"You know I'm good at making a big entrance." He dipped two fingers inside her. "God, you're wet." He noted, slipping in a third finger. "And being fashionably late is a thing, you know."

"I don't know about that." She smiled, trying not to gasp as he found just the right spot and applied more pressure. "I think there's something to be said for coming on time."

"I think it's about time for your first coming."

He smiled, slowly massaging her to the brink with his thumb, then lessening up, and letting her fall back a little from her release, holding it at bay, like a prize she was straining to grasp. When her breathing steadied, he reapplied the pressure, quickly bringing her back to the edge, and swiftly pushing her over. Her sounds filled in the holes he'd been hiding in his heart as her body wracked with quakes.

"And I can't wait to see, and hear, your second coming," he whispered in her ear, nuzzling his nose into the silky strands of her hair.

"I think you should join me. I don't like to come alone."

"Want to know what I want?" he asked.

She nodded, wondering.

"I want to be inside you and just look at you. That's what I want."

Lining herself up, she slowly moved down the mattress, until she could feel him. Opening her legs, she reached down to guide him in, sliding down the length of him and taking him deep inside her.

"Much better," she commented.

Neither one moved. Lying very still, they stared at one another in silence having wordless conversations that spilled their darkest moments, as they uttered words they would never say for fear of scaring the other off. And in silence, they let the words fill pages and create chapters, that they'd one day revisit. But not today. Today's pages were yet to be written.

It was Aiden who finally spoke. "This was my fantasy. This." Except this time, he was in the present. Connected. Something he had successfully avoided since the day he had told her that they were through. What ended that day was any true connection to another human being as he carried out his self-imposed preservation mission of exile.

Wrapping his hands around her bottom, he pressed her to him, as they continued to silently gaze at one another. The pressure, combined with the sensitivity from her first orgasm, and the sublime sensation of him filling her, sent her up the wave a lot faster than she expected, and she propelled herself to the edge by squeezing him.

"It would be really impolite to come without the host." His voice was hoarse.

"Hurry up, because I can't wait."

With that, he flipped her onto her back and pressing her legs back toward her shoulders, plowed into her. "This is so much better than the fantasy." Changing his motion into a circular grind was all he needed to do to bring on the second coming.

"Did I doze off?" Holly asked Aiden across the pillow.

"Doze? You were snoring like a buzz saw," he teased.

"Someone wore me out." Softly, she traced a long scar down his cheek, exhilarated by his comfort when he didn't flinch.

"Get used to it, Angel."

"Can I ask you a question?"

"Anything."

"Right now, you feel like you to me. You know what I mean? But do you find it hard maintaining you? Is it work not to go to a dark place?

"That is a really great question." Pausing to think for a moment before sharing his thoughts, "What I've found so far is being at work for a long stretch of time definitely takes its toll on me. I am totally depleted after a shift. Being in the bars when there's a crowd, I can only do for a limited time and I just have to leave. I'm getting better, with the help of my therapist, in evaluating where I am in a situation. So, like if I feel I'm at a seven, I probably need to bring myself back down to a two, and most likely the best thing for me to do is disengage and be someplace quiet."

Nodding, Holly thought, *this is good to know, so I know when he needs his space, and don't take it personally.* "How do you recharge?" she wondered.

"I come back here. I put on headphones and listen to music or watch the Mets lose, and I draw. That really pulls my focus in and calms and relaxes me." Rolling over, he went to grab his sketchpad from the nightstand to show her his work, but instead was met by the pencil tin and not the pad. Picking up the tin, there was a perplexed look on his face from finding it out of place, not in the drawer. And the sketchbook was not where it was supposed to be.

Seeing his confusion, Holly confessed. "I picked up your sketchpad last night looking to see if there was any information about your whereabouts. I didn't expect to find the drawings, and they were just so beautiful, and I cried on the *Acebo* sign," she admitted. "I was waiting for it to dry and I was going to try and fix it. And that's when I fell asleep."

"You cried on the *Acebo* sign?" He looked both amused and confused.

"I did." She nodded. "One big fat tear hit it like a bullseye. Splat and smudge."

Laughing, he asked, "Why did it make you cry?"

"It's your first restaurant, and a man's first always has a special place in his heart."

"That's why it's the perfect name."

"Aiden..."

"Holly..."

"I have felt like a puppet on a string. And then to see you're naming your restaurant after me, and yet, still telling me to get out of your life, well I just got really emotional. But when I saw that drawing..."

"What?"

"I stopped worrying that something bad had happened to you. I knew you were okay. And I also knew that you loved me. Whether you were admitting it to yourself or not."

"Mostly not. But when I walked in this morning and you were fast asleep in my bed, I was so happy to see you here. And I haven't felt that happy in a really long time. After the great meetings of the last few days, it felt like my lucky streak continued and you were going to be the first person I was going to get to share it with. And nothing could be more right than that."

"The sketchpad is on the counter." She pointed across the room.

"Let me survey the damage." He smiled and ruffled her hair as he got out of bed.

"Nice ass," she commented as he walked away.

"Yours is pretty nice, too." He surveyed the drawing. "Oh, this is easily fixable."

Sitting back down on the bed, he grabbed the eraser and began to work on the drawing.

"Aiden, I've known you for years. We were together every day. How did I not know you have this insane artistic talent?"

"I hadn't picked up my pencils in years." He smiled. "I started drawing again in the hospital after my third surgery. It was really therapeutic." Putting the eraser down on the nightstand, he opened the tin and selected a pencil.

"How many surgeries have you had?" The gap in her knowledge of his life over the past year and a half was sobering and painful. Suddenly she felt like they were strangers for the first time since he'd arrived back home.

He looked up from the drawing. "Nine."

She just nodded. *I don't even know what happened to him. Was he alone? Was he with other members of his squad? Were they injured? Killed? What did he see out there? And can I ask him about it?*

"That was an easy fix. You didn't do too much damage." He looked up and smiled at her, holding the pad for her to see.

I wish everything was such an easy fix, she thought.

"Can't even tell I cried on it."

Putting the pad in its rightful place on the nightstand, Aiden slipped back under the covers. "It's almost two o'clock, but I am so jetlagged. I could definitely take another nap."

"That does sound like a good idea," she agreed. "But first, can you hand me my phone? I need to text Billy and let him know you are home and okay, and I should let Mia know that I'm still alive."

Aiden is home. He was in LA doing a restaurant deal. We'll come over later to see you. She knew Billy would be relieved to see the message.

We? ☺

We. ;-) See you later.

And then to Mia, **I have not been abducted by aliens. Aiden is back. He was in LA working on a restaurant deal.**

Breathing a sigh of relief. Glad he's back and well.

Taking the phone from her hand, he placed it back on the nightstand and pulled her into his chest.

"This is so nice." She settled her head into a comfortable spot.

More than you will ever know, Angel.

It was almost six o'clock by the time they'd showered and got dressed.

"Where to first?" he asked.

"Let's save Billy for later so we can hang out. Are you up for dinner with Mia and the kids?"

He was surprised by the warm feeling that spread over him from just the suggestion. "Yeah. I'd like that."

"Let me text Mia. See if they haven't eaten yet."

Have you eaten? Want to do dinner with me and Aiden?

Only if I don't have to cook.

"Mia doesn't want to cook." Holly looked up from her phone, smiling.

"There's comfort in knowing some things haven't changed." He laughed.

"Should I tell her we'll meet them at The 'Tross?"

The 'Tross?

A bay scallop salad. Say no more. Nathaniel is tying his shoes and then we're out of here.

LOL. Ok. Meet u there.

"Okay, they're leaving now and will meet us there."

"Hey, before we go." He picked up the extra key from the counter and handed it to her. "Put this on your keychain." And opened the door for her.

As he turned away from locking the front door, he reached for her hand and led them down the slate path to the street. Seeing the emotional look on Holly's face as she stepped onto the pavement, he asked, "What?"

She looked down at their joined hands and he tightened his grip.

"I'm still not totally convinced it's not a mistake, that this is not the wrong thing to do to you." He looked up to the sky and sighed. "But I'm happy when we're together, and I've spent so much time not being happy that I don't want to give this up again. I know that may be selfish, and if it is," he looked her in the eyes, "I'm really sorry."

"Have you thought that maybe it's not selfish, that maybe you're happy because it's right?"

"Are you happy?" he asked.

"Honestly?"

"Yeah, honestly." He stopped walking and faced her.

"Honestly, I'm bouncing back and forth between ecstatically happy and scared shitless, without hitting any of the emotions in between. Just those two ends of the spectrum."

Pulling her to him for a hug, he whispered, "Angel, we're on the same page."

"Please don't let me go again."

"Not happening. I'm here for as long as you'll put up with my shit."

Mia was out on the deck working when Holly got home the next morning.

"Hey, there's a fresh pot of coffee if you want some."

"You said the magic word. Do you want me to bring the pot out here to warm yours up?"

"Yes, please," Mia responded while looking at her computer screen and typing.

Holly emerged with a mug for herself and the coffee pot, refreshing Mia's cup before sitting down.

"That was a nice dinner last night," Mia commented, grabbing her coffee and sitting back in her chair.

"It really felt like old times, didn't it?"

"It did, and it seemed seamless between the two of you. You both looked really happy."

Holly nodded, taking the first sip of her coffee and letting the caffeine dissipate the fog still hanging onto the edges of her mind. "I want to be with him more than anything," she started. "But I also want to be realistic, because this whole thing might blow up in my face, so I think I have a healthy amount of skepticism, even though my heart wants nothing more than for us to be together."

"I think healthy skepticism is good."

"Me too. I worry... is this just a manic phase for him because some psychotropic drugs kicked in? How close is he capable of getting in a relationship, or will it end up being a fraction of what it was?"

"I think those are all valid concerns."

"Or maybe I'm just being emotional?" she questioned.

Shaking her head, Mia disagreed. "You've been deeply hurt. I don't think it's unusual to want to protect yourself."

"I really love him, Mia."

"I know, sweetie. And you know what? He really loves you, too. So, yes, there's going to be bumps. Probably some bigger than average ones for you guys. But he is your love. And you are his. And nothing is ever going to change that."

Holly smiled at her stepmother. "He's my Mia."

Flooded with the memory of meeting Mia for the first time, and seeing what her father looked like truly happy, was a moment in time Holly would never forget. That weekend was also her first time on Fire Island, she mused. Never did she ever think this beautiful sandbar would be more to her than a place where her father bought a beach house.

"Yes, he is," she agreed. "He's your one." Laughing at a memory, Mia added, "I remember the first time I realized he had a crush on you. But you were still seeing Jared back then, and I just remember Aiden looking at you like, I can't get that girl off my mind."

Holly laughed, covering her face with her hands. "I totally didn't see it and when I came out here that spring we got together, I asked him if I had a chance with him."

The sip of coffee Mia had just drank sprayed all over her keyboard as she began to laugh. "Oh, shit." She grabbed a napkin and began mopping it up. "Did he laugh at you?"

"I think he was too shocked to laugh."

"I bet he was, because I'm sure he never thought he'd have a chance with you and he was crazy about you from the start."

"I was always really intrigued by him. You know, he was a man, and I'd only been with boys. And he was charming and flirtatious and had this kind of rough edge, but at the same time was so smooth. When he looked at me, I got this feeling that I'd never had before. I think I kind of got shy around him, because this *man* made me feel like I was the sexiest woman on the planet even though we weren't having any provocative conversations or anything."

"He's coming back, Holly. His journey may take a circuitous route, and it would be a mistake to put any kind of time limit on it, because his healing, and yours, for that matter, will come in their own time. But, mark my words, he is coming back to you. And honestly, as he heals, I don't think anything could keep him away."

The front door to the place on Bayberry Walk was open when Schooner passed it on Thursday afternoon. He couldn't remember ever seeing it open before and thought he'd check if anyone was inside. Slowly inching the wood door open created a sound that would have made a horror movie producer proud. Aiden was standing in the middle of the room and looked sharply at the door upon hearing the sound.

"Aiden, so this is the place?" With the sun's glare pouring in from the windows, Schooner wanted to make sure Aiden knew it was him if his face was in the shadows.

"Schooner, hey. Yeah, this is the place." He couldn't contain his smile.

Surveying the main room, Schooner took in the details. "I had no idea it had this vaulted ceiling. I just assumed there was an attic up there. It really opens the space. Wow. So, what are you thinking?"

Uncrossing his arms, Aiden pointed to the long wall. "Bar the full length with a large, rectangular window centered that looks into the kitchen. That's not a load-bearing wall, so I can do it. Kitchen and deep freeze taking up the entire length behind the wall. Restrooms and offices and storage back there. There's a staircase at the back that leads to a small second floor. You know that second pitched roofline on the southeast corner, that's where it is, and I'd put my private office up there."

"So, do you have everything in place to put this together?"

"I'm working on it. I expect to get a draft of the contract within the next few days from the LA group."

"LA group?"

It was clear from his response that Schooner didn't know anything about his trip. "Did Mia or Holly mention that I was out in LA earlier this week with a restaurant group that has done this kind of concept?"

When Schooner shook his head, Aiden realized he probably didn't know about him and Holly either.

"Cut a good deal?"

"I think so." Aiden felt pretty confident.

"I've got great contract attorneys if you need someone to look over the paperwork."

"Oh, yeah, I'd really love to have your guys take a look at it." It was for resources like that where he felt comfortable with Schooner's offer. He knew at some point he would be asked the question, by someone, as to why he didn't turn to Schooner for a partnership. But he knew the one person who would not be asking him the question was Schooner himself. He already knew the answer.

"I'll get you his number. Are you looking to be open for next summer?"

Aiden nodded. "I can do a lot of the work myself, if I can get most of the materials out before late fall. It's a totally enclosed structure. A lot of the guys who work out here, like Billy and Mikey and a couple of the other guys, all our families were in the trades, so electricians and plumbers and tile guys. I think the inspections will hold me up more than anything."

Schooner laughed, thinking of his own building and remodeling experience. "You're probably right."

"I'll show you some drawings I've put together. I'd love your feedback."

"Yeah, my pleasure. So, what are you calling the place?" Schooner asked, taking a last look around.

"*Acebo.*" Aiden waited for a reaction.

Schooner just nodded his head. "*Acebo.* Okay. Good name."

Aiden took a deep breath. *Best he hear it from me*, he thought. "And, Schooner, you kinda missed a watershed week here."

"Oh, yeah, what happened?"

"Holly and I are back together."

Raising his eyebrows, he shook his head and waited a moment before speaking. "It appears I missed quite a bit this week. And I learn more from you than I do from either my wife or daughter."

"I'm sure Holly was just waiting for you to come out here to tell you everything in person. But I'm actually glad I had the opportunity to do it, and that you're hearing it from me," he paused. "I'm sure you have concerns. To be honest, I do, too. I've got a lot to deal with, but I love your daughter."

"Well, that's something we certainly have in common." And with a wave, Schooner turned and headed for the door.

Walking out into the sunshine and onto Bayberry Walk, Schooner smiled and thought *I like that guy,* not even realizing he was thinking out loud.

Stepping onto the deck where his wife and older daughter were stretched out on chaise lounges sunbathing, Schooner took a second to assess the waves and decided the surf was rough enough to be interesting, and after a chat with these two he was going to change into a bathing suit. The tide was coming in, the wind was stiff and steady, and the swells were calling to him.

Lifting a wide-brimmed straw hat off Holly's face, he looked down at his daughter. "I understand I missed a watershed week."

"Watershed week?" She was caught off guard and confused.

"Yeah, watershed. That was Aiden's word."

Snapping out of her fog, "You talked to Aiden?" Holly's surprise was evident.

"The front door to the Bayberry building was open, so I wandered in, and I found him there."

"So, what did he tell you?" she asked nervously.

"Well, let's see. That he met with people in LA who he's going to partner with on the project. That the restaurant's name is *Acebo* and that the two of you are back together. Did I miss anything?"

"No. You're pretty well caught up now." She placed the hat back over her face.

Shaking his head with a smirk, he lifted the hat. "We'll talk more later." And he put it back down covering her face.

"I told him I'd put him in touch with my contracts people when he gets the paperwork in. I'll rest easier knowing he's protected in the deal."

"I wonder why he didn't come to you to talk about a partnership," Mia speculated.

Schooner shook his head. "Not an option for him. And I respect that. He did the right thing and he's going to do just fine. This is his deal. How he makes his mark." There was respect in Schooner's tone.

Holly pulled the hat off her face.

Looking over at his daughter, he added, "And he's going to need to be a self-made man to take on this one. She's pretty high maintenance."

"I am not," protested Holly. "I think I'm pretty down to Earth."

"Yeah, for a rich girl you are," Schooner agreed, with a smile. "But you've never been poor." He gestured to the ocean right in their backyard. "Your family's summer house is located on one of the most exclusive beaches in the United States, you have an Ivy League education. You grew up harborside in Newport Beach. The man's going to need a lot of money to keep you."

Abruptly rising from the chaise lounge, she crushed the brim of the straw hat in her clenched hand. "Well, maybe if you'd sent me to Africa, I wouldn't be so spoiled," she screamed, storming off and slamming the french doors behind her with such force the glass panes rattled.

"What the fuck?" Schooner looked at Mia in disbelief. "That was quite an overreaction."

"Wow."

"I'll give her a few minutes to calm down and then I'll go and talk to her." Bending down to kiss his wife, "I didn't even say hello to you, Baby Girl."

"It's been quite a week."

Laughing, Schooner shook his head. "And just think, I come out here to relax." He looked at the ocean longingly, knowing he wouldn't be getting in it soon enough.

"And just think, *this* is the quiet time, before Natie and Po get home."

"Let me go change and talk to Holly because I want to get into that surf before those two bandits arrive." As he walked toward the door, he stopped and turned to Mia. "And what is it with her and the Africa thing. This is the second time we've heard about it in the middle of a meltdown."

Mia shook her head. "I have no freaking idea."

Stopping off in the kitchen, Schooner grabbed two bottles of cold water and headed upstairs.

"Hey, can I come in?" He knocked on Holly's door. Entering he found her stretched out on the bed, pillow hugged to her chest.

"Yeah."

Schooner sat down on the edge of his daughter's bed. "You've had a pretty emotional week, huh?"

She nodded, and he knew if she spoke, she would cry.

"Are you happy about what happened this week?"

"Very." She nodded and took a deep breath before continuing. "I know we should be together. But I'm also scared. This is the guy who dumped me and broke my heart."

He loved that she was leading with a balanced combination of her head and her heart.

"Building back trust takes time."

"Dad, I think I'm finally just starting to admit to myself what the last year and a half has done to me. I have been out of my mind, insane, crazy, and miserable."

"Come here." He held open his arms and she sprang into them. Tightening his hug around his first born surfaced a thousand memories of comforting her throughout the years, from the loss of beloved pets to the antics of mean girls. He was the parent she ran to, and in whom she confided. "I know you feel like you're on a rollercoaster that is speeding out of control."

"I do. I really do." Her arms tightened around him. No one understood things like her father.

"Okay, just remember, you have the ability to steer, brake, speed up, drive off the rails, if you want to. You have that control."

Opening his embrace, she sat back and met his gaze.

"How'd you get to be so smart?"

He smiled. "You want the truth?"

"Yeah."

"By making mistakes and letting go of my ego enough to admit them and then learn from them."

She shook her head and smiled. "Then you must've screwed up a lot of stuff because you are really smart."

He let out a hearty laugh. "Now you've got my number." Turning serious again, he added, "I can't tell you what to do. There's no right or wrong in this situation. But you know where I'm coming from, you are my princess, and I want the best for you." He had discovered that even in her twenties, she was still his little girl. And although he wanted to protect her from anything that caused her pain, the best thing he could do for her was to be there when she needed him. He had learned from *that* mistake last summer.

"And you don't think that's Aiden?"

"I didn't say that at all. I like Aiden. I actually like him a lot. I don't like what he did to you, and I'm talking about the past year and a half, not the neck thing, even though I don't like that either. I'm hoping that how he handled things with you is a screw-up that he's learned from."

"I really love him, Dad."

"I know you do, sweetheart," he acknowledged. "So, from my conversation with him, it appears he's going to spend the winter out here renovating the building so that he's open for the start of next season."

"We haven't even gotten that far in our conversations yet."

"Winters are rough out here. And with only a handful of people around, I imagine it's rather isolating."

"My reality hasn't extended past what craziness the next twenty-four hours might bring."

He stood and smiled down at his daughter. "There's something to be said for living in the moment."

He was physically more touchy than she remembered him being in the past. *And he was always pretty touchy back then,* she thought.

Tonight at Castaway, there was never a moment where Aiden wasn't touching some part of her. Her hand, her fingertips, an arm slung over her shoulder, or standing close behind her, an arm draped over one shoulder and wrapped around her.

The pre-Labor Day crowd getting a head start before the weekend had the already summer-sized crowd swelling, and with every passing moment, Castaway's crowd thickened.

"I have to work every dinner and night shift over the next few days, including Labor Day." He put his lips close to her ear so that he wouldn't have to shout over the crowd.

"I figured you'd be on." It wasn't a surprise. Every establishment on the island was at full staff on the final weekend of the season. They had worked it together in the past, always ending up exhausted by Tumbleweed Tuesday, when the island became a ghost town.

"Come hang out with me and keep me company, okay?"

"Only if you promise not to make me drink Malibu Barbie's." She smiled.

"Deal." His embrace from behind tightened and she could feel the tension in his body. Craning her neck back to look at him, Holly could see him scanning the crowd.

Tugging at his arm to get him to bend down so that she could whisper in his ear, she asked, "What number are you at?"

"About a six."

"What were you at when we got here?"

"About a two."

"Do you want to head out?" In just the past few days, she'd figured out at least some of the questions that needed to be asked.

"Yeah. Let me finish this drink."

At first, she thought it odd that he'd want to stay with his anxiety on the rise, even to finish a drink, but when he lifted the plastic cup to his mouth, downing the drink like a cold glass of water on a sweltering afternoon, she had her answer.

"Okay, let's get out of here." He was more than ready.

Taking Holly by the hand, he led her through the crowd toward the door, his grip tightening to vise-like as they went along, making it almost unbearable by the time they were out on the street.

"Aiden, you're hurting my hand." She tried to yank away from him, but he didn't respond. "Aiden," her voice was sharp and loud enough for heads on Bayview Walk to turn. Still he didn't respond. "Aiden!" She grabbed his forearm with her free hand.

Turning to her, he appeared totally unaware that she'd been trying to get his attention, regarding her with a questioning look on his face.

"Aiden, you're hurting me." She shifted her gaze from his face to their joined hands.

It took him a moment to process what she was saying before he loosened his grip. "Sorry, I didn't realize..." His voice trailed off. "Why don't I walk you home," he suggested.

"Home?"

"Yeah, I'm just going to go back to my place and get my shit together."

"And you don't want me there?" The hurt in her eyes was unmistakable.

"Nah. I'm just gonna throw on some headphones and draw or something."

"And you don't want me there." This time it wasn't a question. She turned to walk toward home.

Within a few feet, he caught up to her, falling into stride. "Angel, it's not that I don't want you there. This isn't about you, so please don't take it personally. I just need to go into my own space and regroup, you know."

She didn't answer and they fell into an uncomfortable silence as they walked along.

"I guess I just wish you wanted me there no matter what." They'd arrived at the Moore's house.

"We'll get there."

They both feared his words might not be true. And with a quick kiss on the cheek, he was gone before she could respond, never seeing the tears that filled her eyes as she watched him walk away.

Coming in from her run early the next morning, she found Mia sitting alone on the deck drinking coffee from her *Not my circus, not my monkeys* mug.

"Hey, are you just getting home?" she asked.

"No. I was home all night. I just went out for a run."

"You came home last night?" Mia was surprised.

"Yeah, Aiden was having a tough time with the crowds last night and just wanted to go home and chill out." Making a face, "By himself," she added.

"Well, that might be the case for a little bit until he figures out how to integrate you fully into his new reality. It's a change. And change might come a little slower now for him."

"I know. I just want it to be the way it was and sometimes it feels like it and then reality hits and it's clear that things are really different now." Looking up at the hazy sky, Holly wiped away the tears that unexpectedly made their escape. "Ugh, I'm so emotional. I must be PMSing." Pulling her phone out of her running pouch, she scrolled through, looking for something.

"Everything okay?" Mia asked, noting her stepdaughter's furrowed brow.

Looking up from her phone, she shrugged it off. "Yeah, fine," she said with a forced smile.

Not wanting to push it, Mia just nodded, thinking Holly shared something else with her father, whom she was so very much like. They both had a real smile, and if you knew them well enough, it was easy to discern when a smile was real and when it wasn't.

Standing abruptly, she announced, "I'm out of contact lens solution. I'm going to run into town and get some."

"I have plenty if you need to borrow," Mia offered.

"Thanks, but I really need a bottle. I'll get a twin-pack, so I can leave one at Aiden's, too," she said with another fake smile, trying to look as natural as possible. "Anything you need while I'm there?"

"No. I'm good. Thanks." Mia flipped open her laptop and pulled up her email.

As Holly reached the door to the house, she stopped and turned back to Mia. "Is my dad home?"

"No. He has that doubles tournament today."

"Oh, right. I forgot about that," she said absentmindedly. "You sure you don't need anything?"

"I'm good," reiterated Mia and wondered if the same could be said for her stepdaughter.

"Okay, I'll be back in a few minutes."

Just over an hour later, a freshly showered Holly left the house again, this time headed for Denhoff Walk. Oblivious to her surroundings, she practiced lines in her head, scrapped them, tried a new tact, and scrapped that, too, knowing only one thing for certain, that she had no clue as to how her words would be received.

He was standing toe to toe with her, hands on her upper arms, bringing her to a dead halt. "You're in your own world. You didn't even see me walking toward you for an entire block." Smiling, he bent down to place a soft kiss on her lips.

"Wow." She hadn't realized that she had totally spaced out her surroundings, heading toward his house on autopilot. "I was on my way to come see you."

"Well, that's funny, because I was on my way to come see you."

"You were?" She looked surprised.

"Yeah, there's something I need to say to you and something I need to ask you."

"Well, there's something I need to tell you." Her tone sounded absolute.

Aiden immediately tensed, picking up on her stress. He could see it in every muscle in her face, and the way her eyes were darting everywhere, looking at every person who passed.

With emotion swiftly fleeting across her face, his mind spun out of control. *She just can't do this thing with me. Who could blame her? I really fucked up last night, shutting her out like that. I never should have dragged her into my shit to start with. It's really just so much easier for her to be with fucking Bun Man. She's always smiling when she's with him. I don't make her smile anymore. And she deserves to smile. This was a selfish mistake what I've done to her. And now she's going to tell me goodbye. And deservedly so.*

"Why don't you go first," he finally said, knowing what he had to say might be moot if she was breaking up with him.

Looking around, her eyes still darted nervously as she muttered, "I don't want to do this publicly."

Nodding, his heart sank. "I understand. Come with me." He grabbed her hand, holding it firmly, this time without hurting her.

Walking fast, it was a struggle for Holly to keep up with him as they turned on Bayberry Walk and approached the building with the long porch. Digging in his jeans' pocket with his free hand, Aiden pulled out his keys and unlocked the door, leading her into the space that would be transformed into *Acebo*.

Like her father earlier in the week, she slowly surveyed the space. "It's going to be beautiful," she commented, doing a second visual sweep of what would become a tapas restaurant next summer.

Defensively, as if protecting his heart, he crossed his arms over his chest. "So, what did you want to tell me?" He couldn't wait a minute longer, and at least in here, they would have total privacy for what he was certain would be a very emotional conversation.

Meeting his gaze, she started gnawing at her bottom lip.

"Please just say it," he begged. *Why was I so stupid to think things could be okay, that I could still have it all? That she'd come back to me and just deal with all my fucked-up shit. Dumb ass.*

"I was trying to figure out what I was going to say when I was walking to your place, but I couldn't figure it out. I don't know how to tell you."

"Just do it, Holly. Tell me." He sounded resigned.

Taking a deep breath, she nervously pushed her hair behind her ear and nodded. "Okay, I'll just say it. There's no way to make this anything but what it is." She paused, taking another deep breath, wishing there was something in the empty room to hold onto, but the only thing surrounding her was empty space. "So, it seems that the night of our infamous great fuck..."

He winced at the words. His words. Words that he would forever regret.

"Was more than a choke and fuck." She tried to smile, but the muscles in her face quivered too much to successfully pull it off.

"I'm not sure I'm following you."

"I'm pregnant, Aiden. I conceived that night."

Cocking his head, he smirked. "You know, I remember thinking at the time, I should stop and ask you if we should go on, and then I thought, no, I'm not stopping, this is going to end the same way, no matter what. I guess that was pretty selfish of me, huh?"

She shook her head. "We were trying to claw our way out of a year and a half of hell. Control wasn't in the cards for anything that happened that night. For either of us."

Shaking his head, he had an amused look on his face. "I choked you and knocked you up. In another context that would actually sound hot and kinky."

"And in our context?" she asked, still waiting for some kind of real reaction out of him.

"In our context. Wow. Umm... mind blowing. Surprising. Scary. It sounds scary." Focused on some indeterminate spot on the floor, he raked his hand through his hair, his mind clearly going a million miles an hour. Looking back up, he met her gaze. "I want to be a great father. I hope I'm not too fucked up to be a great father." He then surveyed the room and vocalized what was going through his mind. "Shit, I need to get my ass working on this place and get it open. I have a family I need to support." Looking back at her, he asked. "How long have you known?"

"About forty minutes."

"Oh, wow, you just found out."

She nodded. "I'm sorry, Aiden. That night just happened, and I know this isn't the best thing to spring on you now. It's a lot to handle in the best of circumstances and our circumstances are far from optimal."

And as the thought occurred to him, he asked, "You do want this baby, don't you? I mean, I can understand why you might not. You've got your whole life in front of you and your career and as you've seen multiple times now, I'm pretty fucked up and we're..."

"Yes, I want this baby," she cut him off.

His shoulders sank as the tension he was holding dissipated with her words. Uncrossing his arms, he held them open for her, each taking steps toward the other until the distance no longer existed.

"I'm hugging you whether you want me to or not," he whispered in her ear.

"I want you to."

Smiling as he held her tight, "I'm hugging you and our baby together for the first time." He was silent for a moment. "Wow, Angel, we're having a baby." He tightened his embrace. "We're having a baby," he repeated into her hair.

Pulling back to look at his face, she asked, "Are you okay with this?"

"Honestly?"

"Yes, please."

"I'm processing it. I thought you were dumping me today, not telling me we're going to be a family. Full disclosure, I'm scared as hell that I'm not going to be the man I want to be. But that just means I have to work harder to make sure that happens, for you, and for our baby." He paused, "I still haven't answered your question, have I? So, let me answer it this way. There is no one, and I mean no one, I would want more, to be the mother of my children than you. You even wanting to have my baby is just mind blowing to me. Is the timing something we didn't expect? Yeah. Is it made even more crazy because we're just finding our way back to each other? Definitely. Am I okay with it? I'm a lot more than okay with it, Angel. My dreams just got fast-tracked, that's a good thing, not a bad thing."

Those were the words of Aiden McManus, her Aiden McManus. Reminding her, yet one more time, exactly why her heart was never able to shut the door on their story.

Looking up at him, she asked, "What did you want to say to me and what did you want to ask me?"

"Well, the first thing I want to say to you is I'm sorry about last night. The minute I got home I realized that what worked for me before doesn't work for me now that you're back in my life. That solitude I thought I needed was not what I needed. What I needed was you."

Looking up from his chest, she couldn't speak, overwhelmed by the conclusion he came to on his own.

He went on. "So, I am really sorry about last night. Really sorry. Not being able to handle a crowd doesn't mean I need to be alone. It means I shouldn't be in a crowd. That doesn't include shutting you out. So, I learned that last night. I was alone and all I wanted was to be holding you and to not be alone."

"That's a good lesson. I like that."

"Yeah. I didn't know. I just thought it was like it was before, where I needed to be alone, so it was really kind of an epiphany for me."

"Okay, and so what did you want to ask me?"

"I wanted to ask you if you were leaving on Tumbleweed Tuesday with the rest of your family?" He didn't wait for an answer. "Because I wanted to know if you would stay. I've got an appointment with my shrink on Wednesday morning at ten, and I wanted to know if you would come with me?"

He had finally opened the door. Wide. Unprompted. His decision to do so.

"Thank you for asking. And the answer is yes. Even without my news today, the answer would have been yes. But now, it's a yes in capital letters."

He laughed, pushing her hair behind her ears. His face took on an earnest expression as he said, "Holly, I have not wanted to ask you to wait for me while I work through all this shit and get my life back on track." Momentarily closing his eyes, he shook his head. "But you know what I really want?"

"What?"

"I want you to wait for me."

"Forever and a day." She smiled. *I will wait for you forever and a day.*

"And I have one more question to ask you." He looked very serious.

"Ask away."

Taking her face in his hands, his expression remaining inscrutable. There was a long pause before he spoke again. "Does your father have any guns?" he deadpanned.

CHAPTER
Eight

Thanksgiving...Again

"YOU LIED TO ME, WOMAN." Schooner pointed a finger at his wife. "Flat-out lied."

"I was wrong. Enjoy hearing me say those three words, because it's going to be a long time before you hear them come out of my mouth again, Pretty Boy. Now, grow a pair and go make that phone call. Now!"

"Grow a pair? I can't believe you just said that to me." He shook his head and laughed. "So how much does she know?"

"You're asking me? It's not my ex." She smiled at him before muttering, "Thank God."

"Does she know about the baby?" he asked, opening the cabinet, looking for a bottle of scotch. This phone call required alcohol. He eyed the larger water glasses, just for a moment thinking *even that might not be enough*, then poured two fingers into a rocks glass.

"Not unless Zac mentioned it to her, and I can't imagine he'd want to be the one to share *that* news."

"Well, I'm certainly not telling her." He took a sip of his scotch. "She is going to be pissed when she finds out everyone knew, and no one told her."

Mia held up her hands. "Not my circus, not my monkeys."

"And Holly's going to shit when she sees her there. I think last Thanksgiving was the last time they spoke." He and Mia walked into the office.

"I'm pretty sure Holly has not spoken to her since," Mia confirmed.

As he sat down behind the desk, he asked, "And why are we inviting her again?"

Squinting her eyes at him, Mia didn't need to say a word.

"You may be little, but you are scary." He gave her a side-eye.

"Dial."

"And bossy." He laughed.

He put the phone on speaker and dialed. With each ring, he whispered the number. *One. Two. Please go to voicemail.*

"I hear there's good skiing in Hell now that it's frozen over." Answering the phone with a barb, CJ was clearly surprised by the call from her ex.

"You always did like doing the snow bunny thing. Will you be spending Thanksgiving there?" *Please say you have plans.*

"Well, it would certainly be an improvement over last year's Thanksgiving."

"You won't have any argument from me on that." Schooner laughed. "That's something we actually agree on. So, the reason I'm calling is..."

She cut him off, "To torture me with another Thanksgiving with *your* family?"

"As a matter of fact, yes."

"Well, thank you, but no thank you." Her voice dripped with sarcasm.

"Hey, CJ, it's Mia."

Schooner's eyes widened, and he picked up his scotch, smiling as he lifted the glass to his lips.

"Oh, how nice, you've had me on speaker."

Mia continued, paying no attention to Schooner's exes comment. "CJ, you need to be here this year. We're going to be having Thanksgiving out at the beach and Holly doesn't know this yet, but she'll be getting engaged that day."

"What? Who is she getting engaged to?"

Schooner looked surprised and whispered to Mia, "She really doesn't know anything."

"She's getting engaged to Aiden. They got back together over the summer," Schooner explained, picking up a black enamel pen and rolling it between his fingers.

"Aiden is the bartender she was seeing for a few years after she dumped that nice boy from Brown?"

Her condescending tone caused Mia to sneer. "Actually, he's a restaurant owner and he's a really great guy, CJ. I know you don't want to miss your daughter getting engaged."

"Of course, I don't. Does she know I'm coming?"

It was Schooner's turn to sneer. "She's coming," he whispered, with a mortified look on his face.

"No. But she doesn't know she's getting engaged either," he explained.

"Will I be able to take a cab from the airport out to the beach? And what hotels are close by?"

"No. You'll have to take a ferry out and there really aren't any hotels open on the island in winter, so you'll have to stay with us."

There was dead silence on the other end of the line.

"Or if that doesn't work for you, you can take a late ferry back to Long Island and then the train into the city. It will take you right to Penn Station." Mia offered the alternative.

"Will that take long?"

"A few hours."

"A few hours," her voice was shrill. "Where the hell do you people have a beach house?"

Covering her mouth so CJ couldn't hear her laugh, they heard a resigned sigh over the line.

"So, how do I get there?" she asked.

"We'll have Zac and Lily pick you up at JFK and you can drive out with them."

"Oh, so you *can* drive there."

"No. He'll be driving to the ferry and then you'll take that over. There are no cars on the island." Schooner drained his drink and opened the bottom drawer of his desk, pulling out a bottle of Hennessy and an extra glass for Mia. He decided having a second drink and moving to cognac was permissible, given the circumstances.

"CJ," Mia began after taking a sip of the cognac. "You'll want to wear comfortable shoes to walk from the ferry to the house. And make sure you have warm clothes, sweaters, a good jacket. It's cold out on the beach this time of year."

"I have to walk to the house? This is making last year's Thanksgiving sound good. All I had to do last year was take a cab from the Four Seasons."

"Just think of this as an adventure." Mia laughed.

"If I wanted an adventure, Mia, I'd go to Canyon Ranch."

Mia rolled her eyes. *A pampered adventure? Seriously?* "Yeah, well, you might need to go there for a little rest and relaxation after another Thanksgiving with us."

Mia took another sip and whispered to Schooner, "It's a lot more fun when you have a buzz."

Smiling, he nodded and whispered, "Exactly why I started before dialing."

"Will Henry be there?" she asked.

"Yes, Henry and Seth will be there," confirmed Schooner, now sitting back in his chair.

"Oh, good, I liked Seth, even though he reminded me of you, Mia. What about your parents? I liked your mother."

"No, my parents will be on a cruise over Thanksgiving week."

"Oh, what a shame."

"Don't worry, I don't think you'll be needing the extra firepower this time."

"Oh, what a shame," she repeated. "Last year was some of my best work to date."

"On that note, let Zac know when your flight gets in. See you Thanksgiving." Rushing her off, he hit the button and disconnected the call. Looking at Mia, he just shook his head, "Sorry, I just could not do anymore.

"No apology necessary." Mia held up her glass as if toasting Schooner.

Your mother is joining us for Thanksgiving. I'm going to need you to pick her up at the airport and bring her out to Fire Island with you. Schooner texted Zac.

k.

She doesn't know Holly's pregnant, so don't mention it.

Sweet. The good child has dropped out of her masters program and is preggers. And not married. She's going to shit. This should be fun.

Mia said to tell you we're not recuperated from last year yet.

Ha-Ha. Lily just said the same thing.

Putting down the phone, Schooner looked at Mia, his expression was beyond amused. "She actually said last year was some of her best work to date. I did hear that correctly, didn't I?"

"Yup, she said that." Mia couldn't wipe the smile off her face.

"You are my witness, I'm saying a prayer, right here and now, to the Ex-Wife god. Please Ex-Wife god, I don't ask much of you. I've paid all my alimony, supported my children, given them great educations, left my ex financially stable, so much so that she supported my ex-friend, so in essence, I supported his lame ass, which is way beyond ex expectations. So please, Ex-Wife god, please make sure we don't have any encore performances this year." Smiling at his wife, he added, "I used to love Thanksgiving. Why are we doing this again?"

"You married her. Not my circus, not my," she paused, looking truly confused, "whatever she is."

Laughing, he pointed a finger at her as she got up to leave the office. "And by the way, I'm still not over that grow a pair comment."

That, she knew, was far from the truth.

"You've gotten a lot accomplished." Schooner looked around at the progress the contractors had made on *Acebo* in the three months since summer ended. The bones of the bar were built, plumbing was in for the bar area and the kitchen. The electrical work was in progress.

"I see it every day, so it feels slow for me and I'm seeing all that needs to get done versus what we've accomplished."

"I think that's just a natural thing we do in all aspects of our life," Schooner commented.

"True, I definitely do that with my personal progress," confided Aiden.

"How's that going?" Now that he'd opened the door, Schooner felt comfortable walking through. Something he'd never do without Aiden making the initial overture.

"Much better than I expected. When I started the process, I was skeptical of it working. You know, it was Mia who told me that I was going to have to work my ass off, but that if I wanted it badly enough, I could make it happen."

Schooner nodded.

"And she was right. Holly does one day a week with me in therapy and has really gotten involved in the Vets' group meetings. They love her 7-layer dip."

"My daughter can cook?" Schooner looked shocked.

"No. She definitely cannot cook." Aiden couldn't help but laugh. Holly's many talents did not include culinary skills. "But she can layer food in a bowl with the best of 'em." Aiden's smile was the true barometer of his happiness. "Luckily for her, I've got fifteen-plus years in the restaurant business, or we might be resorting to cannibalism over the winter months out here."

"I'm glad she's in therapy with you. I was pretty worried about her," Schooner admitted.

"I'm sorry about that. I know I sent her life into a tailspin and totally blindsided her. The truth is, when I broke up with her, it wasn't like I'd been thinking about it for a long time, it was totally unplanned and done during a freak out about what might happen overseas and how it would affect her. And I did a great job of rationalizing it every which way I could, and then I stuck to my guns." He shook his head, a solemn grimace on his face. "Unfortunately, I left a lot of carnage in my wake."

"And now you're fixing it." Learning from mistakes was something Schooner knew well and prided himself on the lessons he learned and on making the changes accordingly.

"That's my focus. That and this place. And this will be done by the time the baby comes."

"You'll have a newborn when you open." Schooner commented, thinking Aiden and Holly had no idea of the exhaustion that lay ahead. Either event was all-encompassing, successfully melding the two would galvanize their relationship in a way they could not yet fathom.

Looking up at the transformation of the cathedral ceiling which was now covered with exquisite raw wood and beams, Schooner could totally visualize the concept he had seen in Aiden's renderings. This place was going to do exceptionally well and wouldn't be the last restaurant this young man opened.

"I'm ready for it. We just need to find a place to live." They'd been staying at the Moore's house, and at Holly's insistence, he had continued to rent the studio apartment so that he'd have a 'cave' to go to if he needed alone time. He rarely stepped foot into the place anymore and was ready to let it go.

"If there's anything you need, let me know," Schooner offered, knowing his future son-in-law well enough to know that Aiden would never take him up on it.

Aiden nodded. "Thank you. I appreciate that, and I also want to thank you for not judging me for needing help to get my life back on track."

"Oh, but I do judge you." Schooner took Aiden by surprise with his response.

Aiden nodded, devastated he'd let down a man he deeply respected.

"It takes a secure man to admit he needs help," Schooner went on, his response not what the younger man expected. "And I'm glad my daughter is with a strong man."

"Thank you. That means a lot to me."

"Admitting there's an issue is a big step. Actually doing something about it, and being dedicated to beating the demons, takes a lot of inner fortitude." He stopped and smiled, a thought obviously occurring to him. "And you are going to need a lot of courage and bravery," he paused, "to deal with Holly's mother."

Aiden laughed. "Do you have some words of advice for me?"

"Do not let her get you alone. Seriously, if you need to go to the bathroom, take Natie with you."

"Should I be scared?"

"Yes." Schooner looked dead serious. "We want this baby to grow up with a father."

"You're scaring me," the former Army officer said with a smile. "She can't be that bad."

Schooner just laughed. "You've been warned."

***

"Zac and Lily are here, and they brought that lady." Nathaniel had been looking out the window, waiting for them, when he saw them coming down the street.

"What lady?" Holly asked from the kitchen, looking up from slicing the apples for her pie.

"The one who looks like you, Holly." He called over his shoulder as he ran to the door, flinging it open. "Zac!" he screamed, running out into the cold without a jacket to greet his older brother.

Holly met her father's eyes with disdain. "I hate you," she declared through clenched teeth.

"Get over it." He smiled at his oldest child, an amused look on his handsome face.

"I really hate you," she reiterated, punctuating her point with the sharp paring knife in her hand.

Coming up behind her, he put his hands on her shoulders. Leaning down he whispered in her ear, the amusement evident in his voice, "And you can't drink."

"Have I told you today how much I hate you?"

Kissing her cheek, he said, "This had to happen at some point. Let's get it over with."

Turning her head to look up at her father, she begged, "Please don't let her run Aiden off."

And although it was said in jest, Schooner could see her unbridled fear. CJ was her very own apocalypse and the smoldering wake was always unfortunately very real. "Not a chance," he promised. "Now put down the knife."

Holly smiled at her father and shook her head.

"God, I love you."

"Yeah, well that's good, because I hate you."

As they entered the house, Mia looked over at Schooner and Holly and smiled. "Let ShitStorm2.0 begin," she said just loud enough for the two of them to hear. "Holly, put down that knife."

Her stepdaughter shook her head. "Protect Aiden. I don't want my baby to grow up without a daddy," she whispered to Mia. "You of all people know this, she makes men disappear."

Mia couldn't help but snort, immediately attracting CJ's attention, the two women locking gazes. Time passing would never diminish the deep-seated emotion that accompanied their history.

Walking over to the kitchen island across from where they were working, CJ smiled, it was again her practiced, close-mouthed smile. "What a beautiful home you have. Although it is kind of remote out here."

Mia smiled at the backhanded compliment and bit her tongue to stop from saying, *not far enough from you.* "Please take off your coat." *Or don't.*

CJ ignored Mia and set her sights on her daughter. "Hello, Holly. It's been a while."

"Dad didn't tell me you were coming."

"Well, then, surprise." CJ mustered another close-mouthed smile.

"You ain't seen nothing yet," Mia said under her breath and moved to the counter along the wall.

"CJ," Henry came up behind her, saving the day. Giving her a big hug, he then stood at arm's length, "Don't you look beautiful. Let me take your coat."

CJ shrugged out of her winter white cashmere coat revealing a pale pink sheath dress with an asymmetrical neckline.

"St. John's Collection is perfect for you," Seth commented, as he stepped up for an air kiss.

"Thank you, Steve. I feel that exact same way every time I try on one of their pieces."

Excusing himself and leaving her with Henry, Seth joined Mia and Holly in the kitchen. "Okay, my love affair with her is over. She called me Steve."

"Want this?" Holly held out a six-inch chef's knife.

He was seething. "I want the eight-inch."

"Of course, you do, Princess," Mia smirked.

"Well, she's a little overdressed for the occasion," Holly remarked, checking out her mother's head-to-toe perfection.

"I guess I should have told her this was casual. My bad." Mia smiled at Holly.

"I'm afraid to come out from behind the counter." Holly had begun to show, but dressed in black yoga pants, a partially buttoned oversized black, grey, and white flannel shirt, with a white tank underneath, she was well camouflaged.

"Can't tell. Black plaid hides everything." Mia gave her a once over. "Your face is a little fuller, but that's about it."

"Ugh. I wish Aiden would get here already." He had gone back to *Acebo* and was going to meet his parents at the terminal and accompany them to the house.

"Are his folks on the next ferry?" Mia opened the oven to baste the turkey.

Holly nodded.

"Mommy, I'm hungry." Nathaniel came into the kitchen.

"Hmm, what can we feed you that won't ruin your appetite or make you throw up all over the dinner table?"

"Want to help me, Natie? I'm making pies and I think there's some extra apples with cinnamon on them." She pulled out a stepstool for him to stand on.

CJ wandered into the kitchen. "When did you learn to cook?" she asked her daughter.

"I haven't. I'm watching a YouTube how-to video." She pointed to her phone propped up on the counter. "I don't have to cook. Aiden is an amazing chef."

"Clearly." CJ gave her daughter a disapproving once over. "Someone's fat and happy," her judgmental tone rang strong.

"That's not nice to call somebody fat." Nathaniel had an apple slice halfway to his mouth when he stopped to defend his big sister in a loud voice. "We don't talk like that. And my sister is not fat, lady. She's having a baby."

A silence fell over the room as no one moved.

Schooner broke the silence, "Nathaniel, we don't talk that way to our guests."

"But, Daddy, the lady called Holly fat." He was not backing down from the defense of his sister. A true gallant Moore man in the making.

"You knew?" she turned to Schooner. "And you didn't think that you should share that with me?"

"It was not my place to share that."

"What is wrong with you?" She was livid. Looking across the room at Zac, "And you knew, too, I suppose."

"Like Dad said, it was not my place to share the news."

"Fine." She turned her sights back on her daughter. "And you didn't think I should know about this?"

"I don't want to raise this child alone and I have to worry about you running off the men in my life." Holly lost her cool. A year's worth of anger was raging in her eyes.

"So *that* is what this is about? You should be thanking me for that. I did you a huge favor."

"I do not need any favors from you, Mother." Holly spit the words out through clenched teeth.

"And you," a livid CJ turned her sights on Mia. "I can't count on you as a fellow mother to do the right thing?"

CJ wants me to do the right thing? There's irony somewhere in this moment. "Is this like Mom-code?" Mia asked innocently.

"Put yourself in my position."

In that moment, Mia actually felt bad for her. "CJ, put yourself in mine."

Turning to her daughter, ex, and son, she pointed at each of them, "You, you, and you," and then looked at Schooner, "where can we talk?"

"Follow me." Schooner crooked his hand and opened the french doors to the deck.

"This should be good, it's not me getting in trouble for once." Zac was clearly taking pleasure in seeing his big sister on the hot seat.

"It's freezing out here," CJ bitched, stepping out onto the deck. "Isn't there a room in the house where we can have some privacy?"

"Cooler heads prevail." Schooner smiled at her.

"Were you ever going to tell me?" CJ locked eyes with her daughter.

"I would have sent you a baby picture." Holly smiled, taking great pleasure in pissing off her mother.

"That is not funny."

"You're right. It's not. And I was wrong for not sharing this with you. I'm sorry." Holly knew her mother was actually right.

"Oh, man, you rolled over way too soon. Didn't I teach you anything?" Zac gave his sister a disgusted look, enjoying instigating the situation.

"And you have nothing to say for yourself?" CJ gave her ex a hard look.

Leaning against the weathered wooden railing, arms crossed across his broad chest, Schooner smiled at CJ. "We're going to be grandparents. Let's enjoy our good fortune. And I think you need a glass of wine." He added as an afterthought, pushing off the railing and walking toward the door, letting everyone know the conversation had officially ended.

The McManus's entered the front door at the exact same moment that Schooner, Holly, CJ, and Zac were walking in from the deck.

"Oh, thank God," Holly muttered.

"Coming simultaneously. I hope that's what got you knocked up," Zac whispered to his sister.

"You're lucky I love you, you brat." She swatted her brother in the arm and then went to greet Aiden, his parents, and his grandmother.

"Lift your shirt, I need to see that belly." His mother was overjoyed as she inspected Holly's baby bump.

"I think I'm carrying in my butt. I've kind of widened out."

"I'll bet it's a girl. The boys are all in front and the girls make you go wide. That's just how I carried."

As Holly introduced them to her family, her anxiety catapulted as she finally made the introduction she was dreading. "Aiden, this is my mother, CJ."

"So nice to meet you," he greeted her warmly with a hug, immediately taking her out of her comfort zone. "If this baby is a girl, I just hope she looks like you and your mom." He looked at Holly. "And then I'm buying a shotgun."

Holly looked at her mother. "You approve?"

"Absolutely." She took in the charming, handsome man standing before her. "A significant improvement." She couldn't forgo the barb at her daughter.

In the kitchen, Seth donned an apron over his cashmere sweater. "I'm staying in here with you, where it's safe."

"Good idea, Steve," Mia teased.

"Did I tell you I hate her?"

"Took you long enough." She handed him a spoon and directed him toward the stove.

"Hello, everyone." The front door opened again, and Charles and Gaby came in, Paola and Portia, running in past them.

"It smells wonderful in here, Meezie," Charles called out to Mia.

"Did you just see that?" Seth asked Mia.

"I did."

They had both watched CJ give Gaby a once over, checking out her competition.

"She is one competitive bitch." Seth continued to watch the cool blonde, fascinated by her actions, both subtle and overt.

"You have no idea." Mia shook her head.

Sensing their eyes on her, CJ turned and smiled her close-mouthed smile, and made her way toward the kitchen.

"Great, you've summoned the evil spirits, Princess." Mia nudged Seth in the ribs.

"So, what did you do to Tom?" Mia had been dying to ask the question for a year.

"Nothing you hadn't already done."

Looking out into the great room at Aiden standing behind Holly, with his arms wrapped around her, CJ commented, "He's really attractive. Those scars are actually hot. Did you sleep with this one, too?" She smiled at Mia, clearly amused at her own dig.

Mia put down the slotted spoon in her hand. "You know I've wanted to tell you something for nearly thirty years," she paused to smile at her nemesis. "You are a bitch."

"Thirty years and that's the best you can do?"

Mia was dying to say, "No wonder he left you," but just smiled at CJ and asked, "So, what are you going to have the baby call you, Granny or Grandma?" Continuing to smile, she went on, "Since I'm not a blood relative, I'm thinking Mimi for me. So, I've got dibs on that. You can't have it, Granny." Granny. Ha! That was much worse than calling her a bitch.

"What does he see in you?" Shaking her head, she left the kitchen.

"It kills her that he's crazy about you." Seth commented. "She hates seeing you and Schooner so happy."

"Good." Mia smiled. Nearly thirty years and this little psychodrama was still in full swing. She thought about how much they'd all grown and experienced, and yet, the old wounds needed little provocation, ripping wide open at just the slightest tug, releasing three teens, whenever they were in one another's presence.

Catching Schooner's eye, Mia motioned for him to come into the kitchen. "Let's just set up everything here on the island, and everyone can come and get their own plates." She had set two long tables, with no place cards this year, hoping everyone would mix it up and mingle. "And make sure Aiden's parents are with us."

"Do you want me to carve the turkey?" he asked. Looking to see if he could help, he picked up the carving knife.

"After what you did to it last year? No." Seth answered for her.

"I'm deferring to Princess." She smiled at her husband.

"Smart move, BBC." Seth held out his hand for Schooner to turn over the knife.

"Okay, I'll go be a good host and see if anyone needs a drink." Looking out at the room, he turned to Seth, "Your partner really is a saint," he was referring to Henry keeping CJ occupied.

"He'd have to be a saint to put up with this one," quipped Mia, smiling at her BFF.

"Not smart, BBC. I'm holding the sharpest knife in the house."

"Schooner," Mia grabbed him before he could get away and motioned for him to bend down so that she could whisper in his ear. "No speeches this year, Pretty Boy. This is Aiden's show today."

"Willingly handing over that torch." He gave her a quick kiss and went to attend to their guests.

A few minutes later, Seth had completed his masterful carving, creating a Martha Stewart-worthy platter with a turkey meticulously surrounded with greens, citrus slices, and grapes.

"Okay, everyone, come grab a plate and help yourselves and sit anywhere you'd like," Mia announced to the group in the great room.

Standing in the kitchen, waiting for the guests to fill their plates and be seated, Mia leaned back on Schooner.

"Tired, Baby Girl?" He kissed the top of her head.

"Yes, very, but excited, too."

"I know... me, too."

When everyone was seated, Schooner and Mia filled their plates and joined their guests. Before sitting down, Schooner announced, "No longwinded speech from me this year. I just wanted to welcome everyone and say how thankful and pleased I am that you are all here and healthy. And, of course, Go Chargers!"

"Huh?" Seth turned to Henry.

"Football," Henry explained. "He's a San Diego Chargers fan."

"Jets," both Charles and Aiden yelled out simultaneously.

"My condolences. That's just downright sad," responded a smiling Schooner.

"Can't argue with you there," agreed Charles.

When everyone had finished their first plate, and people were either sitting back stuffed, or starting on round two, Aiden stood, picking up his wine glass, and clanging the side of the glass with a spoon, to get everyone's attention.

"Schooner may not have made a longwinded speech, but I'm going to. So, sit back, undo the top button on your pants and get comfortable, because this might take a while. First, I'd like to thank Schooner and Mia for having us in their beautiful home to celebrate Thanksgiving and for making us this delicious meal. Oh, wait, I mean, thank you, Seth." Everyone laughed and Aiden smiled at Mia.

"I get no respect." Mia shook her head, smiling.

"So, first toast is to our hosts, Schooner and Mia."

When everyone finished sipping their wine or cider, he went on. "I'm also really thankful that we could all be together this holiday. Honestly, I'm just thankful to be here. So many men and women who serve our country are not with their families today. Some are on bases, eating their Thanksgiving dinner in mess halls with their fellow soldiers, while others are out on missions, not celebrating at all. And for the families that are stateside or stationed somewhere around the world, whose loved one isn't with them, I can't help but think how bittersweet today is for them. So, I'd like the second toast to go to the men and women serving our country, especially those who are not with their families this holiday."

With a resounding "Here, here," from both tables, everyone took another sip.

"I'm also thankful to finally meet Holly's lovely mother CJ. This has taken way too long to happen, and it is evident where Holly gets her beauty. If this baby is a girl, she had better look like the two of you."

CJ preened.

"And I'd better get a shotgun." Aiden deadpanned, then continued. "I'm also really happy my family is here today, especially my other girlfriend, my Grandma Rose."

"I thought I was your other girlfriend," Portia yelled out from the other end of the table, sending a ripple of laughter through the room.

"You're my third girlfriend," Aiden clarified, with a wink.

"Okay." Portia was satisfied.

"He should be a politician," Schooner whispered to Mia. "Charms all the women."

"So, quite a few years back now, I was here in the winter, and I was hanging out on a cold Saturday afternoon with my friend, Billy. He was working that day, and I was just taking up space on a barstool, and watching some college football. A party of four walked into Castaway, four people I'd never seen before, so I figured they were day-trippers. There was this big, handsome guy, a pretty little lady, some younger guy, but I didn't pay much attention to him, and the most beautiful girl I'd ever seen in my life. And, hey, this is Fire Island, I've seen some beautiful girls."

"You were there that day?" Holly's hands flew to her mouth in surprise.

"This is my story." He gave her a hard look that melted into a smile. "But, to answer your question, yes, I was there that day. I spent the next two hours watching this girl. I was so drawn to her, and I don't think she ever looked up at me. Not even once. And I was better looking than the guy she was with." He smiled. "So, the other guy, the big guy," he looked at Schooner, "got up and got one of the local newspapers with all the real estate in it from one of the racks along the wall. And then they spent the next few hours looking through that. They left, and the most beautiful girl in the world never even looked at me. Just my luck, right. I figured they were probably on the next ferry out. But the following morning, I'm out early running on the beach, and who's running toward me? You guessed it, the most beautiful girl in the world. We nodded at one another and she was gone again."

"You were in a blue knit cap." Holly was astounded, her hand covering her mouth again as she put together his tale with pieces of her memory.

"I was. Very good." He smiled. "And then I didn't see her again until the next summer and she was still seeing that guy, but she and I became friends and had a lot of good times laughing together. Now, I would think about her too much. And truth be told, I would also think about ways to get rid of the boyfriend."

"Oh, I like him." The words flew out of CJ's mouth, causing the McManus's to laugh. The Moores, not so much.

"But I didn't have to get rid of the boyfriend, because she did it for me, and then let me know that I wasn't imagining this *thing* between us. It was there, and it was real, and she was feeling it too. So, here was this girl I was crazy attracted to, totally enjoyed being with, got along great with. And, yeah, she's beautiful and smart and funny, but I still had no idea who this woman really was. And as time went on and I really got to know her, I was even more blown away. But it was on July 4th this year, when I was literally falling apart in the streets, she was there to catch me, and give me her strength. I was in an alleyway shaking, and she held me and said to me 'I've got you. You're going to be okay. I've got you.'" Aiden stopped for a moment to gather himself, his eyes brimming. "Yeah, she's beautiful and smart, but she's also tenacious and relentless and she loves so hard. And lucky for me, I'm the guy she loves, because this is the woman I want at my side every day, for the rest of my life."

Pulling a black velvet box from his pocket, Aiden dropped to one knee next to Holly's chair, "Angel, everything I do in my life, for the rest of my days, I want to do with you by my side. When I look at you, I see my forever in your eyes, and I'm whole again because you are a part of me. Will you marry me? Be mine forever?"

"Forever and a day."

"That works, too." He smiled, slipping the ring on her finger. "Forever and a day." Leaning forward he took her face in his hands, looking into her eyes with a smile, before sealing it with a kiss.

Before their lips were apart, they heard the muffled pop of a champagne bottle being uncorked, perfectly done, by turning the bottle and not the cork, keeping the sound to a minimum. Still, she could feel his muscles tighten.

"I've got you," she whispered, taking his face in her hands for a second kiss.

"Yeah, and this time it's forever and a day." He stole her phrase.

Enjoying a glass of champagne, CJ congratulated her daughter, admiring her cushion-cut ring. "That is lovely," she remarked. "And you know, I knew about this and you didn't."

"Well, then, that makes us even." Holly referred to being shocked by her mother's presence.

"Have you thought about when you'd like to get married?"

"This ring has been on my finger for like five minutes. Why, do you have a trip to Europe planned or something? We can get married then."

"Don't get pissy with me, young lady. I got that letch out of your life. You need to let it go already."

To anyone looking on, they appeared to be a mother and daughter having a pleasant conversation, maybe talking about decorating a baby nursery. Through smiling, clenched teeth, Holly hissed, "Don't you do anything to Aiden."

"I like Aiden. Why would I do anything to him?" She glanced over at her future son-in-law, eyeing him appreciatively.

"Don't touch him. I'm not kidding." There were furrows between Holly's brows.

"I wouldn't dream of it. He's my grandchild's father. Even I have boundaries, Holly." Her tone was indignant.

Hearing the end of the conversation as CJ walked away, Zac slung an arm over his sister's shoulder. "Today is the day you got engaged. Don't let anyone rob you of that joy. Come, let's go talk to Grandma Rose, she's a hoot."

As she watched her mother walk toward the kitchen, Holly sat down next to Aiden. "Promise me you will never be alone with her."

"That's so weird, your father said the same thing to me."

"He did?" Holly was surprised.

"Yeah, he told me if I had to, I should take Natie with me to the bathroom." Aiden laughed, thinking it was a joke.

"That's where she did it," Holly said, thinking aloud. *Holy crap!*

"What?"

"Nothing, just putting two and two together." Holly again looked over toward the kitchen where her mother had joined Mia, Seth, Henry, and Gaby.

Half cleaning, half just enjoying champagne, Mia was trying to get everything washed and put away before she started serving dessert.

"Gaby, will you pull the cheesecake out of the fridge? I want it to warm up and get to the right consistency."

Grabbing the red-and-white-striped box, Gaby's eyes lit up, "Junior's," she sighed, pulling out the famed-baker's specialty.

"You're welcome." Seth knew his addition to the dessert menu would be a crowd pleaser.

"Congratulations," Henry clinked champagne glasses with CJ when she walked in. "Looks like you're going to have a wedding to make."

"I think I might have to make a baby shower first." Turning to Mia, CJ interrupted the conversation she was having with Gaby. "I want to help with the baby shower."

Gaby just smiled and took a step back, as she sipped her champagne.

"Of course, you're her mother. This should be yours." Mia knew when to jump out of the driver's seat.

"I don't know where to throw it or who to hire here. In Newport Beach, I have all my people in place. So, I think we'll need to do this together."

Caught by surprise, Mia was astonished that CJ would reach across the aisle. "Well, I'll help a little bit. But I think it would be a lot more fabulous if you and Seth worked on it."

Nodding at Mia, she smiled. "I like that idea a lot better."

Of course, you do. Mia just smiled back, congratulating herself on her stellar self-restraint.

With a nod, CJ went back into the great room and sat down on the couch next to Aiden's mother.

Picking up an open bottle of champagne off the marble countertop, Mia refilled Seth's flute and smiled. "She's all yours, Steve."

"I'm doing this for Holly, not for that *Real Housewife*." And turning to Henry, he shook his head. "You should be nominated for sainthood."

Picking up Holly's hot apple pie off the counter, Mia handed it to Seth, "Time for something sweet," she smiled. "Let's just serve dessert from the island counter again." Mia pulled a pumpkin pie and a Key Lime pie out of the refrigerator. "I think we've already lost Schooner, Chazicle, Aiden, and his dad to that football game."

"It's a Junior's cheesecake, that should get them all off the couch," predicted Gaby, saying it loud enough for the men to hear.

"Junior's cheesecake?" Charles and Schooner said in unison, both getting up from the couch.

"You used to eat so healthy," CJ said to her ex. "You really should watch yourself. You're not getting any younger."

He just looked at her and squinted. Slowly lifting a forkful of the creamy cheesecake to his mouth, he leisurely savored Brooklyn's finest confection, licking a dab off his bottom lip, before he turned away from her, and headed back to the game without ever saying a single word.

"Do you have any herbal tea, Mia?" CJ asked, taking a plate of grapes to the table from the fruit bowl Mia thought no one would touch.

"Yes, we've got jasmine and chamomile. Which would you prefer?"

"I'll take the chamomile. Thank you."

"Good, hopefully that will put her to sleep," muttered Schooner, loud enough for CJ to hear.

"Ever the gracious host." She shot him a deadly glance. "At least now you don't walk out on your own parties. Maybe you're maturing. Or just getting lazy." Turning to Holly who was sitting across the table, she announced, "I want to throw you a baby shower."

"Okay. That's nice." Holly looked skeptical, waiting to hear her mother's ulterior motive.

"This is the first grandchild for both the Moores and the MacAllisters."

"You want to do it in California?" Besides grandparents, Holly didn't have ties there anymore, having gone to school in New England and then stayed on the east coast.

"No. I was thinking here in New York. Seth and I will be coordinating and putting together the whole thing."

"You and Seth?" Mia's best friend and her nemesis teaming up? Holly wasn't sure what to think of that.

"Don't look so worried, I'm still planning on inviting Mia." She added with a close- mouthed smile.

"That's Mimi to you, Granny." Mia returned the close-mouthed smile with one of her very own.

"I have never liked you. Right from the freshman retreat on." CJ was livid knowing her grandchild would have a closer relationship with the woman who had been a thorn in her side since she was eighteen. She couldn't believe it then, watching Schooner Moore at that retreat, just a few weeks into their freshman year, totally entranced by the bespectacled little hippie girl. And she couldn't believe it now, nearly thirty years later, he still looked at her like a lovesick teen. And she hated it.

Mia rolled her eyes. "I know. Get over it already. You really do need to go to Canyon Ranch to cleanse and get rid of some of that toxicity. You know that shit'll kill ya." Mia smiled her big, beautiful, devil grin at CJ.

It was too many hours later when Mia crawled into bed, exhausted and aching from being on her feet all day.

Schooner opening his arms, ready to feel her head nestled on his chest. "And that concludes ShitStorm2.0." He kissed the top of her head.

"Not nearly as bad as its predecessor. It could have been a whole lot worse," was Mia's assessment.

"I don't think we scared the McManus's too badly. Even though there was definitely some bad behavior tonight."

"The three of us cannot be around each other without turning into eighteen- and sixteen-year-olds again. We are responsible, successful adults who are generally good role models for our kids. But put the three of us in a room, and that anger is so deep, that the emotions are still like raw nerves." Looking up at him, she sighed. "I love you, I really do. But that is one monkey I don't want in my circus."

"Unfortunately, she came with the big top. So, we've got her for life."

"Ugh. Thanks for that reality check. Hopefully the addition of the baby at Thanksgiving 3.0 will help curb some of the unbridled hostility."

Schooner laughed. "Not if you keep calling her Granny."

Mia smiled into his chest. "It's going to be a shitstorm."

EPILOGUE

July 4th

AIDEN TURNED ON THE TV, flipping stations until he got to PBS where *A Capitol 4th* was about to begin. Turning toward the windows, he could see the beach getting crowded, people standing shoulder to shoulder, ten deep. The Moores and their friends were all on the deck comfortably settled on padded deck chairs and chaise lounges, waiting for the start of the annual July 4th fireworks.

Adjusting the television's volume a little louder, he was looking forward to hearing the National Symphony Orchestra and the U.S. Army Band "Pershing's Own."

It was exactly a year ago that Holly had found him in the alleyway. And now tonight, he had anxiety about having anxiety, wondering if he'd be able to handle it. Tonight would prove to be the litmus test for how far he'd come since last year. Or not. The pressure to be '*better already*' had been choking him all day.

"Do you think this is too loud for her?" he asked Holly as she came down the stairs.

She stood for a moment, listening. "No, I think she'll be fine. I think Daddy needs to see how yummy you smell." She said to her blanket-swaddled daughter, handing the baby to Aiden.

His nose went right to her neck. "Please always smell like this."

Amelia Moore McManus had been born two weeks before the opening of *Acebo* and had attended opening night, greeting all the

251

guests alongside her mother. Today was the first day Aiden and Holly had taken off since the restaurant's opening the week before Memorial Day. Concerned with leaving the staff alone on such a busy night, they decided to go over there to check on everything after the fireworks ended.

Poppop and Mimi would be babysitting Amelia alone for the first time with the help of Auntie Po, Uncle Natie, and the rest of the Moore entourage.

"What do you think of this music, Beautiful?" Aiden asked the baby. "It's pretty, isn't it? We'll see how much it hides those loud bangs for me. For you, we've got noise cancelling ear muffs." He placed the little pink earmuffs over her ears.

"Do you want some noise cancelling earphones?" Holly asked, digging through her bag.

"Not yet." Aiden shook his head. "Let's first see how I do with just the music from the TV. If it gets bad, let's have them on standby."

"It should start any moment now." She stood next to him by the french doors.

"Are you ready for your first Fire Island July 4th?" He kissed the baby's cheek. Looking at Holly, he laughed, "How about we start a new family tradition?"

"What's that? Never work on the 4th?"

"That would be part of it, but I was thinking we go on vacation, out of the country, over July 4th."

"That's one way to not have to be around fireworks. Here we go, they're starting."

The first lights started to flash in the sky, white streams cascaded in graceful arcs, the tips of the smoky ribbons turning red. And then, the much anticipated, and feared, first blast. Holly put a hand on Aiden's back. The truth was, she was as tense as he was. The vision of last year was so fresh in her mind that she could still feel the angst of watching him on the beach the year before.

They both flinched a little with the first blast.

"How's she doing?" Holly asked, distracting him.

"So far so good." Aiden knew focusing in on his daughter would alleviate his tension. Just looking at her made him smile and gave him a peace he thought he'd never experience again in this lifetime. He could spend hours looking at her, studying the funny faces she made. Amelia was the spitting image of Holly, but with his dark hair.

Tensing a little with the next blast, he took a deep breath, then turned his focus back to the baby in his arms. "We've got a couple of summers before you're going to want to go out and see those pretty lights in the sky, which gives me a couple of years to work on getting used to it." Nuzzling her again, he promised, "Yeah, we're both going to be ready together." *Goal set.*

Rubbing his back softly, Holly could feel the tension with each blast, but it was a fraction of what it had been the summer before.

Turning suddenly toward the TV, he said, "Amelia, this is the U.S. Army Band. Don't they sound great? Daddy was in the Army." As he sang *Yankee Doodle* to Amelia, he swayed with her in his arms, moving in time to the U.S. Army Band.

"They are so great." He turned to Holly with a huge smile and was caught off guard. "Why are you crying?"

"Because last year we were in an alley and nothing was right. We weren't together. You were drowning right before my eyes and I had no idea how to save you. And here we are, just one year later. And we're together and you are dancing with our daughter on July 4th. That's why I'm crying. I stood in this room and cried in my father's arms after the alleyway last year, feeling totally hopeless. And look at our world, just one year later. And next year will be even better. I know it will. I'm crying because now I have hope."

"Come here." He held out his free arm to her, pulling her into a hug with the baby. "I could not have done any of this without you."

"Well, thank you. But you've done all the heavy lifting."

"And you're right, next year will be better, because by then we'll be married." With building and opening a restaurant, and the baby, getting married had come in a distant third, mostly because he wanted Holly to have the wedding of her dreams and the focus to put it together.

The frequency of the fireworks was starting to pick up and Aiden could feel his anxiety beginning to rise just knowing the finale was not far off. A vision of last year wormed its way to the forefront of his consciousness.

"I think I should sit." He was afraid to be standing with Amelia if he became overwhelmed. "How much longer do you think?" he asked.

"Probably within the next five minutes." She predicted when the finale would begin. "She must've liked your dancing." Holly motioned to the baby, who was now fast asleep in Aiden's arms.

"I think I'll take those headphones now, Angel."

Grabbing the headphones, Holly put them over his ears so that he wouldn't have to jostle the sleeping Amelia. Curling up on the couch next to him, she watched the fireworks light the Washington, DC sky on the television, feeling the non-synchronized vibrations from the finale blasts being shot off over the ocean outside their door.

"Oh, man, she's now getting in on the blasting action." He turned to Holly.

Sitting up, Holly looked at Aiden, her nose scrunched.

"It wasn't me." He laughed. "How could someone so tiny and so beautiful emit an odor so repulsive? Ugh, she did it again. I can feel the blasts."

"Eww, it smells like something that would come out of my brother." Holly looked like she was going to be sick. "I wonder if it's from the corn-on-the-cob I ate. I don't usually have that. Maybe it was too much for her."

"Oh, man, I'm dying." Aiden laughed as the baby did it again.

As the french doors opened and everyone filed back into the room, Aiden pulled off his headphones. July 4th had been a lot less painful than he'd anticipated, and Holly was right, if he looked at where he was last year to this year, it was evident exactly what therapy, being active in veterans' groups, and her love had done for him. He had taken his life back, vowing not to let the enemy defeat him at home and ruin his relationship with either the woman he loved or his precious baby daughter.

"Oh, that smell is nasty." Lily screwed up her face in disgust as she got near the couch.

"Oh wow, that is foul." Zac looked like he was going to be sick.

Aiden pointed to the baby.

"That is gross. We are not having kids," Zac said to Lily.

"Zac, that smells just like yours." Lily swatted him in the arm.

Aiden looked at Holly and laughed. "Well, we've now established she definitely gets that from your side of the family."

"It feels so weird to be out without the baby, doesn't it?"

Aiden smiled, reaching for Holly's hand, and pulling her closer to him as they walked toward *Acebo*. "It does feel weird."

"I miss her. Is that weird, too? I mean we've only been gone a few minutes."

Aiden laughed. "How about we just check and make sure the staff are doing okay, and if they are, we get the heck out of there."

"I like that idea."

"And I'll buy you an ice cream." He gave her hand a playful tug.

"And I'll even let you lick it," she smiled suggestively.

"I'm going to hold you to that." He raised his eyebrows. "Maybe we should get the ice cream first and then go in the back way directly upstairs to my office. We can check on the staff later. As in much."

"Are you promising me fireworks?"

"Fireworks and ice cream. July 4th doesn't get much better than that, Angel."

As they turned onto Midway, she said, "You did so great tonight. I am so proud of you. Do you feel good about it?" All her anxiety about how the night was going to affect him was now gone. She knew she had been tense all day, but it wasn't until the fireworks ended that she could really allow herself to acknowledge just how on edge she had truly been.

"I do. I really do." He nodded, a look of pride on his handsome face. "You know it better than anyone. One year ago tonight was the watershed moment for me, and I had to make a choice. I either needed to listen to everything you said to me in that alley, or I was going to die."

His admission was a sobering thought, especially because it was most likely true. He would have died. And she feared it would have either occurred at his own hand or through sheer recklessness and negligence.

But that was a year ago. And a lot had changed in a year.

"Come with me," she turned onto Ocean Breeze Walk, tugging his hand and quickening their pace.

It took only a moment for him to realize why they were going down Ocean Breeze Walk and not Bayberry Walk where *Acebo* was located. And he wasn't wrong as she tugged his arm, pulling him down the alley. That alley.

"What are we doing here?"

"Last summer after the fireworks ended, when you and I were going at it, all I really wanted was for you to kiss me." She backed up against the building's weathered shingles, pulling him to her. "And I didn't get that kiss."

"And you want it now?" he whispered, with a wolfish grin.

When she nodded, he placed a hand on the back of her neck and pulled her in for the long-overdue kiss for which she had yearned, allowing the flood of raw and overwhelming memories to ignite and fuel their urgency.

When their kiss finally ended, Aiden looked down at Holly and reached for her hand, bringing it to his lips. "I could not let go of your hand that night." He threaded his fingers with hers, placing a kiss on the inside of her wrist. "You want to know what *I* wanted?"

"Tell me what you wanted." She nodded, still breathless from their kiss and the resurrection of the gut-wrenching emotion that had never been fully laid to rest in this alleyway.

"I wanted to never, ever let you go again. That's what I wanted that night."

"Well, it looks like we both got what we wanted, because I would never, ever let that ferry sail without you."

"Yeah, well, you know what that means, right?" Aiden brushed the hair from her face.

"What?"

"It means you're stuck with me. Forever and a day."

Mission accomplished. She smiled up at her handsome man.

"Come on, Angel." He took her hand and led her out of the alley. "I owe you that ice cream and some fireworks."

AUTHOR'S NOTE

It has truly been an honor for me to bring to light an issue facing those who have served our country. The mental health aspect, including PTSD, are just a small part of the issues facing the men and women who have served our country. As mentioned in the book, twenty veterans take their own lives every single day.

If you, or someone you know in the military, is having a rough time, please reach out to:
U.S. Dept. of Veteran's Affairs: National Center for PTSD: https://www.ptsd.va.gov/public/where-to-get-help.asp
Make the Connection: https://maketheconnection.net/what-is-mtc
Wounded Warrior Project - https://www.woundedwarriorproject.org/
https://www.military.com/spouse/military-life/wounded-warriors/supporting-a-family-member-with-ptsd.html

Depression, PTSD, anxiety disorders, and many other mental health afflictions are pervasive. If you are suffering and need someone to talk to – please don't suffer in silence.
This webpage contains a handy resource of hotline numbers, where help is just a phone call away: https://www.healthyplace.com/other-info/resources/mental-health-hotline-numbers-and-referral-resources

ACKNOWLEDGEMENTS

Thank you to all the readers and blogger/readers who have embraced the Moore stories and me over the past 5 years. This book is for you. Since the release of Moore than Forever, you have asked me repeatedly for Holly's story, and I've been kind of reticent about writing it. And that was for a few reasons. The first reason being, I didn't know her story yet, and although I'm somewhat of a pantser, I generally know the rough outline of a story when I sit down to write it (the exception to that was Searching for Moore – I had no clue I was going to write that book and even less of a clue as to where it was going or how it was going to get there) and with Holly and Aiden's story, I didn't for a long time. The second reason was fear that an additional Moore story might not live up to the rest of the Moore books, and that is the last thing I wanted to see happen. I want readers to walk away from this feeling it was worthy of being part of the Moore works, and I hope that is what I have given you.

So, thank you all for asking me to write this book – I had so much fun getting to develop and know Holly and Aiden as much more than secondary characters. It was also a treat to spend a lot of time with Schooner and Mia, and to see how their relationship and rapport has grown, and the comfort level with which they navigate life as a couple and as a team. Putting Schooner, Mia, and CJ in a room together is a writer's joy. There are so many unresolved issues in that triangle, and the tightrope they walk, as they readily regress into their teenaged selves when in one another's presence, is a blast for me – and I hope for you, too.

Again, thank you dear readers and bloggers for wanting Moore...

A special thank you to my Facebook readers group, Richman's Rogue BBCs – you guys make what I do so much fun. I adore all the positive attitudes and the respect everyone shows to one another. It is truly a drama-free zone and that is because of all of you. Thank you for your love and support.

Vi and P – Having people that "get" it and can laugh with me at the good, bad, and ugly is truly a blessing and I am so thankful that you two are only a PM box away. Thank you for making me snort!

Cleida and Kristen – One of the great things about being in this community is that our paths crossed, and you became part of my life. (Thanks, Schooner) We need to plan a trip!

Jena – I so appreciate your patience and positive attitude as I try to convey what I am seeing inside my head. You have brilliantly translated my somewhat cryptic thoughts into beautiful covers. And Moore than a Feeling is yet another one.

Tiffany – Thank you for taking the time to read this manuscript and share your expertise and advice. I really appreciate your input and perspective and truly admire your ability to handle life with poise and a smile.

Kelly – You are like an oasis in the midst of a chaotic storm. Thank you for your guidance and support.

Eric – Our first time working together and I'm sure it won't be our last. Thanks for Will and the perfect Aiden.

Elaine – Thank you for ensuring everything is perfect and ready to roll. I promise my 'bad habits' will be corrected.

Elena – "Do you have something for me yet?" ☺ You will be the one to make sure I'm never a slacker! Thank you for taking your personal time to make sure everything looks okay.

And last, but not least, the hugest thank you in the world to my family. Mark and Max, you put up with so many nights and weekends where I'm squirreling away in my cave, as we live in a home filled with German Shepherd hair, that I easily walk past and ignore while I'm listening to the characters in my head tell me their story. Dog hair tumbleweed... every home should have some.

And while I'm thanking family, there are two ladies that always get my manuscript moments after the last word is typed (if we still used pens, the ink would still be wet). I love these two women more than you can imagine. Deepest thank you and love to my mom, and my best friend, Mindy, for your love and support in all I do and all that I am.

And if you're wondering... I don't know when, but I'm sure there will always be Moore...

Thank you all for your support and for loving the Moores.

ABOUT THE AUTHOR

Author Julie A. Richman is a native New Yorker living deep in the heart of Texas. A creative writing major in college, reading and writing fiction has always been a passion. Julie began her corporate career in publishing in NYC and writing played a major role throughout her career as she created and wrote marketing, advertising, direct mail and fundraising materials for Fortune 500 corporations, advertising agencies and non-profit organizations. She is an award-winning nature photographer plagued with insatiable wanderlust. Julie and her husband have one son and a white German Shepherd named Juneau.

Contact Julie

Twitter
@JulieARichman (http://twitter.com/JulieARichman)

Website
www.juliearichman.com

Facebook
www.facebook.com/AuthorJulieARichman

Instagram
www.instagram.com/authorjuliearichman

Thank you for purchasing and reading this Book. If you enjoyed it please leave a short review on book-related sites such as Goodreads. Readers rely on reviews, as do authors.

BOOKS BY
JULIE A. RICHMAN

Searching for Moore

Moore to Lose

Moore than Forever

Needing Moore: The Complete Series (Boxed Set)

Bad Son Rising

Henry's End

Slave to Love

The Do-Over

Love on the Edge of Time

www.ingramcontent.com/pod-product-compliance
Lightning Source LLC
Chambersburg PA
CBHW070853250626
47159CB00003B/1042